KNIFE EDGE

(THE EMPIRE'S CORPS—BOOK XVII)

CHRISTOPHER G. NUTTALL

The characters and events portrayed in this book are fictitious. Any similarity to real persons, living or dead, is coincidental and not intended by the author.

Text copyright © 2020 Christopher G. Nuttall

All rights reserved.

Printed in the United States of America.

ISBN: 9798653269769

No part of this book may be reproduced, or stored in a retrieval system, or transmitted in any form or by any means, electronic, mechanical, photocopying, recording, or other-wise, without express written permission of the publisher.

Cover By Tan Ho Sim
https://www.artstation.com/alientan

Book One: The Empire's Corps
Book Two: No Worse Enemy
Book Three: When The Bough Breaks
Book Four: Semper Fi
Book Five: The Outcast
Book Six: To The Shores
Book Seven: Reality Check
Book Eight: Retreat Hell
Book Nine: The Thin Blue Line
Book Ten: Never Surrender
Book Eleven: First To Fight
Book Twelve: They Shall Not Pass
Book Thirteen: Culture Shock
Book Fourteen: Wolf's Bane
Book Fifteen: Cry Wolf
Book Sixteen: Favour The Bold
Book Seventeen: Knife Edge

http://www.chrishanger.net
http://chrishanger.wordpress.com/
http://www.facebook.com/ChristopherGNuttall
All Comments Welcome!

HISTORIAN'S NOTE

I'VE DONE MY BEST TO MAKE THIS BOOK, the second of a series exploring what happens in the Core Worlds after Earthfall, as self-contained as possible. It should be comprehensible without ever having read any of the prior books, save for *Favour the Bold*. However, I would advise you to read *When The Bough Breaks* to set the scene, as it covers Earthfall itself.

CGN

CONTENTS

HISTORIAN'S NOTE v
PROLOGUE I ix
PROLOGUE II xii

Chapter One 1
Chapter Two 10
Chapter Three 19
Chapter Four 28
Chapter Five 37
Chapter Six 46
Chapter Seven 55
Chapter Eight 64
Chapter Nine 73
Chapter Ten 81
Chapter Eleven 90
Chapter Twelve 99
Chapter Thirteen 108
Chapter Fourteen 117
Chapter Fifteen 126
Chapter Sixteen 135
Chapter Seventeen 144
Chapter Eighteen 153
Chapter Nineteen 162
Chapter Twenty 171
Chapter Twenty-One 180
Chapter Twenty-Two 189
Chapter Twenty-Three 198
Chapter Twenty-Four 207

Chapter Twenty-Five	216
Chapter Twenty-Six	225
Chapter Twenty-Seven	234
Chapter Twenty-Eight	243
Chapter Twenty-Nine	252
Chapter Thirty	261
Chapter Thirty-One	270
Chapter Thirty-Two	279
Chapter Thirty-Three	288
Chapter Thirty-Four	297
Chapter Thirty-Five	306
Chapter Thirty-Six	315
Chapter Thirty-Seven	325
Chapter Thirty-Eight	335
Chapter Thirty-Nine	344
Chapter Forty	354

AFTERWORD 361
DEBT OF HONOR PREVIEW:
Prologue	368
Chapter One	375
Chapter Two	384

PROLOGUE I

FROM: *The Dying Days: The Death of the Old Order and the Birth of the New.* Professor Leo Caesius. Avalon. 206PE.

IN HINDSIGHT, Earthfall was pretty much inevitable. We saw it coming.

I suppose we should have wondered, when we finally realised that all hell was going to break loose, who *else* might have reached the same conclusion.

It wasn't as if anything was *secret*. Sure, it was hard to get a completely accurate picture of what was going on, thanks to lies being written into the official record and prevalent official censorship, but enough leaked through for *me* to see it. The Terran Marine Corps saw it. I should have wondered… why not others? Who else knew—or guessed—what was coming?

But I'm getting a little ahead of myself.

As we saw in previous volumes, the Terran Marine Corps saw Earthfall coming and took steps to preserve themselves and—hopefully—rebuild the Empire they'd sworn to serve. Small groups of marines were assigned to isolated worlds at the edge of explored space—including Avalon, a story explored in my earlier volumes—with a mandate to protect and preserve what remnants of civilisation they could. Others were withdrawn from more populated—and inevitably doomed—worlds to await the final end. And, when Earthfall finally came—somehow catching us all by surprise despite years of planning and preparations—the corps started liberating and recruiting the trained and experienced workers who would assist the marines to preserve civilisation.

All of this did not take place in a vacuum. Earthfall led to utter chaos, to wave after wave of destruction sweeping across the Core Worlds. Planetary governors seized power, only to be consumed by the chaos as uncounted billions were swept out of work and unemployment benefits came to a sudden end. Imperial Navy officers declared themselves warlords and started building empires of their own, most falling prey to ambitious subordinates or supply shortages within a very short space of time. Old grudges burst into flame, unleashing a cycle of attacks and revenge attacks that ended with entire planetary systems burnt to ashes. We do not know how many people died in the first few months. It remains beyond calculation.

It was during a recruitment mission, as detailed in the prior volume, that the marines discovered they had a major rival. The Onge Corporation, previously ruled by Grand Senator Stephen Onge (who died during Earthfall), had established a major base on an isolated world, Hameau. This alone would be concerning, but further investigation revealed that Hameau was a corporate paradise, a seemingly-ordered world held in stasis by a combination of extreme surveillance and a cold-blooded willingness to remove and terminate troublemakers before they became a serious threat. It was clear, to the marines, that Hameau represented the future…as seen by the Onge Family. The upper classes would have considerable freedom, while the lower classes would be trapped within a social system that would keep them from either rising or rebelling. If this wasn't bad enough, the sociologists believed the long-term result would be utterly disastrous. Hameau would either stagnate to the point it entered a steep decline—not unknown, amongst worlds that refused to permit a degree of social mobility—or eventually be destroyed by a brutal and uncontrolled (and uncontrollable) uprising.

The marines therefore decided to intervene. Landing troops on the surface—the planetary defences were strong enough to keep the starships from securing the high orbitals and demanding surrender—the marines carried out a brilliant campaign that ended with the capture of the capital city, the effective destruction of the planetary government and them being firmly in control. Everything seemed to have gone their way until the enemy reinforcements arrived, too late to save the world...but quickly enough, perhaps, to destroy the marines.

Now read on...

PROLOGUE II

PARADISE ISLAND, PARADISE
(TEN YEARS PRIOR TO EARTHFALL)

COMMODORE NELSON AGATE had heard the expression *killing someone with kindness*, but he'd never realised it might be applicable to the Imperial Navy. The Admiralty had plenty of ways to deal with officers it didn't like, from assigning them to dead-end desk jobs or dispatching them to asteroid mining facilities in the middle of nowhere. Nelson had expected *some* kind of punishment for daring to disagree with Admiral Valentine, but being ordered to take a long shore leave on Paradise wasn't *quite* what he'd expected. And yet, the more he sunned himself on a remote island, the more he wondered if his career hadn't been cunningly destroyed. Who'd take a complaint about being ordered to go on leave seriously?

Paradise Island lived up to the name, he admitted privately. The beaches were utterly pristine. The water was warm. The local girls were beautiful and willing. The bars never ran out of alcohol. The games weren't rigged. If he'd wanted to have a long holiday, he wouldn't have wanted to go anywhere else. But three months of paradise had left him bored and jaded, convinced he'd sooner go somewhere—anywhere—else. He'd almost *pay* for an assignment to an asteroid facility.

He lay back on his deckchair, wondering if he should signal the waitress for another beer. It was too early in the morning to be drunk, but…there was little else to do. He'd swum, he'd played beach ball, he'd…he'd done too many things, all of which bored him now. The waitress was pretty, but…*all* the waitresses were pretty. It was funny, he reflected sourly, how quickly one could grow sick of something when there was an unlimited supply. There was no longer any thrill, let alone pleasure, in victory. What was the point of playing when the game was rigged?

I'm wasting away here, he thought, morbidly. *In Paradise!*

A shadow fell across him. He looked up, at a pretty young woman wearing a thong bikini and little else. She looked like another guest, yet…there was something in the way that she held herself that set alarm bells ringing in his mind. Nelson forced himself to sit up as she knelt beside him, her bare breasts somehow…unnoticeable. She might have dressed to fit in, he noted, but she wasn't one of the staff. She was something else.

"Commodore Nelson Agate, is it not?" The woman's voice was calm. She spoke with a corporate accent. "I'm Julia. Julia Ganister."

"A pleasure," Nelson said. He shook her hand firmly. "What can I do for you?"

Julia sat next to him. "Why are you here, Commodore?"

"I was ordered to go on leave, an all-expenses-paid leave," Nelson said. "Why are *you* here?"

"I'm looking for people who interest me," Julia said. "And you do."

Nelson frowned. Julia held herself like someone with authority, which meant…what? An intelligence service? A military unit? She didn't look as muscular as he would expect from a uniformed woman, but that was meaningless. Standards had been slipping for years. He'd been in the Admiralty's bad books well before they'd found a way to get rid of him, just by complaining about officers who hired their staff based on looks rather than qualifications and experience. Bad enough in a staff office; sheer, fucking disaster onboard ship. He was tempted to say as much, just to see what Julia made of it. If she was collecting information for the Inspectorate General…

"I see," he said, neutrally. His career was already on the rocks. Better to say nothing incriminating until he knew the lie of the land. "And how do I interest you?"

"A competent officer," Julia said. "A cadet who graduated top of his class, when the rating system was stripped of all ID tags. A midshipman who saved his ship when his drunken supervisor nearly crashed her into an asteroid. A captain who stood against a rebel militia and defeated them, despite being outnumbered five to one. And a commodore who dared to tell Admiral Valentine that his planned operation was going to fail and fail spectacularly."

Nelson sat up. "Who are you?"

"Julia." Julia smiled, as if she found his question amusing. "Tell me something, Commodore. Where do you see your career going in the next few years?"

"Nowhere," Nelson said, sourly.

"We agree," Julia said. "And where do you see the *Empire* going in the next few decades?"

Nelson blinked. It was treason to even *suggest* the Empire might be going through a very rough patch. He dreaded to think what it might be to suggest the Empire was falling to destruction. And yet, he'd heard enough whispered rumours, seen enough failing sectors, to know something was deeply wrong. He'd kept that thought to himself, not daring to utter it aloud where anyone could hear, yet...it had plagued him, in the dead of night. The Imperial Navy that had fought the Unification Wars would not have tolerated Admiral Valentine. The officers would have rebelled against him and the spacers would have used him for target practice. It was hard to escape the sense the entire universe was heading for a fall.

"I'm not a traitor," he managed, finally. He studied her face, noting—for the first time—that it was pretty yet bland. A few minutes with a cosmetic set and she'd look very different. "And I..."

Julia rested her hand on his arm. "We're not asking you to be a traitor," she said. "We're asking you to think about the future."

Nelson swung his legs over the side of the deckchair. "And what do you want me to *think* about the future?"

"I'm not here to lead you into saying something incriminating," Julia said. Her voice was so calm that Nelson found himself believing every word. "Believe me, your enemies already have enough lined up to ensure your career hits a dead end. Admiral Valentine has spent the last three weeks making certain you'll be on your way to the deep black once your leave finally comes to an end. I'm here to offer you an alternative."

"Like what?" Nelson felt ice congealing around his heart. "Who are you?"

Julia stood. "There are some people you should meet," she said. "Will you come with me?"

"Perhaps," Nelson said. "And I ask again—who are you?"

"Julia," Julia said. "Julia Ganister-Onge. And we're trying to salvage something from the ruins. Perhaps that answers your question?"

"It does," Nelson said.

Julia nodded, then turned and walked away.

After a moment, Nelson followed her.

CHAPTER ONE

It is often said, when discussing communist, fascist, theocratic, corpocratic and other unpleasant regimes, that they might have survived if they'd possessed computers and—at the same time— avoided a dictator. This is, for better or worse, untrue.
—**Professor Leo Caesius**
The Right to be Wrong: How Silencing People Hurts You

CAPTAIN KERRI STUMBAUGH kept her face under tight control as she stared at the display.

One of her instructors had told her, years ago, that if things started going suspiciously well it was a clear sign she was about to lose. Experience had taught her there was a degree of truth in that statement. Things going well wasn't a sign of incoming trouble, but the mindset it bred *was*. The idea that she could relax, that she could assume the matter was going to end without further intervention from her...she shook her head, dismissing the thought. They'd been caught with their pants down. They were in deep shit.

Her eyes narrowed as the red icons took on shape and form. Nineteen warships, led by the missing battlecruiser; nineteen warships and seven troop transports, probably crammed to the gunwales with soldiers itching for a fight. Nineteen warships...more than enough to destroy her squadron in a straight engagement. She wanted to believe her superior training would give her the edge, if push came to shove, but it was clear the enemy ships were manned by trained and experienced personnel. Her lips curved into a grim smile. They weren't Imperial Navy officers, then. They'd been skimping on training and exercises for years, mothballing ships and discharging crewmen while pocketing their wages and skimming billions of credits from the budget for ships and facilities that only existed on paper. *These guys knew what they were doing.*

"Captain," Lieutenant Tomas said. The tactical officer sounded grim. "They'll be within engagement range in thirty minutes."

Kerri nodded. The enemy was playing it safe. They were advancing directly towards Hameau, forcing her to either block their path or get out of their way. If she did the former, they'd crush her; if she did the latter, she'd be unable to help the groundpounders on the planet's surface. She forced herself to think, her mind racing as she tried to find a way to even the odds. But she knew, all too well, there was none. She didn't have the time or equipment to do more than delay the enemy ships.

"Prepare for a long-range engagement," she ordered, coolly. An exchange of missile fire wouldn't slow the enemy ships for long, if it had *any* effect on their plans, but the only alternative was withdrawing and waiting for a chance to regain control of the high orbitals. She doubted they'd give her that chance anytime soon. Hameau had been important…was *still* important. They'd be fools to let her retake the planet. "And pass the warning to General Anderson. Inform him that we cannot delay the enemy for long."

She felt a surge of frustrated rage as the squadron rapidly prepared for battle. She knew, better than most, the role sheer random chance played in human affairs, but…she gritted her teeth in silent fury. They'd won, damn it! They'd defeated the enemy forces, they'd occupied the enemy cities, they'd taken out the enemy government…only to have a relief fleet arrive to undo all they'd done. She knew they'd screwed up by the numbers. There'd been no hint the enemy possessed *that* many ships until they showed themselves. It was agonisingly clear Hameau was merely a tiny fragment of a much greater operation.

And in hindsight, that shouldn't have surprised us, she thought, coldly. There was no time for recriminations, but even the Terran Marine Corps was not immune to people using hindsight to score cheap points. Thankfully, they'd probably wait until the campaign was over. Probably. *One world might preserve something of civilisation, and an industrial base, but it couldn't hope to retake the galaxy.*

She wished, suddenly, that she could communicate with someone higher up the chain of command. Major-General Anderson was in command of the operation, but the communications lag would ensure he wouldn't receive her messages until it was too late for him to countermand her orders. There'd been times, in her career, when that would have seemed an advantage. She'd met too many Imperial Navy officers who'd been promoted because of connections or bribes, rather than merit. But Anderson was an experienced officer. He might have something else in mind for her ships.

"The enemy ships are sweeping us with tactical sensors," Tomas warned. "But they're not altering course."

"They don't have to," Kerri said. Whoever was in command of the enemy fleet knew what he was doing. It was tempting to think she could lure the enemy ships into a stern chase, forcing them to push their drives to the limit in a fruitless bid to run down her command, but she doubted they'd take the bait. "They know they can force us to fight on their terms."

She keyed her console, bringing up the latest sensor reports. The enemy fleet hadn't opened fire—yet—but she'd be astonished if their weapons weren't in full working order. Their sensors were certainly top of the range, military-grade systems that shouldn't have been in civilian or corporate hands. She wondered, idly, how they'd secured them, then dismissed the thought. The Onge Corporation had built ships and weapons for the Imperial Navy. It would have been simplicity itself, back then, to produce a handful of extra units—and hulls—and squirrel them away. The Asset Tracking department on Safehouse was going to have to look at the data and try to deduce what had happened, as if it mattered. The only important thing, right now, was that the enemy ships were bearing down on her.

And some of those ships might have non-typical configurations, she mused. Starship design had plateaued over the last few decades—the enemy hulls *looked* like standard navy hulls—but tacticians had been talking about fitting the ships with newer or different weapons for years. *Her* ship's configuration owed much to their planning. *The enemy might have been trying to hide an ace or two up their sleeve too.*

Her eyes narrowed as another report flashed up in front of her. The enemy transports looked more like colonist-carriers. Repurposed transports? Or...or what? She doubted it mattered. The transports would be sitting ducks, if her ships closed to engagement range. It was the enemy warships that posed the *real* threat.

She felt an icy hand clench her heart as the range steadily closed. There was no hope of doing more than delaying the enemy, if that. There was nothing she could do for the marines on the planet. They controlled enough of the PDCs—she thought—to keep the enemy from simply smashing their positions from orbit, but...if nothing else, control of the high orbitals would give them a chance to land troops and retake the world. Or simply let the marines wither on the vine. Supplying the invasion force had been a problem even when the high orbitals were firmly in their hands. She cursed under her breath, then smiled. Hameau hadn't been an easy target. Hopefully, the factors that had made the planet a difficult world to invade would protect the marines long enough for reinforcements to arrive. The Commandant would dispatch them as soon as he knew the invasion had gone off the rails.

And if he doesn't, she thought as the enemy ships glided closer, *a hundred thousand marines are going to wind up dead.*

• • •

Admiral Nelson Agate, Onge Navy, allowed himself a feeling of grim satisfaction as he watched ONS *Hammerblow's* tactical staff perform their duties.

It hadn't been easy, even with the combination of headhunted officers from the Imperial Navy and very enthusiastic recruits from Onge itself, to escape bad habits and turn the Onge Navy into a lean mean fighting machine. He'd relished the challenge—it helped that his budget had been immense, practically unlimited—but he'd been all too aware that the navy had yet to face its first real test. Now...the staff were performing well, even though they knew they were going into battle. The red icons on the display weren't simulated. They were very real.

He studied the long-range sensor reports thoughtfully. He hadn't believed the reports when they'd first arrived, even though they'd come from unquestionable sources, but now...the marines *were* invading Hameau. He shook his head in disbelief. He'd heard the Terran Marine Corps had been destroyed, that the Slaughterhouse had been turned into a radioactive hellhole and the remainder of the corps had been scattered to the four winds. And yet...the display was very clear. Four giant MEU troop transports held position near Hameau itself, while a small squadron of warships sought to block his path. And yet, they had no hope of stopping him. They were going to die for nothing.

Know when to fold them, you fools, he thought, coldly. He'd known enough marines to know they had the sense to know when they were fighting a losing battle and withdraw before it was too late. *Or is it already too late?*

His lips curved into a smile. The marines were renowned for travelling light, but they'd have problems packing up and retreating before his forces took the high orbitals. They'd have to abandon all their equipment if they wanted to get their men out, if they had time to do even that! He checked his console, silently contemplating the problem. They'd have to get very lucky to pull even a fraction of their men off the surface before it was too late. He didn't think it was possible. The last report from Hameau had warned the marines were advancing on the capital, with little standing between them and victory. There was little chance they'd regrouped before it was too late.

"They shouldn't even be here," Julia Ganister-Onge said. The corporation's commissioner—and his lover—sounded astonished. "What are they *doing* here?"

"Invading, it seems," Nelson said. He shared her astonishment. The Terran Marine Corps was a formidable force, but…what were they *doing*? "The corporation might not be the only people who planned for the future."

Julia gave him a sharp look. "They shouldn't have invaded our world."

Nelson shrugged. He didn't see the logic either, but…no one would have gone to all the trouble of invading a heavily-defended world unless *they* thought there was a good reason. The marines were hardly unthinking brutes, whatever the media claimed. And they'd been at the sharp end of every conflict for the last few centuries. They might have realised Earthfall was coming and planned for it. Why not? The Onge Corporation had been laying its plans for decades.

He felt an odd stab of guilt as the range continued to close. He'd rarely questioned his decision to leave the Imperial Navy, yet…he shook his head. The Imperial Navy had been doomed. The Terran Marine Corps were doomed too, doomed by lack of supplies and—he supposed—a cause. What were they fighting for? Did they intend to put their Commandant on the throne? Or did they think they could find the Childe Roland and put *him* on the throne? The last reports suggested the young emperor had died during Earthfall. Even if he hadn't…what throne? The Core Worlds were burning. By the time the fighting died down, there would be little left of the once-great civilisation. The Empire was gone.

"Prepare firing solutions," he ordered. "Engage them as soon as they enter medium-range."

"Aye, Admiral," the tactical officer said. "Preparing to engage."

Nelson smiled, coldly. Julia had made sure he'd had a fairly free hand. And he'd done his best to create a fleet that could go toe-to-toe with the best in the galaxy. His officers were highly-trained, his crewmen drilled until they could perform their duties in their sleep and his maintenance cycles run to ensure peak efficiency. He had no intention of letting standards slip, even now the principal threat was gone. His crews would never have the chance to pick up bad habits. He'd shoot anyone who so much as suggested an outdated component could be left in place because it hadn't failed *yet*.

Julia glanced at him. "Shouldn't we be trying to defeat the enemy fleet?"

"No." Nelson spoke as much for his own benefit as hers. She was no naval officer—he was all too aware that her duties included keeping an eye on him as well as everything else—but it helped, sometimes, to discuss issues out loud. "They have the edge, when it comes to speed. They'd just keep the range open while trying to lead us into a minefield."

His eyes narrowed. The ships—he smiled suddenly as he remembered the marines weren't supposed to have any *real* warships—were clearly in peak condition, handled by crews who knew *precisely* how to get the best out of them. If they'd had more than three heavy cruisers, he might have feared the worst if he'd taken *Hammerblow* against them alone. He'd have made them pay a heavy price for their victory, but...he shook his head. He had nineteen warships against twelve. Odds like that didn't care if the weaker side had a slight edge in training. Unless the marines had some kind of superweapon he'd never even dreamt existed, he had the edge.

They might be nearly unbeatable, man for man, on the ground, he mused. *But we're facing them in space.*

He indicated the display. "Right now, the folks on the planet know we're coming. They're frantically running around, trying to work out how to evacuate what they can before we take the high orbitals and start shooting holes in their transports. They're going to have to get the transports moving in fifty minutes if they want to get them out of range before we run them down. If we can get there before they start running, we might just trap them on the ground."

"I see," Julia said. "And you are *sure* they're frantically running around?"

"They're caught in a bind," Nelson said. He doubted the marines were *frantic*—he'd never seen marines panic under fire, which was more than could be said for many other military formations—but they were in deep shit. "They have to save what they can, yet they simply don't have time. If we take the high orbitals, they're screwed and they know it."

Probably, his thoughts added. *They've almost certainly taken the remaining PDCs by now.*

"So the whole operation becomes relatively simple," he explained. "They have to get those troop transports moving before we get there. Therefore, their ships will try to either slow us down or lead us away. I have no intention of letting them do either. The ships aren't important, not now. The real priority is the planet, not so much because of the industries as because the enemy has thousands of troops on the ground. We retake the high orbitals and land troops—we win."

He grinned as he looked at the display. "They have to try to slow us down," he repeated. "And if they want to do that, they have to come within weapons range. We'll blow hell out of them."

And if the marines refuse to surrender, he thought with a cold smile, *we can blow hell out of the planet too.*

He sobered. They had strict orders to preserve what they could of the planet's industry and trained workforce. Hameau had served the corporation well, first as a training zone for everything from starship personnel to technical experts and then as a relocation centre for trained and experienced personnel from all over the Core Worlds. The Corporation had done everything in its power to recruit trained personnel, often trying to remove them from worlds and systems that were already starting to collapse into chaos. Nelson had devoted two-thirds of his life to the Empire. It was chilling to watch it fall into ruin, even though it had betrayed him well before he'd turned his back. At least the Corporation was *trying* to save something. It wasn't much, but it was all they had.

"Just remember we need to recover the industries intact," Julia said, as if she'd read his thoughts. She might not be a naval officer, but she was *very* skilled in her field. "We can't replace them."

"Not in a hurry," Nelson agreed. The Corporation had gone further than anyone else—as far as he knew—in creating an entirely separate technical base, but losing Hameau's industrial nodes would hurt. It would take years to rebuild, even if there were no further glitches along the path to galactic domination. "We'll do what we can."

He leaned back in his chair. He'd already *done* everything he could to ensure success. The crews were trained, the ships were in good condition... they'd simulated the coming engagement, running through hundreds of variants in a bid to predict what the enemy was going to do and devise countermeasures. He was entirely sure his squadron could engage and defeat an Imperial Navy squadron twice its size. But the marines? He didn't know. *They* understood the value of good training, preventive maintenance and prior planning.

But I still have the edge, he told himself, firmly. *And that's all that matters.*

"Admiral," the tactical officer said. "The enemy fleet will enter engagement range in ten minutes."

"Good," Nelson said. The enemy had to know their attempts to lure him astray—and perhaps onto a minefield—had failed. "Stand by point defence."

He smiled, coldly. It wouldn't be long now.

CHAPTER TWO

The short-term problem, of course, is that avoiding a dictator (and/or a dictatorship) is not easy. The people you need to maintain a communist (etc) state are precisely the sort of people who should not be trusted with the role. Indeed, those who would found such a state are people who have a yen to control their fellow man.
—**Professor Leo Caesius**
The Right to be Wrong: How Silencing People Hurts You

HAVERFORD WAS A VERY STRANGE CITY.

Captain Haydn Steel felt oddly exposed as he led the platoon down the street, his eyes scanning from side to side. The city felt deserted, as if half the population had decided it would be safer to cross the river and find shelter well away from what had once been the home of the planetary government. The streets themselves were neatly laid out, suggesting the city had been planned instead of being allowed to grow naturally. Dozens of abandoned ground—and air-cars lay everywhere, some burnt-out. There were parts of the city that had been devastated during the thunder runs, with entire blocks reduced to piles of rubble; there were parts that looked utterly untouched, as if nothing more significant than a minor thunderstorm had swept over the city. He felt sweat trickle down his back as they reached a crossroads and peered in both directions. There was no one in sight.

He gritted his teeth. The entire planet seemed to be holding its breath, waiting for something to happen. Two months ago, Hameau had been a peaceful—if repressive—corporate world, untroubled by the chaos sweeping through the galaxy. The population had known their place and stayed there, if only because those who tried to step outside their box quietly disappeared. It wasn't the sort of place Haydn would have cared to live, but he could see the appeal. And then the marines had invaded, falling out of the clear blue sky and shattering the planetary system beyond repair. And now...

Haydn had studied wars, invasions and occupations. The most dangerous moments were the ones immediately after, when everyone was trying to come to grips with the new reality. Some people would hide inside, cowering at the knock on the door; some people would try to continue as normal, even though things would never be the same again; some people would throw off the shackles of their previous life and turn to looting or seek revenge. Haydn had served in places where the old order had been smashed. There'd always been thousands of people with scores to settle, people who'd hated silently and bided their time. And it was the same here. They'd already discovered hundreds of dead bodies scattered across the city. The marines hadn't killed them. They'd been so badly mutilated that hardened marines had blanched.

He kept his face under tight control as they walked down the residential street. The houses seemed abandoned, although his combat-honed senses insisted they were being watched by unseen eyes. The drawn curtains could hide anything, from a cowering family to insurgents or stay-behind units preparing for a final desperate engagement. He thought he spotted one curtain quiver, suggesting they *were* being watched. He hoped the locals weren't planning to cause trouble. It wouldn't do much for hearts and minds if the marines had to raid the entire district, dragging out the locals and tearing their houses apart in a frantic search for guns and ammunition. If they didn't have enemies before the search, they sure as hell would *afterwards*.

Sweat trickled down his back as he kept walking. The streets felt eerie, oppressive. The houses looked nice, but they were strikingly uniform. They were practically identical, with very few signs of individuality. A sense of unreality trickled through his mind as he cast his eyes over the closest houses. The locals didn't seem to like the idea of anyone stepping out of line. Haydn knew the importance of standardisation, but there were limits. The corps had no right to tell him how he should decorate his house.

Something moved, above. He tensed, his grip tightening on his rifle as he looked up. A drone? A helicopter? A combat support platform? No, a bird. He eyed it suspiciously for a long moment—there were combat drones designed to look like birds—before deciding it was probably real. It might not be harmless—there were all sorts of ways to use birds in warfare -—but he couldn't blow the creature out of the sky on suspicion. That probably wouldn't endear them to the locals either. They'd gone to some trouble to establish an Earth-compatible biosphere on their world.

He put the thought aside as he passed a scorched, but still intact building. A school, apparently. He eyed the damage thoughtfully, wondering what had caused it. The thunder runs hadn't come anywhere near the district. A stray missile or shell would have levelled the entire building. Perhaps the local kids had taken advantage of the chaos to set fire to the hated building. Haydn had little *good* to say about his education, but it hadn't been anything like as regimented as schools created by corporate educrats. The kids had been on course to become mindless corprat drones before the invasion had intervened.

I suppose it beats schooling on Earth, he thought. He could see why the parents liked it, even if—in the long-term—it was more destructive than constructive. *The kids learn discipline, if nothing else.*

He snorted as they glanced over the schoolhouse, then continued on their way. The kids clearly hadn't had access to anything *really* dangerous, or the sort of education that taught them how to turn simple household products into dangerous weapons. He supposed he should be relieved. Young men were always the most aggressive, in the early days of occupation. The locals didn't have many weapons, thankfully, but that would change in the coming months. They'd learn how to build IEDs, lay ambushes and other nasty tricks that would get people killed for nothing. And there would be enemy soldiers who'd refuse to surrender, even after they'd been ordered to turn themselves in. They'd either absent themselves or go underground to continue the fight. It felt absurd to think they had a chance, but Haydn had seen too many occupations go bad. The invaders couldn't be strong everywhere. They had to win hearts and minds before attitudes hardened and it was too late.

A line of powered-down cars was parked along the street, looking harmless. Haydn eyed them suspiciously, motioning for the marines to keep their distance. The local traffic control systems had ordered all ground and aircars to stay where they were—a degree of control that struck him as creepy—but that was meaningless. A skilled technician would be able to bypass the control processor or simply reroute the system so it thought it had permission to move. And then the cars could be turned into VBIEDs or simply crashed into marine checkpoints. Even if they were powerless, they weren't harmless. Cars made excellent hiding places for IEDs.

He heard two of his men muttering uneasily behind him as they kept walking. He didn't blame them. They'd been in hundreds of engagements over the past two months, from simple firefights to complex multilevel battles, but they knew how to handle themselves when the bullets started flying. Patrolling, on the other hand, was stressful. The ROE were very clear. They weren't allowed to open fire—or even be extremely aggressive—unless they had good reason to believe they were under threat. The enemy would have a chance to land the first blow, if there *was* an enemy. Haydn scowled. It was impossible to tell. They were practically advancing to ambush, without being certain there *was* one.

It could be worse, he told himself, firmly. *You could be re-enacting the Defence of Duffer's Drift in your underwear.*

The thought made him smile, just as he heard the sound of breaking glass ahead of him. He picked up speed, tensing as they hurried into a shopping street. The uniformity didn't change, even though the shops offered everything from food to fashionable clothes. He gritted his teeth, glancing back and using hand-signals to urge the squad into tactical positions. If they were looters, the marines would have no trouble. But if they were insurgents, trying to lure the marines into a trap...

"Call in," he ordered. The squad could deal with a handful of looters, but it was probably best to alert the QRF. A platoon could be easily trapped in enemy-held streets, if there were no friendly units in close proximity. The idea of being trapped and used as bait to snare the QRF was unpleasant. It would be humiliating, even if they escaped without casualties. He'd seen insurgents try *that* trick before. Sometimes, it even worked. "Tell the QRF to ready themselves."

He braced himself as they approached the shop. It had been a general store, judging by the sign on the broken door. The shelves, the ones within eyeshot, were bare. The locals had purchased everything they could, from food and drink to toilet paper and other essentials, as soon as it had dawned on them that their world *was* being invaded. The planetary government had tried to put a damper on panic-buying, but they'd failed. Haydn wasn't surprised. Even repressive governments knew better than to risk starting a civil uprising in the midst of all-out war.

We did the locals a favour, he thought. There was no privacy in the barracks—he was used to it, after years in the corps—but the locals had been kept under intensive surveillance from birth to death. *He* would never have tolerated it. *If the bad guys had won the war, they'd have punished anyone who panic-bought.*

He levelled his rifle at a shape moving within the darkened interior, then barked a command in his best parade-ground voice. "Come out with your hands up!"

There was a long pause. The dark shape froze. He knew, beyond a shadow of a doubt, that it *was* a living person. He tensed, silently praying the looters—if they were looters—wouldn't do anything stupid. Shooting looters was a good way to establish control as quickly as possible, but it bred resentment and hatred. Better to take them alive, if possible; better to move them to the detention for processing before they were either released or shipped to POW camps. God alone knew what would happen to them. Perhaps they'd simply be dumped on an island and told to learn to farm or else. It wasn't as if they could be shipped to a penal colony now.

"Come on out," he repeated. "Now."

The shape started to move, stumbling into the light. A young man in a civilian outfit, his hands waving frantically in front of him. His clothes were as much a uniform, on Hameau, as Haydn's BDUs. An accountant, perhaps, or a clerk. Or a bureaucrat. Haydn swallowed the flicker of disdain and swept his eyes up and down the young man's body. It didn't look as if he was concealing anything, but that was meaningless. He could easily be hiding an IED behind his back, if someone hadn't implanted an explosive device and turned him into a living bomb. The grinding horrors he'd seen on Han—and a multitude of other worlds—could easily start on Hameau too.

He jabbed his rifle at the looter. The young man blanched, eying the weapon as if it were a poisonous snake rearing to strike. Not a soldier, then. Hameau's defenders had been a mixed bag, from brave soldiers who'd fought with skill and determination to uniformed bureaucrats who'd thought nothing of deserting their men when the tide turned against them, but they'd all had basic weapons training. The looter looked as if he'd never seen a weapon in his life. Haydn felt a stab of pity, mingled with contempt. The right to bear arms, in his experience, was perhaps the most important right in human history. No wonder the empire—and the corprats—had worked so hard to keep weapons out of civilian hands.

Two more looters emerged from the shadows, a young man and a young woman keeping their hands in the air. The woman—she was barely in her twenties, if that—looked tired and resigned, as if she hadn't expected to get away with anything. There was something beaten in her expression, although there were no marks on her face. The man beside her looked as if he was trying to be brave, despite the weapons pointed at him. Haydn resisted the urge to roll his eyes. Bravado was all well and good, but mindless bravado was just annoying.

The marines searched them, removed a handful of possessions and bound their hands with zip-ties. The locals submitted without protest, something that surprised Haydn more than he cared to admit. They were in no danger, as long as they behaved themselves, but *they* wouldn't know it. They certainly wouldn't believe it. The remains of the planetary communications network had broadcast assurances no one would be harmed, let alone robbed, raped or murdered, but the locals probably hadn't believed them. They'd been told too many horror stories over the last few weeks.

And famous flicks didn't help either, Haydn thought, as he searched the store. It had been stripped bare—and abandoned. The bedrooms on the upper level showed every sign of a hasty departure. Drawers lay open, clothes lay where they'd fallen, some of them very high quality indeed. Whoever had packed the bags had been ruthlessly practical. *They thought the hordes of Ming the Merciless were bearing down on them.*

He breathed a sigh of relief when it became clear the store had been abandoned when the looters had broken in. It wouldn't have been *easy* to deal with looters who were also murderers, not when it might upset the locals *whatever* they did. He took a final look around, noting the paint someone had slapped over the webcams and other surveillance devices, then headed back outside. The prisoners were looking around despondently, clearly assessing their futures and finding them dark. They'd be in no real danger, but they'd probably be put to work. The POWs were already helping to clear the roads into the city, unless they had specialised training. The medics were working overtime, trying to help people who'd been wounded in the crossfire.

"On your feet," he ordered. He wondered, idly, why they'd turned to looting. Were they starving? Were they trying to hoard whatever they found, in the hope of selling it later? Or were they blowing off steam? They didn't *look* starving. That meant nothing, he reminded himself. Civilians rarely prepared for disaster until it was too late. "You're going to the camps."

The young woman—girl, really—looked at him as she was helped to her feet. "What's going to happen to us?"

"Very little," Haydn said, as reassuringly as he could. "You'll go to the camps. You'll probably be fed, in exchange for work. And then you'll be released."

Unless we have some reason to think you're a threat, he added, silently. The marines had seen too many enemies released by political fiat, only to take up weapons again as soon as they were clear. This time, things would be better. The prisoners wouldn't be mistreated, but they wouldn't be released in a hurry either. *We'll be running your DNA against the captured files too. If you're hiding something from us, we'll know it.*

He kept an eye on the prisoners as the patrol resumed their walk. The street looked to have been thoroughly stripped, probably during the hours between the surrender and the occupation. The owners appeared to have vanished, save for a pair of bodies outside one of the shops. Their clothes suggested they were storekeepers, although it was impossible to be sure. He checked them quickly, noting they'd been shot. Not civilian looters, then. Enemy soldiers? Former policemen? Or...he shook his head. There was no way to know. The interior of their store was as dark and silent as the grave.

The young man snorted, rudely. "Why did you come here?"

Haydn hid his amusement. It was *unwise* to challenge one's captors, even if one *did* want to look brave. It would just get someone marked as a troublemaker, someone who would be turned into an example or merely watched closely for signs he was planning an escape. There were marines who'd do it to distract the enemy, but...he shook his head. There was no sign the captives had ever taken anything akin to the Conduct After Capture course. He'd known experienced marines who still broke into a sweat at the mere *thought* of taking it again.

"Quiet," Command Sergeant Mark Mayberry growled.

Haydn frowned as he saw a pair of shuttles skimming over the city, heading for the FOB the marines had established in the remains of a former enemy garrison. The last he'd heard, shuttle pilots were being told to stay away from the city. It only took one enemy soldier with an HVM to *really* ruin a shuttle pilot's day. Even if he missed, the pilot would probably win the brown pants award *and* supply flights would be badly disrupted. Haydn knew, better than most, just how close they'd come to running out of supplies. He hoped any lingering enemy forces didn't know it. A prolonged insurgency might end with the marines running out of bullets.

Although we can use their factories, given time, he thought. *And...*

His headset buzzed. "Captain, terminate your patrol and report to the FOB immediately," the dispatcher ordered. "I say again..."

"I got it," Haydn said. Terminate his patrol *immediately*? What was going on? "We're on our way."

CHAPTER THREE

The problem therefore can be posed like this: one must either become a dictator, in order to impose one's values, or be pushed aside by a subordinate who not only wants to become a dictator, but is also practiced in the use of the power you have unwisely granted him.
—**Professor Leo Caesius**
The Right to be Wrong: How Silencing People Hurts You

THERE WAS SOMETHING PLEASING, Major-General Gerald Anderson had always thought, in a military campaign executed without political interference. Politicos never knew the *first* thing about military operations, which led them to demand bombing campaigns that took out industrial complexes without killing a single enemy soldier or invasions that were carried out without any of the invaders so much as getting a paper cut. It had been a constant frustration to him, back in the days before Earthfall, that marines—his marines—would fight bravely to give their political masters their best chance of establishing a permanent settlement, only to watch the politicos throw it away for nothing. The enemy frequently lost all the battles and won all the negotiations. Gerald had long-since come to believe the only solution to the endless series of brushfire wars was to put political interference aside and bang heads together until the idiots got the message.

He snorted at his own hubris as he cast an eye over the makeshift command and control centre. It was a scene of organised chaos. His staff had commandeered a hangar, installed hundreds of foldable tables and covered them with computer terminals and communications nodes. They sat or stood at their stations, snapping orders into headsets as they struggled to build an accurate picture and report to him. A team of marine officers were being briefed in the far corner, staring at a map someone had pinned to the wall. They looked to Gerald for leadership. They expected him to set the objectives, then trust them to carry them out. He felt a flicker of envy for the younger men. They could afford to look at their tiny fragment of the picture, as if the bigger picture didn't exist. *He* couldn't afford such a luxury.

The timing was diabolical, he acknowledged sourly. If the enemy had planned it that way…he shook his head in droll amusement. Only a complete idiot would draw up such a plan and expect it to work. He'd find a way to bust any of his subordinates who suggested it all the way back to rifleman—or, more likely, send them back to the field. And yet…it was possible, he supposed, the enemy CO had always had the plan at the back of his mind. Only a fool would *expect* it to work, but only a fool *wouldn't* take advantage if it happened naturally. God knew *he* made sure to keep a handful of contingency plans in his head, even if he never expected to have the chance to use them.

They caught us with our pants down and our cocks on the chopping block, he admitted, to himself if no one else. Denying reality—as unpleasant as it happened to be—was the first sign of terminal stupidity. *And we have only a short space of time to make corrections.*

He didn't touch his terminal or datapad. He'd seen the figures. He'd served in countless campaigns. He *knew* there was no hope of lifting more than a few hundred marines off the surface before the hammer came down. It was sheer luck they'd secured most of the PDCs and orbital industries. If the enemy fleet had arrived even a few days earlier…he'd have been thoroughly screwed. As it was, the campaign hadn't failed, but...he shook his head. Their options had narrowed to fight or surrender. And he had no intention of giving up just yet.

"Sir." Lieutenant Hemet saluted, sharply. "The MEUs are preparing to leave orbit."

Gerald nodded. He was no expert in space warfare, but he knew enough to understand the giant MEUs were sitting ducks. They'd draw fire the moment the enemy fleet entered orbit, ensuring he couldn't hope to evacuate the planet in time. The spacers would do what they could, but it wouldn't be enough. He could calculate the odds as well as anyone else. The spacers could delay the newcomers. They couldn't *stop* them.

"Order them to prepare to receive shuttles," he said. He had *a* contingency plan, but it was one he'd *really* never expected to use. "Get me a list of space-specialists and prioritise them for evacuation."

"Yes, sir," Lieutenant Hemet said. "They won't want to go."

"No," Gerald agreed. "But they have their orders."

He frowned as he heard shouting from outside the hangar. Word was spreading. The marines wouldn't panic, but their local allies probably *would*. He couldn't blame them. Collaborators tended to get the worst of it, if it turned out they'd switched sides too early. It was never easy to make such a judgement. He privately hoped he'd never have to make it himself.

"And inform Captain Steel that I want to see him as soon as he returns," Gerald added. It had been bad luck sending Captain Steel on patrol just before the enemy fleet had shown itself. There was no *good* time for an enemy fleet to arrive, but this one had picked a particularly *bad* time. They'd thrown all of Gerald's plans for a loop. "Dismissed."

Lieutenant Hemet saluted and hurried away. Gerald winced inwardly, wondering if it was time to rotate the younger man back to a combat unit. A good staff officer was worth his weight in whatever previous substance one cared to name, but—as they forgot the lessons of combat—they tended to make mistakes. The corps tried to handle the problem by rotating officers from combat posts to staff duties and back again, yet...by the time a staff officer learnt to be a *good* staff officer it was often time for him to go back. He grimaced. Perhaps it was time to put Auxiliaries in staff positions. They wouldn't be promoted, so they'd do better...

He cursed under his breath as he looked at the display. The enemy fleet was steadily advancing on the planet, ignoring all attempts to lure it away. He felt a twinge of admiration for the enemy CO, tempered by the grim awareness that any tactical officer worthy of the name would *know* there was no point in altering course. Why bother to play the game if it was rigged?

And they know the rules as well as we do, he thought. His analysts had studied the captured files. They'd cautioned that the enemy had been headhunting experienced officers from the imperial forces. *If they'd given their officers freedom to act without regard for politics and political correctness, they could have built a formidable force.*

Gerald strode outside, watching as flights of helicopters and assault shuttles rose and fell around the former enemy base. There was no way to hide the activity from prying eyes. If the remnants of the enemy army were still active, they'd know *something* had gone wrong even if they didn't know precisely *what*. The marines were sweeping the area outside the city, trying to ensure no one sneaked close enough to fire mortar shells or launch missiles into the throng, but there was no way to be *certain*. If the enemy knew something had happened—or that a relief force was on the way—they might gamble everything on a bid to impede the evacuation. They'd be killed, but they'd do immense damage before they were wiped out. They might lose the engagement, yet win the war.

He glanced towards the gates as a marine platoon—and a trio of prisoners—entered the complex. The MPs—marine MPs—hurried to take control of the prisoners, rushing them away before they could see anything incriminating. Gerald suspected it was a waste of time—the garrison would have to be evacuated before enemy forces landed or simply bombed it to shit—but there was no point in taking silly chances. Captain Steel disengaged himself from his men and headed towards the main hangar, his eyes going wide as he spotted Gerald waiting for him. Gerald kept his face as impassive as possible.

"General." Steel saluted, sharply. "You recalled me?"

Gerald nodded, hearing the unspoken question. Why? "There've been developments," he said. "The enemy relief fleet has arrived."

Steel looked grim. He was a rifleman first—*all* marines were riflemen first, even the handful who tried to make careers flying desks—but he was also a space-specialist. He understood the realities of space warfare better than Gerald, who'd spent most of his career on the ground. In hindsight...Gerald dismissed the thought with a flicker of irritation. Hindsight was always clearer than foresight. Sure, it would have been smarter to leave Steel on the MEUs...but only if he'd *known* he'd need Steel up there. And he hadn't.

"We hold the PDCs," Steel said, in tones that suggested he was looking desperately for the bright side. "They can't smash us from orbit."

"No, but they *can* cut us off from Safehouse," Gerald said. Their supply chain had always been weak, despite the mobile factory ships the corps wasn't supposed to have. He hoped the enemy hadn't thought to look for them. "And they can fight us on the ground until we run out of ammunition."

He met the younger man's eyes. "You and your platoon are going to be evacuated shortly," he said. "Grab what you can and join the line."

"Sir." Steel gathered himself to make a protest. "I can't run out on you..."

"Those are your orders, *Captain*, which you may have in writing if you wish." Gerald composed himself with an effort. He understood Steel's feelings. He would have shared them, if they'd swapped places. But there was no time to deal with them. "I need you up there, not patrolling the streets or fighting a rearguard action. You may have a more important role in space."

Steel frowned. "You have a mission for me, sir?"

"I have half a plan," Gerald said. He'd already forwarded what he could to Captain Stumbaugh and the other spacers. They'd have to turn the concept into something workable—if they could—and then put it into action. "Report to the shuttles, Captain. And good luck."

"Yes, sir," Steel said, stiffly. It was just one step short of insubordination. "I'll see you on the far side."

Gerald nodded, keeping his expression blank as Steel turned and strode away. He understood, better than he cared to admit. Marines were taught to be *loyal*. Deserting one's comrades was an unpardonable sin, even if one was *ordered* to leave. Steel—and Gerald, truth be told -would have risked dozens of marines to save one. And yet, there was no point in keeping Steel on the ground. Gerald had thousands of groundpounders under his command. Space-specialists were rarer. In hindsight, he would sooner have left Steel in space. He hoped—as he turned to watch the armoured vehicles and air defence units being moved towards the gates in preparation for the coming struggle—that Steel wouldn't do anything stupid and try to remain on the ground. He'd break the younger man, even though he'd understand. Steel would have problems living with himself if he survived while his comrades died.

And if the worst happens, he thought grimly, *I'll die with my men*.

• • •

Specialist Rachel Green did her level best to look like a harmless—and hopeless—civilian medic as she walked through the makeshift refugee camp. The locals had fled the government complex and surrounding districts, crossing the river and taking up residence in a multitude of abandoned warehouses, schools and colonist barracks that had—somehow—survived the waves of civil unrest that had shaken the city before the thunder runs. They looked pitiful to her eyes, cowering as if they couldn't decide if they were more scared of the marines or their fellow civilians. The planet had always been a hotbed of resentment, made worse by the government's refusal to allow its people to vent. She wasn't surprised that hundreds of downtrodden civilians had thrown off the veneer of civilisation and turned into monsters. The only real surprise was that it wasn't a great deal worse.

These people are sheep, she thought. They'd been born and raised in a cage, with bars both visible and invisible. They acted as if they thought they were being watched at every moment, which—she conceded sourly—was more or less true. *The bars are removed and yet most of them are still pacing the cage, too scared to leave.*

She grimaced as she cast her eye over a battered-looking family. Their clothes suggested they'd been wealthy, once upon a time. The planet's upper classes had enjoyed a little more freedom than the commoners. Now…they looked too scared to move. Rachel felt a twinge of pity for the children, reflecting on how their world had turned upside down practically overnight. Their mother looked too frightened to meet her gaze. There was no sign of any father or uncle or anyone else. It didn't bode well for their future.

Specialist Steven Phelps followed her, acting as assistant and bodyguard. Rachel had little fear of the hapless refugees, even the ones who were steadily turning into wolves, but it was probably better to deter aggression than deal with it after it became a problem. She moved from wounded refugee to wounded refugee, offering what help she could while listening to whispers and rumours flying through the air. The refugees were unaware of her true nature. They talked freely in front of her, exchanging wider and wider rumours that bore little resemblance to reality. The marines had slaughtered the entire city. The marines were rounding up women for secret breeding purposes. The marines were lizard-aliens in disguise. The marines were…the stories got more and more absurd as they passed around the refugee encampment. She supposed they made a certain kind of sense. The refugees had been dependent on the planetary news service, a heavily-censored network that had no qualms about rewriting history to create favourable facts. No, there were no reliable sources of information. There were no private networks, radio broadcasts…not even old-fashioned newspapers. No wonder the rumours were growing out of control. The population couldn't hope to sort truth from lies.

Although one hopes they don't believe we're really *man-eating lizards,* she thought, as they moved to the next encampment. *That's too absurd for words.*

She shivered as she tasted the despondency in the air. The refugee camp looked a little more organised than the last, something that bothered her on a very primal level. Dozens of refugees sat on the ground, almost all women. Young and attractive women. She glanced at Phelps, who also looked concerned. The camp was starting to look like a prison. She braced herself as the guards stood and ambled towards her. They looked like thugs, but thugs with some military or police experience. She guessed they'd deserted when the enemy government had collapsed.

The leader sneered at them both. "Who are you?"

"Doctor Moonchild and Nurse Robb," Rachel lied smoothly. The Opel Moonchild identity had the great advantage of being both useful and harmless, as far as the thugs were concerned. "We're doing what we can to help."

The thugs exchanged glances. "You're working for us now," the leader said. "This way."

Rachel pasted a nervous expression on her face as the thugs led them though the camp and into the warehouse. They'd turned it into a brothel. The warehouse was crammed with beds. Her eyes swept the chamber, noting that there were only five thugs in total. Five! A couple carried visible weapons—military rifles, a common design—but the locals could have taken them out if they'd plucked up the nerve. But they were too beaten down to realise.

"You can treat these bitches," the thug said. "And then…"

Rachel made a sign to Phelps, then hit the thug in the throat. He folded, making a gurgling sound as he hit the ground. Phelps took out the second thug, drawing his pistol a second later and shooting the remaining thugs before they could raise their weapons. Rachel was almost disappointed. The thugs could have been taken out at any moment, if the locals had stood up to them. She'd been in more dangerous situations on the Slaughterhouse.

"Call HQ, get them to send a patrol out here," she said, as she checked the nearest bed. The women didn't look like hardened prostitutes. A number were badly bruised. She guessed they'd been told they were going to whore for the gang and been beaten savagely when they'd refused. "This place needs help."

She gritted her teeth as she searched the warehouse, making sure they hadn't missed anyone. She was used to horror, but...

"They're telling us to report back," Phelps said, in surprise. "They don't have time to send out a patrol."

"Fuck," Rachel said. "Tell them..."

"They put out a Red One alert," Phelps said. "I don't think they'll listen."

"Fuck," Rachel repeated. "Tell them we're on our way."

She looked around for women who seemed ready to fight, then picked up the rifles and passed them around. The bullets wouldn't last—thankfully, the rifles were designed to endure all sorts of abuse—but they'd give the women a chance. She hoped it would be enough. Phelps was right. A Red One alert admitted of no ambiguity. They *had* to report back ASAP.

And see what's gone wrong now, she thought. The invasion force had been transitioning into occupation mode. If something had derailed that...she scowled. *It's going to be bad.*

CHAPTER FOUR

The long-term problem, however, is more serious (particularly as the regime outlasts its founder). That is the problem of receiving accurate information from one's underlings.
—**Professor Leo Caesius**
The Right to be Wrong: How Silencing People Hurts You

DEREK WASN'T SURE, IN ALL HONESTY, if he was a prisoner, an ally or merely someone the marines felt a certain obligation towards. They hadn't given him any good answer, after they'd escorted him from the government bunker to the commandeered HQ, then reunited him with Jenny Alyson. His girlfriend—he supposed he could call Jenny his girlfriend now—had been swept up as the marines secured Bouchon. He was glad they'd sent her to him, yet…he didn't know *why*. Keeping him happy hardly seemed one of their priorities.

And everyone thinks I'm a traitor, he thought, numbly. He'd been *assured* no one outside the marines—and Derek himself, of course—knew what had happened in the command bunker, but he didn't believe it. He'd spent most of his life in a small town, then the army. There were few secrets in such an environment. He knew more than he wanted to know about his neighbours. *If I stick my head out of the camp, I'll be shot.*

He paced the small room, wondering—again—what the marines were going to do with him. He'd been too angry to think about the future, when he'd levelled his gun at the planetary governors and shot them. He'd been too bitter at their failings, too bitter at watching too many good men—friends and enemies alike—die because they'd been betrayed or abandoned by their political leaders. And now…it was a wonder Jenny could even *look* at him. Her father was a Town Councillor. She'd been on the road to greatness, before the invasion. Everyone had known it, particularly her. Now…

Jenny shifted, sitting up in bed. They'd spent a lot of time making love over the last few days, if only because there was nothing else to do. The marines hadn't provided anything in the way of entertainment. Their rations were better than the crap he'd eaten during the war—he honestly couldn't imagine them eating anything worse—but there were only so many ways one could eat ration bars before one got sick of them. Derek wondered, grimly, what Jenny would do if something better came along. Before the war, she'd been way out of his league. Her father would have broken anyone who so much as *looked* at his daughter. Now…

You don't even know you have a future, he told himself, savagely. He'd seen too many people die over the last couple of months. *Why worry about it?*

"Come here," Jenny said. "I think we can try…"

She cupped her breasts in her hands, squeezing them lightly. Derek stared, feeling blood rushing out of his brain and down to his groin. He'd never *dreamed* anyone could be so forward, not outside bad porno flicks. Jenny had seemed as reserved as the handful of other upper-class girls he'd met, girls who appeared convinced they were under the spotlight all hours of the day. And yet…he stumbled forward, reaching for her. All the old rules, official and unofficial, were gone. They could do whatever they liked.

There was a sharp knock at the door. Jenny squeaked, then grabbed the blanket and clutched it to her chest. Derek muttered a word he'd learnt in the barracks, before turning and picking up the nearest towel. He'd lost his sense of modesty long ago—there'd never been any privacy in his life—but he'd always felt a little defenceless when he was naked. He wrapped the towel around his waist, then opened the door. A grim-faced marine, vaguely familiar, stood on the far side. He showed no sign of surprise at their state of undress.

We might be being watched, Derek reminded himself. He stepped back, glancing around even though he knew any surveillance devices would be too small to see. *They won't be that interested in watching us, will they?*

"General Anderson," he said, remembering the marine's name. "It's good to see you again."

Jenny cleared her throat. "General, I…"

Anderson glanced at her, then looked away. "There have been developments," he said. "The relief fleet has entered the system. It will enter orbit in"—he looked at his wristcom—"roughly thirty minutes. We don't have much time to react, let alone evacuate."

"…Shit," Derek said. He was a traitor. They were going to hang him, the moment they laid hands on him. "I…"

"You have several options," Anderson said. "First, we can give you a slot on one of the evacuation shuttles. We *should* be able to get you into space, then well away from the enemy ships, before it's too late. However, there is a slight chance things will go wrong. If that happens, we can't guarantee your safety."

"Oh." Derek swallowed, hard. He didn't doubt his bravery, but there was a difference between fighting on the ground, where he might be able to save himself, and sitting helplessly in a vulnerable shuttle. "What are the other options?"

"Second, you can join us," Anderson said. "We should be able to hold out long enough for reinforcements to arrive…"

"I don't like the sound of that *should*," Jenny injected. "Are you sure?"

"There's little *sure* in wartime," Anderson pointed out, stiffly. "We cannot guarantee anything. We're going to need to carry out a fighting retreat, doing everything in our power to impede them to buy time. You can help us, either by fighting on the front lines or by taking up position within the city. It'll give you a fair chance to fight back."

"Right." Derek had seen more fighting in the last two months than he'd wanted to see in his entire life. "And the third option?"

"You can vanish," Anderson said. "Very few people know *precisely* what happened in the bunker. Those who do have either been put somewhere safe or know to keep their mouths firmly shut. We're looking through the POW camps now, reshuffling prisoners in hopes of sorting the dangerous ones—or the ones guilty of war crimes—from the ones who can be released. You can be added to the latter set and released, with no one aware of quite what you were doing when you were captured. I think we owe you that much."

Derek frowned. He was tempted, very tempted, to walk away. The planetary government had had hellishly complete records, but the stresses and strains of wartime *had* to have broken the system...right? The relief force might know he'd been in the army, if they recovered the records or had copies, but they couldn't know he'd been promoted, or that he'd been in Haverford when the city fell. They'd have no reason to assume he was anything other than a common infantryman. Losing the promotion would hurt, but it would be a small price to pay for vanishing into history. And yet...

He looked at Jenny. She was wonderful and...what sort of life would she have if the world changed hands again? What sort of life would *they* have? Her father was a collaborator, from what she'd said. The newcomers might put him and his entire family up against the nearest wall, if—when—they found out. And they *would* find out. Councillor Alyson had *not* been popular. *Someone* would rat him out, sooner rather than later. And then Jenny would die.

Jenny leaned forward. "How long do we have?"

"To decide?" Anderson frowned. "Ten minutes, probably. I'll have to assign your slots to others if you don't want them."

And you have to go back to work, Derek added. *You're not going to abandon your men and start running...*

"I'll stay," Derek said. "Jenny can take the shuttle and..."

"I'm not leaving you," Jenny said, cutting him off. "We'll *both* stay."

"The front lines aren't safe for women," Derek said. "And..."

Anderson laughed as Jenny flushed angrily. "Dangerous waters, young man; dangerous waters."

Derek glared at the older man. "It's true!"

"Right now, there isn't anywhere safe for anyone," Anderson said, quietly. "And women can be in dreadful danger even if they're far from the front lines."

He shook his head. "If you both want to stay..."

"I want her to *live*," Derek said. "You can take her away while I stay and fight."

"I'm staying." Jenny swung her legs over the side of the bed and stood, wrapping the blanket around her like a shroud. "And that's final."

Derek tried to think of an argument, but nothing came to mind. Jenny had made up her mind and...he wanted to order her to go, to tell her to go, to threaten her with everything from desertion to violence to make her go. And yet...he looked at the older man, who seemed uncommonly amused by the whole affair. Jenny wasn't a soldier. It just wasn't *fair* to put her in danger.

"We'll stay in the city, then," he said, desperately. It would bring its own dangers, he was sure, but at least they wouldn't be on the front lines. "If we pretend to be a married couple..."

"The records are shot to hell," Anderson confirmed. "But we'd still advise you to remain out of sight, for the moment."

He looked from Derek to Jenny and back again. "Get dressed. We've a handful of other volunteers to stay behind, so you'll be joining them. We'll get you into the city, armed and ready, before the shit hits the fan. We hope."

"You hope," Derek echoed. "Nothing is easy in war, is it?"

"No." Anderson turned and opened the door. "It never is."

He closed the door behind him. Derek took a breath, then turned to face Jenny. She'd dropped the blanket and started to dress. Derek forced himself to look away. Jenny looked stunning. It was hard to believe, sometimes, that they'd spent the last few days in bed together. It felt like a dream.

"You could get killed, or worse," he said. He wasn't sure what Jenny had been through, the night Eddisford had fallen, but it couldn't have been pleasant. She'd been very tight-lipped about how she'd travelled from Eddisford to Bouchon. "Jenny..."

"And the only other choice is running and hiding," Jenny said. "And I've done enough of both."

"I know." Derek felt his anger flow away. "I don't want you dead."

"I should hope not," Jenny said, primly. She pulled her sweater over her head. "Get dressed, unless you intend to fight naked."

"It might frighten the enemy," Derek said. He reached for his pants and started to pull them on. "Good tactic, do you think?"

"I think it's much more likely they'll be incapacitated with laughter," Jenny said, with a faint chuckle. "But I suppose you'd be able to shoot them while they were helpless. Is that fair?"

Derek sobered. "I don't care if it's fair or not," he said. "I just want to stay alive."

• • •

"It feels like we're running away," someone said, as the company formed ranks and marched towards the shuttlecraft. "Really."

Haydn resisted the urge to look back and see who'd spoken. He didn't recognise the voice. One of the newbies probably, transferred from another company because his experience in space was more important than skill on the ground. He couldn't help agreeing with the newbie, even though—as a senior officer—he had to hide it. It *did* feel like they were running away, abandoning their comrades to save themselves. The corps never ran from a fight. It was an ethos that had been drilled into him the very first day at Boot Camp. And yet, he had his orders. They had to leave now, before it was too late.

A dozen ideas ran through his head for staying behind, each one more ridiculous than the last. He could leave the company in his XO's hands and *accidentally* miss the shuttle. He could force the shuttle to make an emergency landing. He could bail out as they clawed their way into space. He could hastily rewrite the computer files to suggest he'd never actually passed the space-specialist training course…But none of the ideas were remotely practical. Orders were orders, unless they were illegal. And ordering him to leave the planet was far from illegal. There would be nothing, but a court-martial and a dishonourable discharge in his future if he disobeyed.

Perhaps I should have asked for the orders in writing, he thought. A gust of metallic air struck him as he clambered into the shuttle. As always, the craft smelt of too many men in too close proximity. *Perhaps that would have made General Anderson think twice.*

"Take your seats," he ordered. He stowed his carryall in the overhead locker before finding his own seat. "And please keep the chatter to a dull roar."

He sat and strapped himself in, then pulled his datapad from his belt and accessed the live feed from the command network. The enemy fleet was closing rapidly, preparing to engage the marine starships. The MEUs were already pulling out of orbit. The shuttles were going to have to race to catch up with them. And then…he felt the craft lurch underneath him as the pilot powered up the drives. The shuttle was about to depart.

"Please remember to put your head between your legs," the pilot said, through the intercom. "It won't do any good if we get hit, but it'll make it easier to kiss your ass goodbye before you die."

Haydn scowled. He'd heard too much of what passed for pilot humour. They might be Auxiliaries, but they'd earned respect. They didn't *need* to make immature jokes about stewardesses, buckling one's seatbelts and generally staying put until the shuttle reached its destination. He supposed it was a way of coping with the grim reality that the shuttles were too small and fragile to survive a single hit. If they were fired upon by starship-grade weapons, they'd be dead before they knew what'd hit them.

The shuttle lurched, then clawed into the sky. Haydn swallowed hard. The pilots seemed to go out of their way to make takeoffs and landings as rough as possible. He'd been assured it was a side-effect of the military-grade drives and compensators, but he didn't believe it. The pilots joked too much about turbulence and airsickness.

He leaned back in his chair, trying to relax. They'd reach the MEUs before it was too late and then…and then, he promised himself, they'd find a way to fight back.

It won't have been for nothing, he promised himself. Too many marines had died during the invasion for him to just cut and run. *We'll make damn sure of it.*

...

"General?"

Gerald looked up from his console. "Yes?"

"The last of the shuttles just departed," Lieutenant Hemet reported. "We're moving the captured aircraft and assault drones now."

"Make sure we spike what we can't take," Gerald ordered. A number of former enemy airmen had volunteered to join the marines, but he wasn't about to put them in control of an armed helicopter or a drone. The risk was too great. "Did you set up the alternate command post?"

"It's up and running," Lieutenant Hemet confirmed. "But there's no way to know how long it'll last. We can't depend on the landlines."

Gerald nodded. They'd grown far too used to having the advantage of better weapons, training and communications. No insurgency had been able to match them, let alone take down the command and control network long enough to inflict serious damage. But the corprats *could*. He made a mental note to insist that training exercises be improved, in hopes of ensuring the marines were better-prepared next time. It was terrifying to realise they'd been overconfident for so long. They could have lost if the enemy had been ready to take advantage of it.

And we still can, he thought. *They're going to give us a very hard time.*

"Good," he said. Right now, he had to concentrate on the present. "And the recruits?"

"They're being armed now," Lieutenant Hemet said. He looked doubtful. "Is it wise to trust them?"

"Perhaps, perhaps not." Gerald shrugged. "Turning one's coat *does* tend to be habit-forming. But we risk little by sending them back to the city and stand to gain much, if they accomplish something—anything. It's worth trying."

"Yes, sir." Lieutenant Hemet didn't sound convinced. Gerald didn't blame him. "They might just hide again."

"I doubt it," Gerald said. A handful of the turncoats would be executed, if they fell into enemy hands. The others would probably be executed too. "But it doesn't matter."

He cleared his throat. "Order the beta, delta and gamma units to take up their positions as quickly as possible. And then evacuate the alpha units. I want this base empty by the time the enemy ships come within missile range. If we can land missiles here, they can."

"Yes, sir," Lieutenant Hemet said. "I'll see to it at once."

Gerald nodded, watching as his command staff packed up and hurried to the transports. They'd drilled endlessly, making sure they could move to a new location and set up again as quickly as possible, but it wouldn't be a smooth process. Something always went wrong, even in drills. One delay would lead to more, each one adding up to a real problem. And now...the missiles heading through space were *real*. All hell was about to break loose.

And all we can do is prepare to take it, he thought. *And hope we can hold out long enough for help to arrive.*

CHAPTER FIVE

This is, of course, a problem everywhere. There isn't a politician, corporate CEO or military officer who hasn't faced the issue of his subordinates lying to him, for reasons ranging between self-promotion and self-preservation. A man with a habit of shooting the messenger—i.e. blaming the messenger for the message—is a man who will grow uncomfortably used to hearing nothing but good news.
—**Professor Leo Caesius**
The Right to be Wrong: How Silencing People Hurts You

"Fire," Captain Kerri Stumbaugh ordered.

Havoc rocked as she unleashed a salvo of missiles. The remainder of the squadron fired a second later, salvos merging into a single, giant barrage remorselessly advancing towards the enemy ships. Their point defence sensors went active, filling space with sensor pulses as they targeted the missiles. If she had one advantage, she reflected grimly, it was that the enemy practically *had* to impale themselves on her weapons. It wouldn't be enough to tip the balance in her favour.

"The enemy has returned fire," Lieutenant Tomas reported, needlessly. The display sparkled with red icons. "Point defence online, ready to fire; defence grid online, ready to fire."

"Engage as soon as they enter range," Kerri said. The enemy had flushed their external racks, trying to knock her out with a single barrage. They were going to be disappointed. Her fleet had drilled extensively, against simulated missiles that only existed in her nightmares. Reality would be different, but not *that* different. "Assess the enemy point defence for weaknesses, then adjust our fire to match."

"Aye, Captain," Tomas said.

Kerri leaned forward, bracing herself as her missiles flew into the enemy engagement envelope and vanished. The enemy had clearly trained extensively too, working their ships and crews until they were practically a single entity. She nodded in sour admiration at how their smaller ships provided point defence for the larger ships, particularly the battlecruiser. Standard tactics in mass fleet engagements were to strip away the smaller ships *first*, but she didn't have the time. The enemy formation was simply too powerful.

An analysis popped up in front of her. She glanced at it—the enemy command ship was evidently the battlecruiser, as if she hadn't known that already—and then looked back at the display. The enemy point defence was just too good. It was unlikely she'd do any real damage, unless she closed the range to the point she could bring her energy weapons to bear. And if she did that, she'd be torn to ribbons in short order. The enemy CO was probably hoping she'd oblige him. But she might as well have committed suicide if she tried.

Her eyes narrowed as the last of the missiles swept into attack range and lanced into a handful of enemy ships. Laser warheads detonated, stabbing beams of ravening energy into enemy hulls. Their armour was good, solid. A handful of icons flashed up in front of her, suggesting damage was minimal. One ship staggered under the weight of her fire, threatening to fall out of formation before her crew steadied her. The remainder seemed untroubled as they launched another wave of missiles. She simply didn't have the throw weight to make a serious impression.

Havoc shuddered as a laser warhead detonated nearby, the beam striking her ship. Alerts flashed up in front of her, rapidly updating as the onboard datanet struggled to assess the damage. It veered between total disaster to a mere scratch…she smiled, humourlessly, as her XO directed damage control teams to the hull breach. The hullmetal had absorbed most of the blow. The enemy should have tried to target her drives.

Which they will, when we try to break contact, she thought. The range was steady, her fleet holding position between the enemy ships and the planet, but that was going to change. She'd find herself caught between the devil and the deep blue sea very quickly, once they pushed her right back to the planet itself. *We'll have to show them our rears as we turn and run.*

She watched, grimly, as the engagement continued. There was no point in issuing orders. Her crew knew what to do, allowing her to concentrate on the overall picture. It wasn't good. The enemy ships pressed them hard, as if they literally wanted to drive her ships into the planet. Death through ramming an entire *planet* would be embarrassing. She'd heard of a particularly idiotic officer who'd rammed an asteroid, but—outside bad holoflicks—that was very rare. The man had to have been more than *just* an idiot. He would have had to have been very unlucky as well.

Her lips thinned, eyes tracking the enemy missiles. She had the advantage of trying to keep the range open, giving the enemy missiles a chance to burn themselves out and go ballistic before they reached her formation, but she couldn't keep the range *that* open. They were already too close to the planet for her peace of mind. She dared not let them close with her, not given their firepower. The results would be disastrous.

She glanced at the communications officer. "Confirm the MEUs have made it clear."

"Confirmed," the communications officer said. "They're heading to the RV point now."

And planning to cloak as soon as they're out of active sensor range, Kerri thought. The MEUs weren't warships, and wouldn't last a minute if they ran into an enemy warship, but their stealth systems were second to none. *They'll sneak around the system and link up with us as planned.*

She frowned as she studied the enemy ships. The Imperial Navy had the best stealth systems in the known galaxy—and the Terran Marine Corps had copied their designs—but what about the *unknown* galaxy? The Onge Corporation had been on the cutting edge of starship design for centuries. They'd had all sorts of technical concepts that had never, officially, received funding. What if they'd secretly funded a project that had produced better weapons or sensors than any known to exist? They couldn't have *known* when they'd find themselves on their own. They might have prepared for a clash with the Imperial Navy before Earthfall. And advanced weapons would give them the edge...

Better training alone would give them the edge, she thought, coldly. The Imperial Navy had skimped on training, before the end. The Onge Corporation clearly had *not*. Their crews didn't *need* wonder-weapons. They just needed to know how to get the best out of their systems. Their point defence was good, their targeting depressingly accurate...she gritted her teeth as another missile slipped through her fleet's defences. *There's no doubt they know what they're doing.*

"Captain," Tomas said. "*Lightning* took a major hit. She's losing power."

"Order her to break contact, if possible," Kerri said. "And prepare to evacuate if they can't."

She grimaced. The light cruiser wasn't designed for battle. She wished for a formation of battleships, although she knew the monstrous ships had their limitations. Her fellow cadets had joked battleships had been designed for admirals with penis envy. And yet...they might be ponderously slow, but right now a single battleship would have turned the tide in her favour. The enemy *had* to come into her range if they wanted to retake the planet.

"Aye, Captain," Tomas said.

Kerri nodded. Evacuating *Lightning* under fire would be far from easy—the shuttles and escape pods might be mistaken for mines and blown out of space before the enemy realised their mistake—but she was damned if she was leaving her crew to be picked up by the enemy ships. If nothing else, they knew too much. There was no reason to think the enemy would mistreat prisoners, but *Kerri* would want to know what her prisoners knew. The corprats had surprised her—she admitted that, grudgingly—yet the marines had also surprised *them*. They'd want to know what *else* they'd missed.

And if we'd known they were preparing for Earthfall too, she mused, *what would we have done about it?*

She shook her head. There was no point in dwelling on what might have been. Right now, she had to buy time for the folks on the surface. And hope, when she finally broke contact, that she'd bought them enough time. It was going to be tight. They just hadn't planned for an enemy relief fleet.

We were too used to fighting at a time and a place of our choosing, she told herself. *And now it's bitten us on the bum.*

...

"Why are they wasting their missiles?"

Admiral Nelson Agate glanced at Julia as the engagement continued to develop. The frustration in her voice was clear—and understandable. People who gleaned their idea of space combat from flicks, and simulations where the umpire was on their side, had no concept of just how *long* a major engagement could last. The enemy ships knew what they were doing. They were forcing him to expend his missiles fruitlessly, delaying him for a few short moments as he crawled towards the planet. It looked as though they were wasting their time, but he knew better. He probably wouldn't be able to recover the missiles he'd fired.

Particularly as we're heading straight towards the planet, he thought. *If we accidentally* hit *the planet...*

"They're trying to slow us down," he said, putting the thought aside. If a missile hit a planet at a respectable fraction of the speed of light, the damage would be beyond calculation. The warhead wouldn't need to detonate to do a hell of a lot of damage. "And they're wasting their time."

He smiled, coldly. The enemy *hadn't* had any silver bullets in their guns. That much was evident from how they'd chosen to fight, keeping the range open instead of trying to close. Their missiles were good, top-of-the-range, but nothing *new*. The Imperial Navy could have matched them, if it had been willing to expend time and effort in training and maintenance. And to think the marines weren't supposed to have any warships! They were better at flying them than their naval counterparts.

But not as good as us, he thought, with a hint of amusement. *They could have done better...*

Julia frowned. "So what do we do?"

"They can't stop us from retaking the high orbitals," Nelson reminded her, again. "They'll have no choice but to retreat or fight us on our terms."

He forced himself to watch as the engagement continued, the planet steadily coming closer as his fleet advanced. There were risks in firing missiles through the high orbitals, even if they *didn't* hit the planet itself. The orbital industries *had* to remain intact. He'd done his best to explain that accidents happened, that there was no way to *guarantee* a stray missile wouldn't hit a platform—or the enemy wouldn't destroy them after they evacuated—but Julia had been insistent. Very insistent. He saw her point—the orbital industries were effectively irreplaceable, at least for the next decade—but he couldn't make promises. That was a good way to wind up with egg on one's face.

And a grudge the size of a small planet, he thought. He'd known too many officers, passed over for promotion or simply turned into scapegoats, who'd allowed their resentment to curdle into hatred. *That's when people start plotting trouble.*

"Admiral," the tactical officer said. "The remaining enemy freighters are breaking orbit."

Nelson briefly considered altering course and trying to run them down. Freighters couldn't hope to outrun his ships, although if they scattered he'd have to break up the formation to catch the majority before they crossed the phase line and vanished. But it looked very much as if someone had built the freighters on military hulls and given them military-grade drives. Q-Ships? Or simply a fleet train built to keep up with the warships? *That* was something *he* wanted, something he intended to insist his superiors build as quickly as possible. They weren't going to be *just* defending the cluster, unless he missed his guess. Sooner or later, they were going to start conquering the galaxy. And they'd need a fleet train that was up to the task of keeping the fleet resupplied.

A shame the Imperial Navy never considered the issue, he mused. *But then, the last time it fought a serious war was over a thousand years ago.*

"Let them go," he ordered. "How long until we reach the high orbitals?"

"Ten minutes, unless we reduce speed," the tactical officer said. A dull quiver ran through the ship as a missile impacted on her hull. "The enemy fleet will have to break contact in seven."

Unless they want to try to keep us busy, Nelson thought. *But the worst they can do is snipe at us.*

He allowed himself a moment of satisfaction as the engagement continued. The fleet—*his* fleet—had performed well. His officers had proved they could engage the enemy in real life, as well as in the simulators. There'd been no panic, no hesitation…sooner or later, it would dawn on the raw recruits that the icons they'd seen vanish from the display had represented entire starships, each one with a crew in the hundreds. He wondered, grimly, how they'd cope. Space warfare was supposed to be genteel. Starships met in engagements that were as much elegant dances as anything else. And yet, when a hull was breached, the crew would suffocate unless they sealed off the section or patched the hole. And *that* assumed an enemy missile didn't detonate *inside* the hull. The crew would be dead before they knew what had hit them.

"They have to alter course shortly," he said. "I wonder which way they'll jump."

Julia gave him a sharp look. "What do you mean?"

"They can slow us a little more if they remain where they are," Nelson said. "But it'll expose them to more and more of our fire. And give us a chance to put a missile or two into their drives as they run. Or they can break off now, giving them their best chance to evade us at the cost of losing the opportunity to slow us further."

He shrugged. "It'll be interesting to see what they'll pick."

Another quiver ran through the giant battlecruiser. Nelson smiled, coldly. The engagement was becoming predictable. The enemy could see it as clearly as himself. They'd know what they had to do, even if they didn't want to admit it. And they'd do it. It wouldn't be long now.

Then we can reclaim the planet, he thought. *And that will be just the beginning.*

...

"Captain," Commander Joaquin said. The helmsman sounded concerned. "We're running out of manoeuvring room."

"It's starting to look that way," Kerri agreed. There were thousands of kilometres between *Havoc* and the planet—and tens of kilometres between her and her fellow ships—but, at the speeds starships travelled, it was hardly any room at all. The enemy were increasing their rate of fire, daring her to turn her back. "Communications, signal the fleet. We'll execute Bravo-Two in sixty seconds."

"Aye, Captain," the communications officer said. "Bravo-Two in sixty seconds."

Kerri nodded as a timer appeared on the display. She'd done all she could, slowing the enemy as much as possible without putting her ships in danger. It galled her to turn and run, though she knew there was no choice. Her ships were effectively irreplaceable. She had no idea how the operations to seize navy shipyards were proceeding, let alone the plans to establish new shipyards in hidden locations, but she'd been warned not to expect replacements in a hurry. Even if the shipyards had been taken intact, with their trained workforces, it would take years to smooth out the bureaucratic nightmares and start churning out new ships. There was a *reason* the Imperial Navy hadn't built any new battleships for centuries.

And that reason has nothing to do with their limitations, she mused. *Right now, a squadron of battleships would come in very handy.*

"Execute Bravo-Two," she ordered, as the timer reached zero. "Now!"

Havoc's drives grew louder, the gravity field twitching uncomfortably as the starship spun on her axis and reversed course. The enemy fleet seemed to leap forward, a moment before the range started to open sharply. They'd have a window of opportunity to put a missile into her drives…she braced herself, watching as the fleet deployed sensor drones to confuse the enemy sensors. The Imperial Navy's officers would have problems separating the drones from the real ships—their computer programs were too limited—but she had no idea if the corprats would have the same problem. If they gave their sensor crews their heads, if they trusted them to use their intuition…

She breathed a sigh of relief as the range grew wider. The enemy had lost their one chance to weaken—if not destroy—her fleet. She scowled, wishing she knew *why* they'd let her go. Did they think it a trap? Had the drones confused them? Or were they too intent on recovering the planet to target her fleet? The latter made no sense. They had to know it would be difficult to replace any lost ships. They could win the battle and lose the war, if she returned with reinforcements.

"Captain," Tomas said. "We have successfully broken contact."

"Then take us to the first waypoint before we enter stealth," Kerri ordered. Hopefully, the enemy would think she was running for the Phase Limit. If she was really lucky, they'd assume she would *keep* running until she'd put several light years between them. "And alert General Anderson. He's about to have company."

"Aye, Captain."

CHAPTER SIX

However, the problem is magnified in dictatorial states. The dictator, a man who can and will punish the bearer of bad news, simply cannot afford to trust everything he hears. And yet, once he develops a reputation for killing the messenger, there is no way he can keep his people from lying to him.
—**Professor Leo Caesius**
The Right to be Wrong: How Silencing People Hurts You

THERE WERE TIMES IN HIS CAREER when Gerald would have preferred to command his forces from a battlesuit or a modified AFV. It would have combined the advantage of mobility with the advantage of making it hard for his political superiors to bug him, particularly in the middle of a complex military operation. But, he'd come to realise, in the last few minutes, it also had a considerable downside. The AFV he'd turned into a command post simply didn't have the room to properly pace.

He stared at the display, watching the red icons as they crawled towards the high orbitals. Captain Stumbaugh and her ships had done what they could, but Gerald—and everyone else—had known the outcome was preordained from the moment the enemy ships revealed themselves. She couldn't have stopped them, even if she'd thrown everything into a single, desperate charge. And now…she was retreating, falling back to the first waypoint with a half-formed plan to tip the balance back in their favour. Gerald gritted his teeth in frustration. He was no stranger to the fog of war, or how a military operation could shift from well-ordered precision to utter chaos in a heartbeat, but it was still irritating. His forces were in disarray. Too many of his men were going to be caught in the open when the shit hit the fan.

"General," Lieutenant Salmon said. "The enemy fleet is altering formation. I think they're trying to avoid the PDCs."

"Wise of them," Gerald muttered. The PDCs could pump out enough firepower to deter anyone from approaching the planet. Hameau's orbital space was extremely cluttered, to say the least, but the PDCs could still do a lot of damage. The enemy CO was lucky Gerald wanted to preserve as much of the orbital industry as possible. "Can you get a target lock?"

"Yes sir, but I doubt we'd hit anything." Salmon shook his head. "The range is simply too great."

"Then we wait," Gerald said. "And see."

...

"The enemy fleet has broken contact," the tactical officer reported. "They're accelerating away from the planet."

"And heading straight for the Phase Limit," Nelson mused. He doubted the enemy ships were *really* running in panic. So far, the marines had made good use of what they had. They were much more likely to start haunting the system, hacking away at his supply lines…it was probably their best option, unless they had more ships on the way. "Dispatch two destroyers to shadow them, under cloak."

"Aye, sir."

Nelson turned back to the display. The enemy fleet might be gone—and the orbiting defences were also gone, wiped out during the first invasion—but the planet wasn't defenceless. It was…*infuriating*…that the planetary government hadn't destroyed the PDCs before they'd surrendered. The bastards had sold out for the best terms they could get. Nelson would have been a little more compassionate if they hadn't sold him and his men out too. Their stupidity and selfishness would force him to land troops in the face of enemy fire. Even if the plan worked perfectly, the cost would be high.

We can pay it, he thought, *but we don't want to.*

"Alert the fleet," he ordered. "Begin bombardment pattern, Charlie-Alpha."

He gritted his teeth. His staff had devised a dozen plans for softening up the planet before the landings began, but Charlie-Alpha was the most comprehensive. The missiles and kinetic projectiles would be targeted on everything from known enemy bases and locations to captured garrisons and PDCs. The beancounters would make a fuss, when the dust cleared and they realised billions of credits—perhaps trillions—in infrastructure had gone up in smoke. But he knew better than to assume that retaking the planet would be easy. The marines were tough. They wouldn't surrender. They'd dig in and fight to the last.

Julia said nothing. She'd seen the plans; she'd watched as they'd been devised. She knew what he was going to do, but…she also knew it was necessary. There was no choice. The defenders knew he was coming. There was no hope of taking them by surprise. Better to hammer them from orbit than let the bastards take a bite out of his forces.

"Admiral," the tactical officer said. "The missiles are firing…now."

"Good." Nelson frowned. Hameau presented a unique tactical problem, but not an insolvable one. The marines had taken the defences down through a combination of cunning and brute force. *He'd* just have to rely on brute force. "And ready the landing force. I want them dispatched as soon as we weaken the defences."

He let out a breath. He'd *seen* Hameau. It was…odd, by any reasonable standard. Better than Earth, but Earth had been a wretched hive of scum and villainy even before it had turned itself into a wasteland. The refugees might know they were swimming in cream, if they were lucky enough to reach Hameau, but the locals…he wondered, sourly, just how many of them might have sided with the marines. He knew how *he* would have reacted to living his life in a goldfish bowl, even if he trusted the watching eyes. And experience had taught him the watching eyes could *not* be trusted.

The Inspectorate General had been the most corrupt branch of the navy. It was, he supposed, quite a remarkable achievement.

A shame they didn't do their job, he thought, as the missiles started to enter the planet's atmosphere. *We might not be in this mess.*

• • •

"It could be worse," Jenny said, as she parked the groundcar outside the abandoned and commandeered home. "It really could be worse."

Derek wasn't so sure. The planetary communications network was screwed. There were few—if any—radios or independent communicators on the surface. The marines had resorted to driving through the streets, issuing orders via loudspeaker, but it was hard to tell if anyone was listening. The idea of being completely cut off from his fellows was terrifying, even though he knew the old communications network had been constantly monitored for signs of dissatisfaction. His universe had shrunk to what little he could see. It was hard to believe there was an enemy fleet bearing down on the planet. He sure as hell couldn't see it.

He jumped out of the car and hurried up the path to the house. The marines had inspected it a few days ago, searching for a missing government official, then marked it as abandoned, open to whoever wanted to lay a claim. There were hundreds of abandoned houses within the city, Derek had been told. No one should pay any particular attention to *this* one…or so the planners had claimed. Derek wasn't so sure. He'd *lived* in a small community. Everyone knew everyone else's business. And it only took one person to spill the beans to have them arrested.

The door opened when he touched the keycard to the slot. He stepped inside, one hand reaching inside his coat for the pistol. Society had been breaking down even before the thunder runs. The entire population seemed to have gone collectively mad. There might be a squatter in the house already, if the missing government official hadn't sneaked home to collect his belongings. He felt oddly dirty as he moved from room to room, as if he were doing something wrong. The house wasn't *his*. He hadn't been amused when he'd heard someone had moved into his family's house, back home. Here…he was doing the same. And the previous occupant hadn't even had time to move out. His family's possessions lay everywhere.

Jenny stepped into the house. "You'd better help Roger with the junk," she said, as she took off her cap and looked around. "We don't want to be caught in the open."

Derek nodded and headed back outside. Roger Dashan and Gayle Jalil were two more collaborators, a young man and woman who didn't dare fall into enemy hands. They'd gone too far, Derek had been assured, to survive if the newcomers caught them. Derek would have preferred people he'd known, either from Eddisford Garrison or one of the scratch units that had been hastily thrown together during the invasion, but that wasn't an option. The marines hadn't captured many survivors and most of them, it seemed, preferred to remain as POWs. Derek didn't blame them. They couldn't—wouldn't—commit themselves until a clear winner emerged.

"You take the bigger suitcase," Roger said, as he passed Gayle a large rucksack. "I'll take the other one."

"Got it." Derek wondered, as he hefted the load, where Roger had served. The man was a year or two older then Derek, clearly a veteran… and probably someone who'd volunteered to stay in the army after completing his six months of planetary service. But he'd been very tight-lipped about his past. "Are you…?"

A flash of light—*lightning*, he thought—darted across the city. He glanced up, just in time to see a streak fall from the sky and land several miles to the west. Another flash of light rent the air, followed by a colossal fireball. Rumbling thunder echoed moments later, a low tremor running through the ground. He cringed, mentally, as he realised the planet was under attack. The enemy fleet was bombarding the planetary defences.

"That's the garrison," Roger said, quietly. "They just dropped a rock on it."

Derek swallowed, hard, as he carried the suitcase into the house. Roger followed him, closing the door firmly as more thunder echoed. Derek almost laughed as Roger carefully piled chairs and tables in front of the door, as if it would save them from a kinetic strike. A stray missile or shell would smash the house and kill all of them…he shook his head. If someone had seen them move in, if someone realised who they were or what they were doing, the makeshift barricade might *just* give them enough time to grab their weapons and sell their lives dearly.

"There're two bedrooms," Jenny called from the top of the stairs. "Roger? Which room do you and Gayle want?"

"I'll take the sofa," Roger said, flatly. "We really need to have someone on watch at all times."

Jenny shrugged. "Derek? You come help me choose?"

"Coming," Derek called. He put the suitcase down, marvelling at its weight. The marines had been generous—or so it seemed. He was all too aware they'd expend their ammunition very quickly. Another rumble shook the house. "What are they *doing* up there?"

Roger spoke like a man who didn't want to think about what he was saying. "The system is full of junk. They can gather asteroid rock and compress it into kinetic projectiles, then use it to take out as much of us as possible before landing. Quick, easy and cheap."

Derek said nothing as he hurried up the stairs. The sense of doing something wrong only grew stronger as he peeked into the bedrooms as he passed. A room that had clearly belonged to a young boy, probably in his first decade; a room that had probably belonged to a teenage girl, walls covered with posters of heartthrobs and bed strewn with clothing; a bigger room that had evidently been the master bedroom, with its own bathroom and shower. Jenny lay on the bed, smiling at the ceiling. Derek started to join her, then stopped as he saw the picture on the wall. A middle-aged man, a woman a year or two younger and their children. He wondered, morbidly, how burglars coped with the guilt. The urge to turn and leave—and pretend he'd never been anywhere near the house—was almost overwhelming.

"I was told I'd have a house like this." Jenny sat up, smiling at him. "This isn't how I thought I'd get it."

"This isn't *our* house," Derek reminded her. He sat on the bed and wrapped an arm around her. "We don't belong here."

Jenny gave him an odd look. "They gave the house to us."

"No." Derek shook his head as another thunder crack split the air. "This isn't *our* house."

He looked around, feeling a pang of envy. The house *was* a nice house. He couldn't have afforded it, not on his army salary. He'd have had to work his way up the corporate ladder to have any hope at all of affording anything like it, even in tiny Eddisford. He was sure the owner was an asshole, if only because all government ministers were assholes. That didn't justify stealing his house and destroying his possessions.

"We'll have to pack up his stuff," he said, tiredly. "We shouldn't destroy it."

"After we celebrate being alive," Jenny said. "We're meant to remain indoors, remember?"

"For the moment." Derek started to take off his shoes. "But it's only a matter of time until someone betrays us."

Jenny snorted. "Are you always so distrustful?"

"Back home, they used to reward people for snooping on their neighbours," Derek reminded her. "Here…it only takes one person to betray us."

He sighed, then smiled as he turned and slipped into her arms. There was nothing else to do, not until the invaders occupied the city. They had orders to keep their heads down, whatever happened, until the enemy troops were within their range. If, of course…Derek felt a wave of despondency, even as their lips met. He had to pray the marines won. He'd be dead if anyone ever figured out what he did. And Jenny would be dead with him.

•••

"The PDCs are holding firm," the tactical officer reported. "But we've scored some good hits on the military infrastructure."

"Good." Nelson wasn't sure that was true, but it behoved him to claim it was. "Have you taken down the planetary datanet?"

"I believe so," the tactical officer said. "But there's no way to be sure."

Nelson kept his thoughts to himself. The planetary datanet was practically *designed* to be easy to take down, being only a handful of datacores, linked to buried landlines that tied thousands of houses, schools, businesses and government facilities together. They could have hardened the network by making it decentralised, but that would have made it far harder to police. A *decent* network treated censorship as a malfunction and rerouted around it. This planetary network had been designed by people who wanted to make damn sure they controlled the flow of information. One could *not* make snarky remarks, let alone plan an uprising, without being caught and punished.

"Continue the bombardment," he ordered. It was a shame the PDCs had survived—the campaign could have been ended quickly if he'd been able to take them out—but he'd planned on the assumption they'd survive. "Do we have solid locks on their positions?"

"No, sir," the tactical officer said. "We don't have very good visuals at this range. They keep shooting down our drones."

And our KEWs, Nelson thought. It wasn't as if he was short of ammunition, except…he *was*. His fleet didn't have the capability to convert raw material into ballistic projectiles. In hindsight, that was a serious oversight. The marines had certainly brought a factory ship with them when they'd invaded. He simply hadn't thought to do it himself. *That's another lesson we're going to have to remember.*

He made a mental note of it—if nothing else, the entire campaign was going to remind them *precisely* what they'd forgotten over the centuries since the *last* interstellar war—and put the thought out of his mind. There were too many other concerns. And…he *had* brought hundreds of projectiles with him. Enough, at least in theory, to take down most of the planetary defences without resupply. But no one had ever actually *tested* the theory.

Of course not. The thought mocked him. *One does not test expensive fortifications by trying to destroy them.*

"We need to land troops near Haverford," he said. "Divert the bombardment. I want every suspicious target near the landing zone, outside the city itself, smashed before we start landing troops."

Julia frowned. "That would mean taking out property belonging to the planetary governors," she said. "Is that wise?"

"The governors are dead or captured," Nelson pointed out. The fleet had heard nothing from the planetary government. If there was anything left of them, it was buried so deeply they probably didn't know the relief fleet had arrived. The bombardment might wake them up, but…he doubted it mattered. "I think we can afford to discount their opinions."

He dismissed the thought with a shrug as the attack pattern continued to develop. The marines would *not* have a chance to surprise his forces, even if they survived. He'd sooner tear up the landscape and turn it into a battered nightmare than risk losing hundreds of soldiers. The men were keen, according to the reports, but inexperienced. They simply didn't know what they faced.

"Admiral," the tactical officer said. The display updated, showing hundreds of KEW strikes around the city. Haverford hadn't been hit directly, but the sound and thunder had to have scared the civilians. "The bombardment pattern has been completed."

"Good." Nelson glanced at Julia. "It's time."

He raised his voice. "Signal the transports. Order them to commence the landings."

CHAPTER SEVEN

This undermines his rule, in ways both subtle and gross. On one hand, a revolt might go unnoticed until it becomes too obvious to ignore. On the other hand, his subordinates might easily decide that it would be better to turn on him—in simple self-preservation—or merely hold him in contempt, as his decisions will be based on a dangerously flawed conception of reality.
—**Professor Leo Caesius**
The Right to be Wrong: How Silencing People Hurts You

I MUST HAVE BEEN OUT OF MY MIND, Lieutenant Garfield Onge thought, as the landing pod detached itself from the giant transport. *What the fuck was I thinking?*

He swallowed hard, trying to resist the temptation to reach for his water bottle and take a swig. He'd been told, when he reached his majority, that he was expected to serve the corporate family or else. The military had seemed ideal. He was too junior to climb to the very top, while a mid-level corporate position promised nothing but endless boredom and resentment of his higher-ranked kin. And the promise of rapid promotion had overcome what few doubts he'd had, when the recruiter came calling. In hindsight…

The pod shivered as gravity took control, yanking it down towards the planet. Garfield had carried out high-altitude drops before, from air—and space-craft, but this was different. This time, someone would be trying to kill him as he made the drop. This time...he tried not to look back at his platoon. He'd been told to work his way up the ranks, to gain experience before he could be considered for promotion...corporate royalty or not, he had to know what he was doing before he started making the *really* big decisions. And every man under his command was...was *his*. The slightest mistake on his part could lead them to death—or worse. Garfield's tutors had spared nothing, as they'd prepared him for officer training. They'd made sure he knew how bad it could get, if he screwed up. He could condemn his men to a fate worse than death.

It would have been better to use an assault shuttle, he thought, *or risk dropping men in armoured battlesuits into the teeth of enemy fire.*

He felt as if he'd left his stomach on the transport. The pod was falling faster now...the concept had seemed so clear, when he'd read the notes, but now that he was actually putting the plan into action it felt like the stupidest idea in the entire universe. The idea would be brilliant, if it worked. If it failed, a lot of men—including him—were about to die.

I could have stayed home, he thought. He'd been raised in the lap of luxury, with servants competing to fulfil his slightest whim. It wouldn't have been hard. Sure, he would have had to abandon all hope of doing *something* with his life—at least until he grew bored of luxury and sought something new—but he would have been safe. *I could have stayed home and...*

Something *slapped* the pod. It rolled over, g-forces tugging at him as the pod spun madly before steadying itself. Garfield heard someone loudly praying behind him, something that was technically against regulations... right now, he didn't care. The rational part of his mind insisted there were no gods, that religion was nothing more than a mental trick to explain the unexplainable, but the *feeling* part of his mind thought a prayer or two might be a very good idea. If the pod failed, if they hit the ground at speed, no one would ever find enough of their bodies to bury. He counted silently under his breath, trying to remain calm. This wasn't his first orbital drop. The falls were rough—he'd wet himself, the first time—but the pods were automated, unbothered by the drop from high orbit. They could handle the drop, leaving him to do nothing but wait. He almost wished he was flying his own shuttle. He knew how to fly. He'd be in control...

Perhaps I should have gone into piloting instead, he thought. There was little room for career development, but he'd already mastered most of the skills. No one could question his nerve if he flew shuttles in combat zones. *It might not have been safer, but at least I would have been in control.*

A low bleep echoed through the cramped compartment. Garfield went limp, an instant before a bone-jarring *thud* shook the pod so violently he heard pieces of debris crash to the ground. Gravity pressed down on him a moment later, reminding him they'd landed. He forced his fingers to work, unbuckling himself and stumbling to his feet. The platoon was following suit, led by Sergeant Janelle Richmond. Garfield's tutors had told him to pay close attention to anything she had to say. A woman wouldn't reach sergeant's rank in the Imperial Army—let alone transfer to the corporate forces—unless she was at least three times as good as her male counterparts. Garfield had never admitted it, not even to himself, but he found the heavy-world woman hellishly scary. He hoped she intimidated the enemy as much as she intimidated him.

"Out, out now!" Janelle's voice was harsh, the legacy of decades in the military. "Move it!"

Garfield forced himself to turn and run through the crack in the hull. A wave of heat struck him as he jumped, landing neatly on the ground. The ground was smouldering, a grim reminder they'd dropped so quickly the pod had had little time to cool. He took a sniff of the air and regretted it. The smoke burned his lungs, despite the genetic enhancements spliced into his DNA. He wondered if the enemy had hit the LZ with area denial agents, even though it was against interstellar law. The laws had died with Earth...he shuddered, silently grateful the detectors weren't going off. If someone coated the LZ in nerve gas, they'd kill most of the lead units—including him—in seconds.

Another pod fell from the skies, retrorockets slowing its descent a moment before it hit the ground. It opened, the platoon hurrying out and taking up position. Behind them, a giant colonial dumpster fell and hit the ground with an immense *thud*. Garfield smiled, caught up in the sheer thrill of the invasion. The idea had seemed a joke when it had first been proposed, but he had to admit it had worked. Colonial dumpsters were *designed* to transport vast amounts of men and materiel to a planetary surface. If one didn't care about retrieving the supplies, at least in a hurry, it was also the quickest way to get supplies dropped to the surface. Anyone who'd expected a leisurely invasion was going to be in for a shock.

Janelle grabbed his arm. "This way!"

Garfield flushed as he followed her towards the muster point. The sound of falling pods—and kinetic projectiles—was overwhelming, testing even *his* ears to the limit. The enemy could be shelling them now and he wouldn't even *know*. The final briefing had insisted the enemy positions near the city had been thoroughly pasted, but even *Garfield* knew there was no way to be sure. It wasn't *that* hard to conceal armoured vehicles and fighting positions from prying eyes. There was so much smoke drifting across the LZ he was sure the second and third waves were going to have problems landing without coming down on top of one of the forward units.

He lifted his eyes and peered into the distance. Billowing plumes of smoke rose up in all directions, suggesting that *someone* had definitely gotten a pasting. The KEWs had torn the ground up, turning the once-pretty countryside into a cratered wasteland. He'd seen maps, but it was hard to reconcile his memories with the sight in front of him. The distant forest was burning brightly, flames spreading in all directions. He shuddered, despite himself. Their CO had told his subordinates they were going to unleash hell. It looked as if he'd been right.

A line of vehicles—light tanks—rumbled past, heading for what remained of the road. They were followed by half-empty troop transports and air defence units, the latter already taking up position around the landing site. Garfield admitted, grudgingly, that the dumpster plan—he couldn't help smiling at the name—had worked very well. The enemy would barely have any time to react before the armoured units started pushing towards the city. Haverford hadn't been *designed* to withstand a siege, or a direct assault. The marines had taken it once. And now the city was going to be taken again.

He found himself inspecting the platoon as it formed up, joining the rest of the company. A platoon was missing, absent without leave. He hoped that meant their pod had been held back, rather than simply being blasted out of the air while they made their descent. It wouldn't be the first time someone on the ships had ordered a sudden change in the landing timetable, even if the knock-on effects disrupted the entire invasion. The spacers never seemed to realise that the landings were little more than barely organised chaos. Garfield had been drilled endlessly on what to do if he suddenly found himself in command, something that could easily happen if the captain and his senior officers were killed in transit, but he'd never had to try outside exercises. And *they*, as Janelle had pointed out sourly, tended to leave out the *real* emergency.

"Form up by platoons," Colonel Foster bellowed. The man looked stressed, alternating between glancing at a datapad in his hand and waving it around like a weapon. "I want the forward positions occupied before they react!"

There's nothing left of them to react, Garfield thought, as the platoon hurried through the desolate hellscape. *We hammered them from orbit before we even started to land.*

He glanced up as three more dumpsters fell from the skies. The fleet was still launching projectiles towards the planet, hopefully aiming at targets on the other side of the city. Garfield had been *told* the kinetic projectiles were very accurate, but he'd taken part in live-fire exercises where the spacers had missed their targets or accidentally fired on friendly units… thankfully simulated. Even if their shots were perfectly accurate, they'd risk damaging their own side if they dropped them too close to the advancing units. He'd just have to hope the spacers were being careful.

"They'll have pulled back to the city, sir," Janelle said. "And we'll have to dig them out."

"Assuming there's a city left," Garfield said. The ground shook, again and again. He saw a flash of light in the distance and cringed. "At this rate, there won't be much of one by the time we arrive."

• • •

"That's fucking impressive," Phelps said. He sounded incredulous, as if he didn't believe his own eyes. "They're fucking using dumpsters to dump troops on the ground."

Rachel barely heard him as she peered through the visors. The enemy trick *was* impressive, she admitted sourly. It would turn into an utter disaster if the LZ was rapidly overrun and destroyed—they'd have no way to evacuate their soldiers, let alone their material—but she was all too aware the marines were in no position to hit the LZ. The enemy had smashed every structure between the LZ and the city. It seemed as if they'd dropped a KEW on anything that looked even *remotely* suspicious. Most of those shots had been wasted, but they'd done enough damage to ensure they could land and deploy in relative peace.

Relative peace, she thought, sweeping her gaze over the enemy formation. A handful of troops were lagging, clearly suffering the side effects of their violent drop, but the vast majority were hurrying towards makeshift muster points. She could see MPs sorting them out, barking orders at the soldiers as they passed. Behind them, a dumpster started to disgorge a convoy of tanks. *We can slow them down a little.*

"We should probably drop a nuke on them," Phelps muttered. "It'll take most of them out."

"Perhaps." Rachel wasn't so sure. The dumpsters were tough. They'd passed through the planet's atmosphere and landed—roughly—on the surface. "We'd only take out the ones in the open."

And encourage them to use weapons of mass destruction themselves, she thought. Sure, there were hundreds of ways to make the invaders miserable…

if one didn't mind encouraging them to retaliate in kind. *A few nuclear shells would take out a sizable chunk of the civilian population as well as us.*

She reached for the pointer and fitted it, carefully, to her rifle. "Call Gamma," she ordered, as she peered through the scope. It wasn't as good as her visor, but she could pick out what looked like an enemy command vehicle. At the very least, it was a communications unit. They'd have been wiser to make it look identical to the supply trucks or AFVs. "Tell them I have a target."

"Got it." Phelps muttered into the microburst communicator as Rachel turned on the laser pointer. "You got them?"

"Got them," Rachel confirmed. The laser beam was supposed to be invisible to the naked eye, but it was quite possible the enemy vehicle's sensors would realise it was being targeted and take countermeasures. "Tell them to hurry."

She waited, counting the seconds as the enemy air defence units raised their weapons and opened fire. The artillery units had been placed just outside the city itself, too close—the planners thought—to draw enemy fire. Rachel wasn't sure how she felt about *that*—there was a better than even chance that any counterbattery fire would land within the city, killing innocent civilians—but they needed to buy time to move back under the protective umbrella before it was too late. The retreat plans had been drawn up in a hurry, yet... even the worst-case planning hadn't quite grasped what was coming. She cursed under her breath as shells exploded in mid-air, picked off by enemy lasers. If she was lucky...

A shell struck the command vehicle. It exploded, too quickly for any of the staff to bail out. Rachel hoped they'd taken out someone important, although she was fairly sure the man's death—if indeed they *had* killed someone important—wouldn't slow the enemy for long. A force capable of launching an interstellar invasion would have contingency plans for losing their commanding officer. Hell, she would be surprised if they'd taken out the *supreme* commander. The *real* commander would be safely in orbit.

Unless they took a leaf out of our book, she mused, as the last of the shells rained down on the enemy positions. *Their CO might have landed with the first wave.*

She crawled back, scrambling to her feet and starting to run as the enemy troops continued their advance. They'd know they were being watched now. The shellfire would grow more random, now the laser pointer had been turned off. Their guns were already starting to return fire, despite the risk to the city. She saw a drone moving high overhead, invisible to normal eyes. Thankfully, it was heading towards the city...although that didn't mean it couldn't see them. Their uniforms were designed to provide a staggering amount of concealment, from the naked eye as well as prying sensors, but she knew better than to assume they were invisible. The Empire had spent a lot of money on trying to make sensors that could see through any level of concealment. It would be unwise to assume the corprats hadn't bought or stolen copies of the latest technologies.

A missile lanced up from the west, blowing the drone into a fireball. Rachel smiled in relief. An HVM team, positioned nearer the city. Losing the drone would hurt the enemy, as well as serving as a stark warning they didn't control the skies. Neither side would be able to rely on air or space power to win the war. They'd have to win or lose on the ground. She gritted her teeth as she picked up speed, sweat trickling down her back. Their plans had been smashed to flinders, first by the arrival of the enemy fleet and then by their rapid landing and deployment. Her enhanced ears had no trouble picking out the sound of tanks and AFVs advancing in their general direction.

"Crap," Phelps breathed.

Rachel followed his gaze. The farm had once been a sweet place. She'd seen it during their march to the OP. A neat little farmhouse, a cluster of barns and a handful of fields, populated by cows and sheep. Now, it was a ruin. The farmhouse was gone, the barns nothing more than firewood and the animals...the animals lay dead in the muddy ruins. There was no sign of the farmer and his family. She hoped they'd had the sense to run before their farm had been wiped out, merely for existing.

We brought the war here, she thought, morbidly. It was hardly her first campaign—she'd been in the corps for over a decade—but it was the first invasion the marines had genuinely started. Every other time, they'd been called in when the regulars had been unable to cope...too late to end the conflict without major bloodshed. *And they were caught in the middle.*

She shook her head. It was never easy to see how high morals and good intentions collided with reality. Or discover—again—that the locals were unwilling or unable to welcome them. Or...

There's nothing we can do for them now, save win the war, she told herself. *And we have to do it quickly.*

CHAPTER EIGHT

This becomes worse as the dictatorial state outgrows the dictator himself. The lying—which will be epidemic throughout the system—will ensure that no one, not even the liars, will really know what is going on.
—**Professor Leo Caesius**
The Right to be Wrong: How Silencing People Hurts You

"THE FIRST WAVE HAS LANDED SUCCESSFULLY," General Rask reported. "The LZ has been secured and we're readying ourselves to advance on the city."

Nelson frowned as he studied the display. He was no ground forces expert—the groundpounders looked as if they were barely moving, even though he knew they were fighting desperately to establish a lodgement—and he had severe doubts about the landing plan, but he trusted Rask's judgement. The man had been cashiered for daring to disagree with his aristocratic commander, back in the bad old days. Nelson had faith the older man knew what he was doing.

"Good," he said. "You do understand we're running short of kinetic projectiles?"

"Yes." Rask looked unconcerned. "We can't drop them so freely within the city."

"No," Nelson agreed. He cared little for the city itself, but the relief force had strict orders to recover as much of the population as possible. Haverford housed thousands of technical experts and their families, as well as a small army of bureaucrats. He'd sooner have watched the latter die, but he knew they were needed. They were useful, as long as they were kept under close supervision. "I assume you can proceed as planned?"

"Yes, sir," Rask said. "The marines appear to be retreating in good order. I suspect they had a contingency plan all along."

"That's their style," Nelson agreed. He wasn't so sure. The marines had exposed themselves, for what? Either they had an immensely cunning plan or there'd been a giant screw-up somewhere along the line. Not, he supposed, that it mattered. The marines could neither surrender nor withdraw. "Can you take them?"

"I think we're about to find out," Rask said. He raised a hand in salute. "See you on the far side, Admiral."

His image vanished. Nelson stared at the empty space for a moment, then raised his eyes to the system display. The enemy fleet had vanished, seemingly into nothingness. They were either on their way out of the system or, more likely, lurking somewhere near the asteroid belt. They'd run out of supplies eventually, he told himself, but it would probably take some time. He wondered, idly, if they had reinforcements on the way. If the Onge Corporation had been trying to seize shipyards and naval bases, why not the marines? A single battleship could tip the balance either way.

Assuming they could crew the giant white elephant, he thought. He'd served on battleships. They might be formidable, in theory, but in practice they drained resources that could have been better used elsewhere. It wasn't as if the Imperial Navy had ever been going to face a peer power. There were no other major powers within the known galaxy. *And yet...*

Julia cleared her throat. "How long until we can secure the orbital industries?"

"Right now, we can't," Nelson said. "They're far too exposed to the planetside defences. If we board and storm the facilities, the PDCs will blow them out of space. Better to push the offensive on the ground, take out the PDCs and then force the orbital platforms to surrender."

"I see," Julia said. Her face was artfully blank. "And are you sure they won't destroy the platforms anyway?"

"No," Nelson said, bluntly. "But there's nothing we can do about it."

He felt a stab of sympathy, mingled with irritation. He didn't pretend to understand corporate politics, but it was clear that Julia's future depended on the success of their mission. Either she'd be raised to higher levels, if not the *very* highest level, or be cast down to the very deepest depths of corporate hell. Julia had every reason to want the mission to succeed, quickly, but there was no way they could speed things up. The marines were in a sheltered position. Winkling them out would take time.

"In a sense, we're both hostage to the orbital platforms remaining intact," he said, as reassuringly as he could. "They need them as much as we do. They won't destroy them unless they feel they have no other choice."

And they can use them as bargaining chips when the time comes to negotiate a surrender, he mused. The marines wouldn't give up as long as there was a slight hope of victory, but they had to know they were in a bad spot. Their survival depended on a relief fleet of their own arriving before it was too late. *We'll do everything in our power to make it clear we'll honour surrenders and treat prisoners well.*

He keyed the display, drawing the starchart back until it showed the Core Worlds. A dozen stars—Sol and its closest neighbours—were marked with red icons, each telling an emotionless tale of horror. Planets nuked, asteroid colonies cracked open...he'd long since given up trying to calculate how many people had died in the last few months. Billions, perhaps trillions. The figure was so high he couldn't even begin to grasp it. It was hard to believe that each of the icons represented billions of deaths...

Julia stepped up beside him. "Credit for your thoughts?"

"I'm wondering how long we have," Nelson said. "Where *are* the marines?"

He leaned forward, as if it would draw answers from the display. The Slaughterhouse was a radioactive ruin. Nelson had no idea who'd bombed the Slaughterhouse, or why, but it was obvious they'd failed to take out the Marine Corps. The corps had clearly been planning for Earthfall...where had they gone? Nelson knew, better than most, just how hard it was to move hundreds of thousands of men at a moment's notice. The corps must have set up a fallback position, but where? He shook his head in irritation. There were hundreds of possible answers, from Sol itself to an isolated red dwarf in the middle of nowhere. He wasn't going to get an answer just by glaring at the starchart. The datacores didn't *know* where the marines were hiding.

And we have no idea how long it took them to get here, he thought. They'd interrogate the prisoners, when they *took* some, but he doubted the rank and file would know anything useful. Their superiors would only tell them what little they needed to know. The riflemen didn't need to know where the base was, let alone what it was called in the navy database. *They could have set up shop anywhere.*

"We'll see how long it takes for their reinforcements to arrive," he said. The marines hadn't known his fleet was coming, or they would have assumed better positions before he actually arrived. If it took a week for their message to reach their base, their relief fleet could arrive within the next two to three weeks...assuming, of course, it departed at once. "It'll give us a rough idea of where they have to be."

Julia nodded. "And can we find them?"

"Perhaps," Nelson said. "But it depends."

He knew it wouldn't be easy. Searching every star system within a hundred light years would be a nightmare, even if he had every starship in the universe under his command. The marines could remain hidden from all but the closest inspection, if they were paranoid enough to conceal their emissions. They'd have problems operating a shipyard and a fleet, but...he scowled. The marines could establish a base in the middle of interstellar space and the searchers wouldn't have a hope in hell of finding it. They'd have to get impossibly lucky.

"Right now, we have other things to worry about," he said. "We'll deal with their relief fleet when it arrives."

...

"Based on current estimates, they managed to land at least twenty thousand troops within the space of a few minutes," Colonel Harkin said. The intelligence analyst was grim. "The dumpsters were a nasty surprise."

"Tell me about it," Gerald growled. He'd heard the concept discussed, but always as something the corps would never dare try. The enemy had committed their men to a do-or-die operation, knowing—they could hardly be ignorant—there was no way to retreat if they ran into something they couldn't handle. "They must be very confident of victory."

He felt his frown deepen as he studied the map. Both sides were fighting a vigorous campaign of surveillance and counter-surveillance. Drones were being shot down, remote sensor platforms were being blasted by long-range fire and constant ECM barrages were making it hard to pick up any *real* data. The fog of war had thoroughly enveloped the enemy LZ, ensuring he couldn't plan any operations. Constant alerts flashed in front of him, including a sensor report that over a *billion* enemy troops were crammed into a tiny space. Gerald guessed that someone had pissed on the sensor. It was a trick that dated all the way back to the pre-spaceflight days.

At least we know someone is there, he mused. The gunners had hurled a few shells towards the compromised sensors, in hopes of hitting *something. We just don't have any hard data.*

"The enemy fleet is pulling back," another officer said. "They're holding position outside engagement range."

"That's something, at least," Gerald said. The enemy bombardment had been staggeringly extensive, for an interstellar power that—presumably—wanted to recover the planet and its facilities intact. He didn't think there was a single, intact structure between Haverford and the enemy LZ. Dozens of marines were reported missing, presumed dead. "Keep harassing them as we pull back to defensible lines."

He cursed his luck under his breath, trying to ignore the guilt in his heart. He was relatively safe, unless his staffers made an unsecured transmission that drew enemy fire. His men, on the other hand, were caught in a meatgrinder. They were trained and experienced, but even the best soldiers had problems withdrawing under fire. And the planetary population was caught between two fires. Those who'd been too friendly to the marines, over the last few days, would probably be rounded up and shot. Gerald knew the score. He'd served in countless places where the locals had hated the insurgents, but were too scared to resist. What choice did they have?

At least we destroyed their records, he thought. He had no way to know if there were *copies* off-world. It was possible, all too possible. *It'll take them a long time to rebuild.*

"Contact report," another officer called. "They're crossing MW-09!"

"Which puts them a few, short miles from Haverford," Gerald said. The enemy was expanding their foothold, trying to seize as much territory as possible before the marines rallied and counterattacked. "And with the prongs heading north and south, they can lay siege to the city soon enough."

He wanted to reach for the console and issue orders, but there was no point. His men already knew what to do. They were being caught in a vise, one that would steadily close until the retreating marines were crushed between two pincers. He wondered, suddenly, just who was in command of the enemy forces and what his objectives actually *were*. A skilled general would try to destroy the marines on the ground, before they could rally, but a political general—or someone overruled by his superiors—would concentrate on the city. Gerald knew, all too well, that he should hope for the latter, despite the grim truth that thousands of civilians would die. It would buy time for his troops to rally and reinforcements to arrive.

A young officer stepped up to him. "Coffee, sir?"

"No, thank you," Gerald said.

He shook his head. It was pointless to deprive himself of coffee, just because his men in the field had no time to relax, but he would have felt worse if he'd taken the drink. He wished someone senior would arrive, just so he could take the field himself. But duty insisted he keep out of harm's way.

All we can do is try to get out of the trap before it's too late, he told himself. The fog of war was growing thicker. He'd lost touch with positions on both sides of the city. He hoped that meant the marines had managed to retreat; he feared they were dead. *And then hold the line.*

He gritted his teeth as more reports flashed up. It would take nearly six weeks for reinforcements to arrive, assuming they were dispatched the moment his report reached his superiors. He knew it wouldn't be that easy. There weren't that many troops—and starships—based at Safehouse itself. The Commandant would do his best—Gerald knew Major-General Jeremy Damiani well enough to be sure of it—but there would be hard limits on what he could do before it was too late. If he couldn't get a relief force to Gerald in time…

They'll be here, Gerald told himself. Marines did *not* abandon their own. *We just have to hold out long enough for them to arrive.*

...

"Good to see you again," Specialist Michael Bonkowski said. The Pathfinder looked like a refugee from a horror flick. "I thought we'd lost you."

"Likewise," Rachel said. Splitting the squad had seemed like a good idea at the time, she reflected sourly. "They came damn close to killing us."

She glanced back. The distant forest was still burning brightly, clouds of poisonous smoke drifting through the air. The sound of fighting echoed over the torn-up fields and smashed buildings. Streaks of light flew through the air, each a missile or shell aimed at targets on the other side of the line. She tensed as she heard rumbling in the distance, suggesting that the enemy tanks were on the move again. They were heading right towards the city, as far as she could tell. She was fairly sure they were moving to cut off the city, too. They had no choice, unless they wanted to launch a set of thunder runs of their own.

"We'd better get moving," Bonkowski said. "They're not going to invite us for lunch when they catch up."

"No," Rachel agreed.

Phelps leaned forward. "Any news on what they do with prisoners?"

Bonkowski shrugged as the squad started to walk. "Nothing so far," he said. "If they bothered to demand surrender before they started landing, it never got forwarded to us."

Rachel frowned. It was customary to demand surrender during the landing period, although she knew from grim experience that very few took the invaders up on the offer until they'd fired at least one shot for the honour of the flag. The enemy force behind her had practically *had* to land quickly, whatever happened. They couldn't have wanted to give the marines more time to regroup. But they wouldn't have lost anything by demanding surrender. It wasn't as if they had anything to lose. Who knew? The marines might have surrendered without a second thought.

Not that we would have, she thought. *Falling into enemy hands means certain death.*

She kept the thought to herself. She'd been warned, when she'd first joined the corps, that she couldn't expect prospective captors to be *gentle*. The enemies they'd faced before Earthfall hadn't had the facilities to take prisoners, even if they'd *wanted* to. And the stories of what happened to marines—male as well as female—who fell into enemy hands were gruesome. Now...perhaps the enemy would be civilised to the *average* marine. They wouldn't be civilised to her. If they realised she was a Pathfinder...

The sound of distant shooting—and explosions—grew louder as they made their way towards the city. A handful of refugees—civilians, not marines—waved feebly as they passed, as if they thought Rachel and her comrades could help them. Rachel wanted to tell the poor bastards they were heading in precisely the wrong direction, that the city would be a death trap, but there was no point. The marines might manage to make it out of the trap before it was too late. The civilians might be safer in the city than trying to run the gauntlet.

"Poor bastards," Phelps muttered. He raised his voice. "Lie low! You're in no danger as long as you lie low."

Rachel didn't look to see how the refugees reacted. She wasn't sure Phelps was right. In theory, sure; the refugees would be unharmed. A disciplined military force would make sure they were harmless, then either ship them to a detention camp or simply point them on their way. But she had no idea how the invaders would treat civilians. Human history showed a wide range of possibilities, from all kinds of abuse to simple slaughter. She'd seen Civil Guardsmen gun down civilians for kicks. Who knew if the invaders would be any better?

They want to recover the planet, she told herself. *They won't be too beastly to the locals, will they?*

She winced, inwardly. That might not be true. If the invaders thought the locals were collaborators...

"Nearly there," Bonkowski called. "You can thank me later."

"For what?" Phelps spoke with an arch tone that betrayed his true feelings. "You just led us into a trap."

"At least we have a chance," Bonkowski pointed out. "Those poor bastards back there don't."

"It depends," Rachel said. Their orders had been more than a little vague. She was used to that, but...there were times when she would have appreciated clearer guidance. "Are we supposed to hold the city, hole up *in* the city so we can make their lives miserable, or sneak through the city and out the other side?"

"God knows," Bonkowski said. "We'll find out when we get there."

CHAPTER NINE

Worse, the further the system becomes divorced from reality, the more erratic (and insane, from an outside POV) its decisions will become.
—**Professor Leo Caesius**
The Right to be Wrong: How Silencing People Hurts You

IT WAS HOT, TERRIBLY HOT.

Lieutenant Garfield Onge's back was sweaty. The sweat had even pooled in his boots as he led the platoon through the blackened, battered landscape. The air stank of smoke and blood, his throat burning despite the combination of genetic enhancements and protective mask. He tasted bile as he saw a body lying in a mud puddle, so badly burned that he couldn't tell if the dead man had been a friend, an enemy, or a civilian caught up in the fighting. Explosions shook the ground, the constant thrumming of the distant guns echoing through the air. He saw flashes of light everywhere, followed by expanding fireballs as the shells crashed down.

Fear gripped him. He felt alone, even though he had nine men—and one woman—behind him; even though he knew he was in the midst of a vast army. The fog of war was creeping over him, insisting he was cut off from his friends and comrades even though cold logic told him it couldn't be true. He just needed to reach for his communicator to call, but…he'd been warned not to use it unless they made contact with the enemy. A single communication might be enough to tell the enemy *precisely* where he was.

Another body lay in a ditch. Garfield swallowed hard, trying not to be sick. This body was so badly mutilated that it was impossible to determine if the body was male or female, let alone friendly or hostile. He stared, trying to convince himself the dead body was an enemy soldier who thoroughly deserved to die. The reports suggested the enemy troops were retreating in good order, and there were no civilians on the battlefield, but it was impossible to be sure. The training exercises had insisted that everything would run like clockwork. The live-fire exercises had suggested otherwise. His first taste of *real* combat had taught him that *something* would always go wrong.

He frowned as they advanced towards the motorway. It had been designed by a soulless planner; the road drew a straight line between two cities, never so much as curving as it carved through the landscape. He could understand the appeal, but didn't share it. The motorway was practical, but it was also a blight. A handful of broken vehicles lay on the tarmac, burned out by…something. The road was covered in potholes. He was sure *someone* had shelled the motorway only a few short hours ago.

A chill ran down his spine as he looked towards the city. The motorway was completely deserted. There were no moving vehicles, no refugees trying to get in or out of the city…it was deserted, as dark and silent as the grave. He forced himself to keep moving, unwilling to show fear in front of his men. The instructors had made it very clear that he could *not* show weakness of any sort, even if it meant girding his loins in brown pants. The joke had been funny, until it wasn't. Now…he smiled, grimly. He wasn't the only one who'd wet himself during his first drop.

He tensed as he heard more shellfire, the sound echoing through the air. He couldn't tell who was shooting at whom…it sounded, as the shellfire intensified, as if both sets of guns were trying to destroy the other. He forced himself forward, feeling oddly naked as he slipped down the grassy slope and onto the motorway. He'd enjoyed driving, as a younger man; he'd taken ruthless advantage of his birth to ensure he could drive the groundcar himself, rather than rely on the onboard driving system. Just standing on the motorway made him feel as if he was going to be run down at any moment when a car raced down the street at several times the speed limit. But there were no moving vehicles in sight.

The sergeant moved up behind him. "Stay away from the burned-out cars," she muttered, pitching her voice to ensure the men couldn't hear her. "They can conceal traps."

"Understood," Garfield said. He could have kicked himself. The cars provided the only real cover for several miles in both directions. "Let's move."

He wanted to call in as he resumed the advance down the motorway, keeping a steady distance from the wrecked cars. He knew better than to try. The closer they got to the city, the greater the chance of running into an enemy ambush. The platoon was uncomfortably exposed. He kept a wary eye out for traps, hoping that the horror stories he'd heard from the old sweats were exaggerated. Getting covered in bright pink paint during drills had been embarrassing, but in the real world—the instructors had said, time and time again—he would be dead. Sure, the medics could repair almost anything—as long as it wasn't immediately fatal—but it would be difficult to get to them if one's legs were blown off. A sucking chest wound would kill him, enhancements or no, if he didn't get medical treatment before it was too late.

And we spent months drilling on what to do if someone was hit, he reminded himself. *We just never tried it under battle conditions.*

The sense of unreality grew as they inched down the motorway, passing a pair of cold concrete bridges that linked the motorway to villages outside the city. A handful of buildings were clearly visible, all smashed from orbit. Garfield noted the debris scattered across the motorway, although he was sure it wouldn't slow the tanks for more than a few seconds. The combat engineers wouldn't be needed to clear the way. He smiled, remembering how the heavy tanks had torn up the landscape during exercises. No wonder they'd been cautioned to get off the roads as quickly as possible…

He looked up, just in time to see a distant bridge collapse into a makeshift barricade. He hit the ground a second later, as bullets started flying. He cringed inwardly—it was the first time someone had tried to kill him—and then started crawling forward, trying to assess the situation. It sounded as if there were hundreds of shooters in front of them, but he was fairly sure his estimate was off by at least *one* order of magnitude. The marines couldn't have spared more than a handful of men to slow him down.

Janelle spoke rapidly into her communicator, calling down shellfire. Garfield stayed low as shells crashed down around what remained of the bridge—he was mildly surprised that the gunners had been allowed to fire on the motorway—and then jumped to his feet and ran as the aftershocks died away. The bridge had been small by local standards, but it had been big enough for the debris to provide plenty of cover. He forced himself forward, keeping as low as he could as he scrambled over the pile and into the enemy position. A body—wearing civilian clothes—lay on the edge of the crater. The other enemy soldiers had either been blown to bits or simply retreated as the shells crashed down. He tried to tell himself they'd been killed. He didn't believe it.

Janelle examined the body. "Sir...what do you make of it?"

Garfield felt a hot flash of anger. He had no qualms about learning from experienced soldiers, even ones he outranked, but the middle of a battlefield was no place for a lesson. Not that kind of lesson, at least. He leaned forward, studying the body. It was hard to believe it had once been a soldier. Garfield hadn't met any marines, but he'd met elite corporate soldiers as well as the infantrymen he'd been trained to lead. The body didn't look anything like as fit as the lowliest private.

He frowned as it hit him. "This was a civilian."

"Yeah." Janelle sounded unsurprised. "They gave someone a gun and told him to blaze away at us."

Garfield shook his head. He didn't know why she was so unsurprised. He'd seen the briefing notes. The local population *loved* their society. It was so much better than Earth, before and after Earthfall, that they had no reason to rock the boat. The corporation provided everything they needed, from safe places to live to schools that actually *educated* the kids, and in return they were loyal. And yet...his mind spun as he tried to come up with an explanation. The poor bastard could have been too stupid to know what was good for him. The poor bastard could have been blackmailed into carrying out an ambush. The poor bastard...Garfield's mind spun. It didn't make sense.

"Why?" It was almost a cry of pain. "Why?"

Janelle shrugged. "In every society, there are people who are dissatisfied or discontented," she said. A faint sneer crossed her face. "And some of them will act to pay back grudges as soon as they have a chance."

Garfield said nothing as they made a brief report, then resumed their march. He found what she'd said hard to believe. The corporation was good at putting round pegs in round holes. If someone was unhappy in one position, the corporation's HR specialists could find them a position somewhere else. He'd seen it in action during basic training. Officer candidates who were better at supporting troops rather than leading them in combat were steered into roles where their talents could be used to the fullest.

It made no sense! Why would someone be discontented on Hameau?

He wanted to ask her more questions, but he didn't dare. Not in front of the troops. Instead, he forced himself to remain calm as they started to approach the city. The ring road surrounding the city looked untouched, but—beyond it—he could see a barricade. It didn't look like a very *threatening* barricade—a handful of tanks could smash it easily—yet...he had a feeling the enemy intended to use the barricade to slow the invaders down while they rained shells on their positions. He peered into the distance, noting there were more civilians amongst the defenders. They looked ready to fight.

It makes no sense, he thought, numbly. The civilians were fighting their liberators. Were they being held at gunpoint? It didn't look like it. *Why?*

He caught himself and started to snap orders. There was no point in trying to get any closer to the city, not yet. The enemy barricade would eat his squad alive. If the original plan was still working—and he had his doubts—the other intersections would be secured quickly, allowing the invaders to surround and seal off the town. He wasn't sure what would happen then. The planners had admitted—he'd heard, through the grapevine—that they weren't sure what the enemy would do either.

Garfield nodded to himself as he peered at the city. It was bigger than he'd expected, for a city on a relatively new colony world. Towering skyscrapers loomed over the streets, massive warehouses, colonist barracks... it didn't look very welcoming, but the map *had* insisted the more expensive accommodations were on the other side of the river, well away from the lower-class districts. It made a certain kind of sense, he guessed. The colonists were expected to either move up in the world, as they found positions within the planet's industrial sector, or moved out to the countryside to run the farms. There was nothing to be gained by making the temporary accommodation too welcoming. The colonists might not want to leave.

The wind shifted. He tasted something unpleasant—piss, shit, and fear—in the air. A low humming echoed behind and he glanced back, smiling in relief as he saw a handful of light hovertanks making their way towards him. They weren't heavily armoured, he recalled, but they'd provide cover if—when—the assault began. He saluted as an officer jumped out of the lead tank and landed neatly on the ground. Brave man. The lead tank would almost certainly draw the most fire. If the enemy disabled or destroyed it, the wreckage would slow the other tanks...

"Sir," he said. "I beg leave to report the intersection is secure."

The officer—a colonel—gave him a sharp look. "Good," he said. "Follow-up units are already on their way. I dare say we'll receive orders once they arrive."

Garfield wanted to ask when and where they were going to go into the city, or even if they *were* going to force their way into the city, but he knew the colonel probably wouldn't know anything more than he did. It didn't *look* as if the city intended to surrender...he reminded himself, again, that the original plan had been to seal the city off from the rest of the world *first*. Perhaps General Rask would leave a blocking force in place to *keep* the city sealed up while the remainder of the force chased the marines back into the hinterland, overrunning the PDCs as they moved. Or...perhaps he'd see political advantage in recapturing the city quickly. Haverford had little military value, but it had a *lot* of symbolic importance. Leaving it in enemy hands would look bad.

He forced himself to relax, slightly, as more troops and vehicles arrived. The enemy was shelling the ring road, launching a handful of mortar rounds at convoys as they tried to link the intersections together. Garfield suspected there was no point in trying until they recaptured the city. The ring road was just too close to the buildings, particularly given the reluctance to fire into the city. Too many civilians, some of whom had powerful friends, would be at risk.

And their friends would make a fuss, he thought. He was young, but he wasn't naïve. *What would that do to the General's career?*

"Look at me," someone called. "I'm on top of the world!"

Garfield looked up, sharply. A soldier—still in his teens—was standing on top of a tank, waving cheerfully towards the enemy positions. Garfield understood—he would have liked to mock the enemy too—but it was dangerous. The enemy snipers were good.

"Get down at once, you bloody fool," Janelle snapped. "Now..."

The soldier tumbled to the ground. Garfield thought, just for a moment, that he'd lost his footing and slipped. Tanks were *designed* to make life difficult for people who wanted to climb on them. He heard the shot a second later and knew, with a sick certainty, what had happened. He ran forward as a cluster of friendly soldiers retaliated, firing a volley towards the enemy. Their sniper would have to duck and sneak out if he wanted to survive the next few hours. Garfield's men had orders to take prisoners, but no one wanted to march a sniper into the POW camps. The troops would kill a sniper as soon as look at one.

He bent over the injured man, searching for the wound. The man looked unharmed...no, he was bleeding from the chest. Janelle tore his uniform open, removing the layers of body armour the techs had sworn blind would stop—or at least deflect—a bullet. The armour had failed. The bullet had cut through it and punctured a lung. Janelle swore as Garfield yanked a medical pack from his belt, tore it open with his teeth and pressed it against the wound. It might just keep the poor bastard stable long enough to get him to the medics.

"Dumb bastard." The colonel seemed unconcerned. His voice sounded almost bored. "He shouldn't have shown himself so openly."

Garfield barely—just barely—kept himself from saying something that would have earned him a court-martial, despite his exalted birth. The colonel was right, he supposed, but...it wasn't good for discipline to express that opinion too openly. The medics arrived a second later, waving the colonel away as they hoisted the wounded man onto a stretcher and carried him back down the motorway. Garfield hoped *they* wouldn't be fired upon. The old sweats had cautioned him that *some* of their enemies had used the red cross as a target.

The marines won't do that, will they? He tried to convince himself the answer was *no*. The briefings had been clear. The marines were civilised opponents. And besides, the corporation wouldn't hesitate to retaliate if it was the only way to deter atrocities. *They know that we'll start killing their medics if they start killing ours.*

Janelle touched his arm. "They'll get him back in time, sir."

"I hope so," Garfield muttered. He'd seen men die before...no, he hadn't. Not really. They'd been simulated deaths, deaths that—no matter how horrible—only lasted until the simulation came to an end. A man could have his head blown off, then rise from the dead moments later. Now...the men who died would not be coming back. His stomach heaved as it struck him. "I..."

He swallowed, hard. He didn't want to throw up. Not here. Not in front of the men. "I...does it get any easier?"

"No." Janelle's eyes were hard. "But you do get used to it."

"I don't think I'll ever get used to it," Garfield confessed.

"Yeah." Janelle shrugged. "I said that too, when I was your age."

CHAPTER TEN

This is, of course, common in bureaucratic states. The bureaucrats will determine targets—based on their faulty understanding of the possible—and demand they be met...or else.
—**Professor Leo Caesius**
The Right to be Wrong: How Silencing People Hurts You

"I THINK IT'S JUST A MATTER OF TIME," Bonkowski muttered.

Rachel nodded in agreement. The barricades looked tough, to the untrained eye, but they wouldn't last more than a few minutes if a professional force wanted in. The defenders were nothing more than a handful of marines, including the specialists, and a number of locals who'd volunteered to make a stand. Rachel had a private suspicion that half of them would desert, the moment the shit hit the fan. The only reason they'd volunteered in the first place was because they had nowhere else to go.

She lifted her visor and peered east, towards the intersection. The enemy force was gathering, pushing tanks and armoured vehicles forward to discourage sniping. They'd proved themselves quite adept at returning fire too, although they hadn't managed to kill her and the others when they'd sniped at exposed targets. And they were learning fast. She'd sniped an officer, after he'd been saluted. She hadn't seen any of the others—officers or men—exchange salutes since.

They hadn't seen real action, she told herself. She was fairly sure of it. The enemy soldiers were competent, but they'd moved with the squeamish determination of inexperienced troops…at least at first. *But that's changed now.*

She sighed inwardly as she surveyed the barricade. Given time, the marines could have put up one hell of a defence. They could have turned the entire city into a death trap, crammed with pitfalls and traps intended to bleed the enemy white. Haverford was nowhere near as random as some of the other cities she'd seen—she was grimly aware the enemy would have perfect maps too—but there was plenty of room for organised resistance. Given time…she looked up, noting the sun steadily falling towards the horizon. The enemy had moved with terrifying speed, but…they didn't have long if they wanted to start the attack before sundown. Even marines would have hesitated to attack the city after nightfall. The best night-vision gear in the universe wasn't good enough to even the odds.

"But the longer they give us, the tougher we can make the defences," she muttered. "A week or two and we could really hurt them."

Phelps glanced at her. "Huh?"

"Just wool gathering," Rachel said. She cursed the timing under her breath. The marines had invaded the city, smashing defences they desperately needed—now—to *defend* the city. She was well aware that, sometimes, the timing just didn't work out…but it was still frustrating as hell. "We could have put up one hell of a fight if…if things had been different."

"Yeah." Phelps raised his bottle and took a sip. "I could be drinking alcohol, if I had alcohol."

"And then you'd be brutally murdered for being drunk on duty," Rachel said. Marine enhancements were supposed to make it impossible to get drunk, but a lot of her fellow riflemen—back when she'd been a regular marine—had done their level best to push the enhancements to the breaking point. "If you weren't shot by the enemy first."

She glanced back as she heard an explosion, deeper within the city. The marines had lost control of large swathes of territory, territory now dominated by street gangs and self-proclaimed defence associations. The latter might have been useful, once upon a time; now, they were just another headache for the defenders. She had a feeling the invaders would disarm them, as soon as they could. Or simply wait for the associations to run out of ammunition. It wouldn't take long. The planet had once had very strict laws on gun control.

"The spooks insist the enemy assault is about to begin," Bonkowski called. "They're picking up lots of organised chatter."

"And hopefully fucking them good and proper with shellfire," Phelps called back. "Or are they asleep at the switch? Again?"

Rachel snorted as she eyed the enemy force. They *had* moved quickly. They'd nearly overrun the city within the day. She was fairly sure they were pushing their supply lines to the limit, but…she glanced at her terminal, noting that over a hundred full-sized dumpsters had hit the ground. A good logistics staff would have no problem sorting the supplies out, then getting them where they were needed. She had to admit the enemy forces had done well. If they'd taken their time…

"I see movement," Phelps announced. "Their tanks are moving forwards."

"Light tanks," Rachel corrected. "Where are the Landsharks?"

"They don't have them, perhaps?" Phelps grinned at her. "Or maybe they didn't think to bring them?"

"Whistling in the dark," Bonkowski growled, as he ambled up to their position. "And you know it."

Rachel nodded. The enemy *would* have Landsharks…or a tank design roughly comparable to Landsharks. They'd have no choice, unless they'd designed plasma weapons capable of burning through Landshark armour in one shot. They *had* to know the marines had Landsharks of their own, now holding position to the west. They'd do whatever it took to match them, then take them out. They sure as hell wouldn't let the marines have the advantage of heavy—and mobile—firepower if there was any other choice.

"Yes, sir," she said. She peered into the distance. Only a fool would drive a Landshark down a motorway if there was any other choice, but the enemy would have no trouble driving the massive vehicles over the fields and straight down to the city. "They might be reluctant to risk them in the streets, though. It wasn't easy carrying out the thunder runs."

"No," Bonkowski agreed. "But they want to recapture the city as quickly as possible."

Phelps opened his mouth to say something, then shut it again and ducked down as the enemy opened fire. Rockets—antitank rockets—lanced towards the barricades, exploding as soon as they struck the makeshift structures. Rachel gritted her teeth as the defences shattered, dead or wounded defenders flying in all directions. A handful stood their ground, defiantly returning fire before they were targeted and picked off by rockets or shellfire. The tanks kept moving in a smooth line, firing as they came. They were coming too close for comfort...if there'd been much in place to stop them.

"One rocket each," Bonkowski ordered, as the enemy tanks reached the edge of the former barricades. Behind them, Rachel could see a multitude of troops using the tanks for cover. "Mark your men and make it count."

"Got it." Phelps levelled his rocket launcher at the nearest tank. "I've marked my man."

Rachel hastily followed suit, aiming at the next tank. There were only four rocket launchers left, facing a small army of enemy tanks. They'd give the enemy a fright, and slow them down a little, but not for long. She told herself it wouldn't matter. They couldn't hope to hold Haverford. Even if they tried, they'd be nothing left of the city when the reinforcements finally arrived. She braced herself, knowing it was only a matter of time before they were spotted. It would be ironic if they died because they showed themselves—they were trained to remain in the shadows—but...

"Fire," Bonkowski snapped.

The launcher jerked in Rachel's hands as she fired. She tossed it aside and scrambled for the ropes, half-abseiling down to the ground. Her legs hit the ground hard, but she ignored the pain and ran. The other three joined her a second later, just as a hail of fire slammed into the building they'd been using as a base. She didn't know what the rockets had hit, but they'd definitely hit *something*. The enemy had just expended one hell of a lot of firepower on an empty building. She could hear it crumbling behind them.

We probably killed four tanks, assuming each of us hit a target, she thought. Her enhanced ears picked out someone screaming. She glanced into an alleyway and saw a badly wounded man lying there. *Shit.*

She hesitated, just long enough to assess his condition. He was torn and broken, in desperate need of medical attention. She knew he wouldn't get it. Haverford's hospitals were already overwhelmed, treating the victims of the *last* invasion. The doctors were short of everything from face masks to nanite packages. And the enemy troops might take what little they had left. She wanted to take him to the nearest safe zone, but…there wasn't one. There was nothing she could do for him.

"I'm sorry," she said. He didn't stand a chance. "I'm sorry."

She drew her gun and shot him, telling herself it was a mercy kill. Cold logic told her she was right. He *wouldn't* have stood a chance of survival. But…she didn't really believe it.

And things are just going to get worse, she thought. She heard a mortar banging away, lobbing shells towards the advancing enemy troops. *There might not be much left of the city by the time we're done.*

"Rachel," Bonkowski yelled. "Come on!"

"Yes, sir," Rachel muttered. "Coming!"

• • •

Garfield hit the ground, again, as an antitank rocket punched into the tank he'd been using for cover and turned it into a massive fireball. He rolled over and over, trying to put as much distance as he could between himself and the vehicle as it burned, hoping and praying the crew would make it out before it was too late. He thought he saw a shape within the flames... no, it was too late. The crew was dead. He picked himself up, glancing at the line of tanks. Two more were burning; a third looked to have stalled. It took him a moment to realise the antitank rocket had punched through one side and blasted straight through the other before exploding. The warhead had detonated too late.

And the crew might be dead anyway, he thought, as he shouted for the platoon to continue the advance. *The heat from the passage would probably have been enough to kill them.*

There was no time for further thought as he ran towards what remained of the enemy barricade, using the surviving tanks to cover the squad. Haverford's network of outer warehouses and barracks had taken a terrific beating, a number either nothing more than piles of rubble or looking as if they were on the verge of collapse at any moment. Garfield kept moving as he mounted the barricade, swinging his weapon as he searched for targets. But all he saw were dead bodies. The barricade had been smashed so completely it had taken the defenders with it.

He led the way into the nearest warehouse, searching for targets. A pair of wounded men lay on the floor, staring at him in horror. They didn't look like marines; they appeared to be civilians. Traitors. His finger tightened on the trigger—it would be so easy to put them out of their misery—before he caught himself. They had orders to take prisoners, didn't they? Damn it. He snapped orders to his men, commanding them to march the wounded men to the detention centres. They could wait there until their fate was decided. Who knew? Perhaps they'd be given medical care and put on hard labour for the rest of their lives. Or simply left to die in the streets...

"This way," Janelle called, as more shooting echoed over the city. "Quickly!"

Garfield kept moving, somehow, as more and more troops flooded into the city. The enemy seemed to have defended all the ways *into* the city, if the snatches of chatter he heard over the network were accurate, but they didn't seem to have bothered to establish inner defence lines. A handful of traps, a handful of ambushes that lasted only bare seconds before the enemy broke contact and withdrew...it felt as if they were merely being delayed, not stopped. A tank moved past him, heading too close to an unsearched house. Garfield had no time to shout a warning before an antitank rocket blew it to hell. The tank exploded into another fireball, the crew dead before they knew what had hit them. Flaming debris flew everywhere.

He yanked a directional blasting charge from his belt, crammed it against the wall and triggered it. The explosion blew a hole, large enough for two men. Janelle threw a grenade into the room, then two more down the corridor as the building quivered uneasily. The roof fell in a moment later, sending a man in a strange uniform crashing to the floor. He was shot four times before he could stand, his body rolling over and over before finally lying still. Garfield knelt beside him as he breathed his last, feeling an odd twinge of admiration mingled with hate. The marine—it *was* a marine—had died well, but he'd died for nothing. He checked the man's body, removing a pair of weapons, a multitool and a datanet terminal that went dead the moment Garfield touched it. He put it to one side. The intelligence staff might be able to make use of it, although he doubted it. The device had clearly been designed to respond only to its assigned bearer.

They checked the rest of the house, then continued sweeping the city. The firing started to die, although it never faded completely. Each ambush drained his men, wearing them out as they kept moving forward. It was growing clear, all too clear, that the marines simply hadn't had the *time* to set up a proper defence. What little they'd done was quite bad enough, he reflected. The attackers had hit the city from all directions, ensuring the enemy had no chance to deploy their reserves to seal off a breach, but they'd still be slowed by heavy fire and constant ambushes.

A pair of tanks rumbled past as they reached the river. The map insisted there were six bridges—imaginatively named one to six—but the first bridge had been dropped at some point during the fighting. Garfield couldn't tell who'd blown the hell out of the bridge or why. The foundations poked out of the water, oddly desolate and alone. He surveyed the far side with a sinking feeling as they reached the second bridge. It was intact, suspiciously so. A sniper round snapping through the air, far too close for comfort, confirmed his suspicions. The enemy intended to force him to cross the bridge, straight into the teeth of their fire.

The tanks returned fire as Garfield took cover and tried to decide what to do. He seemed to have inherited command of an entire company's worth of soldiers, although they came from a dozen different scattered units. Janelle barked orders, rounding them up into squads. Garfield gritted his teeth. He couldn't see any way to cross the river. He'd bet half his inheritance the structure was mined, just waiting for a small body of troops—or tanks—to cross. They'd be dropped into the churning waters to drown, if they survived. And there weren't any other ways to cross. No boats...

Janelle appeared beside him. "Your orders, sir?"

"I don't know what to do," Garfield admitted. There was no point in pretending otherwise. His sergeant had been in the military longer than he'd been alive. "We have to get across the river, but we can't get across without being killed. What do you suggest, Sergeant?"

He thought he saw a flash of approval in her eyes. "Hold the waterfront and call for combat engineers to remove the charges," she said. She showed no hint of amusement at offering orders to her superior officer. "And have the tanks continue suppressing enemy fire."

"And try not to do too much damage to the houses on the far side," Garfield said. "They might have powerful owners."

He sucked in his breath. The contrast was striking. On his side, homes were massive apartment blocks, each clearly housing hundreds of people; on the other, homes were neat little cottages and bungalows, some with visible jetties and swimming pools. He could even see boats, tied by the distant riverside. The homes were tiny, compared to the mansion he called home, but...he wondered, uneasily, just how the people on his side of the river had felt when they'd looked across the water. Had they seen it as something to aspire to? Or a sign of a world forever out of their reach? Or...

Janelle looked up from her communicator. "They're moving up reinforcements now," she said. "They're also advancing from the other direction, so hopefully most of the city should be in our hands by the end of the day."

And someone else will take command, Garfield thought. It would be a relief, one he couldn't admit out loud. *And then I'll go back to commanding a platoon.*

"There isn't much of the day left," he pointed out, telling himself it was for the best. Recapturing the city had been almost pathetically easy, compared to the great city fights he'd studied during OCS. He felt his heart sink as the truth struck him. "The marines got away, didn't they?"

"I'm afraid so," Janelle said. She pursed her lips as shooting echoed over the waters. "The war is far from over."

CHAPTER ELEVEN

Naturally, the people charged with making those targets will lie. Why not? On one hand, failure to meet the targets will be heavily punished; on the other, the bureaucrats have no independent means of actually checking. The risk of discovery is considerably less dangerous than the certainty of punishment for honesty.
—**Professor Leo Caesius**
The Right to be Wrong: How Silencing People Hurts You

"IS IT WRONG," JENNY ASKED QUIETLY, "for me to be scared?"

Derek shook his head. They were in the basement, trying to sleep under a table that would provide a *little* protection if the roof caved in. The fact that they might wind up trapped if a missile struck the house, buried under a pile of debris, had only occurred to him *after* the shooting started, once it was too late to move. There'd been no messages—the planetary datanet remained as dead as a doornail—but he hadn't needed them. The sound of enemy fire had been enough to tell him the offensive had begun.

He felt oddly exposed, even though he was in the basement. He'd never been anything more than an infantryman—he'd assumed he'd have been discharged the moment his service expired—but he'd heard stories about bunker-busters that could take out entire underground complexes. The house was flimsy in comparison, probably not strong enough to withstand a single shell. They might be killed at any moment, without whoever fired the shot ever knowing what he'd done. The urge to grab his rifle and go upstairs, to stand in defence of the city, was almost overpowering. Only the grim awareness that he'd be killed for nothing kept him in place.

"No," he said, finally. "I'm scared too."

"Fuck," Jenny said. She grimaced. "And there I was planning to cling tightly to you."

"I'm sure I can cling tightly to you too," Derek said. A distant explosion shook the house. A bomb? A shell? An IED? He didn't know. "I think everyone gets scared."

Jenny leaned against him. "What do you want to do, when all this is over?"

Derek blinked. "You want to talk about our future now?"

"It'll distract me," Jenny said. "It'll distract you too."

"True." Derek thought about it. He'd never really considered his future, not since the fighting had begun. "I think…"

He shook his head. Before the war, he'd known he'd have had a menial role. His family didn't have the connections to secure him a higher position. Perhaps he'd have gone into farming. There was plenty of unclaimed land, with loans and government grants for the happy families who were prepared to make a go of it. He'd never thought he might stay in the military. There'd been lads who'd intended to join the regulars, when their service was over. He wondered, tiredly, what had happened to them. Dead? Captured? Or…who knew?

"I suppose it depends on what happens now," he said, finally. "We might not survive the next few days."

Jenny poked him. "Be positive."

Derek laughed. "Well, we *could* get married, have kids, raise a family," he said. "Or we could try to leave the planet and go somewhere else. We might not be welcome here, when all is said and done."

"I hope not," Jenny said. "I don't want to leave."

Another set of explosions vibrated through the walls. Derek held her tightly, keeping his thoughts to himself. Jenny's father hadn't been *liked*, not before the war. Something nasty would have happened to him, if there hadn't been the certainty of punishment. Now…Jenny's father might be collaborating with the marines, but that might not be enough to save him if someone decided they wanted to pay back old scores. Derek had heard the rumours. A bunch of corporate royalty had been lynched by their former subordinates. It was only a matter of time until someone decided to kill Jenny's father.

And target her too, Derek thought. It was hard to believe the girl he'd known and the girl in his arms was the same person. Old Jenny had been so snooty she'd walked around with her nose in the air, unwilling to give a lad like him the time of day. New Jenny was clinging to him as if he were a life raft. *How many people are going to think she's changed?*

He sobered. What about *him*? If the marines won, well and good. Except…there would be people who'd see him as a traitor, a turncoat. And if the marines lost…the winners would *also* see him as a traitor. He hoped—prayed—the marines had managed to destroy *all* the records when they'd purged the datanet. If there were hints he'd been reassigned to Haverford before the end, he could expect some pretty serious questions.

"It's quiet," Jenny breathed. "Have they stopped?"

Derek shrugged. Haverford wasn't heavily defended. The marines had taken control of the city in a day, although it had taken longer for them to secure it. Too long, as it turned out. The newcomers could have done the same. It wasn't as if there were many defenders standing between them and the city. The marines had decided not to turn the city into a real battlefield. He knew he should be relieved, even though he felt as if the jaws were steadily closing. There'd been little left of Bouchon after the marines had fought their way through the bottleneck city.

Ice crawled down his spine as the silence grew and lengthened. His watch insisted it was nearly 2000 hours. Darkness would be falling outside, wrapping the city in shadows. Haverford had had streetlights, once upon a time, but they'd be as useless as everything else without the datanet. He wondered, morbidly, how people were coping. The datanet was the primary source of everything from education and entertainment to news. Parents were probably going mad, just from keeping their kids indoors. He shuddered. Better indoors than dead.

"I hope so," he said, finally.

His mind ran in circles. The city *hadn't* been heavily defended. Not, he supposed, that the newcomers would know it. They'd fear attack constantly, at least until they had the city under firm control. They'd probably wind up shooting innocents. A handful of unarmed men could look very threatening in the semi-darkness. Derek remembered his training and shuddered. The instructors had insisted that anyone stupid enough to walk towards armed troops deserved everything they got. Better to risk shooting innocents than let someone get close enough to do real damage. A lone suicide bomber could take out an entire squad.

Jenny pulled him close and kissed him, hard. Derek gave into her touch, rolling her over until he was on top of her. Sex would banish the darkness pervading his mind, both of their minds. The world would feel a better place, at least for a while. And he'd worry about everything else tomorrow.

• • •

"I thought the streets were paved with gold," someone said dramatically, behind him. "Never have I been so deceived."

Garfield ignored the comment—one thing he'd been taught was that there was a difference between idle talk and *dangerous* grumbling—as he clipped his night-vision goggles into place. Haverford's streetlamps were dead, those that had survived two successive invasions. He was fairly sure *someone*, either the marines or criminal locals, had carefully destroyed as many streetlights as possible. It made sense. The sensors mounted on the streetlights were vitally important for population control.

We might not be able to stop a crime, he thought. He'd been carefully briefed on how the system worked—and its limits. Filtering programming was good, but not good enough to be sure of telling the difference between something innocent and something criminal. *But at least we'd be able to trace the criminal back to his haunts.*

He swept his gaze from side to side as he led the way down the street. The residential area looked surprisingly untouched, for somewhere far too close to the governing complex. The cookie-cutter houses were dark and silent, although his goggles detected hints of people moving behind the curtains. There was no way to be sure. The civilians were helpless without power. He wondered, idly, if any of them had so much as a box of matches or a firestarter. So much technology was dependent on the datanet, these days, that losing it had probably taken down practically *everything*. In hindsight, that might have been a mistake.

His eyes narrowed as he thought he saw shadows move within the darkness. Shapes glinted at the corner of his eye. He stared, chills running down his spine. They couldn't be real people, could they? It was easy to feel alone in the darkness, even though the squad was behind him. He tightened his grip on his rifle, telling himself—firmly—that he was literally jumping at shadows. The goggles would have picked up a living person's heat signature well before they came close enough to be dangerous. Unless...

Garfield tried to put the thought out of his mind as they moved on, keeping their eyes open for possible threats. The main roads in and out of the city had been secured, along with the remaining bridges, but entire districts remained unsecured. He'd been told the marines had lost control, before the assault had begun. He was silently relieved he wasn't assigned to sweep *those* districts. The locals couldn't expect any mercy from the relief force. They'd rebelled against both the legitimate government *and* the occupiers.

And the marines won't give them any mercy either, he thought, as the platoon reached the end of the road. *They distracted them from mounting a proper defence.*

He kept the thought to himself. Their orders had been to patrol, nothing more. Garfield thought General Rask was surprised at how quickly the city had fallen, although it had been a far from cheap victory. Rumour insisted that over thirty tanks had been destroyed and two hundred soldiers were dead. Garfield hoped the rumours were exaggerated. There was a good chance he knew men who'd died in the fighting. He gritted his teeth, promising his dead friends revenge. They wouldn't—they couldn't—have died for nothing.

The buildings grew larger as they approached the government complex. He tensed as a shape loomed up in the darkness, then relaxed as he spotted the AFV holding position by the roadside. An antiaircraft vehicle stood just behind it, sensor nodes constantly sweeping the skies for incoming threats. The marines had seemed reluctant to lob shells into the city, but who knew when—if—that would change? Beyond them, he saw a handful of men standing guard by the doors. The government complex had been swept—he'd been ordered to let the elite units lead the way—but, so far, none of the senior officers had moved into the complex. Garfield didn't blame them. There were plenty of ways to sabotage a building, and the marines were supposed to know all of them.

He tried not to yawn as he saw Colonel Jayson standing by the command vehicle, smoking. The man was a stickler for military protocol, someone who'd reprimand someone for not shaving in the middle of a combat zone. Garfield was mildly surprised he was anywhere near the command vehicle, unless he'd been reassigned to General Rask's staff. It was possible. Jayson was a better staff officer than combat commander.

"Sir." Garfield nodded. Salutes were forbidden in combat zones. "We have orders to report to Captain Hesston once we completed our sweep."

"Captain Hesston is dead." Jayson sounded too tired to care. "He was sniped two hours ago."

Garfield felt a hot flash of anger. Captain Hesston had been a good man, a decent commander who'd treated his subordinates with respect. He'd made sure Garfield and his comrades were ready to take command at a moment's notice, in case something happened to him. Garfield had never thought something *could*. He heard a mutter behind him as the news ran through the platoon. Captain Hesston had been popular. Garfield doubted the sniper would live long enough to reach a POW camp if he were caught.

He turned and gazed over the darkened city. A sniper could be anywhere, from lurking in a skyscraper apartment complex to resting on a rooftop. And they could be hellishly accurate. He'd once heard of a sniper who'd killed a man five miles away. The city was huge…the bastard could be anywhere, if he'd made the mistake of staying still. There was little hope of finding him in the gloom.

"Fuck," he said, finally. "I…*fuck*."

"Perhaps later." Jayson showed the ghost of a smile. "There's a school just down the way. Your platoon has been assigned a classroom. Try not to have flashbacks while you bed down."

Garfield resisted the urge to say something incredulous. A school? He reminded himself he'd slept in worse places. It wasn't as if there'd been military barracks in the heart of the city. The colonist barracks were on the other side of the river, probably crammed with refugees and criminals. Instead, he nodded again and led the platoon down the road. The government complex looked surprisingly active, even though it was nearly midnight. Elite troops stood outside, while intelligence officers and staff made their way in and out of the building. Garfield wondered if they were having any luck. Prisoner interrogations—so far—had proven worse than useless.

The school looked nicer than he'd expected, as they turned into the grounds. A midsized football field, surrounded by a chain link fence, had become a makeshift prison. Garfield silently counted the visible POWs, all sleeping on commandeered bedding or blankets under the watchful eye of armed MPs. He doubted they slept well. The orders from General Rask were clear. Anyone who had served the marines, in any capacity, was to be held until their precise role in affairs was determined. Garfield felt a flash of pity. The lower-ranked bureaucrats probably hadn't been given a choice. It was astonishing what someone would do at gunpoint.

"Garfield." Lieutenant Yeller stood just inside the school, looking as tired as Garfield felt. "I've put you and your squad in Room 101. Bed them down, then come find me."

"Yes, sir," Garfield said. Yeller was senior LT. He'd effectively inherited command of the company, although not the rank that came with it. The army bureaucracy being what it was, Yeller would probably not receive backpay even if he was promoted into Captain Hesston's shoes. And there was no guarantee Yeller *would* be promoted. Who knew? There might be a more experienced LT in another company just waiting to be transferred. "I'll be back in a moment."

He frowned as they made their way through a maze of corridors. The schoolhouse felt creepy, as if it was designed to drain all individuality out of the inmates. They were children, not prisoners. And yet…he silently thanked his family for ensuring he didn't have to attend such a school. The classrooms were crammed with desks and chairs, so many that…he shook his head. It looked as if they'd tried to cram forty children into a room that was barely large enough for twenty. Kids were small, but not *that* small.

"I'll clear the room and bed everyone down, sir," Janelle said. "You'd better go back to the LT."

"Understood." Garfield was too tired to argue. The sooner he found out what Yeller wanted, the sooner he could get some rest. "Do we have bedding?"

Janelle made a face. "I'll have some brought up, if possible," she said. "This isn't a boarding school, I think."

Garfield nodded and headed back down the corridor. More squads were moving in, their commanders bickering over everything from toilet space to who got to feed their units. They'd be eating ration bars until someone set up a proper field kitchen or turned the power back on…Garfield shuddered as he realised the stasis fields had probably failed too. The school's kitchens used them to store food. It would be going rotten now, if it wasn't eaten quickly. It was funny, he reflected as he stepped into what had probably been the headmaster's office, just how few stories of heroism in the face of unimaginable odds covered such details. Troops had to be fed and watered or else they stopped fighting. The logistics officers might not be on the front lines, but that didn't mean they were useless.

"Garfield," Yeller said. He was sitting at the desk, searching the drawers. "How many men are having flashbacks?"

Garfield frowned. "To what?"

"To being in school. Or prison." Yeller sat up. "This guy printed all of his files. I don't think he trusted the datanet."

"Smart guy." Garfield had the odd feeling Yeller was going off the deep end. The invasion was his first taste of combat too. "Did they catch the fucker who killed the captain?"

"I don't think so," Yeller said. "They hurled a shitload of machine gun rounds at the sniper nest, but the QRF didn't find a body. I think the bastard got away."

Garfield nodded. It was possible the body had been reduced to its component atoms—he'd seen bodies disintegrate under machine gun fire—but it was probably wishful thinking.

He let out a breath. "So...what now?"

"Right now, we have orders to sleep," Yeller said. "Tomorrow"—he held up the datapad—"we have to bring the remainder of the city under control while waiting for further orders."

"Yes, sir," Garfield said. "And you'll be in command of the company?"

Yeller nodded. "Until relieved," he said. "A bunch of units got torn up. It might be a while before anyone notices I'm in command."

"Yes, sir," Garfield said. "Right now, there are too many other problems."

CHAPTER TWELVE

This leads to what can probably be best described as a dangerous—and very deadly—version of musical chairs, in which the producers will dance like crazy to avoid being the one caught out when the music finally stops. Accordingly, they will do everything in their power to pass the buck from person to person, praying desperately that they won't be caught with it.
—**Professor Leo Caesius**
The Right to be Wrong: How Silencing People Hurts You

PERHAPS WE SHOULD HAVE WORN OUR UNIFORMS, Rachel thought, as the small squad approached the riverside. *We might not be shot out of hand if we get caught.*

She snorted, inwardly, at the thought. The Pathfinders *would* be shot if they were caught, once the enemy realised what they were. There was little hope of keeping them prisoner without specialised equipment. Even shoving them into a stasis tube wouldn't be enough, not when their implants could counter a stasis field. Being out of uniform—and technically spies—would be the least of their worries. They could *not* be taken alive.

Her enhanced eyes swept the riverside for enemy positions. The fifth bridge had been taken out—she wasn't sure when it had been dropped or why—but the enemy had still placed a squad of men on guard. She had no idea why, given that the bridge was effectively useless to the local civilians. Perhaps the enemy thought the civilians would try to use the bridge anyway. It was possible, particularly if the locals didn't realise just how *badly* the bridge had been damaged. They might think they could still cross.

And staying on this side of the river isn't safe, Rachel thought. The lower-class districts had fallen into chaos. The enemy had enforced a strict curfew—they'd shot a bunch of looters and machine-gunned rioters—but there were limits. They hadn't tried to patrol the colonist barracks or take control of the refugee camps. *The locals might want out.*

She glanced at Phelps, who signalled for the other two to slip into position. The enemy squad didn't look very alert, although they weren't smoking or drinking as they stood on guard. She hoped it was a sign they feared they were being watched, rather than general training and discipline. The Civil Guardsmen had been known to get frequently drunk on duty, when they weren't harassing the local population or selling guns to rebels. She gritted her teeth in annoyance. She'd wished the Civil Guards would vanish. She'd gotten her wish.

Phelps held up three fingers. Rachel counted down, boosting as she reached zero. She lunged forward, sprinting towards the guards at inhuman speed. One of them started to raise a weapon; too late. She was on him before he could so much as point it at her, slamming her fist into his throat hard enough to snap his neck. Another guard grunted as Phelps hit him, his weapon clattering to the ground. Rachel heard a gasp from the riverside and saw a *fifth* guard, zipping up his fly with one hand as he tried to draw his pistol with the other. Rachel almost smiled as she hit him. He should have put his dignity aside and fired a shot. The sound would probably have summoned another enemy patrol before the marines had a chance to escape.

"Their communications network is tight," Bonkowski said, with grudging admiration. He held an enemy datanet terminal in one hand. "I don't think I can hack it, not from this piece of crap."

"They probably don't let the grunts have access to the upper levels," Jones suggested. He picked up the nearest body and searched it roughly. "No papers. No ID. No dog tags. No nothing."

"They probably use implants," Rachel said, as she searched her second victim. He had nothing in his pocket, save a picture of another man and a little boy. A brother? A husband? A son? There was no way to know. She told herself, firmly, that it was better not to think of the enemy as *people*. They would kill her if she didn't kill them first. "Shall we go?"

Bonkowski nodded as he armed a grenade, then hid it under the bodies. It would prove a nasty surprise for the enemy, even if it was—technically—against the laws of war. Rachel found it hard to care. The laws of war were meant to mitigate the horrors of combat, but her experience suggested they did nothing more than hamper the good guys while allowing the bad guys to run free. The cynic in her insisted the enemy had had the right idea, when they'd shot looters out of hand. And yet...she sighed, inwardly. Idealism had its place, but not on a battlefield. The objective was to win as quickly as possible.

She studied the remaining waters, noting the position of the destroyed struts. The bridge supports poked out of the churning foam, looking oddly desolate in the darkness. She braced herself, then clambered down to the nearest and jumped to the second. They'd considered swimming or finding a boat, allowing the river to carry them down to the sea, but it was too dangerous. The enemy had taken up position downriver, ready to hose suspicious objects with automatic fire. Better to creep through the western streets and escape over land.

If we escape, it's a brilliant plan, she thought, as she kept moving. The destroyed supports were slippery, but stable. *If we get caught, it's the stupidest plan since soldiers stood and walked very slowly into machine gun fire.*

She put the thought out of her mind, scanning the nearing riverside for signs of enemy troops. *She* would have made sure to guard both sides of the river, although she could understand why the enemy probably hadn't bothered. It wasn't as if civilians were going to cross the bridge, was it?

Besides, it was unlikely any of the westerners would try to go east. They'd be safer on the western side. It would take time for the newcomers to make themselves really unwelcome, and by then it would be too late. She allowed herself a moment of relief as she reached the far side, keeping her eyes wide. The faint hum of enemy vehicles echoed, but she saw nothing. They should be safe as long as they stayed away from the government complex.

"Good," Bonkowski said, once they were all on the far side. "Now the real fun begins."

Rachel nodded. "Keep your eyes open," she ordered. "And listen carefully for trouble."

She moved down the road, trying to stay in the shadows. Her biological enhancements were supposed to make her invisible to IR sensors, through a process that might as well be magic from what little she'd understood of the explanation, but she was grimly aware it was a lot harder to fool *motion* sensors. The enemy probably hadn't managed to boot the datanet back up—the simple fact they'd been unable to turn the streetlights on suggested they'd been unable to fix whatever the techs had done—yet there was nothing stopping them from scattering automated sensors around the city. A team of good staff officers could easily isolate the false positives and ensure patrols were sent to arrest anyone who violated curfew. And the enemy was probably quite practiced at population control.

Her eyes narrowed as she saw a handful of abandoned and burned-out buildings. The fighting hadn't been so extensive here; she had no idea who'd destroyed the buildings or why. She peered into their darkened interiors, then kept moving. She could worry about it later, if there was time. Instead, she snuck further into the shadows as she heard a vehicle move towards them. She lowered herself quietly as an AFV drove down the street, guns swinging from side to side constantly as they searched for a target. The vehicle was almost silent. An unenhanced civilian would never have heard it. She let out a breath as the enemy headed towards the river, away from them. She'd known the enemy were at least as well-equipped as the marines, but it was still a shock to see it in the flesh.

They had the contract to produce all sorts of crap for the army, she reminded herself. She was sure she knew how it had been done. *And they cooked the books to hide the fact they built twenty vehicles instead of ten.*

She put the thought aside as the squad resumed their crawl westwards, evading two more enemy vehicles and a small platoon on patrol. The enemy soldiers looked professional, although they didn't seem inclined to go smashing through gardens or raiding houses in search of fugitive soldiers or loot. Rachel scowled. It was odd to *wish* the enemy were atrocity prone, but it was a grim fact of life that most civilians would keep their heads down and try not to be noticed unless they were pushed into resistance. She'd *worked* with underground groups, before Earthfall. She was all too aware that, for every hundred people who grumbled, only one or two would pick up a weapon and fight.

The houses grew smaller as they circumnavigated the government complex and continued to head towards the edge of the city. The enemy troops grew thinner on the ground, although they seemed to be constantly running patrols at random. There was no time to see if there was a pattern, to see if they were careless enough to fall into a routine that could be exploited...Rachel shook her head in frustration. It was unlikely anyone, even guardsmen, would make *that* mistake. Not here. The city would have to calm down before they started to relax.

Bonkowski moved up beside her as they neared the ring road. "Troops on the intersection," he muttered. "We're going to have to cross it further south."

"Got it," Rachel muttered. She tensed as she eyed the motorway. Small convoys were moving up and down the road. "We may need a diversion."

She contemplated the possibilities as they crept south. The motorway itself was neatly hidden in a gully, making it all too likely they'd be spotted as they scrambled down and crossed the road. There didn't seem to be any pattern to the convoys, either; she grimaced as she realised they were moving openly, shining their headlights as if they had nothing to fear. The marines would have to teach them the error of their ways, if only to slow them down a little more. The longer it took for the enemy to regroup and head west, the more time the marines would have to prepare defences and bleed them white.

"We should be able to cross there," Phelps said. He pointed downwards. "Drop keyed grenades as we cross?"

"Good idea." Bonkowski studied the scene for the moment, then muttered orders. "Ready? Go."

Rachel led the way down the slippery slope, then onto and across the motorway. The grenades would make ideal mines, if they weren't spotted in time. *She* was sure she'd keep an eye out for surprises, if she was driving down the motorway in a war zone, but the enemy might have gotten careless. Their drivers didn't seem to realise they *were* in a combat zone. She understood the need to keep moving, to rearm the advance units so they could resume the march west as quickly as possible, but still...she tensed as she saw headlights in the distance, putting her head down and running for her life. The others followed her into the darkness, a moment before the convoy came into view. The drivers slammed on the brakes; too late. Rachel smiled coldly as they ran over the grenades, triggering a chain of explosions. The final explosion was bigger than she'd expected. The enemy vehicle must have been transporting ammunition.

She felt her smile grow wider as they hurried into the fields. The enemy would probably still be wary of flying helicopters, skimmers, or drones over the countryside. They knew there were HVM teams out there, watching for targets. What would they do? Would they even realise the convoy had been attacked? They'd be wise to assume so, she thought, but they might not work it out in a hurry. They might even think it was a tragic accident. *Marines* would assume the worst. What would the newcomers do?

Her enhanced hearing picked up hints of vehicles moving in the distance, but there was no sign of pursuit. The enemy had already lost their best chance to run them down. Right now, they'd be fools to give chase when they'd have to follow the marines into the darkness. She kept moving, making sure to glance behind her every so often. The enemy might not try to play it smart. If, of course, they realised the marines were there.

Phelps took point, allowing her to fall back to walk beside Bonkowski, while Jones brought up the rear. Rachel didn't relax, even though she had every faith in her comrades' ability to sense an ambush before they walked into it. The farmland was steadily growing wilder the more they walked west. There were patches of woodland, tracts of land that looked as if the terraforming process had failed...she smiled, realising the locals had tried to create a preserve. It was a surprise, given how...tightly they controlled the rest of the world, but not unpleasing. If nothing else, she supposed it would make a nice place for the children.

"Quiet," Phelps whispered. "Light."

Rachel followed his gaze. There was a faint light in the distance, barely visible even to her enhanced eyes. It looked like a fire. She glanced at Bonkowski, then allowed Phelps to lead her forward as the other two followed at a distance. The sound of men laughing and joking grew louder as they neared the fire. The noise suggested they weren't expecting trouble. She tensed, wondering just who they were. Marines wouldn't have been so careless, not so close to the enemy troops. They were risking attack just by showing themselves so openly.

She leaned forward as the campsite came into view. Troops, enemy troops, were sitting around a fire, eating ration bars as they prepared to rest. Rachel narrowed her eyes, wondering just how inexperienced the enemy troops actually *were*. She understood the importance of relaxation—she knew how stressful combat could be—but someone who relaxed in the middle of a combat zone might not live long enough to realise her mistake. There didn't seem to be a sergeant or a senior officer to put the men back to work, to order them to put out the fire before they were attacked...deserters? Or...her eyes narrowed. A trap?

"It's too easy," Phelps signalled. "We need to sweep the area."

"Stay here," Rachel signalled back. "I'll circle the campsite."

She slipped into the shadows, remaining low as she circled the enemy campsite. There were no waiting troops, ready to mount an ambush; there were no surprises at all. And that made her suspicious. She'd seen ill-disciplined guardsmen do things that exposed them to attack, but the enemy troops hadn't struck her as incompetent. Perhaps this bunch had never really tasted combat. They might have landed after the city fell and been ordered to patrol, rather than go into the city. She frowned as she returned to the rest of the squad. If it was a trap, it was a very odd one.

"We could just slip around them and carry on," Jones signed, when she told them what little she'd found. "Leave them to have their fun."

Rachel frowned, sweeping the visible faces carefully. They all wore uniforms, they all looked to be having fun...she'd seen Civil Guardsmen stop to have *fun* with local women, holding the poor bitches at gunpoint to make them strip, but this lot just looked to be having a friendly party. There were no locals in view, no one who might be a prisoner...she was torn between urging an attack and slipping away, letting the enemy keep a few bad habits. Letting them get careless might make the difference between a successful counterattack, once the reinforcements arrived, and total defeat.

"Yeah," she signed, finally. "Let them live."

Bonkowski frowned. "And what will you say if they're the ones who kill you later?"

"Nothing," Phelps signed. "I'll be dead."

"You know what I mean." Bonkowski made a rude gesture and continued. "If we kill them now, they won't have the chance to kill us later."

"We'd also be giving away our position if one of them manages to get out a warning," Rachel pointed out. There was no way to know if letting the enemy troops live would be useful, later on, but killing them would have one very definite downside. "Better to carry on so we can report to the general."

"I hope you're right," Bonkowski signed. "Let's move."

The sound of laughter grew louder as they circled the campfire, then faded as they crept further into the forest. Rachel felt an odd pang of guilt, although she wasn't sure what she was guilty *of*. Letting them live? Or spying on them as they relaxed? She had few qualms about playing voyeur—she'd had no privacy ever since she'd joined the corps—but she still felt as if she'd done something wrong. They might have made a terrible mistake. Time would tell, she supposed. It always did.

Any Drill Instructor who saw that little party would have to make up some new numbers so he could assign press-ups to the idiots, she thought, with a flicker of amusement. They might not have done the enemy troops any favours. There were limits to NJP, but any officer who heard what the troops had been doing would probably sign off on outright torture. *And he'd probably be so pissed he'd actually hit them.*

Shaking her head, she followed Phelps further west.

CHAPTER THIRTEEN

The results of this percolate through the supply chain. In order to keep production high, standards are allowed to slip—and slip badly. Refined metal is discovered—too late—to be far from perfect. Computer components and codes are glitches—or easy to hack. Sealed vials of medicines are discovered to be water. Components that absolutely must be perfect, machined to very high standards, are inevitably nothing of the sort. It is only a matter of time until disaster strikes.
—**Professor Leo Caesius**
The Right to be Wrong: How Silencing People Hurts You

"I NEED A PISS," GERALD ANNOUNCED, to no one in particular. "Call me if anything happens."

He stepped out of the command vehicle, crawled through the earthen tunnel and out into the night. They'd gone to some trouble to hide their location, using camouflage netting and sensor distorters to ensure prying eyes shouldn't be able to find them, but he was grimly aware the enemy might be better than they thought. The marines had spent years studying all the tricks and learning to counter them. The Onge Corporation might have done the same.

Hell, Gerald thought. *The bastards might have read our tactical manuals.*

He relieved himself in the field latrine, then leaned against a tree and stared up. The night sky was bright with stars, orbital industries, and pieces of space junk. It was surprisingly crammed, compared to the skies of Earth or the Slaughterhouse. Gerald could almost believe the planet was a *lot* closer to the galactic core than it was. But the lights were moving oddly... he shook his head, wondering if any of the visible lights were enemy starships looking down at him. It was unlikely, but a lot had happened in the last few weeks that had been unlikely. A few years ago, he would have said it was impossible.

And we just suffered our biggest defeat in the last few hundred years, he reminded himself, sourly. *We got everything we could out of the trap, but we couldn't save* everything.

He cursed under his breath. The Terrain Marine Corps had a long history—and it had appropriated histories from military formations that practically everyone outside the corps had long forgotten—and they'd suffered their share of defeats. Isolated platoons had been destroyed, entire companies and regiments had been put through the meatgrinder...there'd been incompetent commanding officers and ignorant political superiors and failures that had been no one's fault, but still caused death and destruction on a terrifying scale. And yet, they'd never been beaten in the field, not for over a thousand years. Until now...

It wasn't a fair comparison, he told himself. The marines had only had a few short hours to redeploy their forces to meet the offensive. He'd conceded ground he knew perfectly well he couldn't keep, saving the lives of countless marines who would have been killed in the bombardment if they'd stayed in place. And the fighting was far from over. Wars had been won before by sides that had lost all the battles but the last. He'd settle for losing the early engagements if he won the final—decisive—engagement. But...he had no idea if reinforcements would arrive before the enemy found a way to tip the balance against him.

Or if the fleet can find a way to tip the balance against them, he mused. *It won't be easy.*

He turned and walked back to the command vehicle, feeling the burden of command resting heavily on his shoulders. If there was someone else to take command...he shook his head. There was *no one* else who could, not unless Major-General Damiani himself accompanied the reinforcements. Perhaps he would. Damiani had to feel responsible for the disaster, even though no one—including Gerald himself—had grasped what they were facing. Gerald couldn't point fingers at anyone, not now. It would be a different story if he'd realised the truth before the operation was launched.

A failure of imagination on our part, he thought, sourly. *And the only good sign is that they had the same failure.*

It was...frustrating. The intelligence officers had interrogated the handful of truly *senior* personnel captured during the fighting. They hadn't known much—the highest-ranking officials had been killed when the bunker was stormed—but what little they had known was frightening. Rumours of entire fleets, of entire clusters of worlds...Gerald suspected they were exaggerated, yet there was no way to know how *badly*. The prisoners weren't lying. They just couldn't tell their captors something they didn't know.

He felt a twinge of claustrophobia as he reached the bottom of the tunnel and stepped into the command vehicle. The display had updated again, showing a few enemy transmitters within the city. A handful of contact reports hovered below them, the timer warning him that the messages were already outdated. The force trackers were working perfectly, but the marines had stepped them down as much as possible. Microburst signals were supposed to be impossible to track. He'd ordered his subordinates not to take that for granted. The enemy had every motive to find a way. And they probably had more than enough technical experts under their control to do it.

"General." Lieutenant Sally Hemminge looked disgustingly fresh. She'd slept while Gerald and the alpha staff had been monitoring the battle. "We picked up a lone transmission from the city. The enemy have secured the west side and are moving into the east in force."

Gerald nodded, stiffly. He hadn't expected Haverford to hold out for long, but it offended his professional pride to lose the city in less than a day. The post-battle analysis—and self-criticism session—was going to be painful. Perhaps he should book himself in for a session of dental torture instead. It would be less unpleasant in the long run. The corps might not penalise him—it wasn't as if he'd blatantly ignored warnings while sticking his head in the lion's jaws—but every decision he'd made was going to be examined carefully so the proper lessons could be learnt. And it had to be done.

"It might keep them busy for a few days," he said. The rioters were unlikely to do more than delay a professional military force. It was quite possible the invaders would just seal off the district, then either bomb it into submission or wait for the inhabitants to starve. "But we won't place any faith in it."

He tried not to yawn as he studied the display, as if he could draw new information from it just by looking. His body was intent on reminding him that he wasn't a young man any longer, even though he was still pulling his weight. He needed rest, then…then what? It wasn't as if he could do anything to change things, not in a hurry. He could issue all the orders he liked, and then some, but it wouldn't make any difference. The only thing he could really do was wait.

Gerald told himself, sharply, to be patient. "Did we hear anything from the fleet?"

"Not since the last transmission," Sally said. "They went doggo."

Quiet, Gerald translated, automatically. *It'll be a while before we hear anything, unless the shit hits the fan.*

"Understood." He took one last look at the display. "I'm going to get some rest. Alert me if we come under threat."

"Aye, sir," Sally said.

Gerald felt a flicker of guilt. If he couldn't share the dangers, he could at least watch as his men faced an advancing enemy. Right? But he knew it was pointless. There was nothing to be gained by watching the displays until he collapsed, no point in issuing orders that wouldn't bear any resemblance to the facts on the ground. He'd always hated being micromanaged as a young officer—it was a bad habit, but one so easy to embrace—and yet, he thought he understood the urge. He didn't like feeling useless.

He picked up his bedroll, then found a spot on the edge of the clearing and unrolled it. It wasn't perfect, but better than nothing. Better, too, than taking up residence in the biggest farmhouse in the region. He'd known army officers who'd done just that, only to discover—too late—that the enemy had anticipated them and prepared the commandeered accommodation for destruction. Some of them had been—barely—lucky enough to survive.

I may not be a young man any longer, he told himself, *but at least I can still take the field.*

Closing his eyes, he went to sleep.

• • •

"You could be in the CIC," Julia said, from the bed. "Why are you here?"

Nelson grinned at her as he poured them both a drink. "Sick of my company already?"

"No." Julia made a dismissive gesture. Her bare breasts bobbled invitingly. "I could never get sick of you. But I do wonder why you're not in the CIC."

"Well." Nelson passed her the first glass, then lifted the second to his lips. "To victory!"

"To victory," Julia echoed. She gingerly sipped the wine. "And you haven't answered my question."

Nelson sat on the bed. "Well," he repeated. "There's nothing I can do. I've issued all the orders I can issue. All I can do now is wait until my orders are carried out or something goes spectacularly wrong. Until then...all I can do is wait."

"And see," Julia said. "You can't encourage them to hurry?"

"They can't hurry," Nelson said. "Tell me, does nagging really encourage people to hurry up?"

He went on before she could answer. "If I urge them to move faster, they'll make mistakes. That'll happen with the best will in the world. And if they start to resent me nagging them, they'll start subtly sabotaging the operation. They might not be aware of what they're doing, but they will. I'll have a mess to clear up at the worst possible time."

Julia glanced at him. "You really think so?"

"People are people," Nelson said. "And there's only so many times you can swallow your pride before you start to choke."

He smiled, coldly. Admiral Valentine had been fond of belittling his subordinates and threatening them with relief—or worse—if they failed to carry out impossible orders. He wondered, suddenly, what had happened to the bastard. The last reports suggested he'd died on Earth, although Nelson didn't believe it. The slimy admiral had been a cockroach. He was so good at getting people to take the fall for him that he'd probably got some poor sucker to die in his place. Nelson rather hoped he'd survived. He'd wanted to kill the admiral personally.

"Interesting thought," Julia said. "Do you think someone will try to ruin the mission?"

"Not deliberately," Nelson said. "Leadership is more than just being bossy and issuing orders. It involves skills you have to learn by doing. It's not easy."

"And that's not an answer," Julia said.

Nelson grinned. "Right now, I think the answer is *no*. And I have no intention of engaging in behaviour that might start someone thinking, consciously or not, about ways to change that."

He waved a hand at the display. "We've driven the enemy fleet away and established a blockade," he added. "We have to stay out of range of the planetary defences, but that's not a major concern as long as we can funnel troops through the clear zone to the surface. Our forces on the ground have recovered Haverford and are positioning themselves to drive west. We have done as well as I'd hoped and better than I'd feared. It could be worse."

"It could be better too," Julia said. She stood and started to pace. "Do you think the marines are overrated?"

Nelson watched her for a long moment, admiring her naked body. She had a complete lack of self-consciousness that had surprised him, the first time they'd worked together. Naval officers knew better than to expect any privacy, but still…Julia was exceptional. He rather thought she could walk into a meeting unclothed and, by manner alone, ensure everyone forget it within seconds.

"No," Nelson said. "We caught them by surprise, twice. We surprised them when we arrived and we surprised them, again, when we dumped troops and supplies on the surface. In order to do *that*, we had to literally paste the landing zone with projectiles and turn it into mud. If we'd faced them on even terms…"

He shook his head. General Rask had made it clear there was a difference between a rout and a retreat. The marines had fallen back in good order, escaping from the kill zone before it was too late. It was tempting to believe they'd thrown away their weapons and run for their lives, but he knew the marines too well to believe it. They'd been caught with their pants down and they'd still managed to get most of their people out of the trap.

"We have them in a vise," he said. "But we have to keep the pressure up before their reinforcements arrive."

Julia turned, resting her hands on her hips. "Are you sure they'll call for reinforcements?"

"They must," Nelson said. "They have to have launched the invasion from *somewhere*."

He sucked in his breath. No one had launched a full-scale planetary invasion in hundreds of years. Even the most rebellious planet hadn't had proper planetary defences. There'd been safe places to land and deploy troops, friendly locals…well, friendly until they met the imperial forces and remembered why they'd rebelled in the first place. The marines had caught them by surprise, at least in part, because they'd mounted an operation that seemed to come out of nowhere. No one would take such a risk unless they were sure they could win. And that meant the marines probably had reinforcements on the way.

"How long?" He stared at the display, asking himself the unanswerable question. "How long until their reinforcements arrive?"

Julia smiled. "Is there anything to be gained by stressing about it?"

"It would be nice to know," Nelson said. "Clearly, a lot of things stayed off the books."

Including our preparations, he added, silently. *We surprised them as much as they surprised us.*

He remembered the early reports and frowned. They'd insisted that *billions* of marines were landing, a claim Nelson had dismissed on the grounds there weren't billions of marines in existence and, even if there had been, transporting them across interstellar space would be impossible unless the marines had millions of ships too. How many marines had *really* landed? Nelson's calculations suggested there couldn't be more than two to five divisions on the surface, with a rough total of eighty thousand men. Not *all* of them would be marines, of course. They'd have supply officers, civil affairs officers and bureaucrats as well as war-fighters. Perhaps a hundred thousand at most, if they pushed their life support to the absolute limits...

"I don't know," he said. "If we knew what was coming, it would be a lot easier to make plans."

Julia walked behind him and started to massage his shoulders. "What do you *think* they have coming?"

"I don't know," Nelson said. "Officially, those warships we saw don't exist. But they looked very real for ships that don't exist. And three of their transports weren't in our files either. They could have a battlecruiser of their own, if they wanted, or simply capture some battleships...it could be anything from an entire fleet of cruisers to a couple of heavy-hitters."

He considered the problem as he leaned back, allowing her breasts to brush against his bare skin. "We could try to talk to them, but they'd assume we were trying to stall them."

"And they'd be trying to stall us," Julia pointed out. She wrapped her arms around him, gently. "Right?"

"Probably." Nelson shook his head. "Diplomacy is the art of saying *nice doggy* while you get a big stick. Whose big stick is going to arrive first?"

He grinned. "Is there anyone who has actual experience in diplomacy, anywhere?"

"No." Julia shrugged. "There are a few corporate lawyers who might be diplomatic enough to arrange something, but..."

"They're lawyers," Nelson agreed. "No one will trust them."

Julia poked him. "I trained as a lawyer, I'll have you know."

"Oh." Nelson smiled at her. "Sorry."

"Hah." Julia sounded more amused than angry. "But actual diplomats? I don't think so."

Nelson nodded. The Empire hadn't *needed* diplomats. What it wanted, it took. And woe betide anyone who tried to say no. And yet...he gritted his teeth, remembering endless negotiations where the losers had somehow won and the winners had lost. The negotiators had grown up in a world where nothing was ever truly at risk, where everyone kept their word and matters proceeded in a form of genteel harmony. They'd been ill-prepared to face people who knew how the world *really* worked, people who were quite happy to lie, cheat and steal until they got whatever they wanted. And they'd been loathed by everyone who had to pick up the pieces afterwards.

"We'll have to reinvent diplomacy," he said, as he lay back on the bed. "And find ways to say more than just *nice doggy*."

Julia straddled him. "Are you planning for the future?"

"A few months ago, we thought we were the *only* ones who'd planned for the future," Nelson reminded her. "And now we know better. Who *else* planned, too?"

"Good question," Julia said. She brought her lips to his. "And we'll worry about it later."

CHAPTER FOURTEEN

Indeed, the disastrous first—and last—flight of ISS Dyatlov illustrates the danger nicely. On paper, the ship looked perfect. She was regarded as a marvel of modern starship engineering, the perfect vessel to lead the Imperial Navy into a bold new future. In practice, she suffered a series of catastrophic systems failures within minutes of being ordered to full military power. It was sheer luck the entire ship wasn't blown to atoms.
—**Professor Leo Caesius**
The Right to be Wrong: How Silencing People Hurts You

"WELL," DEREK SAID, as the sound of the loudspeaker truck faded away. "That's *us* told."

"Yeah," Roger Dashan said. "They want us to register."

"And that might not be wise," Jenny pointed out. "If they have our records…"

Derek and Roger exchanged glances. There was no way to *know*. Their details had been stored in dozens of databanks, from birth till military service and invasion. The marines *claimed* they'd purged the datanet before shattering it, but there was no way to be *certain* they'd taken out *all* the records. And if there'd been copies stored off-world…It was all too possible. There was no reason the former couldn't transfer records off-world if necessary.

"If we don't register, then what?" Gayle had a more practical concern. "They're threatening to arrest and detain everyone who isn't registered. How long until they search this house and find us?"

"Good question," Roger said. "How long?"

Derek shrugged. There was no way to know. The enemy might take the time to search the city from top to bottom, if they wanted to make damn sure they knew who was within the perimeter, or simply keep the civilians in lockdown while they continued their war against the marines. And yet, cold logic told him it was only a matter of time before the food started to run out. If nothing was coming in from the countryside…he swallowed, hard. The entire population might start to starve if things didn't go back to normal quickly.

"I think we have to gamble," he said. He thought about the weapons and supplies hidden nearby and shuddered. "The more they tighten their grip, the harder it will be to operate without notice."

"True." Roger smiled, humourlessly. "Do we all have our stories straight?"

"Yeah." Derek let out a breath. "Let's just hope they believe us."

He gritted his teeth. The marines had created a set of false personas for the four, but there was no way to know how well they'd stand up. Or if someone would rat them out. A sneak would make himself massively unpopular—as if he'd torn away what little privacy the population had—but Derek could imagine people trying to curry favour by informing their neighbours. And their cover story wouldn't hold out for long if the enemy decided to spend time tearing it apart. In hindsight, perhaps it would have been wiser to hide on the other side of the river. But—if the distant shooting was any indication—that would have had its own dangers.

"Well," Jenny said. She pulled on her coat. "Shall we go?"

Derek said nothing as they emerged into the bright sunlight. A faint stench—smoke, he thought—hung in the air. The streets were weirdly deserted, even to his eye. He thought he spotted curtains twitch on the other side of the road, as if the neighbours were watching, but it was hard to be sure. The city was eerily quiet. No vehicles moved down the road or flew overhead. Even the distant shooting had stopped. He felt alone.

"This way," Roger said, quietly.

The scene only got eerier as they made their way down the street and into the local schoolhouse. It took him a moment to recognise it, even though the building looked *precisely* like the one in Eddisford. Two AFVs sat outside, surrounded by armed soldiers. They appeared relaxed, but he wasn't reassured. Their eyes followed him as he walked through the gate, trying to pretend to be a scared civilian. It wasn't hard. He *was* scared, for himself and his friends. If the soldiers realised who they were, or simply turned nasty, they were caught.

Sweat prickled down his back as he eyed the armed men, trying not to make it obvious. Their uniforms were exactly like the ones he'd worn, their weapons and equipment were exactly like the gear he'd been taught to use…had it really only been two months ago that he'd been looking forward to his discharge? As far as he knew, he was the last survivor of Eddisford Garrison. The others had died…he didn't know if any of them had been captured. He wanted to believe it. Being the last survivor felt wrong.

A line of people—civilians—waited outside the school. Derek joined the rear, waiting as patiently as he could. The line was slow, very slow. He couldn't help noticing that no one was coming *out* of the school. It felt ominous, even though he was fairly sure there was an exit on the far side of the building. Boys and girls entered from opposite sides…he'd never been sure why they bothered. It wasn't as if they segregated classes by sex.

They probably wanted to get us used to obeying orders, Derek thought. His instructors had made it clear, when he'd started his service, that strict obedience to orders—however irrational—was highly commended. *And they didn't want us thinking about why they gave us the orders.*

The line grew longer as the hours wore on. Derek glanced back, noting how scared most of the civilians looked. It couldn't be *easy* to see the world turned upside down *twice*, not when one had spent most of one's life as a tiny cog in the planetary machine. He felt a twinge of pity, mingled with contempt. Most of the locals would bow the knee to the new-old regime. They'd be too scared to do anything else. Derek smiled, inwardly. At least *he* knew how to fight back.

Not that it matters, he reminded himself. *If they find out what I did, I'm dead.*

He felt his heart start to race as he finally reached the door. Memories of school—bad memories—taunted him as the soldiers ordered him inside, pointing him into a classroom. Jenny and the others were held back, despite their protests. Derek cursed under his breath as the door slammed closed behind him. They were going to be seen separately. If there were any discrepancies in their stories...

"Put your hands on the desk," a grim-faced man in a black uniform ordered. Two green tabs shone on his shoulders. "And don't move."

Derek obeyed orders, gritting his teeth in disgust as the security officer searched him thoroughly. Intimately. He just *knew* the asshole was enjoying it. Derek had been searched before, back when he'd entered the garrison, but that had been utterly impersonal. The security officer was definitely enjoying himself. Derek had to fight to keep from swinging around and punching him. It would be very satisfactory, but he'd be arrested seconds later. Or simply shot.

"Very good," the man said. "I'll buy you dinner later."

He laughed, as if it was the funniest joke in the universe. Derek tried his best to smile, even though he wanted to *hurt* the man. It struck him, a second later, that Jenny and Gayle were going to be subjected to the same experience...he forced himself to look at the man, peering past the green tabs to the slimy face beyond. The security division seemed to attract all the perverts and weirdoes. He promised himself he'd meet the guy again, in a dark alley. The bastard wouldn't walk free.

"So," the officer said. He flipped open a terminal and peered down at the screen. "Name, ID number and occupation?"

Derek forced himself to start talking, using the cover story the marines had devised. The security officer said nothing, his face suggesting he wasn't really listening. Derek reminded himself, sharply, that it could be an act. He'd mastered the art of pretending to pay attention in school. There was no reason an officer couldn't have figured out how to pretend *not* to pay attention. He might hope to catch Derek in a careless lie.

"I see," the officer said. He sounded dismissive, rather than concerned. The cover story artfully avoided mentioning anything that might be *interesting* to the enemy. "Put your palm against the scanner, please."

"Yes, sir." Derek braced himself. If his cover was blown…he might manage to kill the bastard before the soldiers got him. He pressed his hand against the scanner. There was a bleep, then nothing. "I…"

"The records are shot to hell, the bastards," the officer said. He shrugged. "Go through the outer door and head down to the gym. The staff will give you a box of ration bars. I'm afraid you'll be doing grunt labour in a day or two, rather than going to university."

Derek tried to look disappointed. University had seemed the ticket out of Eddisford—and military service—but he'd been nowhere near bright enough to use it. He'd known several students who'd practically worked themselves to death, trying to get in. He wondered, idly, what had happened to them. They'd been conceited little assholes, but he had to admit they'd worked hard. And the man in front of him thought he was one of them.

"Go," the officer repeated.

"Yes, sir," Derek said. "Thank you, sir."

He felt dirty as he stepped through the door and walked down to the gym. Memories rose up in front of him, mocking him. The school was *just* like his old school, right down to the portrait of some old guy in front of the gym. The students had joked it was a painting of the headteacher in his younger days. The old bastard hadn't seen the joke. Derek frowned—the painting was *exactly* like the one he remembered—as he walked into the gym. A bored-looking soldier passed him a box of ration bars and pointed at the door. Derek glanced around, then did as he was ordered. A handful of civilians waited outside. He guessed they were waiting for their friends and families too.

Jenny joined him a second later, looking *pissed*. "She put her hands in my...she...fuck it."

"Not here," Derek muttered. "Are you alright?"

"Just angry," Jenny muttered back. "I need a shower."

"Let's hope they turned the water back on," Derek said. The marines hadn't smashed the city's infrastructure, but the fighting had probably damaged the pipes. "I need a shower too."

They waited for Roger and Gayle, then headed back down the street. There were more civilians in the open, looking around nervously as they went to be registered. Large convoys of armoured vehicles, troop transports and supply trucks roared up and down the bigger roads, platoons of soldiers patrolled the streets. They didn't harass anyone, but Derek was sure it was just a matter of time. They'd wait a few days for everyone to be registered, then start randomly stopping and searching civilians. There was no point in checking anyone until the majority of the population was in their datafiles.

The shopping district was largely closed. Soldiers stood on guard outside the shops, their weapons clearly visible. Large signs warned prospective customers that the banking system was down, that the only way to purchase anything was though verified money orders or cash chips. Derek understood, suddenly, why the system was so flimsy. If all transactions were electronic, it was easy to keep track of who bought what. And yet... the system had gone down. It was hard to believe it could be brought back up. Cash chips were rare. He'd certainly never had one.

A shiver ran down his spine as he saw signs of fighting at the end of the street. Buildings had taken damage, from shooting and bombing; shattered glass lay everywhere, despite the best efforts of the shopkeepers and their families. The bank was closed and shuttered, a large sign on the door ordering the staff to report to the nearest registration point immediately. Derek wondered what the occupiers hoped the staff could do. If the banking records had been destroyed, along with everything else, there'd be no hope of reconstructing them. Who'd know how much money people had?

His lips twitched. *Perhaps I should claim to be a millionaire.*

He sobered. It wasn't really funny. People—families—would starve because they couldn't access their bank accounts. No, their bank accounts had vanished. And their jobs had probably vanished too. How could companies hope to make payroll if they didn't know how much money they had, let alone who they employed or...he glanced down at the ration bars under his arm and shivered, again. The occupiers might be the only thing standing between the population and starvation. All of a sudden, he found himself unsure if resistance was really a *good* idea after all.

Jenny caught his arm. "I came here once," she said. "It was wonderful. Now..."

Derek tried to imagine the street as it had been, before the invasion. Row upon row of shops, each one selling fancy goods from right across the galaxy. Bright lights, welcoming shopkeepers...each offering the very height of fashion, each promising that purchasing his goods would make the owner a star. He rolled his eyes. There'd been a craze for handbags a few years ago, a craze that had gripped the girls—and some of the boys—in Eddisford, even though most of them couldn't have hoped to own an expensive design. Jenny had, he recalled suddenly. She'd worn an expensive handbag for a few weeks, then put it aside when the craze burned itself out. God alone knew what had happened to that handbag.

A scream rent the air. He looked. A family were pressed against a wall, being searched by a team of soldiers. He wasn't sure what they'd done, if they'd done anything. Perhaps they hadn't been respectful enough, or...perhaps the soldiers were shaking them down. He'd been given strict orders on how to treat civilians, but he knew—from bitter experience—that genteel conduct broke down in the heat of war. He wanted to intervene as he saw a man run his hands over a young woman's body, a girl no older than his sister, yet...he knew he couldn't. It would just get them all arrested and killed for nothing.

He forced himself to walk faster, without making it obvious. Jenny walked beside him, her expression grim. Derek wondered what she was thinking, but he didn't know how to ask. The streets were no longer safe... he forced himself to think coldly, trying to understand what the occupiers were doing. If they forced people to stay indoors...

They used to control us through surveillance, he thought, as they passed a streetlight. The sensor above the light was a shattered ruin. *They told us they knew what we were doing, even as we did it. But now...they have to control us through fear instead.*

He didn't feel safe until they reached their house and stepped inside, locking and barring the door behind them. The locks wouldn't buy them more than a few seconds—there'd been no time to turn the house into a small fortress—but it might *just* give them time to grab weapons before a raiding squad burst into the house. Derek supposed it depended on what the baddies expected to find. A police squad would come through the door. A team of elite soldiers might come through the windows, or the ceiling, or even the walls. And there was no way to prepare for anything like that without making it obvious.

"Fuck," Jenny said. "I need a shower."

Derek checked the sink. Water flowed, as normal. "Do you want me to come with you?"

Jenny shook her head. "No. I just want to be alone."

"Fuck," Derek muttered. Gayle seemed to have had the same reaction. "Just...fuck."

"You can help me move the clothes out to the shed," Roger said. "We don't want to get caught with them in the house."

Derek gave him an odd look. "What...?"

"Most of the clothes are useless," Roger said. He sounded like he was trying to distract himself. "To us, at least. There are dresses that don't fit either of the girls, clothes that are clearly for kids...anyone who looks at some of the crap we packed up is going to ask what happened to the kids. And there'll be no good answer we can give."

"And there I was thinking we were part of a *rich* family, that bought a home for their children," Derek said. He saw Roger's point, though. The clothes would suggest they were lying about something, even though any investigators might not know precisely *what*. "We could just say we were storing them."

"And then they'd ask why," Roger pointed out. "Who are we storing them *for*? And where are they? The more we add to the story, the greater the chance of a lie being exposed. Better not to take chances."

"And plan while we do it," Derek said. He winced, remembering the security officer—and the soldiers on the street. They *had* to find a way to make the occupiers feel uncomfortable, to keep them from tightening their grip. "We need to start planning how to hit back."

"Yeah." Roger headed for the door. "And do it before they start putting the surveillance system back online."

CHAPTER FIFTEEN

The Imperial Navy's post-mortem concluded that the reactor cores were poorly engineered, the power conduits incapable of tolerating the strain placed on them and the emergency systems—and their backups—completely unsuited to purpose. The final assessment even stated that it was hard to tell the order in which many of the early failures had occurred, suggesting that instead of one stream of failures there were several separate failures that set off a cascade reaction.
—**Professor Leo Caesius**
The Right to be Wrong: How Silencing People Hurts You

THERE WAS NO POINT, Captain Kerri Stumbaugh had learned years ago, in whispering on a starship, even one trying to hide in the vastness of interplanetary space. Sound didn't travel through a vacuum. The entire crew could hold a keg party—complete with deafening rock and roll music and tuneless singing—and the searchers wouldn't hear *any* of it. They'd be in more danger from a stray electronic emission than the crew singing badly at the top of their voices...

And yet, as *Havoc* drifted near the asteroid belt, an uneasy silence pervaded the ship. Crew—even officers—spoke quietly to each other, barely saying anything beyond the bare necessities. They did their duties, then retired to their bunks to sleep. The privacy tubes were open, but unused; the onboard entertainment facilities were almost untouched. Even *Kerri* felt it, experienced officer though she was. The mere sound of someone raising their voice, even slightly, was enough to make everyone jump.

She sat on the bridge and studied the passive sensors as her crew hastily transferred missile pods from the supply ships to *Havoc*. Resupplying in interstellar space had never been easy, even in the days before they'd faced any significant opposition outside a planet's atmosphere. Kerri was all too aware that a single enemy warship could *really* ruin their day, if it stumbled across *Havoc* while she was vulnerable. Losing the cruiser would hurt—there was no point in denying it—but losing the transport and its supplies would be worse. She'd have to take the enemy ship out, whatever the cost. She certainly couldn't surrender. *Havoc's* datacores held too much information to risk allowing them to fall into enemy hands.

The display updated, showing a pair of enemy starships leaving the planet, heading out on a least-time course towards the Phase Limit. Kerri eyed them sourly, silently calculating their vectors. There were a dozen possible destinations within fifty light years…assuming, of course, they didn't alter course once they were out of range. There'd been no point, before Earthfall, but now…she shook her head. The corps—and their new enemies—were relearning old lessons, lessons they should never have forgotten in the first place. She had a feeling it was going to be a steady theme. The after-action reports were not going to be fun to write.

She leaned back in her chair, gritting her teeth in frustration. Her first major space battle…and she'd lost. She knew, intellectually, that she'd had no choice, but to fight a long-range engagement and retreat when they were pushed back. She knew it and yet she didn't *believe* it. She wanted to believe there'd been a way to win, that some tactical genius would find a way to beat the enemy fleet. But it wasn't true. She'd run a handful of simulations during downtime. They'd all agreed there was no way to win. The best she could do was take out a handful of enemy ships, at the cost of losing her entire fleet.

The planet hung in the centre of the display, a cluster of red icons holding station just outside PDC range. They taunted her, even though she knew they hadn't secured the entire planet. Not yet. They'd need to take out the PDCs, on the ground, before they could occupy the high orbitals and batter the marines into submission. She watched, trying to think of a way to win before it was too late. And yet, she couldn't come up with anything. Her flotilla might be able to take out the battlecruiser, but at a price. And the battlecruiser's escorts were more than enough to safeguard the giant ship.

She tossed ideas around and around in her head, none really plausible. Slipping a nuke onto the ship might work, but only if they could get it inside the hull. The battlecruiser was designed to survive environments that would daunt a mere heavy cruiser like *Havoc*. She mulled over a few options, knowing they'd all depend on *everything* going right for them to succeed. They might be worth trying, but only as a final resort. Trying and failing might be worse than not trying at all.

They'll have to ship more supplies into the system, she mused. *And we can harass them while we wait for reinforcements.*

"Captain," Tomas said. "The last of the supply pods has been transferred."

"Good." Kerri allowed herself a moment of relief. "Order the transport to return to the RV point, then wait."

"Aye, Captain," Tomas said.

Kerri barely heard him. Her ship had her teeth back, but for what? She couldn't fight the battlecruiser and her escorts, not until reinforcements arrived. It would be at least a month before anything arrived from Safehouse, even though a courier boat had been dispatched the moment they'd realised the enemy held more than one planetary system. She'd worked it out. Gathering the squadron would take time, too much time. It left the ball in enemy hands.

"Hold the squadron here," she ordered. "We'll search for a way to even the odds."

"Aye, Captain," Tomas said. "We could always feint at them."

"We might have to," Kerri said. She'd quite happily take suggestions from *anyone*, provided they had a chance of working. She stood. "Mr XO, you have the bridge. I'll be in my ready room."

She didn't allow herself to sag, let alone show any sign of weakness, until she was in the compartment and the hatch was firmly closed. The crew didn't need to see her lose heart, even for a moment. Morale was already heading down. They weren't used to losing, let alone hiding from superior firepower. In hindsight...she shook her head. There was no point in worrying. Sure, there were a *lot* of things she'd do differently...if she knew what was hidden by the fog of war. She walked over to the desk and sat down. The latest set of departmental reports demanded her attention, but she ignored them. They could wait until the fighting was over. The reports from the surface were much more important.

The enemy scored a victory, no matter how much we might like to deny it, she told herself. *And they're no doubt preparing to retake the PDCs and declare victory.*

Kerri let out a breath as she scanned the reports. The war had stalemated, but that wouldn't last. Given time, the enemy would take out enough of the PDCs to allow them to secure the high orbitals and start dropping rocks. She was mildly surprised they hadn't started sniping from orbit already. The cost would be minimal and the rewards enormous, if they scored a hit. They certainly shouldn't have a *shortage* of projectiles. The star system was *full* of junk they could turn into KEWs. And they had to know there was no way they could recover the PDCs intact.

They're winning, she mused. *And we have to find a way to tip the balance back in our favour.*

But, no matter how many options she considered, she couldn't find a way.

• • •

"This is a pretty weird Marine Country," Lieutenant Joseph Wooten observed. "It encompasses the entire ship."

"Yeah," Lieutenant Freckles said. "If every compartment is part of Marine Country, are we all marines?"

Captain Haydn Steel glared at the pair of them. *Havoc* was odd, compared to the Imperial Navy starships he'd known. The entire *ship* was designed for marines, crewed by marines and marine auxiliaries who knew precisely how to treat them. Freckles had a point, for someone who'd only just been assigned to the company. If Marine Country encompassed the entire ship...

He shook his head in disgust. There was no point in worrying about it, not now. He wished he'd stayed on the surface, even if disobeying orders would have earned him a court-martial followed by a dishonourable discharge. Or immediate execution. A division commander *did* have the authority to pronounce a death sentence, although Haydn couldn't remember if anyone actually *had*. Probably not, he decided. The case would have been discussed endlessly, with OCS candidates debating the pros and cons of sentencing an officer to death, if the authority had ever been used. It was far more likely it was just on the books as a deterrent.

He'd half-expected to be blown out of space as the shuttle flew through the atmosphere and raced to catch up with the retreating fleet. He'd feared he'd die without ever knowing what'd hit him...or, perhaps just as bad, the shuttle running out of fuel in interplanetary space, condemning the marines to drift forever unless the enemy deigned to rescue them. Instead, they'd boarded a transport and then told they were being transferred to *Havoc*. Haydn was used to being jerked around by superior officers, as plans and circumstances changed without warning, but it was irritating as hell to keep moving. He stared at the bunk without quite seeing it, then threw his knapsack onto the mattress. He'd slept in worse places. *Havoc* was practically a paradise compared to makeshift barracks in a hostile town.

"Colonel," Command Sergeant Mark Mayberry said, as he stepped through the hatch. "The men are all bedded down."

"Good," Haydn said. *Colonel*. It was traditional to give a captain an honorary promotion onboard ship—there could only ever be *one* captain on a warship, the one in command—but it still felt odd, as if he was claiming an authority that couldn't be his. "Have them rest as much as possible. We'll start drills tomorrow."

"Yes, sir," Mayberry said. "I suggest you get some rest too. How long has it been since you last slept?"

Haydn wasn't sure. He'd been patrolling since sunrise, then he'd been ordered to abandon his comrades and save his own skin…a surge of bitter self-loathing washed through him. He'd had no choice but to obey orders, yet…his friends and comrades were in danger, fighting for their lives, and he'd abandoned them. The guilt mocked him. He'd never understood how someone could betray their people and run, abandoning them to their fate. The urge to do something—anything—to wipe the guilt from his soul was almost overwhelming. He honestly didn't know *how* long it had been since he'd slept.

"I'll sleep shortly," he said. "You go sleep. That's an order."

Mayberry gave him a sharp look, then saluted and retreated. Haydn followed him into the passageway, then turned and walked down the corridor without any clear idea of where he was going. *Havoc* was built on an Imperial Navy hull, but the marine designers had added all sorts of little improvements and special modifications designed to make it easier to fight an engagement in interstellar space or land marines on a hostile surface. Dozens of crewmen passed him as he walked, pushing trolleys of supplies from compartment to compartment or manhandling vast packages through the corridors. They spoke in hushed whispers, as if there'd been a death in the family. Haydn felt a flash of black amusement. There *had* been a death in the family. Their certainty in victory had died.

We lost the battle, he told himself, firmly. He'd downloaded the latest reports when they'd transferred to *Havoc*, but he hadn't had time to review them. *We didn't lose the war.*

His feet carried him to the observation blister. He hesitated, then pushed the switch to open the hatch. The tiny chamber was empty. A single chair—more like a metal bench—was positioned in front of him, allowing anyone who sat to peer out into the universe. The stars glowed, burning with a cold eerie light. They didn't twinkle...he smiled in fond memory, recalling the first day he'd stared into the void. Stars didn't *really* twinkle. It was just an illusion, caused by planetary atmospheres...

He sat, feeling as if a giant weight rested on his shoulders. He knew he was no coward. A coward could not have graduated from Boot Camp, let alone the Slaughterhouse. Marines did not break. They might retreat in good order, they might fall back in good order...they didn't break like civil guardsmen experiencing their first taste of resistance. And yet, he felt as if he'd turned tail and fled. His thoughts mocked him as he stared into the starfield. His orders had been clear. No one was going to torment him over it. And yet...he'd torment himself. How many people had died on the surface? How many people would have lived if he'd been down there? How many of them had names and faces he knew?

The hatch hissed open. He glanced back, raising his eyebrows as a woman in a captain's shipsuit stepped into the blister. Captain Stumbaugh, he remembered. *Kerri* Stumbaugh. He didn't think they'd ever been formally introduced, although they'd probably attended some of the same briefings. She had the short, compact and muscular look of someone who'd trained as a marine and kept going, even after being transferred to the auxiliaries. Maybe not conventionally attractive, Haydn thought, but striking. He told himself, sharply, not to go down that route. It would only end in tears.

"Colonel," Kerri said. "Welcome onboard."

"Thank you." Haydn stood and saluted. Technically, he outranked her, but *Havoc* was her ship. Regulations insisted she was in command, at least until Haydn and his troops were deployed. "I'm sorry to impose upon you."

"I dare say we have room," Kerri said. She stepped past him and peered into interplanetary space. "Did your men get settled in?"

"Yes, Captain," Haydn said. He couldn't keep the guilt and self-reproach out of his voice. "Your ship is practically paradise, compared to some of the hellholes we've had to use."

Kerri laughed. "We had to pack away the bed of nails," she said. "And the bug-infected blankets had to be sent elsewhere."

Haydn had to smile, despite everything. "But I hope you kept the ice-cold showers?"

"The water has been exposed to the vacuum of space," Kerri assured him. "I think the last bunch of visitors we had from the Imperial Navy thought we were trying to torture them."

"You'd think they'd be used to it." Haydn snorted. Imperial Navy crewmen had accommodations little better than Marine Country, but flag officers had palatial quarters and entire *armies* of servants. "Didn't they file a complaint?"

"They must have done," Kerri said. She smiled, although the expression didn't touch her eyes. "I got a commendation."

"Hah." Haydn met her eyes as she turned to face him. "Do you have any plans for us?"

"Not yet," Kerri said. "But I'm working on them."

"Something that will let us make a difference?" Haydn felt another flash of guilt as he jabbed a finger at the transparent blister. "I could have made a difference down there."

"Yes," Kerri agreed. Her voice was suddenly very cold. "You could have added a hundred and twenty names to the list of honoured dead."

Haydn blanched. "How many died?"

"So far, we have over two hundred marines reported missing, presumed dead," Kerri said, grimly. She couldn't hide her grief. "Some of them may yet return to the fold."

"I hope so," Haydn said. He had his doubts. The survivors of a shattered unit might be able to make their way back to friendly territory, or...they might be captured. There was no way to know. The enemy wouldn't be in a hurry to exchange prisoners. A single marine was worth at least ten of their soldiers. "I...fuck it."

"Maybe later," Kerri said. She turned back to interstellar space before Haydn could think of a response. "Reinforcements are on the way. The folks on the ground can hold out that long. And we can give them a hand, by harassing the enemy fleet and raiding their supply lines. And then..."

She stopped. "You know, I think I've just had an idea. Your men are all space-capable, right?"

"Yeah." Haydn scowled. General Anderson had yanked thirty space-capable specialists from a dozen other units and attached them to his command, with nothing more than a hunch they might prove useful. He'd have protested, if there'd been time. And if he'd thought the CO would have listened. "Unit integrity took a pounding, though. I'll need to start running training exercises from tomorrow."

"Work on it," Kerri said. A faint smile, promising confusion and death to their enemies, spread across her face. "I have a cunning plan."

Haydn frowned. In his experience, cunning plans tended to be either impractical or simply idiotic. A plan that relied upon the enemy doing *exactly* as one wanted was doomed to fail, as the enemy would rarely deign to cooperate. And then...he knew from grim experience that it was all too easy to become hypnotised by one's plan, to press on even though it had become obvious the operation had gone off the rails and was heading down the slippery slope into disaster. Sometimes, good training could make the difference when the plan hit reality and went *splat*. Sometimes, all the training in the universe was useless...

"I see," he said. The starship's captain was an experienced officer. She'd know what was practical and what wasn't. Right? "What do you have in mind?"

Kerri told him.

CHAPTER SIXTEEN

Naturally, the report was suppressed. The captain of the ship was officially blamed for the disaster and, along with his entire senior crew, posthumously stripped of all honours, pensions and practically everything else. (The fact that nearly the entire crew had died was of no importance.) The officers who actually wrote the report were reassigned to asteroid mining colonies in the middle of nowhere.
—**Professor Leo Caesius**
The Right to be Wrong: How Silencing People Hurts You

SAFEHOUSE WAS NOT, BY ANY REASONABLE standard, a prime candidate for settlement. A gas giant's moon wouldn't attract much attention at any time, but the poisonous atmosphere, the shortage of known deposits of rare materials and the sheer abundance of other candidates had discouraged just about everyone from giving the system more than a single glance. Even fugitive colonists, trying to hide themselves from a universe that didn't really care about them, preferred to set course for the edge of explored space. A system too close to the Core—practically *part* of the Core, if one went by astrographics alone—was not a safe place to hide.

Major-General Jeremy Damiani, Commandant of the Terran Marine Corps, stood by the window and stared over the hellish landscape. It was almost charming, a winter wonderland from a past that had never truly existed. He'd been raised on stories of Christmas, of Santa Claus and Rudolf the Red-Nosed Reindeer; it was easy, if he felt fanciful, to imagine they were somewhere within the white haze, perhaps just a *little* out of sight. But he knew the environment was poisonous. An unprotected human would be dead within seconds if they set foot on the surface. It would be a toss-up, he supposed as he turned away, which particular lethal hazard would get them first.

He watched, saying nothing, as Colonel Chung Myung-Hee and Major-General Miguel Foxtrot entered the conference room and took their places at the table. Major-General Anderson should be there too, but he was hundreds of light years away on Hameau. The last set of reports had been grim. It looked, very much, as though the enemy relief fleet had arrived. He both hoped for and dreaded the next set of updates. He might have hurled four entire divisions into the fire.

His aide served coffee, then withdrew as silently as she'd come. Jeremy sat at the head of the table and sipped his mug, savouring the sour taste. Marine coffee was strong enough to wake the dead, marines joked. It was hardly expensive, not compared to jars of coffee that had once cost thousands of credits and were now probably priceless, but it did its job. The corps practically *ran* on coffee. There were times, he felt, when it had made the difference between success and failure.

"I don't want any recriminations, not now," he said. "We'll assess just how we got into this mess later, once we've dealt with the looming disaster. Right now, our priority is either winning the engagement on Hameau or cutting our losses and withdrawing."

He felt a hot flash of bitter frustration. It had taken a week for the courier boat to reach Safehouse, a week…anything could happen in a week. No, anything could *have* happened. The enemy ships could have won the engagement, hammered the marines on the ground and declared victory…

or, perhaps, lost the engagement. Major-General Anderson might be alive and victorious, dead and defeated...or anywhere in-between. And it would take another week for any orders *he* issued to reach Hameau. By the time they arrived, they might already be invalidated by events.

Jeremy composed himself. It was clear they'd screwed up, although it wasn't clear how *badly*. Not yet. There'd be time for proper assessments later. They'd have to work hard to learn lessons, to determine what mistakes had been made and assign blame to officers who'd fucked up spectacularly. Jeremy had no intention of starting a witch-hunt, of tearing the corps apart in a desperate search for scapegoats and traitors. He simply didn't have the time.

"Colonel," he said. "What's your assessment?"

Chung took a breath. "Our current assessment is that the enemy will have defeated our fleet or driven it away, allowing them to land troops on the surface. Assuming a dismemberment capability roughly equal to our own, and assuming that all the enemy transports are troopships, they could drop a couple of divisions within the week. If they've found a way to speed the process up, perhaps by cramming additional shuttles into their hulls, our estimates may be a *little* inaccurate."

"A *little*," Jeremy repeated. Intelligence staffers didn't have it easy. They had to put a jigsaw puzzle together, without knowing what it was meant to look like. Thankfully, marine officers were taught to be careful about reading too much into what little hard data they had. "And then?"

"Impossible to say, sir," Chung said. "They'll want to secure the PDCs. Tactically, they'll have no choice. They might be able to do it too, if they snipe at the defenders from orbit while their troops advance on the ground. The planetary settlements are largely immaterial to them, as long as we hold the PDCs. We think they'll land to the east, but beyond it..."

She shrugged. "We don't know."

No, Jeremy agreed, silently. *And at least you're smart enough to admit it.*

"We should have another update in two days, assuming a second courier boat was dispatched," Foxtrot said. "By then, we may know."

"Yes," Jeremy agreed. "Your thoughts?"

"We can't leave Gerald hanging in the wind," Foxtrot said. "We appear to have three options. Reinforce, then kick the shit out of them; reinforce, and then withdraw back into the shadows…or open talks with the enemy."

"Surrender," Chung said. "You're suggesting surrender."

"No," Foxtrot said. "I'm suggesting we talk to the bastards, see what they want."

"Galactic domination," Jeremy said, dryly. He *knew* the Onge Family. Grand Senator Stephen Onge might have died at Sol—Jeremy wasn't sure who'd been in line to succeed him, if the Grand Senator's heir was aware his predecessor was dead—but he was sure the man's hand-picked successor would be just as determined to secure power as the late Grand Senator Onge had been. "And there are limits to what we can give them."

"Yes," Foxtrot agreed. "But, right now, we have a bunch of marines caught like rats in a trap."

"We'll get them out," Jeremy said. It wasn't going to be easy. Pulling a small army off a planetary surface was a logistics headache at the best of times. Doing it under enemy fire would be damned near impossible. "And we can decide—then—if we should continue to seize Hameau or withdraw, back into the shadows."

"And we still don't know what we're facing," Foxtrot pointed out. "If Hameau is not their headquarters, where is it?"

"There's a handful of possible candidates," Chung said. "All places that were under corporate influence, if not outright control. The *real* Corporate Worlds are in deep shit."

"Their base will not be," Jeremy said, firmly. "They wouldn't be launching snatch and run raids if they had problems at home."

"Yes, sir," Chung said. "It's quite possible they played a role in triggering Earthfall."

Jeremy considered it, briefly. It *was* possible. There was no way the enemy could have prepared for a crisis when they had no way of knowing when it was going to happen. Triggering the crisis themselves would be a neat way of getting around the problem, if one didn't mind slaughtering uncounted—and uncountable—billions of people. He could see the logic. Earthfall would take the rest of the Core Worlds with it, shattering the imperial government and ruining their rivals. And then the Onge Family could take over and rebuild the government in their image.

The Grand Senator was certainly ruthless enough to try, he thought. *We still don't know who took out the Slaughterhouse.*

He felt a chill as he contemplated the sheer scale of the enemy plan, as he saw it. The Onge Corporation had had practically *limitless* resources. Setting up a chain of hidden bases would be easy. They could hide the work in the budget, tell the crews they were doing something completely different... hell, they could just construct enough components to build eleven naval starships instead of ten and put the last ship together in a black facility. Given enough time, it would be easy to keep the work completely off the books. He and his cabal had done much the same, just on a smaller scale.

"I think we'll deal with that later," he said. He remembered the incident at Terra Nova and scowled. Belinda Lawson was looking for the perpetrator, but—so far—she hadn't found anything. Whoever had turned a little girl into a killing machine clearly had access to cutting-edge technologies and a complete lack of scruples. "Right now, we have to deal with the crisis at Hameau."

He pursed his lips. There was no way they could slip back into the shadows, even if they managed to evacuate the planet. The Onge Family knew the marines had survived, now. They'd be looking for them...he glanced at the window, reminding himself that no camouflage was perfect. Safehouse would be pretty far down the list of possible locations—it was why the moon had been chosen in the first place—but it would probably be *on* that list. And the slightest mistake would bring the enemy fleet down on them.

"We have already sent out recall orders," Foxtrot said. "But it'll take us at least two weeks to concentrate enough firepower to give them a very hard time."

"And we cannot rely on better training and equipment either," Chung added. "The reports suggest they have access to mil-grade weapons and sensors."

"Which shouldn't surprise us for a moment," Jeremy said, dryly. "The Onge Corporation built a *lot* of material for the Imperial Navy."

He made a mental note to check the list, just to see what else might be coming their way, and leaned forward. "We have to act fast. Miguel, I want you to prepare two divisions and their supplies to accompany the relief force. You'll take command. You and Gerald can fight it out when you reach Hameau."

Foxtrot smiled. "He'll know what's going on," he said. "He'll have the edge."

Assuming he's still alive, Jeremy thought. Not *knowing* wore on him more than anything else. He was alive and well and relatively safe, while his subordinates were in danger on a hostile world. *They might all be dead by now.*

It was a humbling thought. He'd resented micromanagement by politicians who took the credit when things went well and searched for scapegoats when things went badly, who demanded constant updates and sent orders that were laughably out of date when they reached their destination…but he thought he understood them now. They'd felt helpless to do anything, yet they'd known they had to do something. And they'd thought they were doing something.

"If you believe the planet can be secured, with the industries captured intact, do so," Jeremy said. "If not—in your judgement and his—withdraw as best as you can."

"Yes, sir," Foxtrot said, formally. "And if we have a chance to take the war to the enemy?"

Jeremy kept his face impassive. They would be committing themselves…no, they were already committed. He felt another twinge of sympathy for the politicians, the ones who hemmed and hawed and did their level best to avoid making a decision…even a decision everyone who studied the issues knew was not only the right decision, but inevitable. He understood, now, just how they'd felt. The junior officers could see the tactical view. *He* had to focus on the strategic picture.

"If you have a chance…" Jeremy stopped himself before he could say *no*. There might be a window of opportunity, a window that would close before his subordinates could contact him and ask for orders. God alone knew how many opportunities had been lost because the officers on the ground hadn't been given the freedom to exploit them. "If you have a chance, take it. But remember, we can't afford heavy losses."

"Neither can they," Foxtrot said. "But your point is taken."

Jeremy made a face. The training pipeline had been effectively shattered beyond repair. The Slaughterhouse was gone. Safehouse had some facilities, but nowhere near enough to replenish even a relative handful of combat losses. Recruiting officers were already moving amongst the refugees, offering youngsters the chance to join the marines, yet it would be a long time before they'd be ready to serve. Standards were going to slip, despite their best efforts. The newcomers were going to have to learn hard lessons on the battlefield.

We'll have to set up a whole new training camp, he told himself. There were a handful of possible candidates, all of which would require some terraforming before they could support even a minimal population. *But we can only dedicate a planet to ourselves when the fighting is over.*

"We can't afford to lose ships, either," he added. "Replacing them is going to be a pain in the ass."

"We do have leads on shipyards we might be able to secure," Chung reminded him. "It should be doable."

"Yes," Jeremy said. "But everyone will know where they are."

He kicked himself, mentally. It was so fucking *obvious* in hindsight. They'd prepared for Earthfall, for a crisis they knew would come. Why couldn't someone else—anyone else—have drawn the same conclusion? Why couldn't they have started making their own preparations? The signs of impending doom had been clear *decades* before Professor Leo Caesius had gotten himself in hot water by daring to write a book about them. Who knew who'd read his book and taken his words to heart? Who knew...?

They had to have started decades before the professor was even born, Jeremy reminded himself. *They couldn't have settled a dozen possible seedling worlds in less than a century or two.*

"Good luck," he said. "We'll discuss formal orders when you're ready to leave. We should have some more intelligence by then."

"Sir." Foxtrot stood. "See you on the flipside."

He left the room. Jeremy turned to Chung. "How many recon units can we put together in a week or so?"

Chung frowned. "Most of our scouts are scattered across the Core, collecting information," she said. "I only have two holding position at the waypoint. We can gather four more, assuming they return on schedule. One vanished without a trace...it may still turn up."

"It may," Jeremy said. "Send the two you have to recon the possible enemy homeworlds. When the others return, send them out as well. Give them orders to pass through Hameau on their voyage home. If we still have a presence in the system, we might be able to make use of what they find."

"Yes, sir," Chung said. "We only have a list of possible suspects."

Jeremy nodded. They'd have noticed, he hoped, if Hameau was close to any other Onge-dominated world. That meant...he shook his head. The enemy homeworld *had* to be fairly close to Hameau. They couldn't have dispatched a relief force as quickly as they had if it lay anywhere else. And it had to be a fairly major world...the list of suspects wasn't that long. They could scan them all for suspicious emissions from a safe distance. If that didn't turn up anything useful...

We'll have to think of something else, he told himself. *They might have set up shop in a seemingly uninhabitable system too.*

"Make sure you arrange to have every system within fifty light years swept at least once," he ordered. "We might be dealing with more than one enemy world."

"Yes, sir," Chung said. "Do you want me to hang fire on the next recovery mission?"

Jeremy made a face. They'd committed too many men and ships to Hameau. And yet, they were running out of time. They wanted—they *needed*—to save as many trained men and their families as possible, before the waves of chaos swept across the worlds. He turned to stare out the window, watching the white snowflakes drifting through the air. It was hard to believe they were poisonous. Children who saw the snowfield would want to build snowmen. They wouldn't realise the danger.

"No," he said, finally. "We need to keep going."

"Yes, sir." Chung stood. "I'll get right on it."

Jeremy watched her leave, then picked up his coffee and stood. He was used to being active, but there was nothing he could do. Nothing *useful*, at least. He could have joined a drill instructor in the ring or gone to the shooting range or…or something, anything, that might have kept his mind from wandering. Perhaps it had been a mistake, he conceded ruefully, not to establish a brothel. The courtesans who'd worked on the Slaughterhouse—the most highly-paid sex workers in the galaxy—had been moved elsewhere. He had a feeling there were thousands of marines who wished they'd gone to Safehouse instead.

And we have room for them now, he mused. *The diggers have carved out the next set of caves. We could turn one of them into a brothel and…*

He dismissed the thought with a flicker of irritation. He'd made mistakes. He'd made mistakes and his subordinates were going to pay for it. And…he'd done what little he could to fix the mistake, but it wasn't enough. And…all he could do was wait and see what happened. And hope.

And pray, he told himself. It wasn't a cheerful thought. *There's nothing else I can do.*

CHAPTER SEVENTEEN

Indeed, it is something of a surprise the navy never tried to construct another ship of the Dyatlov's class. Clearly, some of the right lessons were learnt.
—**Professor Leo Caesius**
The Right to be Wrong: How Silencing People Hurts You

THE NIGHT AIR FELT UNCOMFORTABLY WARM as Derek slipped through the window and dropped to the ground. He glanced from side to side, wishing he had a pair of night-vision goggles or enhanced eyes or *something* that would have made it easier to see in the dark. The streets were shrouded in darkness, the streetlamps still non-functional despite the power and water being brought back online. Roger dropped down beside him, ducking low as they inched around the house and onto the street. It was silent, but that was meaningless. If they were being watched…

He looked up at the twinkling lights overhead. One could be peering down at him, watching with cold unblinking eyes as they sneaked down the streets. A single drone, holding position over the city, could track him… the marines had promised they'd shoot down anything within range, but they'd need to have an HVM team near the city to shoot down the drone. If, of course, there *was* a drone. He felt a flicker of apprehension, combined with a grim awareness they had to move before the enemy tightened their grip on the city any further. They already dominated the streets. Rumour insisted it was just a matter of time before non-essential personnel went back to work. And then the population would be too busy to resist.

And heartily sick of ration bars, he thought, coldly. The bars weren't *bad*, but they tasted suspiciously of cardboard. *They'll want us working to earn the cash to buy real food.*

He gritted his teeth. They'd watched and listened to rumours as they swirled through the city. The majority of the population was keeping their heads down, waiting to see if the city changed hands a third time. He didn't blame them. Two months ago, they'd had no reason to think anything would change. Now…he shook his head. The entire planet had been turned upside down by two successive invasions. If things had been different, if he'd had the option, he might have chosen to slip into obscurity himself. But he'd lost that chance when he'd gunned down the planetary government.

Roger followed him as they reached the crossroads. Row upon row of parked vehicles, grounded by order, greeted their eyes. The aircars were useless without the ATC system, as far as he knew. They'd been hardwired to require permission to fly before they so much as powered up their drives. He shuddered, realising—once again—just how completely the planet had been controlled. Resistance would have been literally futile. He slipped a little down the road, glancing at the darkened houses. There were no lights in the window, no hint they were being watched. He hoped the homeowners remained quiet. The last thing they needed, right now, was to draw attention to themselves.

The wristcom vibrated, once. Derek dropped down, bracing himself as he heard the enemy patrol march along the street. They'd fallen into a routine of running regular patrols through quiet neighbourhoods, while—if rumour was to be believed—concentrating their forces on the other side of the river or preparing an offensive against the PDCs. He held his pistol as the patrol marched closer, promising himself he'd sell his life dearly if they spotted him. They'd have night-vision gear. He knew it was quite possible they'd be spotted.

Derek felt sweat bead on his back as the patrol marched past and vanished. He stayed still, all too aware that the patrol could be trying to lure him into a false sense of security. He'd been through enough exercises to *know* they might be playing games, even though there was no *need*. They could have tried to grab them both, if they'd known Derek and Roger were there. Unless they were silently tracking them from a distance...

He put the thought out of his mind as he produced his multitool and carefully opened the aircar. The lock offered little resistance, somewhat to his surprise. A groundcar would have been harder to hack. His lips twitched—a groundcar would also have been easier to steal—as Roger hastily passed him the knapsack with the explosives. Derek rigged the charge quickly, hoping the enemy didn't notice anything was wrong before it was too late. They'd march right past the IED. Their radio signals would trigger the bomb.

And we won't be able to watch the results, he thought, as he closed the door silently and led the way back to their street. The next patrol wasn't due for twenty minutes—and there was no way to be sure when the IED would actually detonate—but there was no point in taking chances. Hopefully, the charge would explode before sunrise. *If we catch an innocent in the blast...*

He told himself it wasn't likely. Radios had been banned well before the first invasion, let alone the second. Civilian terminals and wristcoms wouldn't trigger the IED. But...his heart twisted. It was impossible to be *sure*. He wanted to go back and remove the device before it was too late, to find another way to strike at the enemy. And yet, there was *no* other way. They had weapons and equipment—and instructions on how to turn simple household supplies into bombs—but if they tried to fight openly, they'd be slaughtered. They *had* to strike from the shadows.

And if someone gets caught in the blast, he told himself, *it's acceptable.*

His heart twisted again. It wasn't acceptable. He'd been trained to avoid killing civilians. And yet...what choice did he have? His thoughts ran in circles. They had to fight. They had to take the risk of killing their own people. And yet, killing innocents would turn the locals against them. He was all too aware that it would only take one person to betray them, one person who thought the insurgents were terrorists who needed to be exterminated. They were already strangers to the neighbourhood. There were no guarantees they could escape if the shit hit the fan.

I suppose that's why they told us never to shit where we ate. His lips twitched at the thought. *We could have poisoned our own well.*

Jenny met them as they clambered back through the window, holding a scanner in one hand. Derek held himself still as she waved the device over them, then nodded in relief. He wasn't sure what he would have done if it turned out they'd been stung. Military-grade bugs and trackers were so tiny they couldn't be seen with the naked eye. It might not be easy to *accidentally* lose one. The enemy might ask some pretty pointed questions. Or they might just jump to the right conclusion and arrest everyone in the house.

"Did you do it?" Jenny sounded eager. "It'll explode?"

Roger made a show of consulting his watch. "The next patrol is in ten minutes," he said. "We should be able to hear the bang."

"Assuming they use their radios within detection range," Derek reminded him. "There's no way to know when the bomb will actually detonate."

"As long as it doesn't blow up in your face," Jenny said, practically. "You'd better get into your nightclothes. People will talk."

"You make it sound as if we're walking around naked," Roger said, although he headed to the door anyway. "We'd frighten the neighbours."

"You might raise eyebrows if you're fully dressed in the middle of the night," Jenny said, indicating her nightgown. "And what will you say if they ask *why* you're fully dressed?"

Roger snorted as he left the room. Derek had to smile as he stripped quickly, putting the clothes in the washing basket before they headed upstairs. Jenny was right. It wouldn't be easy to explain. The patrollers wouldn't need to be Sherlock of the Yard—whoever that had been, whatever that was—to suspect *something* if they'd stayed fully dressed. Better to walk around in his underwear—and risk them laughing—than have them suspect the truth.

He frowned as he caught sight of himself in the mirror. Did he look too muscular for a civilian? Too scarred? The marines had done what they could for his bumps and bruises, but he was uncomfortably aware he didn't *look* innocent. He made a mental note of where he'd put the pyjamas—he'd change, if someone banged on the door—and crawled into bed. Jenny joined him a moment later, looking pensive. Derek understood. They were committed now.

As if we weren't committed already, he thought, as he held her close. *We were committed the moment we chose to stay behind.*

There was no explosion as he drifted off to sleep. He frowned, dimly aware it might be a problem even though he *knew* it was just a matter of time. He'd used real military gear to build the IED. There should be no room for anything to go wrong. Advanced technology was often surprisingly unreliable, or so the old sweats had claimed, but he'd used very basic stuff. The moment someone used a communicator too close to the IED, it should detonate.

He jerked awake, what felt like seconds later, half-convinced the bomb *had* detonated. Someone was banging on the door. Roger? They'd agreed each couple would have its own private room, as long as they stayed in the house. No, not Roger. Someone was hammering on the door downstairs. Derek sat up and jumped out of bed, grabbing his pyjamas and pulling them on at breakneck speed. Jenny rolled over and stood. She looked winsomely innocent in her nightgown.

"I didn't hear the blast," Jenny said. "Are they…?"

"I don't know," Derek said. He thought, briefly, about the concealed weapons. They could make a fight of it…no, not if an entire enemy squad had come calling. Better to try and bluff it out. "Are you coming?"

Jenny followed him as he inched down the stairs and checked the security camera. A pair of uniformed men stood outside. They looked irked, rather than angry. The fact they weren't trying to break down the door suggested they didn't think they were storming a terrorist's house. Derek knew he wasn't an elite soldier, but even *he* knew there were ways to enter a suspect's house without being depressingly predictable. If one didn't care about the damage, or cleaning up the mess, there were all sorts of options.

He checked the time—it was 0730, shortly after the curfew had been officially lifted—and opened the door. The uniformed men looked him up and down, their expressions suggesting they'd seen more impressive specimens in prison drunk tanks. Their uniforms marked them as army bureaucrats, not real soldiers. Derek allowed himself a moment of relief as their gazes shifted to Jenny and lingered. They definitely weren't suspicious. A suspicious man would have thrown a stun grenade in first and worried about the consequences afterwards.

The leader cleared his throat. "Are you Derek or Roger?"

"Derek Frazer," Derek said. First names only? This was going to be bad. "What can I do for you?"

"You and your…*friend*…are ordered to report to Unit 45 to assist in the clean-up," the leader informed him. "Should you refuse to work, you will not be fed."

Derek tried to sound surprised. "But…"

The leader cut him off. "Report to Unit 45 by 0830," he said. "Lateness will be noted in your permanent record."

I bet you were a schoolteacher in your previous life, Derek thought, as the two men took one last look at Jenny and then turned away. Teachers had been threatening him with red marks in his record for as long as he could remember, although he *did* have to admit it was a valid threat. His record might be dragged up and used against him at some later date. *If they ever manage to cross-reference the educational files with the registry, we're fucked.*

"Charming men," Roger said. Derek hadn't heard him coming down the stairs. "What do they want us to do?"

"Fucked if I know," Derek said. "The bomb hasn't detonated."

"Clearly not," Roger agreed. He strode into the kitchen. "We'd better eat well. Would you like your ration bars roasted, baked, fried or raw?"

"I'd like them edible," Derek said, absently.

"Edible?" Roger's mock-incredulous voice drifted back. "Edible? We don't serve *edible* ration bars around here. You'll have *inedible* and you'll like it."

Derek laughed. "Terrible service," he said. "I'm going to have to give you a bad review."

Roger made crying noises as he opened the box and handed out the ration bars. Derek took his and ate it slowly, more concerned than he wanted to admit. The more time they spent working, the greater the chance of slipping up. The enemy would have their watchful eye on the worker gangs. And...

"You two stay indoors," Roger said, addressing the women. "You don't want to be caught alone."

Jenny looked pissed, but she said nothing. Derek understood. They'd heard enough rumours of women being harassed, molested, and outright raped for them to be concerned about their safety. The enemy commanders didn't seem inclined to punish the rapists, at least not publicly. He had no way to know if there was any truth to the rumours, but he believed them. He'd seen civilisation start to break down during the first invasion.

"Let's go," he said, once he'd changed into his working clothes. "We'll be back."

He frowned as they left the house. The IED had clearly *not* exploded. He was tempted to check on it, but the risk was too great. Instead, he followed Roger down the street to Unit 45. The school was still closed, at least to the children. Derek was sure they were very upset. He kept the thought in his mind as they were greeted by a harassed-looking functionary wearing a fancy uniform—another bureaucrat, he was sure—and ordered to join a gang of youths from all over the city. They looked sullen and resentful as they were marched down the streets towards a pile of rubble. It was hard to believe the debris had once been a house.

They must have made a stand here, he thought, numbly. *And then been driven out.*

"Pick up the rubble and put it in the skips," the functionary ordered. "And no slacking."

"Hey," a young man called. "Is this a paying job?"

"You work, you get fed," the functionary said, in the manner of someone pointing out that two plus two equalled four. "You don't work, you starve."

"And he's lazing around watching us while we do all the work," Roger muttered, as the gang started to work. "How…typical."

Derek nodded absently as he picked up a piece of rubble and tossed it into the skip. The enemy were clearing the streets…for what? His blood ran cold as he pulled a stuffed animal out of the wreckage, so badly torn that it was impossible to tell what it had been. A child had lived in the house, perhaps more than one. He swallowed hard, telling himself the child would have been evacuated long before the house was destroyed. The marines wouldn't have knowingly put civilians in danger. Would they?

The IED hasn't detonated, he thought, numbly. The air was very quiet. *Why not?*

He eyed his fellow labourers as the morning wore on. None of them looked very happy to be doing grunt work; none of them looked used to it. Derek understood, even though he'd done his fair share of bullshit jobs during basic training. The drill instructors had known what they were doing, damn it. They'd made sure their trainees didn't doubt their competence. But the functionary was just smoking and watching them. He wasn't even doing *that* very well.

We can talk to the others, he told himself. The grumbling was quiet, but it was there. *And see how many of them might be interested in forming a resistance movement.*

"Hey," the young man who'd spoken earlier said. "We need some water!"

"And food," another man called.

"It's on the way," the functionary said. He sounded as if he didn't believe himself. "Wait and work."

"I think we need to talk to them," Derek muttered. Clearing the rubble by hand would have taken days, with an enthusiastic team. The conscripted workers were moving as slowly as possible. "And see if they'll work with us."

"Got it," Roger said. "Let me do the talking. I speak their language."

Derek frowned. "Their language?"

"I grew up here," Roger said. "I know how to talk to them."

"Good." Derek straightened, feeling his arms and legs starting to ache. The others looked to be in even worse shape. "Do you know people you can trust?"

"Some of them," Roger said. He snorted, rubbing his filthy hands on his trousers. "It would help if they had a sign there *was* a resistance."

Derek looked west. The IED had *still* not detonated. He made a mental note to consider ways to detonate it himself, perhaps by sending a transmission when an enemy force passed too close to the aircar. They couldn't just leave it there. Sooner or later, as things started to return to normal, it would explode. And if the authorities decided to allow aircars to return to the skies...

"We might have to think of something else," he said. "And quickly."

CHAPTER EIGHTEEN

There are, of course, many smaller incidents that illustrate our point nicely. The political contest between Premier Yang and Senator Hartford on Eleusis should have led to Yang's automatic re-election. Her opponent, however, had found a new way to challenge her in the court of public opinion, while her aides and advisors were unwilling to risk their careers by telling her that matters were not proceeding as smoothly as she might have hoped.
—**Professor Leo Caesius**
The Right to be Wrong: How Silencing People Hurts You

"IS IT WRONG," GARFIELD ASKED as he pulled his body armour into place, "to hate being bored?"

"Yes." Janelle glanced at him, then returned to pulling on her battledress. "Bored is good. Bored means no one is trying to kill you. Bored means…"

"I get the point." Garfield felt his cheeks redden. "But I also feel as if we're wasting our time."

Janelle shrugged. "It could be worse," she said. "You'll be craving boredom when the shit hits the fan. And it will."

Garfield conceded, privately, she had a point. His first taste of combat had been exciting and terrifying. He'd thought himself immortal until he'd discovered—the hard way—that he was as vulnerable as everyone else. The endless marches up and down the streets, when they weren't providing security for the FOBs or escorting grandees around the city, were far better than being in the field. And yet, he felt his edge starting to slip. There'd been no real excitement on their side of the river since the city fell.

He checked his personal weapons, fingered his belt to be sure he had everything from his terminal to emergency medical supplies, then headed for the door. Janelle followed him, her footsteps echoing sharply in the quiet morning air. The school felt eerie as they hurried down the stairs to the playground. The platoon was waiting for them, looking suspiciously innocent. Garfield wondered what they'd been doing and whether he'd be required to take official notice of it. He'd already overhead some of his men bitching about the lack of entertainment, grumbling that the higher-ups hadn't got around to establishing a brothel. Matters hadn't been helped by rumours senior officers already had their own entertainment complex.

They did clear practically everyone out of the government compound, he reminded himself dryly. *Who knows what they're doing in there?*

He checked his terminal, then addressed the platoon. They'd been cautioned they might be transferred to the front, but—for the moment—they were still assigned to patrolling the city. Janelle had grumbled about predictable patterns, cautioning Garfield that it had only been a few days since the city fell. The enemy might still be reeling from the shock. He understood. He'd even taken her concerns to higher authority, only to be told to mind his own business. Their superiors seemed to want to believe they'd taken and secured the city without a fight.

"Viper formation," he ordered, quietly. "Move out."

The sun beat down as they advanced out of the complex and down the street. The city still felt oddly deserted, even though most of the population hadn't been able to flee. There were very few locals, almost all of them men, on the streets. Their faces were so bland Garfield *knew* they were resentful. They'd had a nice city once. Two invasions in quick succession had turned it into a warzone. He could *feel* unfriendly eyes staring whenever he looked away.

We'll be leaving soon, he told himself. *And once the war is over, they'll have their city back.*

He scanned from side to side as they marched down the middle of the road. The roads were lined with air—and groundcars, the latter probably already marked down for commandeering at some later date. The groundcars would be useful for moving troops to the front, when the time came. He'd heard a rumour that the supply lines were already on the verge of snapping. The army simply didn't have enough vehicles to move supplies from the landing zone to the front. He suspected it was just a matter of time before the higher-ups started pressing locals into service.

Janelle moved up beside him. "It's too quiet," she muttered. "It means trouble."

Garfield felt cold, despite the heat. "Are you sure?"

"No," Janelle said. "But something feels wrong."

They kept moving. Viper formation spread the platoon out a little, three men taking point, three men bringing up the rear and five more—including the commander—in the middle. He felt uncomfortably exposed, even though he thought they were relatively safe. The skyscrapers weren't *that* far away. A lone gunman with a sniper rifle could pick some of them off before vanishing into the gloom. He glanced at the nearest skyscraper and shivered. He might be dead before he knew what had hit him…

The world flashed white. Garfield hit the ground before he *quite* registered the sound of the explosion. No, *multiple* explosions. Pieces of glass and debris crashed down all around him, fragments of white-hot metal flying through the air…Janelle yammered out a contact report, even as Garfield pulled himself up. The pleasant street had become a scene from hell. Aircars burned, the flames threatening to spread to the nearest houses. And…

His heart skipped a beat. The point men had been near the blast. Their bodies had taken the full brunt of the explosion. He ran forward—heedless of the heat, heedless of the danger—to check on them. They'd worn their body armour, if only out of fear of the sergeant's wrath, but it hadn't been enough to save them. Their bodies were so badly mutilated Garfield *knew* there was nothing the medics could do.

Janelle ran up to him. "The QRF is on the way," she said. "They'll take over..."

Garfield barely heard her. Three men, three of *his* men, were dead. A wave of pure anger rushed through him, driving him on as the rest of the platoon assembled. His eyes swept the houses, looking for signs of where the bomber was hiding. The fucker couldn't be far away. The bomb had been detonated at *precisely* the right moment to catch three men and blow them to hell. He had to be somewhere nearby.

A curtain twitched. Garfield pointed. "There," he snapped. "Take the house."

The platoon swarmed towards the house, the lead soldier slamming a charge against the door and detonating it seconds later. Garfield knew he should stay at the rear, but instead he led the push into the house itself. Some screamed, drawing him onwards. A woman appeared out of nowhere, shouting something he barely heard over the rage. He slammed his rifle butt into her chest, sending her crashing to the floor. The others could deal with her. He wanted the sniper. Janelle said something, but he didn't hear her as he led the men on a rampage through the house, tearing it apart. Three children stared at him in horror as he crashed into their room. Garfield almost hit them too. Only the certainty they couldn't possibly be snipers kept him from striking the little brats.

Anger led him on. He crashed from room to room, smashing through a bedroom and finding...nothing. There was no bomber, no watchful sniper. There were no adult males in the house. He gritted his teeth, readying himself to go down and demand the woman answered his questions. She'd talk. She'd talk, even if he had to hurt her until she talked. She'd talk...he searched the loft quickly, finding nothing. If there were any hidden chambers in the house, they were very well concealed indeed.

"Secure the prisoners," he ordered, tasting blood in his mouth. "And make damn sure you search them before you do anything else."

Janelle caught his arm as his men headed downstairs. "*Don't* mistreat the prisoners," she said, sharply. "You don't *know* they're enemies."

Garfield glared at her. "They housed a bomber!"

"And where *is* the bomber?" Janelle met his eyes, evenly. "What—exactly—did we find?"

"She might *be* the bomber," Garfield said, sullenly. He'd been told it was rare for women to serve in front-line units—Janelle was the only female soldier he knew—but one didn't need to be a trained soldier to detonate a bomb. The bitch could have watched and waited, pressing the trigger as soon as the point men were within the blast radius. "She could have killed my men."

"You don't know that," Janelle snapped. "And you're *not* going to win any friends by mistreating prisoners."

Garfield found it hard to care. Three of his men were dead. It hadn't been his fault, but…he'd been in command. Their families would blame him, even if his superiors officially cleared him of any blame. Hell, they'd practically *have* to clear him. They'd have problems making the charges against an Onge stick unless they could be proved beyond all doubt. And that wouldn't satisfy the families…

He clenched his teeth, trying to calm himself. Janelle was right. He knew she was right. But he didn't believe it.

Janelle tapped her headpiece. "The QRF is here."

Garfield nodded, looking around before they headed downstairs. The bedroom was clearly for an adult, probably two adults. There were male clothes as well as female lying on the floor, lying where they'd been dropped by the searchers as they made sure no one was hiding in the wardrobe. He felt an odd little pang as they walked past the devastated children's bedroom and down the stairs. The QRF was busily searching the other houses, leading out the prisoners one by one. The poor bastards sat or lay on the street, their hands tied behind their back. A handful were clearly wounded. The soldiers hadn't been *gentle* when they yanked them out of their homes.

An officer—Garfield vaguely recognised him, but he couldn't recall the man's name—nodded to him. "The medics had a look at your men," he said, dispassionately. "They're beyond all help."

It was no surprise, but it still hurt. "What...what did you do with the bodies?"

"We're shipping them back to the compound," the officer informed him. "I don't know what'll happen after that."

Garfield nodded curtly, feeling oddly out of it. The scene felt like a nightmare, something not quite real and yet something he couldn't escape. The stench of burning aircars—and burning flesh—drifted through the air, making his stomach heave in revulsion. He'd been bored, only an hour ago. Janelle had been right. He should have been glad to be bored. He'd have given anything to be bored again.

"Escort the prisoners back to the compound," the officer said. "And then go have a stiff drink or two."

Thanks for nothing, Garfield thought, sourly. He wasn't fool enough to say *that* out loud. Losing three men was a minor offense, but insulting a senior officer was *serious*. He'd be in trouble, with or without the family name. *And where am I supposed to get a fucking drink?*

He nodded, instead. "Yes, sir. I'll deal with it."

Janelle hurried to organise the prisoners, ordering them to stand and prepare to march. Garfield watched, feeling his anger drain away into bitter numbness. The children didn't deserve to be marched away, did they? And yet, what choice did they have? There was a bomber, either amongst the prisoners or lurking nearby. The intelligence teams would extract what the prisoners knew, then...Garfield shrugged. He had no idea what'd happen to them and he didn't much care. It was someone else's problem.

His eyes swept the group as they began to march. They looked shocked, a handful openly crying. Their lives had turned upside down in the blink of an eye...behind him, Garfield could hear the QRF searching their houses time and time again. They'd probably find proof and do a little looting on the side. It was officially forbidden, but who gave a damn about traitors?

The bomber and his family would be lucky if they spent the rest of their days in an arctic work camp. It was more likely they'd be put against a wall and shot.

The marchers stumbled on. Garfield could *feel* eyes following them, staring in horror as the prisoners were escorted to the compound. The handful of people on the streets made themselves scarce, but…he wondered, suddenly, what they'd say to their fellows. He knew just how quickly rumours could grow in the telling. The entire population would believe, sooner or later, that the prisoners had been stripped naked and raped—or worse. He scowled, tiredly. The bomber deserved it. But what about the rest of them?

He kept the thought to himself as they reached the compound. The MPs were already waiting to take custody. The prisoners were searched again, then prodded towards the makeshift POW camp. Garfield tried not to sag. He was still on duty. He didn't want to look weak in front of the men. And yet, the sheer sense of horror at losing three of his troopers to a bomb tore at him. He'd killed them, as surely as if he'd put a gun to their heads and pulled the trigger himself.

"Sir," Janelle said, quietly. "Go to your room. I'll see to the men."

Garfield felt torn, torn between irritation she was babying him and the grim awareness she was probably right. It would be easy to keep the men busy, to keep them from brooding on what had happened and why; he didn't have the luxury of mindless tasks to keep him from thinking. He was meant to be an officer, damn it! The old jokes—officers got men killed, sergeants tried to protect the men from the officers—mocked him. His stomach heaved. He barely managed to get to a toilet before he threw up everything he'd eaten in the last two days. His uniform stunk of burning flesh.

The jokes aren't funny any longer, he thought, as he washed his mouth out with cold water. *They never were.*

He stumbled up the stairs, feeling tired and worn. He'd never really understood what it was like to lose men under his command, not like that.

He understood losing men in honest combat, but striking from ambush…? He glared at the window. Someone had covered it in a protective gauze, but he knew he only had to lift it away to see the city beyond. He felt a surge of pure hatred. The city deserved to be burned to the ground! There were no innocents within the shattered hellscrape. They all deserved to die.

Janelle knocked on the open door, then stepped inside. "I thought you could do with this," she said, as she closed the door. "Finest shipboard rotgut."

Garfield eyed the flask in her hand. "You make it sound *so* enticing."

"Drink," Janelle ordered. "It'll make you feel better."

"Hah." Garfield took the flask and drank. The liquid tasted suspiciously like rifle oil. "What the fuck is this?"

Janelle smiled, humourlessly. "If I told you, you wouldn't want to drink it."

"I don't want to drink it anyway," Garfield said, peevishly. He thought about the fine wines and spirits served at his family's parties, liqueurs so expensive a small bottle would cost more than Janelle made in a year. If he'd served the rotgut at one of the parties…he snorted at the thought. He had to be halfway to drunkenness already if he thought *that* was a good idea. The rotgut was strong enough to make his teeth ache. "It's disgusting."

"But very alcoholic," Janelle said. "Drink."

Garfield took another swig. "I should have taken point myself," he said. "I'd have died instead."

"Yes." Janelle met his eyes, evenly. "You would have died instead." She shook her head. "It wasn't your fault," she added. "You had no reason to suspect trouble."

"You told me something was off," Garfield said. "I should have listened."

"And there was nothing you could have done, if you had," Janelle said. "They were careful to leave no trace of their work. I didn't see anything before the blast went off."

Garfield clenched the flask in his hand. "So how did you know something was wrong?"

"I've been serving for a *long* time," Janelle reminded him. "I have instincts."

"Good ones," Garfield said. "What the fuck are we going to do now?"

"You should have read the reports from Han," Janelle said. "Compared to Han, this place is a goddamned paradise."

"I just lost three men," Garfield said, sharply. He was starting to get a taste for the rotgut, as foul as it was. "This isn't a paradise."

He looked down at his hands. "Does it ever get easier?"

"No," Janelle said. For a moment, she sounded as if she was recalling something she'd prefer to forget. "It never gets easier. But you learn to cope."

She stood. "It sounds as though we'll be reassigned to the front, sooner rather than later," she said. "You should rest, then prepare for it."

"Ouch." Garfield knew he should be pleased, but it felt like a punishment. They'd fouled up and their superiors were sending them away. "I…fuck it."

"Yes, sir," Janelle said. "What would you like me to fuck?"

Garfield blinked, then shook his head. "Fuck up the enemy," he said. It was a terrible joke, but it made him smile. He was *definitely* more than halfway to drunkenness. "Put a knife in the bastards."

"Be glad if we get reassigned," Janelle said. "Fighting an insurgency is never pleasant."

"Yeah." Garfield took a final swig, then passed the flask back to her. "And they've already drawn first blood."

CHAPTER NINETEEN

She didn't change tack out of incompetence or stupidity, although both charges were levelled at her by allies and opponents alike. She didn't change tack because she thought she was winning. She was, in her view, doing everything right. And so she didn't make any changes until it was too late. Her advisors failed her.
—**Professor Leo Caesius**
The Right to be Wrong: How Silencing People Hurts You

FROM A DISTANCE, THE CROSSROADS—and the service station beside it—looked strikingly normal, almost untouched by the war. The staff had vanished long ago, the supply depots had been looted, but otherwise it was remarkably intact. It made a good rally point, Rachel decided as she surveyed the enemy position through her sniper scope. She didn't really blame the enemy for turning the service station into a jump-off point for the forthcoming offensive. They were short of choices.

She lay on her belly, watching the enemy convoy pull into the station. Three AFVs, loaded with troops; five troop transports and a dozen supply trucks…all looking ready for a fight. She tracked them carefully, silently counting the troops as they spilled out of the transports, either heading for the coffee stands or trying to find a place to piss. Rachel frowned as she studied them. They looked to be a mixture of veterans and inexperienced newbies. She did her best to pick out the experienced soldiers as the enemy troops started to relax. If she took out the ones who knew what they were doing, the remainder might panic and run. It would certainly take them longer to learn their lessons...

Her lips quirked into a cold smile. She'd picked her nest with malice aforethought, when the spooks had realised the enemy were turning the crossroads into a jump-off point. They'd have some problems hitting her, once the shooting started, and it would take them a long time to *get* to her... if they worked out where she was. The greatest danger lay in the enemy machine guns, but even *they* could be avoided. She could roll into cover, hurry down the far side and run before they had a chance to throw up a cordon. And she had another surprise waiting for the enemy.

Pity none of their senior officers are visible, she thought. She'd picked out a handful of mid-ranking officers, but she hadn't been able to identify whoever was in overall charge of the convoy. If he had any sense at all, he was probably hiding in one of the AFVs. *I'll just have to make do with whoever I find.*

She took aim, braced herself and squeezed the trigger. It was an easy shot. Her target dropped to the ground, blood leaking from his scalp. Rachel almost regretted not choosing ammunition that would make her target's head explode. It would have shocked the enemy, hampering their ability to react. She put the thought aside as she moved to the next target and shot him too, then the third. Someone was screaming orders, trying to take command as chaos spread. Rachel shot him, noting how many men were responding like experienced troops. It was hard to train troops to prepare for snipers without actually using *real* ammunition. The Slaughterhouse had used a combination of live ammunition, laser beams and pellets to train marines. Rachel felt an old twinge in her arm as she kept shooting. Being shot once with a pellet was an experience she would have preferred not to repeat.

The AFVs turned, bringing their machine guns to bear on her position. Rachel blinked in surprise—that was fast—then rolled over and down the slope. It was utterly undignified, but preferable to being vaporised. Bullets tore through the trees above her head, sending sawdust flying. Rachel caught herself at the bottom of the gully, one hand fumbling for the one-shot transmitter on her belt. The enemy ECM teams might be scanning for her already, but it didn't matter. They had no way of hitting her until they either sent troops to flush her out or unlimbered their mortars and rained shells on her position. She almost hoped they would. They'd waste a lot of ammunition for little return.

She clicked the transmitter, then threw it away as the automated mortars opened fire. She'd sighted them herself, carefully taking the bearings to ensure the shells fell on the enemy vehicles. Hopefully, the enemy would assume there was an entire mortar team in the vicinity, not just one marine. Rachel smiled as she stood and hurried away, forcing herself to move as quickly as possible. It went against the grain to throw the mortars away, but it wasn't as if there was a shortage. They'd captured enough tubes from enemy supply depots that the *real* danger was a shortage of ammunition.

The sound of machine gun fire faded behind her. She'd killed at least four officers, as well as a number of men. The enemy wouldn't be slowed for long, but they'd be forced to be a little more careful as they advanced towards the front lines. She wondered, idly, if they'd try to give chase. They'd want to hunt down the mortar teams, yet…they'd have to worry about running into an ambush. It had happened, more than once. She kept her senses open, trying to avoid starting as animals ran through the undergrowth. She'd have to go as dark as possible if they got close to her.

Unless they're trying to be clever, she mused, coldly. *And follow me back to my base.*

She felt certain, as the day wore on, that she'd broken contact. She'd done her fair share of forced marches, back in the day, when she'd been chased by enemy forces. There were no hints the enemy was following her, no disturbances that might—just—have marked an enemy force closing from the rear. Instead, the woodland might have been almost pleasant if she hadn't known it was about to be torn apart. The enemy were gathering.

It was only a matter of time until they rolled west. Small teams—and Pathfinders like herself—could inflict considerable delay, but they couldn't stop the enemy altogether.

A shape stepped out of the shadows. "Halt! Your money or your life!"

"You'd better take my life," Rachel said, dryly. "I'm saving my money for old age."

"I think old age isn't going to be an issue, if I take your life now," Phelps said. "How'd it go?"

"More or less as planned," Rachel told him. "I don't know how effective the mortar fire was, though. Did you pick up any chatter?"

"Nothing, not even a contact report," Phelps said. "Microbursts or incompetence?"

"Probably microbursts," Rachel said. A unit that had come under attack was supposed to inform its superiors at once. "No way to be sure, of course."

"Of course," Phelps echoed. "You threw a bunch of shells into the target zone. I'm pretty sure you hit something."

Rachel nodded as he fell in beside her. It was tempting to believe she'd wiped out the entire convoy—her imagination showed her a pretty picture of the enemy vehicles burning merrily—but she couldn't allow herself to become convinced. Better to assume the worst and be pleasantly surprised than assume the best and wind up dead. Or worse. The enemy were going to be advancing soon. It was only a matter of time before they started pushing towards the front lines. And then they'd be headed straight for the nearest PDC.

Pity we couldn't put up a real fight in Haverford, she thought. A distant explosion echoed through the air. Someone else was hitting the enemy, she hoped. It could just as easily be an enemy forward column. *We'll just have to meet them under the protective shroud of the PDCs.*

• • •

"Admiral," General Rask said. "I'm afraid there have been developments."

"I was afraid of that," Nelson said. He was only half-joking. "What happened?"

"There's at least one enemy team in Haverford itself," General Rask said. "And we've been meeting increasingly heavy resistance as we prepare to thrust west."

Nelson nodded as he studied the two-dimensional map. It was relatively simple. Hell, *ground* warfare was relatively simple. The enemy couldn't come from above or below…he reminded himself, sharply, that the invasion force he'd dropped on the planet had, technically, come from *above*. And yet…the lines were clear, it seemed. The forward units were marked with a handful of red icons, each one marking an encounter between the two sides. It looked as though there was fighting going on all along the line.

"It looks as if you're barely moving," he said, dryly. "How bad is it?"

"My plans for moving up reinforcements and taking the offensive may have been thrown out of alignment," Rask informed him. "Right now, I have to increase our presence on the streets while continuing to funnel troops to the front. I'm not sure I have enough manpower to do both."

"You should have enough manpower," Nelson said, stiffly. "Can you not transfer soldiers from the landing zone?"

"Not without weakening the defences there," Rask said. "Frankly, sir, if they manage to take out our supply depots we're screwed. We cannot afford to lose the supplies. Really, I'd prefer to loosen our grip on the city."

Julia frowned. "That's a political decision, General," she said. "And I can honestly say that it will *not* be seen as a good move."

Rask's face went blank. "With all due respect, he who would be strong everywhere is strong nowhere. We have three separate priorities, all of which are in widely divergent locations. The city can be recaptured later, once we destroy enough of the PDCs to allow for effective orbital bombardment. Right now, we'd be better off moving the supplies around the city rather than through the city. It wasn't designed for a major war."

"A terrible failure of imagination," Nelson said, dryly. He stroked his chin, trying to look thoughtful although he'd already made up his mind. "How do you suggest we proceed?"

"We can run stronger patrols through the city for a day or two, putting entire districts into lockdown and carrying out random searches in hopes of either capturing an insurgent or simply forcing them to keep their heads down," Rask said. "In the meantime"—the map changed, showing a trio of arrows stabbing west—"we'll gather our troops and thrust towards the PDCs, forcing them to fight us on relatively even terms or give up the PDCs. Either we beat them on the ground or we take out the PDCs."

"Allowing them to be crushed from orbit," Nelson said. "When do you think you can launch the offensive?"

"I'd like to wait for a week," Rask said. His voice suggested he wanted to wait for longer. "That'll give us time to secure the city, move up the troops and establish supply depots nearer the lines."

"And then?" Julia looked uneasy. "How long will it take to...deal... with the PDCs?"

"I can't make any promises," Rask said. "It depends on factors outside my control. The marines may make a stand, or they may harass us until we hit their innermost defence line...there's no way I can promise anything. Not yet."

Julia glanced at Nelson. "Admiral?"

"The General is right," Nelson said. He understood her concern—the longer the fighting lasted, the greater the damage to the planet's infrastructure—but there was no way they could simply smash through all opposition. The marines were hardly idiots from a planet so backwards they thought the sun circled their homeworld, or that prayer and bravery would be enough to stand against tanks and machine guns. "It's worth taking the time to do it properly."

He studied the map for a long moment. The overview suggested it would be a matter of merely moving from the jump-off points to the PDCs. The more detailed view warned that terrain was going to be a major headache.

Nelson winced as he considered the bridges and rivers lying between the two points. In space, there was no such thing as terrain. There were very few systems where local oddities posed a challenge to the invaders.

And this is one of them, he reminded himself. *All that space junk orbiting the planet makes it harder to snipe at the PDCs.*

"Do what you must, General," he said.

"Yes, sir," Rask said. "I must add, as we're talking about issues with political implications, that not all the civilians are happy with us. They seemed to think the marines would make better masters."

"Absurd," Julia hissed.

"Those who considered themselves losers will look to anything that might put them on top," Rask said. "And the marines did them a favour when they purged the datanets. We don't know who's competent, let alone reliable."

Nelson stroked his chin. "How bad is it?"

"It's hard to say," Rask said. "The eastside is rather…restive. Apparently, the former government didn't bother to keep it under tight control even before the invasion. The westside has had the one major incident, but"—he frowned—"I'd say they were just as unhappy, if for different reasons. A lot of people got thrown out of work when the city was invaded. We're trying to feed them, but…"

"I understand." Nelson studied the map for a long moment. "Do what you must, General."

"Without damaging too much of the city," Julia said, sharply. "It is *vital* we recover the planetary infrastructure intact."

"I shall do my best," Rask said. His voice was so flat it was clear he didn't believe it was possible. "But we may need a political solution."

"We'll discuss it," Nelson said. It was a conversation best had away from listening ears. "Until then…"

He tapped the console, terminating the conversation and bringing up the first reports. It wasn't good news. He knew, if only because Julia kept reminding him, just how important it was to recapture the planet largely intact. The only real *value* in the planet lay in its infrastructure...and the human resources, men and women who'd get understandably discontented if they were treated like cattle or terrorists. And yet, deliberately or not, the insurgents had upset his plans. It might be better to have them brought to heel, even if it upset the locals, rather than let them prolong his troubles.

"It's a tiny distance," Julia pointed out. The frustration was almost palpable. "Why can't they take it in a day?"

"It's a tiny distance in a *starship*," Nelson explained. He shouldn't have to explain that planets were *big*. "Or even an aircar. But on the ground, it's a long walk."

"I see," Julia said, slowly.

"And people will be shooting at them," Nelson added. His eyes wandered across the map. It looked as if the troops were barely moving, yet pressing constantly against enemy positions. He didn't envy the troops on the ground. If the reports were accurate, every rock and tree hid a marine with a rifle. "It'll slow them down still further."

Julia nodded, stiffly. "The reinforcement convoy should be here soon," she said. "We need to make progress before it arrives."

Just in case someone senior to you arrives, Nelson thought. The Onge Corporation was better than the Imperial Navy about ensuring the credit went to the person who deserved it, but the bar wasn't set very high. If someone took over command just before victory, it was quite possible they'd get the lion's share of the credit. *That would be awkward, would it not?*

He reached for her hand and gently squeezed . "This is a very minor setback," he said. "One explosion doesn't mean a whole insurgency. Why, on Han there were hundreds of explosions every day."

"It still looks bad," Julie said. She rested her hands on her hips, glaring at the map as if it had personally offended her. "And we told our superiors that we'd secured the lodgement."

"We have." Nelson decided not to point out that the courier boat probably hadn't reached its destination. Not unless the pilot had managed to find a way to push his craft *well* past its limits. "We have yet to lose anything that *matters*."

Julia scowled. "Are you sure?"

"It's like someone pulling a hair out of your scalp," Nelson said. He smiled at the example. It wasn't perfect, but it would have to do. "It's painful and embarrassing, but not really *harmful*. Right now, we can go where we want…in the city, at least. And they can't stop us."

And if they rise against us, we can cut them off at the knees, he added, silently. *They must know it too.*

He frowned, inwardly. Julia was corporate royalty. She couldn't understand, not emotionally, just why some of her subordinates might want to escape. Nelson himself would have shared their feelings, if he hadn't been at the top. Or as far up the ladder as he could climb, at least. His children would have a chance to rise to the *very* top. He was determined to make sure they had all the support they needed to make their mark on the universe. And he knew Julia shared his determination. She might not be executed if she failed here, but it would cost her. She might be shuffled aside, put out of public life.

A fate worse than death, he thought, sardonically.

"All we have to do is take out the PDCs," he said. It sounded so simple, in theory. In practice, it was a whole different story. "And then we can impose our will on the rest of the planet."

CHAPTER TWENTY

But why should they not? Yang had a terrible reputation. She had a long history of destroying the lives of people who challenged her, from her earliest opponents to advisors who dared to suggest she was going in the wrong direction. Dissent was treason, as far as she was concerned. And so no one dared tell her the truth.
—**Professor Leo Caesius**
The Right to be Wrong: How Silencing People Hurts You

"YOU SHOULDN'T HAVE GONE OUTSIDE," Derek snapped. "You could have been caught!"

"I had to see!" Jenny folded her arms under her breasts. "And you wouldn't know what had happened if I hadn't gone outside!"

Derek gritted his teeth. Jenny was going stir-crazy…they were *all* going a little crazy, but it was worse for Jenny and Gayle. They couldn't go out, not alone. The streets were no longer safe. He'd heard enough rumours, when he'd been working on the chain gang, to know the risks were high. Women on their own simply weren't safe. And Jenny had gone out to see what happened after the IED went off.

"You should have stayed indoors," he muttered. "Really."

Roger elbowed him. "I know someone who's going to be sleeping on the couch tonight."

"Hah fucking hah," Derek said. He'd assumed the girls would follow orders. *That* had been a mistake. Neither Jenny nor Gayle had served in the military. "Look..."

"No, *you* look," Jenny said. "I knew the risks. I took a calculated risk. And it paid off."

Derek put firm controls on his temper. "What happened?"

"The blast did a lot of damage," Jenny said. "From what I heard, it killed at least a dozen enemy soldiers. They went mad, rampaging through nearby houses and arresting everyone they found. I slipped away before they could grab me too."

Roger snorted. "They must have thought the bomber was lurking nearby."

"Probably," Jenny said. "You killed a dozen of the bastards. Aren't you pleased?"

Derek said nothing. It was hard to keep his feelings under control. Jenny could have been grabbed off the streets and...his imagination provided too many possibilities, each one worse than the last. And there was no way to *know* if they'd really killed a dozen enemy soldiers. He knew from bitter experience that rumours grew in the telling. By the time the story crossed the city, it would probably insist a *million* enemy soldiers had been killed in the blast, even though it was physically impossible. And other rumours would claim the enemy had slaughtered millions in retaliation.

He felt a pang of guilt. He'd known what he was doing, when he put himself at risk. He'd known there was a possibility of being caught and shot like a dog. But others...the arrested civilians hadn't known what was going to happen, let alone been asked if they wanted to put themselves at risk. Jenny hadn't said anything about civilians being killed, but it was quite likely some had been caught in the blast too. Derek hadn't expected it to take so long for the IED to detonate. He'd assumed it would explode before dawn.

And we don't have a choice, he thought, coldly. *We have to continue to fight.*

"Well?" Jenny scowled at him. "Aren't you happy?"

"Yeah," Derek said. "I suppose."

He sat down, trying to calm himself. There was no room for an argument, not here. The neighbours might hear and...and what? Report them? Or merely shout for them to shut the fuck up? Or...he shook his head. The stress was getting to them. In hindsight, they'd been very lucky. They'd have to be careful, next time, to put more distance between themselves and the IED. The enemy could have stumbled across the house through sheer luck.

"I want you"—he glanced at Gayle—"and you too to stay in the house, when we're not here," he said. "I don't want to lose you."

Jenny glared. "And who died and appointed you boss?"

"If we don't come back, you can do whatever you like," Derek said. He wished, suddenly, for a proper chain of command. "But we don't want to lose you to a random sweep."

"Agreed." Roger looked firm. "Stay inside, prepare our weapons. And plan for what you'll do if we don't come home."

"Fine." Jenny waved a hand at the couch. "You're sleeping there tonight."

Derek gave Roger a cross look. "This is all your fault."

"He's sleeping there tonight too," Gayle said, sweetly. "I'm sure you'll have much to talk about."

"Right." Derek gathered himself. "The good news. We met others who want to fight back too."

He smiled, grimly. They'd spent hours chatting to their fellow workers, trying to determine who could be trusted—and who might be willing to help. Roger had been able to draw a *lot* from them, including names and family connections he could verify for himself. Not *all* the workers would be willing to take up arms, Derek was sure, but even a handful would be able to make life worse for the corprats. The enemy would have to put the city into lockdown—again—if they wanted to crack down on a growing insurgency. And doing *that* would make them even more enemies.

"Good," Jenny said. "*Can* they fight back?"

"They'll probably need some advice," Roger said. "A handful had military training, if not experience, but they're short on weapons."

Derek nodded. He'd been told, in no uncertain terms, that he *wasn't* allowed to take weapons and supplies back home unless he had permission. It had struck him as stupid—the government trusted him enough to train him—but there was no point in arguing. The government had made up its mind. Farmers were allowed shotguns, with strictly limited supplies of ammunition; urban dwellers weren't allowed anything more dangerous than knives and forks. The marines had concealed catches of weapons and supplies around the city—it dawned on Derek, suddenly, that they might not be the only band of insurgents—but not enough. Supplies were going to be a very real problem.

"We'll start work as soon as possible," he said. "When and where?"

Roger leaned forward. "Down by the riverside, there's a bundle of abandoned warehouses and barracks. They were in pretty shitty condition even before the war. We'll have to recon them, just to make sure the bastards haven't turned them into accommodation for their troops, but they should be usable if not. We can hand out some basic weapons, train them in their use…tell them how to make bombs from household crap. It should be doable."

Derek glanced at him. "What did you *do* before you got discharged?"

"They were training me in urban warfare," Roger told him. "I don't know what they had in mind. My CO—dead now, I think—wanted to push a cluster of us forward, into the regulars. I didn't want it for myself."

Jenny leaned forward. "Why not?"

"We're not all born with a silver spoon in our mouths," Roger said. His voice was even, but there was a hint of bitterness in his tone. "I just thought…why was I being asked to put my life at risk for people who'd never reward me? What hope did *I* have of getting promotion? Why did I have to serve people who'd never done anything for me? I had the idea I could get onto a farm and build something for myself. And I was midway there"—he shrugged, expressively—"when I was called back to the colours."

"Ouch," Derek said. "When this is over, you can build a farm for yourself."

"When this is over, assuming we survive, there will be no limits," Roger said. "I'll reach for the skies."

Derek nodded. "Right now, we have work to do," he said. "And plans to make."

He glanced towards the window. "They had a pair of checkpoints down the road," he said. "We'd probably better wait a day or two before we try anything."

"Or you could just try and wander down to the riverside," Jenny pointed out. "It used to be quite a romantic spot."

"Not where I'm thinking," Roger said. "Believe me, there was nothing romantic about those old buildings. We'd probably do better to try and steer the work gang down there."

Gayle grinned. "You two could just say you're wanting some time alone," she said, mischievously. "How does that sound?"

"Terrible," Derek said, dryly. "We'll have to sneak down there after work."

Jenny giggled. "Hand in hand?"

"They want us back there tomorrow," Roger said, firmly. "We'll sneak away afterwards and go down to the riverside. If it seems quiet, we'll start issuing invitations."

"And hope for the best," Derek said. "The more people we bring into the group, the greater the risk of being betrayed."

"Yeah." Roger let out a breath. "Is there anything we can do about it?"

Derek shook his head. Most people kept their mouths firmly closed. That had been true of Eddisford and he was sure it was true of Haverford too. But he was all too aware that it would only take one person to blow the circle wide open. Roger had friends and family within the city, people he trusted not to reveal their presence, yet...how far could they be trusted? They might not want to betray the insurgents, but there were plenty of ways to make someone talk. Derek had heard all kinds of horror stories. Suspects could be drugged or tortured until they broke and talked. He wasn't sure how well he'd stand up to a modest amount of dental torture.

"We'll just have to be careful," he said. "And hope for the best."

• • •

The sun was far too bright.

Garfield tried not to rub his forehead as the patrol marched down the road, keeping a wary distance from parked groundcars, rubbish bins and anything else that could conceal an IED. He hadn't realised, not really, just how many hiding places there *were* until he'd seen his men die. An IED could be anywhere; under a car, hidden in a garden, inside a house... *anywhere*. He eyed a car suspiciously. Had it been opened, since the invasion? Did it even matter?

His head pounded savagely as he kept moving. He shouldn't have drank so much, not when he'd known he might have to go on patrol later in the day. But he'd drank and drank and even the hasty sober-up Janelle had slipped him had done nothing for his headache. He felt dehydrated, tired and worn...he wanted to go back to bed and sleep, or simply put his pistol to his head and pull the trigger. The entire world seemed to be tormenting him. The sunlight glinted off the windows and stabbed daggers into his eyes; people were staring...he craved sleep. But he had to go on.

Fear prickled at the corner of his mind as his eyes wandered from car to car. How many of them hid bombs? How many watching eyes—he saw curtains move as they marched past—were waiting for their chance to set off a bomb? He'd been told there couldn't be many insurgents in the city—so far, there'd only been one bomb—but he didn't believe it. There were hundreds of thousands of people in the city, including countless refugees from the outer towns and farms. If even ten percent of them were angry, and ten percent of *them* were willing to resort to violence, there might be thousands of potential insurgents.

He breathed a sigh of relief as they reached the shopping district. There were dozens of people milling around, suggesting they had no reason to fear.

Garfield wasn't sure that meant anything. The locals would have a better awareness of what was wrong than his soldiers, but it was quite possible the bombers hadn't told anyone about the bomb. The locals would act normally because they didn't realise they shouldn't. His eyes flickered from person to person, noting the vast number of men lining up to shop. There were only a handful of women on the streets and they were all escorted by men.

Probably wise, he thought, sardonically. *Law and order no longer exists outside the range of our guns.*

The crowd scattered as the soldiers marched down the road. Garfield tensed, his spine tingling as he spotted the manhole cover…had it been opened? Had an IED been emplaced underneath? Or…he wanted to think he was being paranoid, yet was he being paranoid enough? He led his men on a detour around the cover, giving it as much room as possible. If it exploded…they might already be within the blast radius. He kept moving, feeling eyes following him…nothing happened. He felt himself begin to sag as they reached the bottom of the street and turned the corner. There hadn't been a bomb. There hadn't…

And how do I know, he asked himself helplessly, *if there's a bomb or not?*

He gritted his teeth, leading the soldiers on. The men were quiet, no laughing or joking. They felt it too; they were constantly on the verge of getting blown up. Garfield would almost have preferred to be facing a platoon of enemy tanks, armed with nothing more dangerous than a water pistol, than an unseen enemy. He didn't even know for sure the enemy was *there*. For all he knew, the patrol was completely unobserved. There had only been *one* IED, after all.

They turned the corner again and saw a teenager writing a message on the wall. The young man, his hair hidden under a cap, jumped, stared at them and ran for his life. Garfield reacted on instinct, bringing up his rifle and firing a single shot. The force of the impact picked the young man up and threw him through the air, cap flying off as he hit the ground. His hair spilled out, flowing. Garfield stared at it numbly, only slowly realising the young boy was actually a young *girl*. She didn't look any older than he did.

"Good shot, sir," someone muttered.

Garfield didn't pay any attention to Janelle lecturing the unfortunate soldier as he inched forward. The girl was dead. The bullet had gone right into her heart. Perhaps she could have been saved, with proper medical attention, but there was no way to get her to one of the ships before it was too late. He eyed her tight clothing, noting there was no way she could have concealed anything, then rolled her over. She'd been pretty, only a few short minutes ago. Now, she was a lifeless corpse. Cold eyes stared accusingly at him as he looked down at her. She'd been young and pretty, the sort of girl he would have chased back home. And now she was dead.

"She was writing rude messages on the wall," Janelle commented. The sergeant sounded unmoved. "She could probably have done with some grammar lessons."

Garfield gave her a sharp look. Was that meant to be funny? He turned and peered at the wall. The spelling was tacky, text-talk, but the message was clear. She was protesting military occupation…it had only been a matter of time, he told himself, before she started throwing bombs instead. She'd deserved to die. She'd deserved…it was hard, so hard, to convince himself it was true.

"Leave the body," he ordered, harshly. He didn't want to so much as *look* at it any longer. "They can throw it in the river for all I care."

He marched past the corpse and led the way onwards, trying to brush his qualms aside. Trouble was best nipped in the bud. A sharp response to insurgents and terrorism was the best guarantee they wouldn't get out of control. He'd had that drummed into his head, time and time again. The instructors had made it clear an occupying force couldn't look weak. People wanted to be on the winning side. If the insurgents looked to be winning, people would flock to their banner before it was too late to pledge their allegiance. They couldn't take the chance.

Guilt still gnawed at him. The girl had been rebellious—yes—but that didn't mean she was an insurgent. It could have been a petty teenage rebellion, a response to parents who told her to stay inside or…or just a desperate attempt to savage some dignity after a bruising encounter with a search party. Garfield was all too aware just how far some people would go to retain fragments of their pride. The girl could have been...

She could have been his sister. She could have been his girlfriend. She could have been...

The thought nagged at him as they completed their patrol and headed to their beds. He tried, time and time again, to tell himself the girl deserved it, to make himself believe...he had to believe it. Otherwise, he would have killed her for nothing and...and he couldn't live with himself if he'd killed her for nothing. He just couldn't.

"Rumour has it we'll be moving to the front in the next few days, sir," Janelle said, after the men were bedded down. "How does that grab you?"

"Great," Garfield said. He hoped the rumour was true. Sergeants often knew what was coming before their nominal superiors, but the regular chain of command was breaking down under the pressures of war. "It can't be worse than fighting here."

"The marines are digging in," Janelle reminded him. She waved a hand westward. "Believe me, it could be a great deal worse."

CHAPTER TWENTY-ONE

The wiser dictators—and dictatorial states—do everything in their power to encourage truth-telling. But there are limits to how far they can encourage it without crippling themselves. One may navigate within a framework of reality, as defined by the state, but not step outside it.
—**Professor Leo Caesius**
The Right to be Wrong: How Silencing People Hurts You

DEREK FELT UNCOMFORTABLY EXPOSED as he and Roger sneaked down to the river, making their way towards the cluster of abandoned warehouses. It was dark, with no hint of anyone—friendly or otherwise—moving in the shadows, but they'd have no excuse if they were caught by a wandering patrol. The last few days had been uncomfortable, to say the least. The occupiers had set up dozens of checkpoints and enforced the curfew vigorously. Rumour insisted that hundreds of people had been arrested for going out after dark.

Not that we have much of a choice, he thought. *They keep us busy during the day.*

He dropped his hand to his pistol as they neared the compound. They'd checked it twice, and discovered the buildings were on the verge of collapse, but it was hard to be *sure* someone hadn't set up shop there. The warehouses had been designated for demolition for *years*. Derek honestly wasn't sure why they hadn't been knocked down well before the first invasion. They were just unsafe for anything, from storing goods to providing makeshift accommodation. And the land could have been used for something else.

He felt a twang of guilt. Jenny had wanted to accompany them, but he'd had to say no. It was too dangerous. The checkpoint guards were already making people strip to their underwear. The process was supposed to be random, but rumour claimed they exclusively picked on pretty girls. Derek understood, more than he cared to admit. He was already trying to think of a way to use it against them. And...

The warehouse was dark and silent as they slipped inside. Derek had seen bigger buildings, but the darkened warehouse still took his breath away. The air smelt foul, although he couldn't identify the stench. Perhaps a sewer pipe had cracked, somewhere further inside the complex, or perhaps they'd abandoned a load of fish long enough to go really rotten. He wished, suddenly, for a mask. He'd hidden his features behind a bandanna, but it wasn't enough to keep out the smell. His clothes were going to *stink* when he got home. Jenny was going to be *very* sarcastic about it.

And she'll make me sleep on the couch again, he thought, as they quickly swept the warehouse for bugs. *That wasn't fun.*

He sighed, inwardly. He didn't blame Jenny for being pissed. She'd had the freedom of the town not too long ago. She could have gone anywhere and done anything and now...she was trapped, locked in a house that wasn't hers, surrounded by the debris of a life that *could* have been hers if things had been different. Gayle seemed to be taking it better, but that meant nothing. She hadn't grown up as one of the elites.

"Here they come," Roger said. "Remember, no names."

Derek nodded, impatiently. They'd picked a handful of their fellow workers, the ones who seemed most solid and reliable...and, perhaps, likely to fight. It hadn't been easy. Each little conversation ran the risk of betrayal, even though social convention demanded people keep their mouths shut. It was a petty defiance, a convention that might not even hold true now the world had been turned upside down. Once, an open betrayer would have been shunned and abhorred. Now...who knew?

Of course, there was little to gain from open betrayal back then too, Derek thought. He frowned, inwardly, as he spotted the masked men. In the gloom, it was hard to see who was who. *Now, there might be a reason to give rewards.*

"Welcome," Roger said. He pitched his voice low. "We've swept this place for bugs. We should be able to speak freely."

"Are you sure?" The speaker was a young man, a year or two younger than Derek. "What if you're wrong?"

"Then we're dead," Roger said, bluntly. "And if we're caught here, we're dead too."

He carried on before anyone could say a word. "Right now, we're caught between the devil and the deep blue sea. If the newcomers win, they'll put things back to the way they were before the marines invaded—only worse. The entire planet will be put into lockdown. There will be little chance for advancement. On the other hand, if the marines win without our help, they won't see any reason to support us either. The only way out is to fight."

His words hung in the air for a long moment. "And if that doesn't convince you," he added, "do it for Kiki."

Derek shivered. Kiki had been a young girl, shot down by an enemy patrol. Details were scarce, but rumourmongers were quite happy to fill the gaps. Kiki had been completely innocent, shot down for the sheer hell of it. Kiki had stood up to a bullying blowhard, then killed for daring to stand up for herself. Kiki had been raped by a dozen men before being shot; Kiki's dead body had been violated before it had cooled. The stories had grown in the telling, he was sure, but one thing was true. Kiki—whoever she'd been—had become a martyr. The entire city was burning with anger because of her death.

He listened, quietly, as Roger spoke on. "There's nothing to be gained by getting yourselves shot," he said. "We're going to show you how to hurt the bastards. The stuff we brought is—mostly—stuff you can get anywhere.

They'll be watching, after the first few blasts, so do what you can to stay unobserved. Those of you who show real potential—and those with military training—will be given real weapons. We'll try and get some more shipped in from outside."

To hide the existence of the weapons dumps, Derek added, silently. *And keep you thinking we're being supplied from the outside.*

"We'll also be discussing ways to communicate, while avoiding leading the enemy from one cell to another," Roger said. "First lesson, *no names*. We want you to assemble other fighters, but tell them nothing. What they don't know they can't tell."

"My friends won't tell," another young man objected.

"Anyone can break," Roger said, flatly. "There are truth drugs out there. They inject you with one of them, you'll be telling them everything from our secrets to the terrible truth that you didn't *really* bonk all those girls. You'll spill your guts. Don't tell me you won't. I won't hold it against you. The strongest person in the world will tell his captors everything after he's injected with the right drug."

"I thought there were ways to immunise people to the drugs," the young man said. "I saw in a flick…"

"Yes," Roger said, cutting him off. His voice was very sharp. "Do you happen to know how to do it? I don't."

He went on, quickly. "Make plans on the assumption you'll end up on your own. People can be arrested, either through carelessness or sheer bad luck. Stay out of sight. If someone who knows you gets caught, make yourself scarce before they start talking. Don't tell yourself your close friends won't betray you. One injection and your wife will be telling everyone you've got a really small cock."

"Point taken," the man muttered.

Another laughed. "You have a small cock?"

"Shut up," Roger said. He placed his rucksack on the ground and opened it. "Now, watch carefully."

Derek leaned forward, watching with interest as Roger produced a handful of household supplies and started to explain how to turn them into bombs. A simple cleaning fluid wouldn't do much damage on its own, but it would turn into an explosive if it was combined with two more. And all it would take to set it off was a simple spark. Roger's explanation grew more complex as he added a cluster of household tools and toys to the mix. It was easy to turn them into makeshift detonators once one realised it could be done.

"Be extremely careful when you put these together," Roger warned, as he wrapped up his talk. "The slightest mistake could lead to an explosion."

"And be watchful of olfactory sensors," Derek added. He'd been caught like that a couple of times, during basic training. The jokes had practically written themselves. They would have been funnier if they hadn't been aimed at him. "Make sure you shower before going outside."

He smiled to himself. He intended to make sure grounded aircars were randomly splashed with cleaning fluid. The sensors would sound the alarm, forcing the enemy to waste their time trying to disarm a bomb that didn't exist. They'd realise what the resistance was doing very quickly, of course, but they wouldn't be able to do anything about it. They couldn't afford to ignore the alerts. It would only take one *real* IED to convince them of the error of their ways.

"Don't stick around to fight," Roger said. "They're *much* better armed than us. They'll come after you if you give them a chance. Get in, hit them, get out. Or lay a bomb and run before it detonates. You do *not* want to let them catch you. The worst of the stories of poor Kiki will seem like a picnic, compared to what they'll do to you."

Derek allowed himself a moment of relief as the small group slowly dispersed. The lessons would take, he hoped. They had to. If they didn't... he was uncomfortably aware they were *very* exposed. The enemy might round the entire group up in a single night. It was just too dangerous, but... what choice did they have?

"We'll plant a couple of surprises as we go back home," Roger said. He repacked his rucksack, then headed for the door. "It's a shame we can't get any closer to the bridges."

"Not with our weapons, no," Derek agreed. The remaining bridges had been reopened, but there were checkpoints on both sides. It was too risky. If they were searched, they'd be arrested or shot before they could run. "We'll have to give it some thought."

He glanced at his watch as they started to leave the compound. It was just past midnight. He was *not* going to get enough sleep before he had to get up, pour coffee down his throat and stumble off to the work gang. The supervisor was a lazy bastard—Derek hadn't seen him so much as pick up a single pebble—but he was sharp enough to notice someone arriving late. And unpleasant enough to report him too. Derek knew—from Jenny—just how much someone could work out from data-mining. If there were reports of bombs being emplaced late at night, and reports of workers turning up late because they were tired, someone might put two and two together. And it was too much to hope they might get five.

And we might be arrested on the spot, when we turn up for work, he mused. *If someone was tracking us...*

They crossed a patrol route, waited long enough to be sure they were unobserved, then concealed a pair of IEDs before retreating back into the shadows. He would have preferred to hit the bridges—the security troops really were the worst of the worst—but that wasn't going to be easy. He tossed a handful of ideas around as they hurried home, avoiding a pair of checkpoints and dodging a patrol. He'd get some rest, then...go back to work. And, when night fell, he'd do it again.

• • •

Lieutenant Blair Quigley, Internal Security Division, enjoyed security work. Internal security attracted and retained a certain kind of person, people who not only had no qualms about invading someone's privacy but a very definite willingness to do just that. Blair had been recruited straight out of school and put to work, first as an investigator and later as a security officer. He'd been fascinated, he admitted openly, by what people did when they thought they weren't being watched. And he took pleasure in spying on them. Catching malcontents, spies, and saboteurs was just a bonus.

He studied the young woman as she slowly lifted her shirt to prove she wasn't hiding anything. Her breasts were perfect, soft and round. It was a pleasant view—he'd snatched her out of the crowd because she was young and pretty—but he didn't care about that. Not really. He wouldn't really have cared if he was subjecting a man, instead of a woman, to such humiliating treatment. It was the sheer pleasure of forcing someone to expose themselves, forcing someone to humiliate themselves, that drove him on. He licked his lips as the girl lowered her shirt, glancing at the bridge as if she hoped he'd let her go. Or someone would come to her aid.

"Pants," he ordered. The crowd was watching, murmuring. Blair could *feel* their anticipation, the pleasure of seeing a young woman exposed; he could feel their shame and guilt in how he'd made them compliant, how he'd made them enjoy themselves. "Drop them. Now."

The girl looked from side to side, all too aware she had an audience. It was easy to forget the hidden cameras and monitors, easy to pretend they didn't exist…but she couldn't ignore the rest of the security patrol, or the watching civilians, or…everything. Her eyes pleaded silently, promising him the world if only he'd let her go. Or even search her in private. Blair was almost tempted. It would be great if he could make her degrade herself still further, to go down on him, to…he shook his head.

"Drop them," he repeated. A thrill of excitement ran through the crowd. A handful looked away, unwittingly marking themselves for later attention. "Now."

The girl lowered her pants and panties in one sharp motion. Blair felt his heart start to beat faster as he eyed her legs, eyes lingering on her bush. She turned without being told, bending over and spreading her cheeks to show him her rear. He could tell she'd reached the point of no resistance, that she'd do anything she was told…he sighed, feeling the pleasure slowly start to fade. Who cared about someone who'd *willingly* do whatever she was told?

"Pull them up, then go," he ordered, curtly. The fun was gone. "Fuck off."

He watched the girl scurry away, frightened and broken. Contempt and disgust washed through him. She could have put up more of a fight, made it more fun for him. There were plenty of ways to degrade someone, plenty of things to do that were only fun if the victim didn't want them. He smirked, remembering some of the people he'd broken. It was making them his playthings that *really* got to them. And then turning them into his willing allies and collaborators.

The day wore on. Fewer and fewer people seemed to want to cross the bridge. He didn't care. A mobile population was a dangerous population. If the price of crossing was being searched, only people who really *needed* to cross the river would use the bridge. His superiors wouldn't care. They'd been on edge, ever since the first IEDs. A handful of explosions had shaken the city…a handful, but too many. Blair knew the sky would be the limit if he caught one of the bombers. No one would question his methods if he brought his superiors a living bomber. And he'd be allowed to do whatever he liked to make the bastard talk. He smiled in anticipation. He was going to have so much fun.

He searched a handful of young men and women, then an elderly woman who tried to remonstrate with him. She was an old bag who was well past her prime, if she'd ever been in it, but she put up more of a fight than any of the others. He was tempted to drum up an excuse to arrest her, then have her shipped to the security HQ and broken properly. He'd enjoy it. By the time he was done, she'd be telling him things she didn't know she knew.

Blair's eyes narrowed as he spotted a young man wearing a heavy knapsack. His finely-tuned instincts sounded the alarm. The man was hiding something. It was clear, just from the way he avoided Blair's stare. Blair smirked, then beckoned him over. His squad tensed, ready to grab the man if he tried to run. Blair had authority to shoot runners, but where was the fun in that? He felt his smirk grow wider as he studied the young man.

Nineteen, at a guess; young and fit and handsome, just like the assholes who'd mocked Blair as a teenager. He'd had the last laugh, ensuring his childhood tormentors spent the rest of their days in work camps. He didn't care if they were guilty or innocent. All that mattered was teaching them a lesson they'd never forget.

"Well," he said. He made a show of snapping on his gloves. That never failed to intimidate. And yet, the young man seemed oddly unconcerned. Blair felt a hot flash of anger. Perhaps he'd do worse than a public strip search. Prisoners *had* been known to hide things in indelicate places, after all. "ID card. Now."

The young man was holding something in his hand. "For Kiki," he said. "Fuck you."

Blair stumbled back, but it was far too late.

The world went white, then dark.

CHAPTER TWENTY-TWO

Therefore, one may question aspects of policy—communism's economic policy, for example, or the precise interpretation of God's Word—without ever being allowed to question either communism or the bedrock of the religion itself.
—**Professor Leo Caesius**
The Right to be Wrong: How Silencing People Hurts You

"WELCOME TO FOB KNIGHT," Captain Lopez said. "Our all-new home from home."

Garfield looked around. Dusk had fallen, but he could see enough to pick out details. The FOB had once been a small town, before the local inhabitants had been displaced and the buildings converted into barracks and warehouses. It didn't look very impressive, no matter how many tanks, AFVs and supply trucks had been piled up behind the ramparts. A dozen antiaircraft vehicles were evenly spaced around the edge of the compound, unblinking electronic eyes watching for incoming threats. His eyes lingered on the distant mountains and the PDC beyond. The peak was lost in the haze, but...

He swallowed, hard. The marines were waiting for them.

"Thank you, sir," he said. The platoon had been hastily reassigned to Lopez's company, after he'd received three sets of different orders that had been cancelled before he'd managed to get started on carrying them out. His superiors seemed unable to decide how best to use the men at their disposal, either in patrolling the city or preparing for the grand offensive. "I won't let you down."

"Glad to hear it," Lopez said. He jerked his head east. "I heard a whole security company was blown to hell."

"Yes, sir." Garfield wasn't sure how he felt about *that*. On one hand, security troops were assholes, even worse than MPs. On the other, they were—nominally—on his side. "But it was just a platoon, not a company."

"Oh, what a shame." Lopez didn't seem too concerned. "What's it like, back there?"

Garfield tried to put it into words. The bombing campaign was a strange mixture of professional and amateurish. One would-be bomber had blown himself up, something that had frustrated investigators who'd hoped the idiot's corpse could lead them to the rest of the gang. He'd learnt the hard way to ensure they stayed a safe distance from *anything* that might be a bomb. But the rest of the growing insurrection was almost worse. Lone soldiers had been attacked and knifed, platoons on patrol had been shot at from ambush...a handful of mortar shells had been fired into the government complex itself. It didn't seem the time to be mounting a major offensive.

"Bad," he said, finally. "It's pretty damn bad."

"Noted," Lopez said. "There's been some harassment out here too."

"Yes, sir." Garfield had read the reports during the march upcountry. "But at least it's a cleaner war."

"We'll see." Lopez gave him an odd look. "For the moment, the offensive itself is scheduled to launch in two days. There's been a bunch of clashes over the last few hours, brief engagements between our probes and their counter-probes, but nothing major. The higher-ups believe we probably won't have the advantage of surprise, though. Their scouts are damn good at what they do."

Garfield grimaced. "And they're probably listening to our chatter too."

"Probably," Lopez agreed. "Tell your men to watch what they say. Or write down. Bastards killed an entire patrol, then stripped the bodies of everything before they withdrew. The spooks insist they're learning lots from us, just by examining our garbage."

He shrugged. "Make sure you get some rest. There's a brothel for officers in the nearby town. You can go there, after the briefings. We probably won't have time for proper exercises, but I want your men joining the patrols and working hand in hand with the rest of the company. Make sure you get to know my officers too. You'll be junior man, I'm afraid, which won't stop you from inheriting command if the worst happens."

"Yes, sir," Garfield said. A brothel? He was almost tempted, but... there were no brothels for his men. Someone had started a cruel rumour the insurgents had stopped plans to establish one by killing the prostitutes. "I'll do my best."

"And make damn sure you watch your back," Lopez added. "The marines are *good*."

"Yes, sir." Garfield looked towards the distant mountains. They looked scenic, but they were hundreds of miles away. There could be thousands of marines between him and the PDCs, hundreds of tanks and guns just waiting for him and his men. He'd be surprised if they didn't have countless guns already zeroed in on their position. It was the smart move. "I'll bear that in mind."

He nodded—he didn't dare salute—then turned and walked back to the barracks. A couple of men stood outside, smoking. Garfield stepped past them and into the makeshift chamber. He had no idea what it had been, once upon a time, but it didn't matter. Right now, the floor was covered with sleeping bags and bedrolls. The sound of snoring echoed. He walked past, remembering the first night he'd spent in the barracks. He'd hadn't gotten any sleep.

And the trick is to keep working, he reminded himself. *If you go to bed tired, you'll sleep through a bomb.*

Janelle met him when he reached their bedding. "Everyone went to bed, sir," she said. "Do we have any new orders?"

"We're starting joint patrols tomorrow," Garfield said. "And we're launching in two days."

He breathed a sigh of relief as he lay on his bedroll and closed his eyes. The marines were tough—and there was a very real risk of dying before he saw his next birthday—but at least they were honest. There'd be no risk of being blown to hell by a suicide bomber or...or worse. He'd seen a couple of badly-wounded men being flown back to the ships. They might survive, if they reached the medics in time, but they'd bear the scars for the rest of their lives. And he knew there was a price on his head. The girl he'd shot—the girl he kept telling himself deserved to die—had become a martyr.

And we can fight a cleaner war here, he told himself, as he drifted off to sleep. *Maybe we can win without killing everyone.*

...

I need a bigger gun, Rachel mused, as she lay on her belly and peered into the enemy camp through her visor. *And perhaps a nuke or two.*

She cursed under her breath. Sneaking up to the vantage point hadn't been easy. She'd considered trying to sneak into the camp itself, but there was row upon row of checkpoints designed to make sure of a visitor's *bona fides* before they were allowed past the fence and into the enemy lair. And she'd spotted only a handful of uniformed women amongst the enemy troops. The guards would probably know them all by name. She'd have to suggest it to one of the men.

If we can put together a proper cover story, she thought, sourly. She'd walked into an enemy camp during an earlier mission, before Earthfall, but the entire complex had been utterly chaotic. *They're pretty damn good at checking everything that goes in and out of the town.*

She scanned it slowly, carefully counting the visible infantrymen, tanks and self-propelled guns. It looked as if the offensive would begin in a day or two, which matched the information the spooks had picked up from enemy transmissions. They were doing their level best to avoid hostile terrain, but they practically *had* to go for the mountains if they wanted to take out the PDCs. She frowned as she inspected the enemy soldiers, preparing themselves for the offensive. It looked, very much, as if they thought they were going to go sooner.

And they might be right, she thought, as she finished her sweep and started to crawl backwards. *Their superiors could easily have lied to them about when the offensive is due to begin.*

The thought made her smile as she inched through the foliage. She disliked the idea of not being trusted—she'd survived Boot Camp, the Slaughterhouse and Recon Training—but she had to admit she couldn't share what she didn't know. The enemy troops would talk—troops always talked—and listening ears might pick up something useful. They wouldn't know they were hearing lies because the talkers wouldn't know they were lying. The offensive might start in a day instead, and then...

She tensed as she heard someone crunch through the foliage. A patrol? It sounded like one man, but...she braced herself as someone came into view. He wasn't paying any attention to his surroundings as he found a convenient tree. She heard the sound of a zipper, followed by running liquid. He was taking a piss! She inched forward, senses scanning for signs there was anyone else in the vicinity. A smart soldier wouldn't go too far from his comrades, even if he needed to pass water. She could understand a degree of embarrassment, but he really should have lost it by the time he boarded ship. Basic training removed all sense of privacy.

The soldier zipped up his fly. Rachel stood and darted forward in one smooth motion, grabbing him with one hand and covering his mouth with the other. He struggled long enough to confirm he couldn't break her grip, then sagged. It wasn't *that* easy to snap someone's neck with one's bare hands, but her enhanced strength would be more than up to the task. Rachel leaned forward, pressing her fingertips against his veins. It wouldn't be as reliable as a lie detector test, but it should work.

"When I move my hand, speak quietly," she ordered. She felt a start of surprise when he heard her feminine voice. "When's the offensive due to begin?"

The soldier trembled against her. "Two...two days."

Truth, Rachel noted. Or, at least, true as far as he knew. She frisked him with one hand, her fingers brushing against his terminal before she yanked it out. His fingerprints unlocked it, allowing her to open the user interface. It was painfully simple, compared to hers. She supposed it made sense. The Imperial Army had made its systems as simple as possible too.

She tightened her grip. The soldier whimpered, too scared to fight. He was almost painfully young. The marine corps had a small number of volunteers who'd probably lied about their age in order to enlist, but...she was surprised to see it here. A big corporation should have been able to catch that. She gritted her teeth, then pressed her fingers against his neck, injecting him with a drug. His memories would be scrambled so badly, he'd forget ever meeting her. He went limp, an unpleasant stench rising from his pants. Rachel grimaced as she lowered him to the ground. His sergeant would assume he'd been sleeping on the job and beat the hell out of him, but at least he was alive. She kept a wary eye on him as she poked at the terminal, trying to unlock it further. It was futile. The device had been designed for a common soldier. It was too much to expect it carried the entire invasion plans within its database.

Rachel snorted at the thought, then returned the device and hurried off as quickly as she dared. It wouldn't be long before *someone* realised the soldier was missing and sent out a search party. He certainly hadn't known he needed to hide his tracks when he left his unit. She heard the sounds of moving people, but none came into view. It was surprisingly lax, for a force that *knew* it was in bandit country. She supposed there were fools in every organisation. The commanders might have ordered their men to stay together, but they couldn't account for someone who wandered off to take a piss.

She picked up speed as she crossed the stream into no-man's land. The map suggested the two forces were practically touching each other, but the facts on the ground were different. The disputed territory between them was fought over constantly, marines and soldiers exchanging blows as they each tried to keep the other as far from their lines as possible. She knew both sides held immense forces in reserve. It was just a matter of time before they clashed. Again.

And we're going to hurt them, she thought, as she reached the RV point. *We're going to bleed them white.*

Bonkowski was waiting for her, looking worried. Rachel's eyes narrowed. There was no sign of the other two. They should have been back before her. Their destinations had been a little closer.

"They're supposed to be on their way," Bonkowski said. His voice was flat, a sure sign he was worried. "But the enemy garrisons have been changing their patrol schedules."

"Damn it," Rachel said. "We'll just have to wait."

"No," Bonkowski said. His voice was very firm, cutting off her objections before she could even verbalise them. "You take the intelligence back home. I'll wait for them here."

Rachel wanted to object, but she knew her duty. "Yes, sir."

• • •

Gerald found himself reflecting, as he stared down at the map, just how *irritating* it was to try to plan a battle on a battlefield enveloped by the fog of war. It was easy to track his own forces, even though they'd disabled most of the force trackers to prevent the enemy from using them too; it was harder, much harder, to keep track of the *enemy* forces. Their point defence and ECM capabilities were good, fully the equal of anything under his command. Both sides had launched drones, in hopes of spying on the other side; both sides had watched hopelessly as the drones were blown out of the sky. They were both reduced to methods that had been outdated when humanity took its first fumbling footsteps into space.

He stroked his chin and studied the latest updates. The enemy forces were clearly massing in position to drive across the smaller river, seize the town and bridges and then push onwards towards the PDC. He had to admit their plan had the virtue of simplicity, although he could put a spoke in their wheels simply by taking out the bridges. They'd have to replace them, which would take time they didn't have. He hoped. He had no way to know which side would get reinforcements first. And then...

If we can regain the high orbitals, we can force them to surrender, he thought. It was practically a mantra by now. The enemy CO was probably dwelling on it too. *And if they gain control of them first...*

He dismissed the thought. There was no point in worrying about something he couldn't control. Instead, he turned his attention to the terrain. There *were* some options for using it against the enemy, with a little work. He had teams already exploring the question, trying to figure out if theory could be turned into practice. That too was out of his control. The forces under his command, on the other hand, had been carefully emplaced. They should be able to stall the enemy—repeatedly—until they were right where Gerald wanted them. Or the reinforcements arrived.

"And they have more than enough firepower to hurt us in a straight fight," he muttered. It was frustrating to see how well the dumpster gambit had paid off for them. They'd taken one hell of a risk and come out ahead. Somehow. And the hell of it was that the corps would never risk copying the tactic. They might lose and wind up thoroughly fucked. "We'll have to bleed them white before we try to catch them in a trap."

He allowed his eyes to wander over the map. There were a dozen options, ranging from simple limited steps to desperate measures that would stake everything on one throw of the dice. They had their attractions, he admitted privately, but they'd have to wait until the enemy fleet was distracted or destroyed. There were definite hints the enemy had run short of KEWs—there was no other explanation for why they weren't trying to snipe his forces—yet they were clearly trying to rearm. And that meant...

"General," Lieutenant Yen said. "We just picked up a report from the Pathfinders. The enemy troops believe the offensive is scheduled for two days from now, but there are signs it might start early."

"Noted." Gerald had suspected as much. It was never *easy* to mass the forces for a full-scale offensive, but the enemy seemed to be proceeding in a surprisingly leisurely manner. Odd…unless they intended to launch early. "Keep an eye on their positions. I want to know the moment their tanks roll."

"Yes, sir," Yen said. "Specialist Green says she interrogated an enemy soldier. The trooper wasn't lying, she thinks, but he might have been lied to."

"Perhaps," Gerald said. He'd never deliberately lied to men under his command. There were reasons—short-term reasons—for doing it, but in the long-term it served to weaken the bonds between officers and men. Besides, anyone who'd survived the Slaughterhouse could be trusted. They'd been through more, before they first heard a shot fired in anger, than just about anyone else. "We'll assume the worst."

He allowed his eyes to drift over the map. The enemy was going to push west. They *had* to push west. And there were limits to how their offensive could develop, unless they had something new up their sleeve. They *had* to send their tanks alongside the roads, they had to push towards the bridges, they *had* to take the town. And then…

"They'll come," he said. He'd done everything he could. "And we'll be ready for them."

CHAPTER TWENTY-THREE

Those who dare to step over the line rapidly find themselves in hot water and sentenced to jail, or exile, or death. They are branded as crazy, or traitors, or whatever particular demon features in the state's pathology, and denounced so completely that they are destroyed and everyone else takes note.
—**Professor Leo Caesius**
The Right to be Wrong: How Silencing People Hurts You

"WE'RE READY, SIR," GENERAL RASK SAID. "I just wish we had more KEWs."

"Me too," Nelson agreed. He'd managed to put together a makeshift asteroid mining operation, but he was grimly aware it was just a matter of time before the enemy realised what he was doing and moved to stop him. "You'll have to make do with what you have."

He studied the map for a long moment, wishing he knew more about ground combat. Julia stood next to him, resting one hand on his arm. The operation looked simple on the display. Drive westwards, capture or knock out the PDCs; force the marines to surrender or simply destroy them from orbit. And yet, he was all too aware everything was riding on their success. If they failed, or if they had to beg for reinforcements, they were likely to suffer the consequences.

"Begin the operation," he said, calmly. There was no point in admitting his fears, not to anyone. Julia was already jittery, with reason. Rask already knew the risks. "The KEWs will be launched in two minutes."

"Aye, sir." Rask saluted. "See you on the far side."

His image vanished. Nelson let out a breath as the display updated, showing the KEWs—and ground-based weapons systems—preparing to fire. The enemy lines would be bombarded heavily, unless their point defence was up to the task of stopping each and every projectile, shell and missile. They'd certainly hunker down, Rask had insisted; they'd be unable to react quickly to his armoured columns as they started to move west. The plan looked perfect. It would continue to look perfect until it ran into the enemy.

Julia glanced at him as the countdown reached zero. "I wish there was something more we could do."

"We can't," Nelson said, flatly. He made a show of looking away. There was nothing to be gained by watching the early stages of the operation. His staff would warn him if matters went wrong. They knew what to do, what little they *could* do from orbit. It was the troops on the ground who'd have to win the war. "All we can do is watch and wait."

...

"Incoming! Rachel glanced up as the shout echoed over the trench. "Incoming!"

She dived into the trench as her senses picked out a wave of shells and missiles falling towards their positions. The ground shook a moment later, an endless grinding shuddering that made her think of earthquakes -—and worse. It looked as if the enemy were hammering everything that *might* be a threat, every position their scouts or prying orbital eyes had picked out and marked for destruction. She hoped the decoys would soak up most of the enemy fire. They might smash their way through the lines if they were prepared to destroy the region in order to save it.

"Fuck," Phelps grunted. "What are they throwing at us? The kitchen sink?"

"And everything else." Bonkowski didn't look up from his terminal. "They're hitting us high and low."

The ground heaved again. Rachel gritted her teeth, willing herself to stay calm until the bombardment finally ended. The enemy wouldn't be mad enough to shell their own troops, would they? Even the marines rarely risked dropping KEWs into positions so tight it was easy, with the best will in the world, to accidentally kill their own people. And the Imperial Navy had never been *that* good at targeting. Rachel had been on Han, during the early stages of the fighting. Someone—either through incompetence or malice—had managed to drop KEWs on a friendly unit, obliterating it to the last man. They'd never recovered the bodies.

"Shells, missiles, projectiles..." Perkins looked decidedly unwell. "They'll detonate most of the surprises before their troops get within engagement range."

"Possibly," Bonkowski said. "But we planned for that, didn't we?"

Rachel nodded. The shaking continued, pieces of dirt falling from the makeshift roof as dull thumps thudded through the ground. Intelligence claimed the enemy was running short on KEWs, although she didn't believe it. They shouldn't have any difficulty producing more. And yet, the bombardment was already starting to slacken. Perhaps the PDCs and point-defence units were doing their jobs, wiping out as many incoming shells as possible before they reached their targets. It wasn't as if the shells were difficult to hit. It was just that there were so *many* of them.

Let them get into the kill zone, she recalled. Their orders had been very clear. The marines had space they could trade for time, space they intended to use ruthlessly. *And then hurt them while they try to push west.*

She grinned to herself as the shaking continued to die away. The enemy was clearly unwilling to destroy large swathes of the planet in order to save it. She glanced at the terminal, noting that only one shell had fallen within the distant town. The enemy wanted to keep the bridges intact.

Good thinking on their part, except they could have severely weakened the marines by dropping the bridges ahead of time. General Anderson would have had no difficulty pulling his troops out of the pocket, but they'd have had to leave most of their heavy equipment behind.

"They're reducing their fire, concentrating on our rear positions," Bonkowski said. "And they're hammering the decoys quite hard."

"Good," Rachel said. "That'll keep them from pounding us."

She thought, fast. How long would it take for the enemy to realise they'd been tricked? Not long, she suspected. Their shooting wasn't *that* bad. Sooner or later, they'd realise they'd wasted a bunch of shells. The deception teams would be doing all sorts of things to delay the realisation as long as possible—panicky messages, transmissions brutally cut off to suggest the shells had taken out something important—but it wouldn't work for long.

"They'll be on their way," Bonkowski said, as the ground heaved one final time. "And we have to give them a hot reception."

"Got it." Rachel stood, feeling her legs wobble as she headed for the hatch. The bombardment had disturbed her on a very deep level. Behind her, the others didn't look much better. "Let's move."

• • •

Private Vincent Tremens ached.

He'd been a corporal, only a day ago. And then…he wasn't quite sure what had happened. They'd found him away from his unit, sleeping beside a tree…his former squadmates insisted he'd gone for a piss, but he didn't remember it. The sergeant had beaten him bloody, screaming in rage and frustration, then marched him off to a penal unit. Being stripped of his stripe—a stripe that had taken him years to earn—would have been a disaster, under other circumstances. Now…

He shivered in fear as he and the rest of the penal unit were ordered forward. The army didn't bother putting soldiers in jail, not when they could serve much more effectively in a penal unit. The punished men were told that, if they survived a month without being killed, they'd be allowed to return to their original units with the slate wiped clean. Vincent didn't believe them. He'd never heard of a penal soldier returning home. They were sent on the most dangerous missions, the ones with the greatest chance of death. And they were used ruthlessly. He'd heard the rumours. Being sent to a penal unit was practically a death sentence.

And it isn't fair, he thought. There were men behind him who'd been caught looting, or raping, or being disrespectful to their officers. He… he honestly wasn't sure what had happened. They deserved it. He didn't. He'd done everything he could to earn and keep the stripe. *It just isn't fair!*

His legs buckled as he forced himself to keep moving across the battered remains of no-man's land. The shelling had been hellishly effective. Small clusters of trees had been smashed to sawdust, fields had been battered so intensely that it was hard to believe they'd once been used to raise animals or grow crops. There'd been a farmhouse ahead, according to the map, but there was no sign of it now. He was tempted to believe they'd taken a wrong turn somewhere along the line. All he could see was mud, an endless sea of mud. His boots slipped as he kept moving. The MPs had made it painfully clear they'd shoot him in the back if he failed to move quickly.

Sweat trickled down his back. It wasn't fair. He'd always been loyal. But there was nothing he could do. He trudged through the mud, wondering why he hadn't been assigned to seizing the motorway and clearing it before the tanks and AFVs were ordered west. The higher-ups had probably given that order to a more motivated unit, one that might not overlook an IED out of spite. He told himself, firmly, to keep his head down as an explosion echoed in the distance. The enemy were out there somewhere, waiting between the front lines and the mountains. Waiting for him.

A pair of missiles flashed overhead, heading west. He looked up, following them with his eyes. One exploded in midair, picked off by a hidden point-defence unit; the other lanced down and hit the ground. There was a flash of light, followed by an immense fireball. The sound of thunder echoed across the plains seconds later. He felt a twinge of sympathy for whoever had been under the blast, followed by irritation at himself. The marines were *tough*. They were going to kill him, if they had a chance. The more killed by missiles, the fewer who'd be able to take shots at him.

He kept going, somehow. The sound of fighting echoed in the distance, but…it never touched them. He felt oddly isolated, as if they were completely alone. It was hard to believe that thousands of soldiers—and hundreds of vehicles—were on the move. Perhaps they'd been forgotten, their unit overlooked by commanders focusing on the real invasion. Or… he glanced back at the MPs, keeping their distance from their charges. He had a rifle. He could kill them…he shook his head. They'd shown how deadly they were, back when he'd been marched into the camp. He'd be shot down in an instant if he tried to bring his weapon to bear on them. And even if he succeeded, where would he go?

They reached a cluster of ruins that might—once—have been a small village. It was hard to tell. The ruins looked shattered, very little surviving above the mud. There were supposed to be roads running through the village, according to the map, but they were drenched so deeply it was impossible to be sure where they were. Vincent wondered, sourly, if they'd been required to clean up the mess. Penal units were never given time to relax, he'd been warned. If they weren't walking into enemy territory stark naked—or as close to naked as possible—they were doing all the crappy duties no one else wanted to do. Digging latrines, filling in trenches…he felt his heart twist at the thought. Nothing would ever be the same again.

The point man fell. Vincent stared, so dazed it took him longer than it should have done to realise he'd been shot. There was a sniper ahead… he hit the ground, feeling the mud squelch under him. He felt sick as he crawled forward, holding his rifle at the ready. Where *was* the bastard? He'd seen snipers on rooftops and other hiding places, but there wasn't much of the village left to use. There was very little cover…he scanned the surroundings, trying to spot the marine. Where was he?

And we can't fall back either, he thought. The MPs were still behind him, guns pointed at his back. They'd *still* shoot him for retreating, even though it was starting to look as if they had no choice. Damn the bastards. And damn him too. *What can we do?*

He barked orders, hoping the remainder of the unit would follow them. They were a surly group, unwilling to do more than the bare minimum. Their supervisors seemed to enjoy setting them against one another, cheerfully pointing out who'd earned the group a collective punishment. Or who'd committed the worst offense. A man who'd molested a child had been beaten to death by the rest of the group, Vincent had been told. No one had cared. They'd probably been relieved the penal unit had saved them the cost of a bullet.

They spread out, trying to approach the remains of what had once been a fairly large house before the shells had slammed down. A house... or a general store. It was hard to tell, but it was the only bit of cover within the area. A good sniper could use it long enough to fire a shot or two, then vanish into the mud before it was too late. Vincent kept moving, wishing he had a grenade or two. He could have thrown one into the ruin, in hopes of killing or injuring the sniper before he exposed himself. But penal units weren't allowed grenades. He cursed under his breath as he glanced at the two men nearest them, trying to convey orders with hand signals. If they went in together...

He hurled himself forward, into the gloom. The shack—it was just a shack now, he thought—was empty. A pair of murder holes had been drilled in the walls, although he wasn't sure why they'd felt the urge to bother. There were plenty of *other* holes within the walls. The shack was empty... no, there was something in the corner, something half-buried under a cloth. He heard a *click*. His instincts sent him stumbling back, too late.

The world went white, then dark.

• • •

Rachel felt a stab of pity, mingled with the grim awareness there'd been little choice, as the IED detonated. The enemy unit had been odd, a strange mixture of competence and incompetence that baffled her. She'd never seen anything like it, outside a handful of Civil Guard units that had been combined into a single unit. A penal unit? It was possible. The soldiers bringing up the rear had looked hellishly like a political unit, with orders to gun the men down if they so much as looked like retreating. She was tempted to find another vantage point and gun the fuckers down, before telling herself she simply didn't have the time. They were pushing forward, slowly but surely. All she could do was leave a handful of surprises in her wake. Hopefully, the blasts would slow them down a little more.

She stayed low as she hurried back to the RV point, smiling coldly as she heard a couple of small explosions behind her. The enemy didn't seem inclined to pick up speed. They knew it wouldn't be easy to check every last inch of the terrain for tricks and traps, let alone hidden snipers. There wasn't much to find, either. Some of their commanders would suspect it, given a chance, but they wouldn't be able to take it for granted. They'd be wise to assume the landscape was festering with unpleasant surprises. The mud alone could hide a hundred IEDs, if not an entire minefield.

Another explosion rang out behind her, followed by a handful of shots. She pressed herself into the ground, half-expecting bullets to snap through the air above her. Nothing happened, save for a single shout. It didn't seem to be directed at her. She glanced behind her, then picked herself up and hurried on. The enemy would be moving faster now, she was sure. They had to get to the town before it was too late. They *needed* the bridges. And that meant their movements would be predictable.

She reached the RV point, jumped into the foxhole and nodded to Phelps. "Any word from higher-up?"

"The bastards are probing forwards slowly," Phelps said. A rumble of shellfire underlined his words. "And we're hitting them everywhere we can."

"Good." Rachel saw shells heading eastwards, trying to take out the enemy forward units before they could start advancing on the town. A moment later, the enemy guns returned fire. She hoped the marine gunners were prepared to change position *fast*, after hitting a handful of targets. "Any specific orders?"

"Nothing new," Phelps assured her. "Get in, hit targets of opportunity, get out again."

Perkins dropped down beside them. "Same old, same old," he said. He sounded surprisingly cheerful, for someone in the path of a full-scale offensive. "Aren't they going to try anything new?"

"Bite your tongue," Phelps advised, making a rude gesture. "If they take out the PDCs, we're fucked."

"Yeah," Perkins agreed. "But the entire planet will also be fucked."

Rachel took a breath, then rearmed herself. "I think we'd better get moving," she said. "They'll overrun this place, sooner or later. And then we really will be fucked."

"Unless we knife them in the back after nightfall," Perkins said. "The fighting won't stop just because the sun's gone down."

"No," Rachel agreed. They couldn't afford to wait until nightfall. There was very little between the enemy spearheads and the town, certainly nothing that would do more than slow them down. "But the more we delay them, the better."

CHAPTER TWENTY-FOUR

This is, of course, common everywhere. Those who dare to stand against the tide of public opinion, however defined, are often penalised. Those who tried to argue that the New Scandinavian Civil War was a bad idea, on the grounds the rebels were dependent on the central government, were smeared as unpatriotic. Ten million dead later, they were finally acknowledged as being right. Too late.
—**Professor Leo Caesius**
The Right to be Wrong: How Silencing People Hurts You

"WE HAVE OUR ORDERS," JANELLE SAID, as the squad held position just before the ramparts. "Go."

Garfield nodded, bracing himself as the tanks rumbled to life. The shelling had lasted for hours, hurling thousands upon thousands of shells into enemy-held territory. A handful of reports, transmitted through the command network, suggested advance elements were already meeting resistance. Details were sparse, but it was clear the shells hadn't smashed the enemy flat. Garfield smiled grimly, although it wasn't good news. The command briefings had made it clear they'd be assuming the worst. They couldn't rely on the gunners hitting their targets.

The platoon advanced slowly, passing the ramparts. The engineers had spent hours opening holes in the defences, ensuring the tanks could move out of the camp and into enemy territory. Garfield half-wished *he* was a tanker, although he knew from bitter experience that the marines had plasma cannons and modern antitank missiles. The tanks were terrifying, but—if the enemy didn't panic—also vulnerable. It was difficult to get out of a tank that had been hit before it was too late. A single plasma burst would kill everyone inside before they knew they'd been hit.

He watched the tanks grind on as they made their way towards the road. It rested on flat ground, unlike the last motorway they'd seized; it looked ugly, but he knew they should be grateful. The shelling had turned the ground to mud, making it harder for the soldiers to advance in good order. The thoroughfare would be useless if it was bathed in a sea of mud. It would be worse than useless if a landslide destroyed the motorway beyond quick repair.

"They're out there, somewhere," Janelle said. "They'll want to slow us down before we reach Riverside."

Garfield nodded. Sweat trickled down his back. Brief transmissions echoed through the command net, warning of enemy contacts that lasted only a few seconds, but left a handful of men dead each time. He eyed the distant mountains, half-wishing the enemy tanks would appear so he could face them in the open. *That* wasn't going to happen. The marines weren't going to let his men chew them to ribbons. They'd fight from the shadows, hitting the invaders quickly before falling back again and again. He'd seen the briefing notes. The marines were *tough*.

He gritted his teeth as one of the lead tanks ran over a mine and skidded to a halt. The idiots had driven too close to the edge, damn it. He barked orders as the tank crew bailed out, directing them to make their way back to the camp. They'd be as safe as anyone else, for the moment. His men inched forward, protecting the tanks as they kept moving. A small hamlet came into view, surprisingly intact. The shelling hadn't done any real damage. But then, the gunners hadn't wanted to risk damaging the motorway.

Fucking waste of time, he thought, as he heard shots coming from the hamlet. The marines had turned it into a strongpoint. *We should just have smashed the buildings and let the engineers clean up the mess.*

"We have to flush them out," he said, grimly. "The tanks can provide covering fire, while we hit them from the side."

He ducked low, Janelle following, as he led the men towards the hamlet. It would have been better, he supposed, if they'd had enough troops to seal off the hamlet first...but the marines would have fought to the death if they'd thought there was no way out. They certainly didn't seem inclined to surrender. The tanks sprayed the buildings with machine gun fire, paying special attention to anything that even *looked* like a murder hole. A few shells would have put an end to the threat, once and for all...Garfield cursed under his breath. The marines just weren't running.

"In five," he muttered, as he unhooked a grenade from his belt and removed the pin. "Now!"

He hurled the grenade, tossing it neatly through the cracks in the wall. The grenade detonated seconds later, the high-ex charge shaking the building and blowing the door open from the inside. He thought he heard a scream as the platoon ran forward, but that might have just been wishful thinking. There were no bodies inside, just a handful of abandoned firing positions. Moments later, he heard shooting from the next building. He gritted his teeth in frustration. The marines had moved to the next building to continue the fight.

"Stay back," Janelle shouted. "Stay back!"

Garfield turned, just in time to see another platoon passing too close to a pile of debris. He opened his mouth to shout another warning, but it was too late. The IED detonated, blowing the men to hell. A salvo of mortar shells landed on top of them, seconds later. If any of them had survived the IED—and there was too much smoke for him to be sure—they sure as hell hadn't survived the mortars. He barked orders, rallying his men to advance to the next set of buildings. They *had* to clear them before it was too late.

The marines fought from the shadows. He barely saw them as they sniped at his forces, or called down hellishly accurate shellfire. They never gave up a position until they'd used it to best effect, then vanished down pre-planned escape routes to the *next* set of fighting positions. Garfield lost count of how many men died, during the final push to drive the marines out. He took a savage delight in ordering the tanks to gun the fleeing marines down before they escaped. The hamlet had been tiny. And yet, over thirty men had been killed before the marines had been driven out.

"Fuck," he breathed, as the tanks rumbled through what remained of the hamlet and headed west. "How bad is it going to be when we hit the town?"

"Bad." Janelle looked tired too, even though they'd made sure to be well-rested before the offensive began. "Really pretty damn bad."

She was right, Garfield discovered as the day wore on. They should have been able to travel from the FOB to Riverside in a few hours. Instead, an endless nightmarish series of engagements slowed the advance to a crawl. The marines had scattered IEDs everywhere, tangling up the supply lines and—sometimes—using the snarl as an opportunity to snipe or shell the advancing forces. Garfield had to call down shellfire on two particularly tough hamlets, his superiors having long-since discarded their reluctance to fire on anything close to the motorway. The engineers were going to be very busy over the next few weeks, Garfield was sure. Getting troops across the river wouldn't be such a great achievement if they ran out of supplies before they could advance any further...

He ducked as a sniper's bullet cracked just above his head. Had the sniper spotted an officer? Garfield wasn't *quite* sure how he'd come to be commanding the remnants of five platoons, only two of which had been part of his original company, but he'd been making a spectacle of himself issuing orders. There was no point in dressing like a common soldier if he'd been barking orders like a sergeant. He stayed low as another bullet pinged off a disabled tank, coming far too close to him for his peace of mind. Janelle peered west, then shook her head.

"I can't see the bastard," she said.

"Order the tanks to spray the area with bullets," Garfield said. He wasn't surprised. The marines were good at hiding, as well as everything else. He'd wondered, weeks ago, if they really *were* as good as all that. The Empire had certainly had an interest in insisting the marines were invincible. Experience had taught him the marines really *were* that good. "And then perhaps a shell or two."

He gritted his teeth as they punched through another hamlet. The town was coming into view, sitting on the river...it *wasn't* going to be easy to take. And the bridges were probably going to be dropped anyway. He'd heard one officer suggest shelling the town to rubble, then clearing away the mess and rebuilding the bridges. It wasn't as if the engineers couldn't have rigged up a few dozen pontoon bridges. They had more than enough supplies.

"Stay low," Janelle said, as another bullet snapped though the air. The tanks had fired madly, but it was clear they hadn't hit anything. "Let someone else relay the orders."

"I can try," Garfield said. "But how many officers are left?"

...

Gerald frowned as red arrows—slightly blurred to remind him of the limits of their knowledge—marched across the map. It *looked* as if the enemy were advancing into a vacuum, although he knew there were hundreds of strongpoints, IEDs and other unpleasant surprises slowing them down. They could have crossed the terrain a hell of a lot quicker if at least *some* of the surprises weren't taking a toll. Gerald rather hoped the enemy's political leadership was breathing down their necks. A unit that tried to attack an enemy it wasn't prepared to defeat yet was one that was going to take one hell of a beating. And there was nothing like political interference to force a commander to act against his better judgement.

He felt his frown deepen. The enemy was pushing forward almost recklessly, something that bothered him greatly. He had no qualms about taking advantage of someone's mistakes, but...there was no hint the enemy commander was actually *incompetent*. Sure, he'd followed a predictable path...Gerald shook his head in dismissive annoyance. The path was predictable because there were few other choices. He supposed the enemy could march *east* instead, in a bid to circle the entire world and take the marines from the rear, but that was the sort of crazy idea that only worked in bad flicks. Planets were *big*, really big. The settled region of the planet was relatively small. The locals had intended to keep developing their planet over the next few *hundred* years.

But that was before the war, he thought. *God alone knows what they're going to do now.*

He shook his head as the latest report came in. The enemy had cleared yet another strongpoint, opening the road to Riverside. Gerald wished them joy of it. The motorway was strewn with IEDs, mostly makeshift devices hidden within the wrecked cars and vehicles taken from the town. They'd have to clear them all before they could start preparing for the main assault, something that would take several days at the very least. He wondered if they'd realised Gerald had evacuated Riverside long ago. There were no civilians to be caught in the middle if the enemy decided to shell the town flat.

And that never works as well as the gunners claim, he reminded himself. *They'd do a lot of damage, but they wouldn't take us out.*

Taking a breath, he mentally stepped back and studied the casualty reports. It wasn't *easy* to estimate how many enemy soldiers had been killed—the first reports, in his experience, were almost always inaccurate—but it looked as if hundreds, perhaps over a thousand, had died during the opening stages of the offensive. Enough to make them think twice? Gerald wasn't sure. Corprats rarely gave much of a damn about human lives—the simple fact they had human resources department was proof enough they didn't care—but trained and experienced soldiers were worth their weight in gold. And they'd have to think about the effects on the survivors. If they became convinced their comrades had died for nothing, they might turn on their masters.

Maybe, Gerald thought. *We sure as hell can't count on it.*

He turned his attention back to the display. The enemy forces were steadily advancing on Riverside. It wouldn't be long before they reached the outskirts of the town and started to surround the eastern side. They'd have to get over the river before they could surround the entire town and *that* wasn't going to be easy. There were no bridges for over thirty kilometres in either direction. The marines had seen to that.

And when they try to take the city, Gerald told himself, *we'll bleed them white*.

• • •

Garfield felt as if he'd gone beyond tiredness, beyond the aches and pains pervading his entire body. He'd fought his way through dozens of enemy hamlets, avoiding hundreds of IEDs as they'd made their way down the motorway. They'd stopped taking chances as Riverside itself came into view, hosing abandoned cars with machine guns in the hopes of detonating any surprises before it was too late. The air was full of smoke and fog from burning cars, further slowing the advance. It was late in the day before they reached the rally point outside the town. He didn't want to think about how badly the planned schedule had slipped. They'd been meant to be there hours ago.

"Captain Lopez is coming," Janelle hissed. "Look alert."

Garfield straightened as much as he dared. The enemy snipers were *very* good. The latest update claimed they'd killed upwards of a dozen officers and wounded two more. He was grimly aware they were probably being watched by snipers in the town or lurking somewhere outside visual range. Bastards. Apparently, one sniper had been caught and systematically beaten to death. Some upper-ranking twit had made a fuss, citing the need to take prisoners. The soldiers hadn't been inclined to care. They'd wanted revenge.

"You did well," Lopez said. "I hear there's promotion in your future."

"Better that than getting the blame for stealing other platoons," Garfield said, tiredly. Unit integrity had seemed so important during basic training, but it had turned into a joke on the battlefield. "Patel is dead, sir. Last I heard, Khan was being rushed to the medics."

"He's stable, but out of the fight for the moment," Lopez said. "I'm sure he'll be glad to hear you took the rest of his platoon."

"Yes, sir," Garfield said. He could have kicked himself. Lopez was a good officer. He'd know what'd happened to his subordinates. "Are we going to push into the town now?"

"It doesn't look like it," Lopez said. "Are your men up for it?"

"No, sir." Garfield had heard about officers who'd shown a lack of enthusiasm, and gotten in trouble for not volunteering for every chance to get a few soldiers killed, but he'd also heard about officers who didn't put their men first. "We—ah, they—need a rest."

"Noted," Lopez said. "It looks as though we will be making camp here, sniping the bastards at night and then hitting them in the morning. Once we get set up here, we'll try and get some rest."

"Aye, sir," Garfield said. "We appreciate it."

Lopez nodded, then turned away with what looked like calculated disrespect. Garfield felt a twinge of annoyance, even though he knew it was necessary. They really *didn't* want snipers deducing they were officers. Bowing and scraping on the battlefield was just *asking* to be shot. He turned to Janelle, resisting the urge to make a rude gesture at Lopez's back. There were limits to calculated disrespect, certainly in front of the men.

"You did well," Janelle said. "You could have volunteered to take the town at once."

Garfield felt a flash of pride. Janelle didn't offer praise easily. A soldier would have to do *really* well to get anything more than a nod from her. Garfield might be corporate royalty, his advancement certain unless he screwed up so badly he was disowned, but *Janelle* had never been impressed. He'd grown to admire her, even as she protected the soldiers from his mistakes. She was…admirable.

"We're not ready to take an entire town," he said, flatly. "If we got hammered taking a handful of tiny hamlets, just how bad will it be when we hit the town?"

He frowned as he saw a pair of heavy tanks moving towards the river, surrounded by infantrymen. Were they planning to take up position by the river and shoot anything moving on the waters? Or drive *across* the river and hit the town from the rear? It was possible, he figured. The tanks were supposed to be able to drive across a seabed. A river wouldn't pose much of a problem. He shook his head. The marines would have anticipated a bid to surround the town. They'd have taken precautions.

And it isn't as if we have time to starve them out, he thought. The marines would have stockpiled ration bars. They could hold out for months, if they wished. They wouldn't enjoy the experience—rumour had it that too many ration bars did unpleasant things to the stomach—but they could do it. *We have to take the town before they drop the bridges.*

He shuddered, inwardly. There could—there *would*—be hundreds of marines in Riverside, waiting. Taking the town was going to hurt. Badly. He shuddered to think how many of his men were going to die. And yet, they had no choice.

If we don't get across the river, he told himself as he accepted a cigarette, *we might as well pack up and go home.*

CHAPTER TWENTY-FIVE

Accordingly, even a relatively mild dictatorship can find it hard to properly assess reality. A smart government may evolve into something more palatable, even developing into a democracy, but in doing so the elite will be forced to give up their power. They tend to find that unpalatable.
—**Professor Leo Caesius**
The Right to be Wrong: How Silencing People Hurts You

"CAPTAIN," COMMANDER JOAQUIN SAID, in a hushed voice. "We are nearing the enemy ship."

Captain Kerri Stumbaugh nodded, stiffly. The enemy ship had been easy to track, too easy. She'd been suspicious right from the start, to the point she'd insisted on spending four days monitoring the asteroid mining operation to make certain the massive freighter was truly alone. Her sensors, the finest in the known galaxy, had picked up nothing. There were no stray electronic transmissions, no faint hints of drive signatures that might—*might*—have suggested the freighter wasn't alone. And yet, she was all too aware the enemy's sensor crews had access to comparable equipment. They'd had plenty of time to figure out how best to hide. There could be an entire fleet lurking far too close to her for comfort and she wouldn't have an inkling it was there before it opened fire.

And the moment we bring up our active sensors, we tell them where to aim their missiles, she thought. She'd give the enemy the first shot, their best chance of doing real damage before she managed to react. *Damn it.*

She clasped her hands on her lap, weighing her options. It was hard to believe the enemy hadn't thought to bring at least one mobile factory with them, although she could see how the oversight had happened. God knew the Imperial Navy and Army had made the same mistake time and time again. It wasn't *easy* to estimate how many bullets, shells and projectiles one would need, particularly when the beancounters were breathing down your neck and insisting you find ways to cut costs. And if someone needed more…? Who cared? The beancounters weren't the ones at risk of having their asses shot off when supplies ran out…

And they probably threw the relief fleet together on the fly, she thought. The corprats couldn't have *known* the marines were planning to invade or…they'd have prepared a much tougher defence, perhaps beating off the invasion before a single marine set foot on the planet. *They didn't realise they'd be committing themselves to a long campaign.*

She sighed, inwardly. They needed time. And so did the marines on the ground.

"Order Colonel Steel to deploy when ready," she said. She'd spent a lot of time with Steel, planning the *real* offensive. "And wish him good luck."

"Aye, Captain."

And if I've made a mistake, she thought grimly, *I've just thrown one of my few cards into the fire.*

She leaned back in her chair. The matter was out of her hands now. All she could do was wait.

• • •

Captain Haydn Steel felt uncomfortably exposed as he jetted out of the airlock and set his course towards the enemy freighter. There was no reason to think the freighter was a Q-Ship—or indeed anything else than a freighter pressed into mining service—but he knew better than to assume she was unarmed. Even tramp freighters carried *some* weapons, even if they were just railguns or plasma cannons that might—just—deter a pirate ship from boarding and doing unspeakable things to the crew. A corporate ship could be armed to the teeth. It might not be enough to stop *Havoc*, but it sure as hell would be enough to take out the marines.

He kept his eyes focused on the freighter's rough location, even though the enemy craft was invisible within the inky darkness of space. Space was big, really big. He felt his heart begin to race as he realised, once again, just how tiny he was…he gritted his teeth, banishing the reaction with an effort. Few people cared to know just how small they were, on a cosmic scale. There were groundpounders who never went into space, for fear of what they might find out about themselves. The stars had burnt brightly for millions of years before the human race had come into existence and would be burning millions of years after the last human had shuffled into the next world. Unless someone really *did* come up with a supernova bomb…

And terrorists have been using that bluff for hundreds of years, he thought, sourly. It was a common threat, although there'd been little real meat to it. If the Imperial Navy's weapons division had been unable to find a way to make a star explode, it was hard to believe a bunch of underfunded terrorists could do any more. *It simply doesn't work.*

He put the thought out of his mind as the enemy freighter slowly came into view. She wasn't trying to hide—or, if she was, she wasn't trying very hard. There were few artificial emissions from her hull, but she'd been tracked when she'd left the enemy fleet and the long-range probes had shadowed her when she'd shut down her drives. The enemy seemed to believe the marine fleet had left the system completely, something that baffled Haydn. They couldn't believe the marines would abandon the forces on the ground, could they? Haydn was starting to like Captain Stumbaugh—in ways, he admitted to himself, that weren't entirely professional—but he'd commit mutiny rather than abandon his comrades. It was bad enough he'd been ordered to leave the surface. Leaving the system would have been a step too far.

And it might be a trap, he mused. *We have to be careful.*

The squad followed him as he glided towards the enemy ship. The freighter was as ugly as hell, a blocky mass that had been chopped open and hastily sealed up once the mining and refining complex had been shoved inside. He wondered, idly, if the crew were committed corprats or independents on a long-term contract. The latter was unlikely. Independent freighters, even ones desperately short of money, tried their level best to remain out of debt to the big corporations. They'd sooner fly smuggling missions into warzones than sign up with the corprats. And yet, the ship looked as if it was constantly on the verge of falling to pieces.

They probably didn't realise they needed a logistics chain, he thought. *It isn't as if the Imperial Navy took logistics very seriously. They were never more than a few days from a supply depot.*

He pushed the thought aside, watching as the enemy crews mined the asteroid and directed pieces of rocky ore towards the freighter. They'd be smelted down and compressed into KEWs, then transhipped back to the fleet. There was nothing *complex* about them, nothing that forced the new-comers to wait for supplies from home. A KEW was nothing more than a piece of rock. The only thing cautioning the enemy to be careful was the simple fact they were bombarding their own world. They might think twice about blowing something up if they genuinely wanted to use it.

And they might change their mind, he thought. *If the shit hits the fan...*

He braced himself as he drifted closer and closer to the freighter, his boots finally making contact with the hull. Up close, the ship looked scarred and pitted by centuries of mistreatment. His lips quirked—one careful owner, shame about the other ten—as the rest of the platoon landed. He'd considered bringing the entire company, but it would have pushed the risk into unacceptable territory. Captain Stumbaugh's plan might succeed without him and the alpha platoon. It would fail—it wouldn't even get off the ground—without the rest of the company.

The hatch was right where he'd expected, yielding instantly to his touch. A warship would have let him and the team get into the airlock—it was standard practice—but sealed them inside until their *bona fides* could be established. A civilian ship, particularly one that had no reason to expect trouble, might be a little more careless. He winced, inwardly, as his helmet picked up alerts. The crew might not have been expecting trouble, but they hadn't been careless either. He shoved one armoured gauntlet against the inner hatch and activated his cutter. The hatch fell off its hinges. He pushed forward as air started to vacate the hull, pouring into vacuum. The enemy crew was about to have worse problems than a team of marines boarding their ship.

But they're probably a military crew, he thought, as he led half the platoon towards the bridge. The other half would take the engineering section. Emergency hatches were snapping closed, threatening to isolate the boarders. He smiled grimly as they picked the codelocks, then pushed onwards. *They'll have trained for emergencies.*

Two men darted out of nowhere, eyes going wide as they spotted the marines. Haydn stunned them both, relieved neither of them had thought to don a proper spacesuit. Shipsuits were good—and both of the enemy crewmen had carried masks—but spacesuits would have made them harder to handle. The stun bolts wouldn't have worked. He'd have had to kill them. He checked to make sure they were relatively safe, if uncomfortable, then hurried down the corridor to the bridge hatch. It was sealed, but unguarded. His lips twitched. Military crew or not, they hadn't thought to prepare for boarders. They could have made his job a great deal harder with a handful of tiny precautions.

They could still blow the ship to hell, if we give them time, he reminded himself. Civilian ships didn't come with self-destructs, but it would be easy for a team of dedicated engineers to rig *something*. If nothing else, they could wipe and destroy the datacores. Haydn didn't care if the freighter was rendered useless or not—the marines didn't need it—but the datacores might point to the enemy homeworld. *And they might wipe them before we seize the ship.*

The hatch hissed open. He charged forward, bracing himself for enemy fire. The enemy crew stared at him, fearfully. Haydn was almost disappointed.

They looked to be reservists, halfway between civilian and military personnel. They'd probably been called into service just after Earthfall, when the corprats had realised their time had come. He would have felt sorry for them, if things had been different. But right now, they were just in the way.

"Keep your hands where I can see them," he said, as his eyes swept the room for the vessel's captain. The man looked older than the rest, his eyes grim and cold. "Order the rest of your crew to come onboard."

The captain glowered. "And what if we don't?"

"We'll take the ship and leave them," Haydn lied, smoothly. "Do you think the corprats will waste time recovering them?"

He felt a twinge of guilt. He didn't know—yet—if the enemy crew had managed to send a distress signal. If they had…it didn't matter. It would take at least an hour for the message to reach the planet, then three more hours for a starship to reach the freighter's last-known position. By then, the stranded miners would probably be dead. Even if there was a ship a little closer, it would still be touch and go.

"Fine," the captain said. "And I request asylum on behalf of my crew."

"Granted, as long as you behave," Haydn said. "And *don't* do anything stupid."

• • •

"Operation completed, Captain," Ensign Susan Perkins reported. "The marines have secured the freighter and the crew."

"Order them to strip as much as they can out of the hull," Kerri said. They'd considered trying to keep the freighter, if only to remind the enemy they existed, but it would be more…irritating if they rendered the ship useless before they left. "And then to rig the hull as planned."

"Aye, Captain."

• • •

Nelson sat in his cabin, studying the latest set of reports from the ground. The offensive hadn't stalled—or at least General Rask had insisted it hadn't—but it had slowed as the advancing troops had run into more and more enemy resistance. Riverside was heavily defended, the marines having repelled a pair of probing attacks before night finally brought an uneasy peace to the region. Not, Nelson reflected sourly, that it was *really* peaceful. Both sides were sniping at the other, trying to keep them from having a proper rest.

The intercom chimed. "Admiral?"

Nelson frowned, recognising the voice. "Ensign Karun?"

"Yes, sir." Karun was young, so young for her role that Nelson was *sure* she had some pretty heavy family connections. She wasn't incompetent, but inexperienced. And she sounded nervous. Bad news? "May I report in person?"

"You can give your report over the intercom," Nelson said. He wasn't the kind of admiral who killed subordinates for reporting bad news. That was a good way to get blindsided, if only because no one would dare tell you things you needed to hear. "What happened?"

Karun swallowed, audibly. "Sir, *Rockall* was attacked. The last message stated they were being boarded and…and that was it. There were no further messages."

Nelson took a moment to compose himself. "Attacked? Attacked by whom?"

"I don't know, sir." Karun sounded as if she expected to be put in front of the wall and shot at any moment. "The message just said they were boarded."

"I see." Nelson glanced at the display. There weren't any unfriendly ships within the system…he cursed himself as he realised his mistake. The marines hadn't retreated completely after all! And he'd made the mistake of not assigning an escort to watch over the miner. It was expendable, in the long term, but…but not in the short term. "Have we detected any explosions? Anything that might suggest the ship had been destroyed?"

"No, sir," Karun said. "It could have been RockRats…"

"No." Nelson shook his head, although he knew the junior officer couldn't see him. "It was the marines."

He frowned. "Detach two destroyers to sweep the area," he added. "If they can recover the ship, they are to do so. If not...they are to return as soon as they've finished their sweep."

"Aye, sir," Karun said. "I..."

"See to it," Nelson said, as Julia emerged from the bedroom. "Inform me if anything changes."

He closed the connection and looked at Julia. "*Rockall* is gone."

Julia blanched. "And there's no way to get her back?"

"I very much doubt it." Nelson stood and started to pace the compartment. "If they take her into interplanetary space and shut her down completely, we'll never find her unless we get very lucky. If they rig her to blow, or destroy her, or wipe her datacores...they'll render her useless. And that means we cannot resupply our KEWs."

"Not until reinforcements arrive," Julia agreed. "Is there nothing we can do?"

"They wrecked most of the asteroid mining facilities during their invasion," Nelson said. He carefully didn't point out that most of the asteroid miners might well have sided with the marines. "We'd need to either rebuild the mining camps we've secured or bring in more equipment from home."

"And that would make us look bad," Julia said, coldly. "Can we win? I mean, without the KEWs?"

Nelson scowled. "Yes. I think so. We assumed we wouldn't be making use of KEWs during the later stages of the offensive anyway, so our plans don't need to be changed that much. But the longer the fighting lasts, the greater the danger of simply running out of everything from bullets and missiles to bandages and ration packs. The marines managed to capture or destroy a *lot* on the surface before we landed."

"Yeah." Julia ran a hand through her hair. "And if we request more reinforcements, we'll look bad."

"Yes." Nelson cursed the timing under his breath. They'd planned on the assumption they were the reinforcements, reinforcing a planetary government and defence force that had been battered bloody, but remained unbowed. Instead, the marines had taken out the government and smashed the defence force. "It will look like we failed."

He wondered, idly, if they could put together an excuse that might—might—save them from the worst. Their superiors hadn't raised any qualms about the plan. There'd been limits to what they'd been able to form into a scratch force, limits to the number of ships and troops they'd been able to redeploy...they'd done their best. And yet, it was starting to look as though their best wasn't good enough. The marines were holding their own.

They must be having supply problems too, he mused. The reports suggested the marines were conserving their forces, rather than daring his men to take them on in open combat. *The victory might go to whoever has only one bullet or bomb left.*

"I'll tell General Rask to speed up the timetable," he said. It wasn't as if the general could do much, beyond urging his subordinates to push harder. His men were already fighting like demons. "And hope for the best."

Julia scowled. "And what if he fails?"

"That's not an option," Nelson said. The alternative was unthinkable. Everything depended on them producing a victory before reinforcements—either side's reinforcements—arrived and changed the balance of power again. "If we can win on the ground, or at least keep the marines in check, we win."

"In all sense of the word," Julia said. She looked as if she wasn't remotely convinced. "I hope you're right."

CHAPTER TWENTY-SIX

This tends to lead to geopolitical, strategic and tactical surprise.
—**Professor Leo Caesius**
The Right to be Wrong: How Silencing People Hurts You

"INCOMING!"

Garfield ducked low as a hail of mortar shells landed near him, debris flying everywhere. The platoon had entered Riverside, following on the heels of a penal unit, only to discover the town was heavily defended and crammed with all manner of nasty surprises. There were no safe places, nowhere they could stop and catch a breath. The marines were never quite seen, yet lurking everywhere. He barely caught a glimpse of their positions—lurking in the shadows—before bursts of terrifyingly accurate fire tore through the air. It was starting to look as though they were going to have to destroy the town in order to save it.

He unhooked a grenade from his belt as they crept up on a small house, then threw it through the nearest window. His squad followed suit, a series of explosions shaking the house a second before they crashed through the doors. The interior had been turned into a small bunker, furniture chopped up and turned into makeshift barricades or simply moved out of the way. He hurled a grenade up the stairs, trusting in the construction to ensure the house survived long enough for the squad to search it. They moved from room to room, throwing grenades ahead of them. They found no trace of the marines.

Garfield cursed as he heard more shooting outside. "They're counterattacking!"

He smashed his rifle through the window and peered down. Three men in urban combat outfits were hosing the house with machine gun fire, spraying bullets into the structure as if they didn't have a care in the world. Garfield jammed his finger on the trigger, forcing them to jump back and vanish into the shadows. Janelle knocked him down a second later, before a pair of bullets cracked through the shattered window. The marine snipers were still out there, searching for targets. Janelle yammered into her communicator as they made their way back downstairs, trying to call down mortar fire. It was anyone's guess if the higher-ups would authorise the shelling. Garfield ground his teeth in frustration. They were desperately trying to keep the goddamned bridges intact.

And we're not anywhere near them yet, he thought, as he rejoined the rest of the squad. They took cover behind a burned-out groundcar, blown up on suspicion of concealing an IED. *At this rate, we won't take the bridges until next year.*

More explosions shook the city as shellfire rained down, falling so close that Garfield ducked into a crater. He couldn't tell who was doing the shelling. The front lines were so ill-defined that there were enemy forces within his lines and vice versa. Marines popped up everywhere, fired a handful of shots of rockets, then dropped back out of sight. He fired a shot at a figure on a distant rooftop. The figure dropped, but he couldn't tell if he'd hit the bastard or not. It wasn't as if anyone would be dumb enough to remain visible for more than a second or two. They'd learnt *that* lesson the hard way.

"They're sending up reinforcements," Janelle called. "They want us to sweep the district before we push to the bridges."

Garfield gritted his teeth as he eyed the innocent-looking houses. They seemed quiet; too quiet. The marines might have turned them into strongpoints...he shook his head. There was no *might* about it. They'd already fallen back as the invaders tried to secure the roads, then returned as soon as the invaders turned their backs. The marines didn't seem inclined to remain still and be killed, damn it. They had no qualms about falling back when they were outnumbered and on the verge of being pinned down, then resuming the offensive moments later. There were patches of ground—and entire buildings—that had changed hands dozens of times in the last few hours. And half the town was burning.

We should just drop the fucking bridges and crush their defenders before pushing across the river, he thought. The marines had managed to keep their supply lines open, just by remaining in possession of the bridges. They were probably floating boats down the river, despite the machine gun posts on the nearside. *Who cares about keeping the bridges intact?*

He dismissed the thought as the reinforced company pressed into the district. He'd been right. The marines were everywhere, popping up to harass his men and falling back whenever he called down fire on their positions. They moved like lightning, luring unprepared soldiers into traps and then slaughtering the poor bastards before they had a chance to retreat. Garfield called down more fire, scattering shells across the remainder of the houses as the day wore on. He was going to catch hell for that later, corporate royalty or not, but he found it hard to care. It wasn't as if he was shelling the bridges. They could do without the houses. Their owners had fled a long time ago.

The nightmarish day turned to darkness. Garfield found a quiet spot for his men to rest, only to discover it wasn't quiet at all. The marines kept testing their defences, hurling shells into his makeshift bunkers while probing their lines for weak spots. A pair of unwary men were sniped from a distance, a handful more killed by a well-aimed rocket. Garfield tried to convince his superiors to rotate the squads out of the city—if it was wearing him down, he hated to think what it was doing to the soldiers—but no one seemed inclined to listen. They wanted to keep the pressure on.

We're going to break, he thought, as he drank cold coffee and readied himself for the second day. *And then what are they going to do?*

The marines didn't seem inclined to break. He wondered, as they pushed against their lines, if they even *had* a breaking point. They'd planned for everything, from holding the places they could to falling back when they couldn't. He'd hoped to isolate and destroy a few strongpoints, but the range was too short. They could protect and support each other long enough to break contact and escape…they'd practiced, he guessed. He'd never seen anything like it, even during the first raids into Haverford. The marines could have turned the entire city into a fortress, at the price of cutting themselves off from all help. Here…

This could go on forever, he told himself. The projections had suggested the town would fall in less than a week. It was starting to look otherwise. *And what will we do then?*

...

"I just got word from the scouts, sir," Rifleman Norton said. "The enemy tanks are on their way."

"Noted," Lieutenant Rupert Yong said. It was hardly his first engagement since he'd joined the corps, but it might be his most significant. "Any ETA?"

"No, sir," Norton said. "But they're heading towards us."

Rupert nodded. The enemy had been surprisingly careless in *not* trying to cross the river above or below the town. The churning waters *were* an effective barrier to infantry—and open-topped vehicles—but the enemy *should* have been able to move a small force across the waters well before trying to take the town itself. It had been starting to look as though they'd been wasting their time. But now…

He peered across the river as the enemy tanks came into view. A shiver ran down his spine, even though he *knew* the armoured giants weren't as dangerous as they looked. Their guns were only effective if they could see their targets…and the platoon was carefully concealed within the undergrowth. They'd have to move, the moment they opened fire, but he'd planned for that. They'd run for their lives as soon as the enemy reacted to their presence.

"I make it nine heavy tanks, five transports," Norton said. "All buttoned up."

"Target the tanks," Rupert ordered. "And fire once they've all emerged from the waters."

He held his breath as the enemy tanks crunched their way down to the riverside and drove straight into the water. It was hard to believe, despite years of training and experience, that the water *wasn't* a formidable barrier. His instincts insisted the tanks should be swept away by the water, their crews drowned…he shook his head in irritation. The tanks were designed to operate in poisonous environments. A little water was nothing. He'd seen Landsharks driven across the seabed with no apparent ill-effects.

The lead tank reappeared, muddy water splashing around its treads as it drove onto the riverside. The waters turned brown, suggesting the riverbed had been torn up pretty badly, but Rupert doubted the muddy bottom would do more than slow the tanks for a few seconds. He hoped the vehicles would sink in the mud, but he knew it was unlikely. The tanks were just too tough. Being caught underwater in a tank—or anything, really—would be a nightmare, but the crews would be safe as long as they didn't panic. He let out a breath as the next tank appeared, followed rapidly by the remainder. It was easy to see why the first men to face tanks had panicked. The vehicles seemed almost unstoppable.

Not quite, he thought. The tanks were pushing forward, guns swinging madly from side to side in search of targets. *We're waiting.*

He cursed under his breath. The last two tanks had yet to emerge, but the lead vehicles would overrun their position within seconds. Time was running out. He'd hoped to make a clean sweep, wiping out all the tanks in a single volley, but it was starting to look as if they wouldn't have a chance. He braced himself, counting down the seconds, then looked at his men.

"Fire," he ordered, quietly.

He tensed as the plasma cannons came online, a high-pitched whine echoing as they flash-woke their containment chambers and spat bursts of blinding white light towards the tanks. The enemy sensors could hardly have failed to miss the cannons as soon as they powered up, but it was already too late. The superhot plasma slammed into the tanks and burned through their armour, rushing through the hulls and incinerating the crews before they could so much as jump. He swore as the two final tanks emerged from the water, their machine guns already spitting fire towards their positions. There was no time to take them out.

"Run," he snapped.

Rupert held his position long enough to make sure his men were on their way, sprinting down the escape route to the fallback bunker, then got out himself. It was just in time. The plasma cannons exploded, waves of heat washing over his back as they lost containment. He smirked, even though he knew it was likely he was about to be gunned down like a dog. Plasma cannons were inherently unreliable—and they could be as dangerous to their users as to their targets—but they'd done their job. The enemy offensive had been stopped in its tracks.

He keyed his mouthpiece, snapping firing coordinates into the network. The self-propelled guns would have a chance to take out the remaining tanks, if they didn't move quickly. He hoped there were guns on call, ready to fire. The enemy counterbattery fire had proven disturbingly effective, forcing the marine gunners to keep changing position. Behind him, he heard a rumble as the remaining tanks crushed the defence position and kept moving. The wave of incoming shells fell too far to the east. He babbled corrections into the network as he fell into the bunker, rolling over to peer at the enemy vehicles. Their infantry had dismounted, advancing forward with grim determination. One of their transports was a burning wreck. Rupert grinned, despite the situation. The shellfire hadn't been as ineffective as he'd thought.

"Sir," Norton said. "Jemsin is dead."

Rupert nodded. Jemsin had been a young man, with two tours under his belt before the current mission...he dismissed the thought with a flash of irritation. There'd be time to mourn later, if they survived. If...the tanks were crunching forward, their flashing guns providing cover to the infantry. A second hail of shells crashed down, too far to the east again. Rupert ignored Norton's sharp comment on the gunner's parentage as he prepared himself to repel attack. If the enemy got a toehold on their side of the river, they could cut off the town and force the marines to either withdraw or be crushed

"Take aim," he ordered. The enemy infantry was still advancing, carefully. "Fire on my command."

He lifted an antitank rocket and aimed at the nearest tank. It wouldn't be easy to disable the vehicle, not without a plasma cannon. The heavy frontal armour might be able to shrug off a direct hit from anything lesser, up to and including an antitank warhead. There was no way to know if the enemy were driving the very latest models, or what covert improvements *they* might have made to the design. The marines had certainly made their own improvements over the past few years.

"Fire," he ordered.

The antitank launcher jerked as he fired the rocket towards the nearest tank. It smashed straight into the vehicle's treads, making it grind to a halt. Some tanks could keep going, even if they lost half their treads...Rupert breathed a sigh of relief as the tank's hatches snapped open, the crew running for their lives. The tank was still shooting, probably on automatic, but it didn't matter. The crew knew their vehicle was a sitting duck. It was only a matter of time before a shell crashed down and destroyed it.

"Hah," Norton shouted. "Got the bastards!"

Rupert wasn't so sure. The second tank was still coming, spraying the marine position with machine gun fire. Its heavy guns were constantly traversing, firing shells into the distance...it dawned on him, slowly, that it was firing on the marine supply lines. And it was going to be a bear to stop. They'd used all their antitank weapons...

"Call in the target," he snapped. In the distance, the enemy troop transports were already heading back to the river. He could see more on the far side, crammed to the gunwales with troops ready to exploit the breach. "And fall back to the third line."

"Yes, sir."

• • •

"General," Lieutenant Yen said. "The enemy has made a crossing at Point Puller."

"Fuck." Gerald wasn't really surprised, but he'd hoped for more time. "How big?"

"One surviving enemy tank, several hundred infantry," Yen said. "Long-range scouts insist more are on the way."

"There'd have to be." Gerald glared at the map. The enemy had made a crossing, but they'd need more troops and tanks to exploit it. And they'd have to move fast. He'd be doing everything in his power to slam the door shut. "Send in Alpha Flight."

"Sir?"

"Do it," Gerald snapped. He understood her concern, but he also knew they had very little time. Once the enemy gained a secure foothold and brought up heavy weapons—and antiaircraft weapons—driving them back into the water would become progressively harder. "Now!"

"Aye, sir," Yen said.

• • •

Lieutenant Arthur Cleaves found himself biting his lip as he flew bare metres above the ground, heading straight towards the enemy pocket. Smoke rose in the distance, a grim reminder—as if he needed one—of the dangers of flying any higher. The enemy antiaircraft weapons were at least as good as the ones covering the marine positions, capable of shooting him out of the sky if he showed himself for more than a second or two. It was humiliating to sit on the ground and wait while others went into danger—he'd even tried to volunteer to pick up a rifle and join the infantry—but there was no choice. The Raptors couldn't operate too close to enemy lines.

Unless we have a chance to catch them with their pants down, he thought, as he selected missiles and bombs. The briefing had stated the enemy had only moved a handful of tanks across the river. That didn't mean they were harmless—most tanks mounted lasers as well as cannons and machine guns—but they weren't designed to shoot down aircraft when they were fighting a battle on the ground. *And we might just have one now.*

His finger tightened on the trigger as he flashed over the marine positions and the advancing front lines. His missiles fired automatically, picking off the tank and a handful of troop transports that exploded into fireballs; he fired his guns, targeting the enemy troops and dropping bombs as he roared over their heads. An enemy vehicle on the far side of the river stopped dead, its hatches snapping open. Arthur blew the vehicle away before more than a couple of soldiers managed to get out. He'd have felt sorrier about it if he hadn't known they'd kill him without a second thought.

The threat receiver shrilled an alarm. He yanked the Raptor into an evasive pattern, firing off flares as he ducked low and flashed back over the river. An enemy soldier fired an HVM, too late. The missile went after the flares, expending itself harmlessly. Arthur breathed a sigh of relief as he fled. That had been too close. He was lucky the enemy hadn't managed to get a proper lock before firing.

He probably thought he was about to be gunned down, Arthur guessed. *And shot the missile as soon as it was pointed in the right direction.*

He keyed his communicator. "Mission accomplished," he said. "Returning to base."

Behind him, the town continued to burn.

CHAPTER TWENTY-SEVEN

On the geopolitical level, a government that (at best) refuses to consider reality and (at worst) is openly deluding itself, is rarely capable of grasping how its actions look to people outside the bubble. What looks, on paper, like a 'mere' border security operation is, in reality, a savage campaign featuring an endless series of atrocities that convince the enemy that they have to keep fighting.
—**Professor Leo Caesius**
The Right to be Wrong: How Silencing People Hurts You

THEY CALL THIS THE HOUR OF THE WOLF, Derek thought, as they slipped through the streets. *The hour when everyone is supposed to be snug in bed, fast asleep.*

He snorted, inwardly, at the thought. His trainers had insisted there were times when people weren't on alert, when attacking their positions might have a good chance of achieving surprise, but he'd often thought that didn't quite make sense. The enemy would know about the hour of the wolf, right? They'd take pains to be on alert when attacks seemed more likely. It was what *he* would have done. And yet, as they moved from shadow to shadow, he was starting to think his trainers had a point. There were only a handful of enemy troops on the streets, almost all guarding important positions.

They are mounting an offensive to the west, he recalled. There was little *definite* information, but they'd heard the rumours. *We're not the most important problem right now.*

He smiled, grimly. The insurgents *were* taking a toll on the enemy forces. Bombs along patrol routes, shooting and sniping...even a handful of soldiers being caught alone and butchered...he wouldn't have blamed the enemy leaders for limiting their contact with the locals as much as possible. They'd lost a couple of men after they'd snuck out to see local prostitutes and a third who'd apparently wandered away from the barracks, although no one was quite sure why. Derek suspected the ban on fraternisation wasn't doing enemy morale any good. He knew from experience that garrison duty could be maddening even if people *weren't* trying to kill you.

Roger stopped as they reached the edge of the town, holding up his hand as they heard vehicles in the distance. Derek crept up beside him, staring towards the motorway. A small convoy of trucks, escorted by heavily-armed soldiers, was driving around the city. They'd learnt the danger of moving supplies *through* the city, he recalled, but they had to use the motorway if they wanted to get supplies to the front before it was too late. He allowed himself a cold smile as he hunkered down, praying the soldiers weren't on alert. They'd picked the spot with malice aforethought, but the enemy could have looked at the map and made the same determination for themselves. Derek allowed himself a moment of relief as the convoy roared into the distance, seemingly untouched. The bastards would never know how close they'd come.

"Now," Roger muttered.

Derek opened his knapsack as they raced down to the motorway, produced a small trowel and started to dig frantically as Roger produced the IED from his pack. They'd put it together carefully, using one of the few military-grade timers in the supply depot. The device should be more reliable than any of the makeshift bombs, but his skin still crawled every time he looked at it. Roger put the device in the hole as soon as it was big enough, keyed to go live in twenty minutes. After that...Derek hastily buried the device, then led the way back up to the city. Once the device went live, any passing weight would be enough to detonate it. He hoped—prayed—it would be a convoy or an enemy patrol. No civilian would dare go anywhere near the motorway in broad daylight.

"Shit," Roger muttered. "Look."

Derek followed his gaze. Dark figures moved along the edge of the city, either insurgents or enemy troops on patrol. It was hard to be sure. They moved furtively, as if they expected to be fired upon at any moment. He stared at them for a moment, then led Roger back into the city. Insurgents or enemy, it didn't matter. They couldn't afford to be caught. Too many people already knew their faces, knew their role in the insurgency. It would only take one person talking, willingly or otherwise, to blow the ring wide open.

And we were careful not to learn names ourselves, Derek thought. He'd done his best to pay as little attention as possible to their allies. *If we're caught, we can't tell anyone what we don't know.*

The thought nagged at his mind as they moved down the street, trying to stay in the shadows as much as possible. The city was eerily quiet, the silence unbroken by shouts, or shots, or bombs exploding on the far side of the river. Derek wished, just for a second, they'd thought to establish themselves on the other side. It would have been far easier to make contact with people who could and would fight. But they'd have had to cross the river to get to the important targets...he shook his head. There was no point in dwelling over what might have been. They had to play the cards they were dealt.

He kept moving, making sure to keep a wary eye out for enemy patrols as they circumvented the enemy bases and headed home. Jenny and Gayle would be asleep, he thought; they'd stopped staying up to wait for them after sneaking out at night had become routine. Derek sighed inwardly as the house came into view, waiting for Roger to check that everything was quiet before they slipped inside. Jenny and Gayle were having a harder time of it. They simply couldn't go outside without an escort.

And the rumours make sure of it, Derek thought. *And they didn't grow much in the telling.*

He shuddered as he headed up to bed. The occupiers had become worse over the last week, as the insurgency really began to bite. People had been snatched off the streets, forced to strip in public, or…Derek knew some of the rumours had been made up of whole cloth, but not *all* of them. The insurgents had made up some of the stories—mass gang rapes, children shot down for shits and giggles—yet others were true. And everyone knew it.

Jenny didn't move as he climbed into bed and closed his eyes. There were only four hours until he had to get up, but he needed his sleep. He couldn't afford to have the overseer notice he was constantly coming in late and tired. There were only so many times he could plead guilty to having a hangover before the excuse wore thin. It felt, as always, as if he hadn't slept at all by the time the alarm went off. Jenny shifted against him, then kissed him lightly on the back of his neck. Derek wished he could stay in bed with her. It wasn't as if there was much else to do.

We really need to find stuff for the girls, he told himself, as he stumbled out of bed and headed for the shower. *Something to keep them busy while we work.*

He shook his head. In hindsight…no, there was no point in worrying about that either. Not now. He allowed himself a smile instead, wondering if the IED had detonated. The patrol—if it had been a patrol—might have been heavy enough to trigger the bomb. And…he hoped, suddenly, the shadowy figures hadn't been insurgents. It would have been ironic as hell to accidentally blow up another insurgent cell. The enemy had already made propaganda capital out of the bomber who'd blown himself to bits. They'd laugh themselves silly over one cell killing another.

If they figure it out, he thought. He dried himself, then dressed in his work clothes. *They might never realise there was more than one cell.*

He shrugged. It didn't matter.

"Good luck," Jenny said, when he hurried downstairs. A mug of coffee was already waiting for him, along with a pair of ration bars. "I'll see you this evening."

"Yeah." Derek eyed the ration bars sourly. He was thoroughly sick of the bars, no matter how many different sauces he splashed on them. There was no hiding the taste of cardboard—and things best not thought about. "I'll see if I can pick up some more food."

"Please." Jenny was an indifferent cook at best, but even Derek's mother would have had problems turning the ration bars into something *edible*. "I'd even settle for fish."

"Me too." Derek had heard there were fish in the river, but he'd never seen them. "I'll see you tonight."

Roger joined him as they headed to the door. "Gayle's pissed," he said. "We're going to have to do something about it."

Derek nodded. "Great idea," he said. "But what *can* we do?"

The question hung in the air, unanswered. It was impossible to answer. There were no distractions in the house, beyond a handful of children's toys and a small collection of bomb-making material. The terminals and datapads were useless without the planetary datanet—the owners hadn't thought to download flicks and music tracks, assuming they'd always have access to the datanet—and there were no books. Jenny really *didn't* have much to do, beyond lying in bed. There wasn't even much *housework*. It wasn't as if they were constantly making a mess.

"We could send them out of the city," he said, finally. He knew it was stupid even as he said it. "It might be doable."

"Sure." Roger snorted, rudely. "And send them where?"

"No idea." Derek kicked a rock on the pavement. "I was hoping you'd have an idea."

His mind raced. If only it was safe to let the girls leave the house! If only there were more of them…he shook his head. If wishes were horses, beggars would ride. Jenny would just have to cope, somehow. They'd look for books or datachips or something to keep the girls busy…

She wanted to come, Derek thought, as they joined the work gang. Fourteen of the eighteen workers were insurgents, although not all of them knew about the others. *She knew the risks.*

He put the thought to one side as he heard a distant explosion. The IED they'd hidden the previous night? He hoped so, but there was no way to know. There was no way to know what they'd hit either. A troop transport? A supply truck? A tank so heavily armoured the IED wouldn't do more than scratch the paint? Who knew?

The enemy knows they got hit, he told himself. *And that will make them more and more paranoid.*

・・・

Jenny had never really experienced *boredom* before.

It simply hadn't been part of her life. As a child, there'd been more entertainment in the datanet than she could explore in a dozen lifetimes. As a teenager, she'd had her girlfriends…and the posse of high-ranking or well-connected girls who'd sneered constantly at everyone they considered beneath them. She'd enjoyed shopping and visiting places denied to the low-rankers and…she knew, now, how shallow she'd been. And as an adult…even during the invasion, when she'd found herself roped into helping with the wounded, she'd had something to do. And…

She liked Derek. It wouldn't have gone anywhere in Eddisford, not when the social gulf between them was so wide it was effectively impassable. She would have lost face for dating him, let alone trying to develop a permanent relationship. Her posse would have sneered—or, perhaps, started a trend of unsuitable dating. And her father…her father wouldn't have cared if she'd dated a lesser man, but marriage would have been completely out of the question. His daughter was going to marry for the good of the family and that was that. And now…she wondered, suddenly, if he'd nag her to marry Derek. There was no question Derek was going places, if he survived. There might be something to be said for a marriage alliance.

But she was bored. Utterly bored. Completely out of her mind with boredom.

She looked at the door, wondering if she could go outside. Derek would throw a fit, but...she found it hard to care. He didn't own her. She wasn't one of his soldiers. And yet, who knew what would happen to a girl on her own? Jenny had heard the rumours the boys had repeated, each more horrific than the last. She wanted to believe they were making them up, but she'd heard enough rumours herself—back when she'd been working in Bouchon—to suspect otherwise. Law and order had been breaking down for weeks, as the planet changed hands and then changed hands again. She was tempted to go upstairs and see if Gayle had any ideas. But they'd already exhausted everything they could do.

The building shook, very slightly. Jenny froze, listening for the explosion. It never came. A bomb? Or...or what? She didn't know. She'd never felt so isolated, not even after the invasion had begun. She liked Gayle—she admitted as much—but they had very little in common beyond femininity. Gayle was lower-class, born and bred to serve. They might have shared a school—if they'd grown up in the same place—but they would never have mingled in the real world. And...

There was a knock at the door. Jenny tensed. People did *not* come visiting. They just *didn't*. Not now. She braced herself, wishing she looked more presentable. The house was her due, the kind of place she'd expected to share with her future husband, but...she knew she didn't look the part of a rich housewife. The neighbours might not talk to the government—any of the governments—yet they'd certainly chat amongst themselves. Jenny was all too aware she didn't look like a sour old biddy, with a rich husband and a small brood of kids. The knock came again, harder this time. She gritted her teeth and headed for the door. Four men in uniforms—with green tabs on their shoulders—stared at her.

Jenny stumbled back, too late. One of them rammed a fist into her gut. She doubled over, gasping in pain. Her assailant turned her around, shoved her to the floor and yanked her hands behind her back before she could so much as muster a reaction. She tried to kick him, but he ignored it as he cuffed her hands and searched her thoroughly. Jenny felt unclean as his hands roamed everywhere, making sure she didn't have anything hidden *anywhere*. She breathed a sigh of relief she hadn't carried a pistol. She hadn't had time to draw it before he'd hit her.

The man picked her up and pushed her against the wall. "Sit. Stay."

I'm not a dog, Jenny thought, numbly. Her mind raced. Gayle was upstairs…hopefully, she'd heard the racket and jumped out the window. They'd calculated it was the easiest way to escape, if someone was careful. And if there were no watching eyes outside the house. *If they find the weapons…*

She winced, trying to look dismayed as the searchers crashed through the house. It was easy. A housewife would be horrified at the bangs and crashes, the shattering sounds as jars broke and spilled their contents all over the floor…she was horrified at the thought of them finding something incriminating. Gayle hadn't been hauled down, which meant…either they hadn't found her or they'd shot her trying to escape. Or…maybe they'd just cuffed her upstairs and left her there as they searched the room. She thought she heard someone catcalling, but it was hard to be sure. Her wrists were starting to ache. The cuffs were just too tight.

It felt like hours before the men returned to the hallway. Jenny's heart sank as soon as she saw what they were carrying. The pamphlet on bombmaking had been thoroughly illegal well before the invasion…both invasions. She wasn't even sure where she would have found it, if any copies had existed on the surface a year or so ago. The marines had given them the instructions, cautioning them to keep the papers out of sight. And they'd failed.

Her captor knelt beside her. His voice, when he spoke, was almost gentle. "Do you have something you want to tell us?"

Jenny gritted her teeth. "No," she said. There was still no sign of Gayle. She hoped—she prayed—that was a good sign. "Let me go."

The man let out a fake sigh. "Let me explain something to you," he said. "You will talk. Willingly or not, you will talk. If you talk freely, you'll be shipped to a detention camp and probably released after the war is over. If not, my men and I will force you to talk. We will not be kind."

Jenny hesitated. How much did she owe Derek, really? How much did she owe the marines? They'd turned her world upside down, shattered the path she'd known her life would take…they'd shown her something better, before the newcomers had taken it away. She wanted to think she didn't owe anyone anything. Perhaps, if she talked, she'd be safe. And she could plead for Derek and the others…

No, she thought. *They wouldn't listen.*

"Go to hell," she said.

The man shrugged. Jenny had expected to be slapped or worse…but the lack of reaction was, somehow, more terrifying than naked violence. She cringed, inside. She'd talk, eventually. And then Derek and the others would be caught…

"You first," the man said, as he hauled Jenny to her feet. "And believe me, the fires will be a relief."

CHAPTER TWENTY-EIGHT

And indeed, a reputation for giving one's word and then breaking it simply makes it impossible for anyone to trust you in the future. But a deluded and/or delusional government may not understand that until it's far too late.
—**Professor Leo Caesius**
The Right to be Wrong: How Silencing People Hurts You

"DEREK! ROGER!"

Derek looked up sharply from the pile of debris—IED debris—they'd been assigned to clear. Gayle was running towards them, her long red hair streaming in the breeze. She wore a nightgown, one that showed her curves to best advantage…Derek found himself staring, a moment before he registered the bruises and cuts on her exposed skin. She'd run for several blocks wearing *that*? It was sheer dumb luck she hadn't been grabbed by an enemy patrol.

The supervisor leered at her. "Come to see your boyfriends, little girl?"

Derek glanced at Roger, then picked up a chunk of debris and hit the supervisor in the back of the neck. The man tumbled, hitting the ground with a thud. Two of the workers started to sidle away, unsure of where they stood; Derek snapped orders, instructing the remaining insurgents to hold them still. There was no time for a fight. Gayle wouldn't have left the house unless it was urgent.

"Gayle," Roger said. "What happened?"

Gayle caught her breath. "They invaded the house," she gasped. "Jenny's a prisoner and...and they know about you."

Derek swore out loud. How? Had they been shadowed back to the house? Or...had it been sheer luck? They'd heard the enemy were doing random searches...he'd assumed their house, in one of the wealthier areas, would be immune. Perhaps he'd been wrong. They wouldn't have been allowed to join the work gang after planting the last IED if the enemy had realised who they were. And now...he thought, fast. The house was crammed with evidence, from fingerprints to DNA samples. A thorough search of the house would turn up enough data to ensure the enemy would know *precisely* who to watch for...

We need to destroy the house, he thought. *And we need to rescue Jenny.*

He looked at the insurgents. "Tie those two up," he said, checking the supervisor to make sure he was really dead. "They'll be freed later."

Roger caught his arm. "What do you have in mind?"

"We have to rescue Jenny before they take her into the governing complex," Derek said, grimly. The building was effectively impregnable, at least to anyone without heavy weapons. Jenny would be made to talk, then discarded. "Once she goes in there, we'll never see her again."

"Got it." Roger didn't look pleased. "You have a plan?"

"Half of one," Derek said. Gayle couldn't have taken *that* long to reach them. The odds were good the invaders were still searching the house. "We'll make up the rest as we go along."

"How very reassuring," Roger muttered.

Derek ignored him. "We have to rescue someone who knows too much," he said, addressing the other insurgents. "If you don't want to join us, go underground now. We've been outed."

"Fuck," someone commented.

"Yes," Derek said. "Choose now."

Derek tried to hide his guilt. What he'd said wasn't entirely true. Jenny had never seen the other insurgents. It was quite possible they could remain undetected, if Derek and the others went underground now. But that would mean leaving Jenny in enemy hands. Derek had no doubt they'd torture her, then throw her into the brothels. The rumours he'd heard were coming back to haunt him. He couldn't leave Jenny to a fate worse than death.

He waited. Nine men agreed to go with them. The remainder said they'd go underground. It wasn't what he'd wanted, but…it wasn't what *anyone* had wanted. He spoke quickly to Gayle as Roger stole the supervisor's clothes. From a distance, he'd look *just* like the man himself. There were enough supervisors wandering the city that it was hard to believe that anyone knew them *all*. And if he was wrong…?

Derek shrugged. He'd cross that bridge when he came to it.

"Let's go," he said, after dismissing the remainder. "This is what we're going to do."

• • •

Captain Franz Gibson allowed himself a cold smile as his team finished searching the insurgent household. It had been sheer luck they'd stumbled across it, although his report would point to a number of traits that—in hindsight—had told them precisely where to look. The inhabitants might *claim* to be upper-class, but they'd made no attempt to claim any special privileges from the occupiers. And they hadn't even tried to worm their way into the command structure. Very suspicious, he thought to himself. His superiors would like it, when he wrote his report. He'd deduced the existence of the insurgent cell from the *absence* of something.

His smile grew wider as he studied the haul. A small amount of illicit material, a collection of household goods that could be turned into bombs… And one girl, barely out of her teens…clearly an insurgent herself, given how reluctant she was to talk. If his assessment was correct, there'd been at least two other insurgents who'd lived in the house, perhaps more. He'd ensure a watch was kept on the house, just in case the others came back.

Who knew? They might not realise their house had been raided. They might not know their cover had been blown.

The girl stared at the floor, looking helpless. Franz was unimpressed. They always tried to look helpless, when they still had hope of escape. The girl was too young to realise she was thoroughly screwed. She'd talk, sooner or later. They always did. Franz didn't enjoy hurting people, but he had no qualms about doing it. The girl would be broken, drained of everything she knew, then dispatched as quickly as possible. She'd had her chance to talk freely and turned it down.

"March," he ordered, pushing her towards the door. The house would look normal, after the forensic teams had been and gone. The insurgents would never know they'd been rumbled until it was far too late. "And don't try to slow us down."

He smiled, again, as they stepped into the warm morning air. The street looked deserted, but he could tell they were being watched. The entire neighbourhood would see the girl being marched down the street and know, even if they didn't want to admit it, that there was no escaping the all-seeing eyes. They'd take warning that no one, no matter how high and mighty, was immune to arrest and detention. And when the girl was never seen again, they'd realise the truth. Their lives no longer belonged to them. But then, on a world that belonged completely to a corporation, that had always been true.

His eyes narrowed as he spotted a worker gang being marched up the street. The supervisor held a neural whip in one hand, cracking it threateningly whenever his workers threatened to slow down. Franz nodded in approval, making a mental note to see if the supervisor wanted a transfer to the security division. You couldn't give the conscripted workers an inch or they'd take a mile. Better to make it clear they'd be heavily punished if they stepped out of line, even once. He motioned for the girl to move to one side as the conscripts marched past, their eyes lingering on the prisoner. They'd better look. The girl could be their sister, their girlfriend, their… who knew? They needed to pay attention…

The neural whip cracked against his skin. Lightning flashed. Franz blinked, then screamed in agony. Every nerve in his body had caught fire. He stumbled, collapsing to his knees as the pain went on and on. The neural whip had been overloaded…he tumbled forward, landing face down on the tarmac. His attacker moved the whip away, but it was already too late. He went limp, utterly helpless. Someone stood next to him…he wanted to scream as he sensed, more than felt, them lifting their foot. And then a crushing weight came down on his neck.

"Die," someone hissed.

. . .

Derek grinned as he slammed the heavy wrench into the security officer's head. The man stumbled, clearly too thick-headed to be severely hurt by the blow. Derek pulled his wrench back, then hit him again. Hard. The man tumbled to the ground and lay still. The others tried to fight, but it was already too late. They'd been surrounded without ever recognising the threat.

Security officers, he thought, as he wrapped his arms around Jenny. *They're all the same.*

"Here." Roger shoved a key at him. "Hurry."

"Strip the bodies of weapons and crap," Derek ordered, as he undid the cuffs. "Leave the terminals. They can track them."

Jenny's eyes were shining as she returned the hug. "You came back for me!"

"I had to, didn't I?" Derek kissed her, hard. "What did they find?"

"Enough." Jenny briefly recounted what had happened. "We're screwed."

"Not yet." Roger grinned. "Derek, burn the house. I'll deal with the bodies."

Derek nodded and let go of Jenny. "Stay with Roger," he said. "I'll meet you in a moment or two."

He hurried into the house, noting how the door had been pulled closed without actually being locked. The searchers had ransacked the place, tearing their way through everything. They must have found them somehow, although Derek had no idea *how*. There was no one who knew where they'd lived who might be a traitor. The enemy might just have gotten lucky or...he shook his head. Right now, he had more important things to worry about.

Scooping up what little he could, he splashed flammable liquid everywhere as he ran back down the stairs, then pulled a firelighter from the drawer and set fire to the room. The liquid wouldn't burn for long, but it burned hot. By the time it burned itself out, the flames would have spread to the rest of the house. Derek felt a pang of guilt, both for burning the house and for leaving Jenny alone, as he hurried through the door. He made sure to close it behind him. It was unlikely the local fire brigade was still active, but they'd taken enough chances over the last hour or two.

"Done," he said, as he met the rest of the gang. "We have to move."

Jenny caught his arm. "Where's Gayle?"

"She went ahead of us," Roger said. "We'll meet her when we get to our new home."

Derek looked at her. "Did you leave the house?"

"No." Jenny sounded very certain. "They arrived about an hour after you left. I thought they were going to break down the door."

"They probably would have done," Derek said. He'd seen enough houses raided in the last few days to be sure of it. "Jenny...how the hell did they find us?"

Jenny scowled. "Someone here told them."

Derek gave her a sharp look. "How do you know?"

"You didn't grow up here, amongst the upper classes," Jenny said. The loathing in her voice was almost a living thing. "There's a *lot* of one-upmanship. Everyone does everything in their power to beat their neighbour, or to make their neighbour look bad. Someone spotted us, realised we weren't who we claimed to be and called in a tip. They'd expect to be rewarded after the war is over."

"Assuming they're on the winning side," Derek said. He had no idea what to make of the rumours, but he couldn't believe the marines would give up easily. "What happens if they lose?"

"Then they think it's just business as usual," Jenny said. "No one will punish them."

"We will," Derek said. "We'll make sure of it."

He brooded as they made their way down to the abandoned warehouses. They'd have to sneak across the river somehow, before the search started in earnest. He'd always known betrayal was a possibility, but…he'd thought, somehow, that the locals would keep their mouths shut. Jenny could have told him otherwise…he shook his head. It was just a theory. They didn't *know* they'd been betrayed. The enemy could have had a stroke of luck. It was possible. He'd had an instructor who'd joked, more than once, that Lady Luck was a whore who flirted with everyone, but went home with no one. Derek hadn't appreciated the humour until he'd found himself on a battlefield.

We'll find out, he promised himself. *And, if we were betrayed, we'll kill them.*

"Try not to make too much noise," Roger advised, as they entered the warehouse. "They'll search this place, sooner or later."

"We'll be quiet," Derek said. The warehouse was about as romantic as a toilet and smelt worse. "Look on the bright side. No more labour."

"Yeah," Roger said. "No more excuse to go strolling around the city too."

• • •

Sergeant Duncan Bothell was aware, all too aware, that his company was going to be shipped to the front within a day or two. The thought nagged at him as he led the platoon down the street, keeping a wary eye out for IEDs and other unpleasant surprises. The platoon hadn't taken part in the first landing or the attack on the city, leaving the men largely unprepared for heavy combat even as they readied themselves to leave. He'd done his best to warn them of the horrors ahead, but he knew his words were falling on deaf ears. They wouldn't understand until the bullets started flying and, by then, it would be far too late. The marines would kill half of them before they even started to shed bad habits.

Although the city itself is pretty dangerous, he thought. The company had patrolled the outer edge of the city, then provided support to the security troops as they guarded the bridges. *We can't take a dump without some bastard taking a shot at us.*

He gritted his teeth. The first victories had boosted morale into orbit. They'd crushed the famed Terran Marine Corps and taken a city right from under their noses. But then the campaign had bogged down to the west, with thousands of men battling over a town barely large enough to hold them, while they'd been bombed and sniped and generally given no time to rest on their laurels. General Rask claimed victory was just a matter of time, but Duncan was experienced enough to know better. They might crush the marines, if their reinforcements didn't arrive before it was too late. They'd find it much harder to rebuild the planet. The locals had come to fear the liberators more than the invaders.

"Sergeant! Look!"

Duncan followed Private Azan's finger. A set of bodies lay in the middle of the road, seemingly untouched. Beyond them, a house was burning. He stared for a moment, then tapped his communicator to make a report. It looked as if no one had bothered to report either the bodies or the burning house. He advanced carefully, circling the bodies to make sure there were no hidden surprises. It was technically illegal to hide grenades—or an IED—under dead bodies, but insurgents rarely played by the rules. Very few people did, unless they saw something to gain. And insurgents never saw *anything* to gain from playing fair.

"Crap," he muttered, as he spotted the half-hidden green tabs. Whoever had killed the men had done what they could to keep them from being recognised. "These were security troops."

He was tempted to throw rocks at them from a safe distance, but instead continued his survey until he was sure the bodies hadn't been booby-trapped. He didn't like security officers—no one did, not even their fellows—yet they didn't deserve to have the bodies left in the streets. He updated his report, then inched closer. The poor bastards looked to have been beaten to death. One appeared to have died in screaming agony. But there were no visible wounds.

His earpiece buzzed. "Sergeant, the forensic teams are on the way. Secure the house."

"Which house?" Duncan didn't recognise the voice. That was probably not a good sign. The regular dispatcher might have been pushed aside by the security officers. If they'd taken over…he groaned. Security matters were never fun. He'd probably wind up carrying the blame for something. Anything, like not doing the impossible. "The burning house?"

He shook his head. He could feel the heat, even from their distance. The garden was already charred. He suspected the framework would hold—it was designed to remain stable—but the rest of the house was doomed. It would be cheaper to knock it down and build a whole new house. There was little hope of recovering anything from the wreckage, from bombs to forensic evidence. He was surprised the bodies hadn't been dumped into the blaze. It would have burned them so badly it would have been tricky to figure out what had happened to them.

Maybe they were in a hurry, he thought. The insurgents couldn't have known his patrol schedule. He'd made sure to randomise it, just to make it harder for ambushes to catch them on the hop. *Or maybe they wanted us to know.*

His gaze swept over the remains of the house. There were no clues, nothing that might suggest what had happened. The security officers had died nearby…why? What had they been doing? The simple fact that no one had reported their deaths was worrying. The locals might have seen something, but…he shook his head. They were losing the battle for hearts and minds. Too many locals had resented the system, before the marines had smashed it. It wouldn't be easy to win them back.

And we'll have to interrogate them, he reminded himself. *That won't make us any friends either.*

CHAPTER TWENTY-NINE

On the strategic level, a government may be surprised by an alliance among other states—victims of the above-mentioned border security policy—that presents a considerably greater challenge than any of those states alone. A government that gets bogged down in a brutal campaign is one that is vulnerable to attack from another direction.
—**Professor Leo Caesius**
The Right to be Wrong: How Silencing People Hurts You

GARFIELD HAD LOST TRACK of how long they'd been fighting in Riverside.

He knew, intellectually, that it couldn't have been more than a few days. A week at most, perhaps. But it felt as if they'd been fighting for months, if not years. Houses, streets, entire districts...they'd changed hands, time and time again. The marines were *good*. They'd rigged half the town to blow, they'd used the sewers to pop up behind his forces, they'd even reconfigured the defunct surveillance systems to monitor troop movements, then call down shells on vulnerable targets. Garfield had thought that was impossible. The marines had proved him wrong.

His company—his new company—had been scattered long ago. The chain of command was a fragmented ruin. Garfield wasn't sure who he reported to, or even if he reported to *anyone*. His world had shrunk to a tiny fragment of the town. It was growing increasingly difficult to believe there was anything outside this nightmare, that General Rask and Admiral Nelson really existed. The men under his command were strangers, newcomers funnelled in to replace the dead and wounded. He'd caught a man blowing off his own foot so he'd be evacuated. Garfield had chewed the idiot out, but—in truth—he didn't blame him. The thought of going somewhere—anywhere—else was enough to make him want to do the same.

Another wave of mortar shells crashed down as they pushed towards the bridges. It felt as if they'd always been advancing on the bridges, inching forward at a steady crawl…he felt his chest heave, painfully, as a man was caught by a burst of machine gun fire and disintegrated. Blood and gore flew everywhere. Garfield lowered his eyes, forcing himself forward. The bridges stood ahead of him, a handful of makeshift pillboxes guarding the nearside. He could see tanks on the farside, their guns hurling death into the town. A bunch of marines—he assumed they were marines—were running across the bridge. Garfield snapped commands, ordering his men to gun them down. He'd long since lost all reluctance to shoot fleeing men in the back.

Not that they were really fleeing, he thought, as the marines hit the bridge and lay still. He'd seen enough of their tactics to be sure of it. *They'd have found new positions and continued to fight.*

"Get the engineers up here, quickly," Janelle said. "The bridges…"

A low rumble echoed through the air. Garfield stared in horror as the bridges swayed, then shattered. Pieces of debris crashed into the river, throwing up gouts of water and splashing waves against the shore. The enemy tanks resumed firing, shells smashing down around their position. Garfield took cover, trying not to swear in front of the men as the bridges were destroyed. They'd failed. Hundreds—perhaps thousands—of men were dead, for nothing. The bridges were gone and, with them, all hope of quickly winning the war.

"Fuck," he said.

He reached for his communicator and started to snap orders. Shells hurtled through the air, a handful exploding in flight. The remainder fell on the enemy tanks, silencing them. Garfield thought he saw a figure swimming through the choppy waters, one hand holding something above his head. The shape vanished before he could rise his rifle and fire. He rubbed his eyes, tiredly. Perhaps he was starting to see things. It felt as if he hadn't slept for a week.

The shooting steadily died away as the marines withdrew, conceding the remnants of the town to the invaders. Garfield snorted at the thought, all too aware there was very little left. Riverside was little more than a pile of debris and blackened ruins. The town might have been a nice place to live once, but it wasn't any longer. Between them, the two sides had utterly destroyed it. He heard bursts of shooting in the distance as search parties stumbled across marines who hadn't been able to make it to the bridges before they were dropped. The searchers had orders to take prisoners, but Garfield doubted anyone would bother. If the higher-ups wanted prisoners, they could damn well take them themselves.

He forced himself to inspect what remained of the platoon as they inched away from the riverside. Twelve men, all but one completely unfamiliar. Half of them came from different companies...he shook his head. There were going to be a *lot* of arguments over who had command authority, in the days and weeks to come. He glanced around, wondering what had happened to Lopez. He hadn't seen his immediate commander in... he wasn't sure. It felt like years. Lopez might be dead or wounded or...or what? Perhaps he'd spent the engagement in a different part of the city.

"Stand straight," Janelle muttered. "We have company."

Garfield blinked, then stared in disbelief as a groundcar made its way through the broken streets. His hand dropped to his pistol. He nearly drew it before he caught himself. The only groundcars he'd seen since the invasion—the only *moving* groundcars, he corrected himself—had been rigged by the marines and used to carry explosive into friendly lines. They'd learnt, quickly, to fire on any moving vehicles that looked harmless. They most certainly weren't anything of the sort.

The groundcar stopped. A colonel, in a uniform so fancy Garfield *knew* he'd never seen active service, clambered out. He was followed by a cluster of reporters, who took up position to film the entire affair. Janelle called the platoon to attention as the colonel surveyed them, his eyes narrowing in disgust at the state of their BDUs. Garfield felt a hot flash of pure rage as the colonel scowled. They'd spent the last week fighting through a very hostile city. They hadn't had time to change! The very thought was absurd.

He did his best to calm himself as the colonel started to yammer, babbling about their great victory and how it would lead to even greater victories in the future. It wasn't easy. The colonel seemed to think he'd won the battle personally. His claim they'd killed thousands of marines was almost certainly nonsense. It was hard to be sure—the marines were generally good at retrieving their bodies—but Garfield thought they'd killed a few hundred at most. He doubted they'd been more than a thousand marines in the entire town.

Oh, for a sniper, he thought. The colonel was an easy target. His uniform was so bright and clean that any sniper worthy of the name shouldn't have any trouble putting a bullet through his brains. *If only he went a little closer to the front lines...*

He controlled himself as the colonel finally stopped chattering and turned back to the groundcar. That was it? Garfield's hand dropped to his pistol again, ready to draw the weapon and shoot the idiot in the head. Janelle nudged him, not gently. He was setting a terrible example for the men, but...but the idiot deserved it. The reporters followed the colonel into the groundcar, which drove off down the street. Garfield glared after it, hoping the driver would be foolish enough to take the vehicle over a bump in the road. He didn't believe they'd taken out *all* the IEDs. The marines had hidden the wretched devices everywhere.

"Be careful," Janelle muttered.

"Yeah." Garfield knew he should be grateful. There were limits to what he could get away with, corporate royalty or not. Shooting a superior officer in the head wasn't a harmless little prank, not like abusing his men or mistreating civilians. "Thanks."

Janelle tapped her headset as the follow-up units arrived. "We have orders to report to the camp," she said. "I dare say we'll have a few days of rest."

"Don't say it too loudly," Garfield said. "We can't count on anything."

He rallied the troops, then led them down the street. The town was definitely nothing more than a ruin. It would probably be cheaper to build a new town, rather than rebuild the old one. The bridges themselves would take months to replace…he shook his head. If the bridges were gone, continuing the offensive was going to be tricky. Getting tanks and troops across the river wouldn't be hard. Moving supplies would be a great deal harder.

Not my problem, he thought, as they made their way towards the makeshift camp. A few hours of sleep, a shower, ration bars…it sounded like heaven. He'd happily accept a suicide mission, if he had a chance to get some sleep first. *Someone else can worry about what we do now.*

...

"You lost the bridges," Nelson said, coldly. "They took them out."

"We assumed they would," General Rask said. His voice was flat, but Nelson had no trouble recognising the telltale signs of someone trying to put a good spin on disaster. "We're already moving up bridging gear."

"And you think they'll let you establish a new bridge?" Nelson gritted his teeth. "We're already short of weapons and supplies."

"They'll have no choice," General Rask assured him. The map changed, showing a bridging location below Riverside. "We'll thrust across the river further down"—the map showed an arrow crossing the waters—"quickly, before they have time to react. I'm already moving tanks into position now. They'll secure a lodgement, while the engineers construct a bridge and put it into place. And then we'll resume our drive on the PDCs."

Nelson sighed. The offensive hadn't gone as well as he'd hoped. It was going to make them *all* look bad, particularly if the reinforcements arrived in time to claim the credit. He knew he had to push things, even at the risk of total defeat. There was no way in hell he was going to lose, either to the marines or his superiors. Julia was already trying to come up with a story to explain the slowdown.

And we didn't really anticipate fighting a long, drawn-out campaign, he thought, sourly. *The only upside is that the marines didn't anticipate it either.*

He rubbed his forehead as he considered the latest reports. The insurgency was comparatively mild, compared to others he'd seen, but it was taking a toll. The occupation authorities had been forced to crack down hard, ensuring the local civilians hated them more than the marines. Given time, Nelson was *sure* they could find a political solution, but they didn't have time. And besides, it was unlikely they could come up with something that would please the locals as well as their distant masters. The minimum one side would accept would be well over the maximum the *other* side was prepared to offer.

"Fuck," he said. "General, it is imperative that you smash the enemy positions. Quickly."

"It'll take some time to do more than develop the lodgement," General Rask warned. "We burned through a *lot* of supplies during the fighting. We're bringing them up now..."

"I know." Nelson cut him off. "Just move as quickly as possible."

"The tanks are crossing the river," General Rask assured him. "And once the lodgement is in place, they'll be unable to push us back into the water."

"I hope you're right, General," Nelson said. "I hope you're right."

• • •

The FOB was minimal, very minimal. There were no bars, no brothels, nothing the soldiers would want to use during what little downtime they had before they went back to the war. But it was heavenly, compared to the town. Garfield enjoyed five minutes under a lukewarm shower, followed by a change of clothes and a pair of ration bars. For once, they almost tasted edible. He was practically feeling like a new man by the time he stumbled into his bedding. A few hours of proper sleep, uninterrupted by mortar shells or enemy raids, would do him wonders.

"Lieutenant," a voice said. "I need a word."

Garfield opened his eyes. It felt as if he hadn't slept at all. Captain Lopez stood by his bedding, looking as tired as Garfield felt. There was a scar—a new one—on his face. Garfield guessed the captain had forgotten to duck when the marines had aimed shells into the trenches. Lopez had been lucky to avoid being killed.

"Captain," he managed. He stumbled to his feet and nodded, then remembered they weren't in a combat zone. He was supposed to salute. "What time is it?"

"Stupid o'clock," Lopez said. "I'd have let you sleep longer if I could."

Colonel Asshole must have complained, Garfield thought. Perhaps one of the reporters had noticed Garfield reaching for his pistol. Reporters were generally unobservant, if the old sweats were to be believed, but it only took *one*. *Lopez wouldn't have woken me for his own amusement.*

"Here." Lopez shoved a cigarette packet at him. "I think you've earned this."

"I'd settle for a few days a long way from the front," Garfield said, as he took a cigarette. He'd never been a smoker, but he'd picked up the habit in the trenches. "What's happening, sir?"

"The company has been shot to ribbons," Lopez said. "You're my only surviving LT. The others are dead."

"I'm sorry to hear that," Garfield said, automatically. In truth, he was relieved he hadn't known the other lieutenants any better. "What about the men?"

"Forty-seven reported dead or badly wounded," Lopez said. "Ten more lightly wounded, all on their way to the medics now. It isn't good news."

"It never is," Garfield said. He felt old, too old. "So…what's my punishment?"

Lopez gave him an odd look. "Punishment?"

Garfield blinked. "You woke me up in the middle of the night," he said. It would probably be best not to mention Colonel Asshole to his superior. If the asshole hadn't noticed anything—and he'd been dumb enough to dress like an officer in the field, well within sniper range—there was no point in stirring the pot. "I thought I was in trouble."

"It's early morning," Lopez said. He shrugged. "I'd like to give you a rest, LT, but the blunt truth is that we're needed. I'm assigning you and your scratch platoon to convoy escort duty. It should give you a break, we hope."

"Thanks, I guess." Garfield knew he should be grateful, but it felt as if he were running away. "What's happening here?"

"From what I heard, the tankers are opening a new front," Lopez said. "But that's just a rumour. We failed to take the bridges."

"I was there," Garfield said. He'd had a chance to think, while he'd been washing multiple layers of dirt from his body. "They'd rigged the bridges from the start."

"Probably." Lopez shrugged. "They're bringing up more supplies. You can escort them and...and hope for the best."

Garfield saluted. "When do we leave?"

"There's a convoy leaving at noon," Lopez said. "You'll take it to the landing zone, then bring it back here. You *might* have a chance to snatch up some goodies while you're there. Bring me a burger if you do."

"I'll do my best," Garfield assured him. "And thanks."

"You're welcome," Lopez said. "I'm not sure what's going to happen to me now. The company, or what's left of it, might be folded into another company. Or...you've already picked up a bunch of men who don't belong to you. It could lead to problems further down the line."

"We're going to have to do more training," Garfield said. "And make sure scratch units come up to"—he smiled at the weak pun—"scratch."

Lopez didn't smile. "Get some rest," he ordered. "You'll be departing at noon. I'll see you when you get back."

"Aye, sir." Garfield saluted. "Be seeing you."

He turned and made his way back into the makeshift barracks. His men were still snoring. It would have bothered him terribly as a young man, but now...he'd learnt how to sleep through shooting, bombing and shelling. He felt a rush of affection, mingled with the grim awareness that almost all of the men he'd trained with before going into battle were dead. He glanced at his terminal, noting a handful of mission briefings that had arrived only to be cancelled before he even looked at them, then sat on his bedroll. Janelle lay next to him, her eyes open. She'd probably been awake ever since Lopez entered the room.

"We're escorting a convoy," he said, quietly. The men were supposed to be able to sleep through anything—anything below their sergeant's bellowing, at least—but he didn't want to test it. "Leaving at noon, to the LZ and back."

"Good," Janelle said, equally quietly. "We need time to catch our breath."

"We'd better hope we get it." Garfield had gone through OCS. If one couldn't meet an enemy in open combat, hacking away at the enemy's supply lines was an excellent way to even the odds. It was a low-risk, high-reward tactic. "I doubt it will be peaceful."

"It'll be better than urban combat," Janelle predicted. "Get some rest. I'll wake you nearer the time."

"Thanks," Garfield said. He hoped he *could* sleep, now he knew what was coming. "I don't suppose you have some *real* coffee in your pack?"

"I can work wonders, but not miracles," Janelle said. "You'll just have to make do with military-grade poison."

Garfield laughed. "I suppose it'll have to do."

CHAPTER THIRTY

*On the tactical level, a government may be surprised to discover—
if it is the aggressor—that its opponents are powerful and advanced
enough to deflect its first offensive and then take the offensive
themselves. The Unification Wars included many battles where one
side believed itself to be superior until it was too late to withdraw.*
—**Professor Leo Caesius**
The Right to be Wrong: How Silencing People Hurts You

THERE WERE TIMES, RACHEL ADMITTED TO HERSELF, that she wished Pathfinders *didn't* have such an intimidating reputation. She'd wanted to be a Pathfinder from the moment she'd heard about them and their reputation, and she knew from the inside that they really *were* almost as good as rumour claimed, but there were limits. She would have been happier carrying out the operation as part of a team, instead of on her own. But the four of them were the only Pathfinders under General Anderson's command. Splitting them up was the only way to ensure they could cause maximum mayhem behind enemy lines.

She lay on her stomach, watching the motorway below her. The enemy had taken Riverside, or what was left of the small town, but they weren't resting on their laurels. From what she'd heard, during the brief flight behind enemy lines, they were crossing the river below the town and pushing onwards. It was good tank country on the far side, she admitted grudgingly. The marines would have trouble doing more than harassing the bastards until they reached the mountainous region to the west. There—perhaps—they could be slowed and stopped.

And if we can hit their supply lines, she mused, *we can slow them still further.*

She waited, patiently, as a handful of vehicles moved up and down the road. There was nothing worthy of her time, save—perhaps—for a pair of cars that were carrying a number of civilians who were clearly reporters. She considered engaging them for a moment, before dismissing it as pointless wishful thinking. She'd be surprised if the reporters were writing anything, but puff pieces. The Onge Corporation had had more than enough clout to bury bad news before Earthfall. Now, they probably executed reporters who dared to tell the truth. Or simply kept them from publishing anything. Rachel would have been surprised if the reporters wrote anything that wasn't wholly in praise of the invaders.

Her lips quirked at the thought as she kept waiting. She'd only get one shot at an enemy convoy, one chance to ruin it before she had to run. The enemy probably didn't have the manpower to patrol the areas as aggressively as they should, but they'd do everything in their power to make it harder for the marines to harass them. She kept glancing into the clear blue sky, relying on her enhanced eyes to spot any drones that might be holding position over the motorway. The enemy might just gamble on the drone not being shot down. It was too far east for anyone on the front lines to take a shot at it.

Rachel frowned as she heard the sound of engines in the distance, multiple engines. She leaned forward eagerly, waiting for the vehicles to come into view. An AFV, a troop transport, nine trucks and, bringing up the rear, two more troop transports. The soldiers looked alert, but tired. Her eyes swept over the visible faces, picking out signs of men who'd been pushed right to the limit. She guessed they'd been on the front lines, only a few days ago. The reports had insisted the enemy hadn't tried to rotate its units in and out of the battle line, but it was hard to be sure. Rachel was experienced enough to know the fog of war enveloped everything.

She reached for the detonator and held it, gingerly. The IED had been carefully hidden when she'd arrived, and she'd done everything she could to ensure it couldn't be triggered by accident, but she'd been all too aware patrolling troops might have spotted it before a target came into range. Or a stray signal might have set it off, no matter what she'd done to prevent it. She hadn't dared set up a landline. *That* would have led the enemy troops to her position instantly.

Her eyes flickered over the convoy. It was tempting, very tempting, to try to take out the troop transports. The men in the vehicles would do their level best to kill her, and her comrades, if she gave them the chance. But they weren't the most important targets, not here. She braced herself as the AFV moved past the IED, gliding in and out of the blast radius before she could push the trigger. It wasn't the target, she told herself. She had to take out the supply trucks. If she was lucky, the IED would set off a chain reaction that would blow the entire convoy to hell. And even if she wasn't lucky...

Now, she thought.

...

Garfield felt uneasy, even though he'd had a pretty good day by army standards. The drive to the landing zone had been uneventful and, once they'd arrived, they'd had a chance to relax and blow off some steam before the convoy was loaded and ready to depart. He'd ordered his men not to drink anything alcoholic, but otherwise to do whatever they wanted as long as they reported for duty on time. They'd headed straight for the brothel. Garfield himself had been more interested in resting, then catching up with his letters home. He almost felt human again by the time the convoy departed the LZ.

He scowled as they made their way down the motorway. The briefing officers had cautioned him that the insurgents were nasty bastards, rigging IEDs everywhere they could to disrupt supply operations. Garfield believed them. He'd seen burned-out vehicles scattered along the ring road, AFVs and supply trucks that had been stripped of anything useful and then simply abandoned. Someone was going to have to clean up the mess, but the briefers had been vague on when that was going to happen. They'd dropped weak hints about trouble with the clear-up crews.

His eyes swept the horizon. The motorway was flat, a straight line leading directly from Haverford to Riverside, but the surrounding landscape offered far too much cover for his peace of mind. They were in friendly territory—they'd yet to pass the original front lines—yet it didn't *feel* friendly. He thought he could feel hostile eyes watching them from the distant hills, biding their time. Rumour insisted that thousands of locals had run away from the towns and cities, fleeing into the hills and surviving by their wits alone. Garfield believed it. The locals knew how to live off the land. It wouldn't be a very pleasant life, but at least they'd be alive.

The explosion shocked him, even though he'd half-expected it. The transport skidded as a blast of heat washed over him, coming to a halt as bullets cracked through the air. Garfield grabbed his rifle and jumped down, a moment before the second explosion. The supply trucks were burning, the arms and ammunition within catching fire and exploding with terrifying speed. He thought he saw bullets—more bullets—flying out of the trucks, spinning in all directions. A troop transport crashed into the rear of the supply trucks, coming to a halt as men jumped for cover. They were still under attack!

"Up there," Janelle shouted. "I saw the flash!"

Garfield waved at the AFV. "Hit it!"

The AFV opened fire, machine guns raking the enemy position. It looked as if nothing could survive, although Garfield knew better than to believe it. The marines could have rigged a cluster of weapons to fire automatically, then retreated the moment the convoy came into view. God knew they'd captured enough arms and ammunition to make it workable. The spooks claimed the marines were running short of ammunition, but Garfield didn't believe it. They'd insisted the planet would be recaptured without a shot being fired and that the marines would surrender. Neither one had happened. Garfield had the scars to prove it.

"Bring up the mortars," he snapped. The shells wouldn't be *that* effective in the undergrowth, but they would serve as a distraction. "Advance by squads!"

He led the way forward, directing the men to fan out and encircle the enemy position as the shells crashed down. The marines might have started running already, but they'd have some problems getting out of the areas before his men started breathing down their necks. He keyed his communicator, ordering the mortar crews to start firing further to the north. If the enemy were retreating, they'd find themselves caught in the middle of the shelling and...

And if we push ahead quickly, he thought grimly, *we might just overrun them before they make their escape.*

...

Rachel cursed under her breath as she rolled out of the hide, machine gun bullets crashing through the trees above her head. She felt a flash of *déjà vu* as she caught herself, clutching her pistol in one hand as she stumbled to her feet and hurried down the hill. Whoever was in command of the enemy troops was sharp, or he'd drilled them well. She'd hoped to harass them a little more, perhaps pick off their leader before she sauntered away, but it wasn't going to happen. They'd shoved back, hard. She hoped they thought they'd killed her.

They probably want my head, with or without my body attached, she thought. By any reasonable standards, she'd done well. Nine supply trucks had been reduced to burning rubble in the blink of an eye, the remainder badly scorched even if they hadn't been destroyed. The secondary explosions had done a lot of damage. *The poor bugger in command is screwed unless he manages to score a kill.*

She glanced up, sharply, as she heard shells dropping through the air. They were too close for comfort...she ducked, an instant before the first shell hit the ground and exploded. The force of the blast picked her up and threw her down the hill, banging her head into a tree trunk. If she hadn't been wearing her helmet, it would have killed her. Even with her helmet, the shock of the impact stunned her. She slid down, hitting the ground hard enough to hurt. Her implants automatically released painkillers into her bloodstream. She'd been damn lucky not to break a leg.

Fuck, she thought. She could *hear* the bastards crashing through the foliage, shouting commands to each other as they advanced. More shells were falling to the north, steadily advancing *away* from her. She felt dazed, but forced herself to clamber to her feet and keep moving. One hand unhooked a grenade from her belt and held it at the ready as she tried to put some distance between her and the searchers. She needed to find a place to hide. *If they search properly...*

A shot cracked through the air. "Stop! Stop right there!"

Rachel threw the grenade behind her, then dropped to the ground and crawled forward. Another bullet snapped over her head, an instant before the grenade exploded. She heard someone scream as she kept moving, hoping the shock of the blast had deterred the enemy from chasing her. Her implants were sounding the alert, warning her that even *Pathfinders* had limits. It might be better to stay low and hide, hoping she could remain out of sight until darkness. It wouldn't be long. Night was already starting to fall.

She heard running footsteps behind her, two...no, *three*...enemy soldiers. She went still, hoping they'd overlook her. No such luck. A weight landed on top of her, hard enough to make her grunt in pain. She readied herself to boost, despite the risk of combining two different drugs in her bloodstream, then froze as someone pressed a pistol to her skull. She was tough, but not tough enough to survive a bullet through her brains at point-blank range.

"Stay very still," a voice cautioned. The weight on her back shifted. The man was sitting up, keeping his knees pressed into the small of her back. He was well-trained, she admitted sourly. She could have dislodged him, if there hadn't been a gun pressed to her head, but only with enhanced strength. A regular woman would have found it impossible. "Don't move a muscle."

"Fucking bastard," another man snapped. His anger was almost a living thing. "Kill the dickhead. Cut off his balls."

Rachel would have smiled, if things hadn't been so grim. They thought she was a man? She said nothing as they yanked her hands behind her back and secured them with a tie...a tie she could break, once she boosted. The endless series of threats continued as they searched her, their hands roving all over her body...they stopped, dead, as they touched her breasts. Rachel had never been well-endowed—military training took its toll—but she very clearly wasn't *male*. She almost laughed as hands poked between her legs, before withdrawing in confusion. Idiots. Didn't they know what could be hidden up there?

"She's a girl," someone said.

"So what?" The one who had threatened to cut off her non-existent balls sounded irked, as if the speaker had said something stupid. "So is the sergeant."

Rachel did her best to look harmless as they rolled her over. The soldiers glared down at her, their eyes suggesting a degree of hatred that worried her. She'd met soldiers who enjoyed doing horrible things—and policemen who thought abusing civilians was one of the perks of an ill-paid job—but these soldiers had been pushed right to the limit. They needed a long period of leave, not convoy escort duties. She assessed them quickly, trying to determine her chances. Five men, all clearly experienced...ignorant enough to assume the zip-tie could hold her, yet probably capable of putting up a real fight when she broke loose. She braced herself, wondering if she dared boost. The drugs might kill her. The enemy certainly *would* when they realised what she was.

The soldiers stepped to one side as two more figures strode into view. A young man, barely out of his teens, wearing a uniform that suggested he was an officer. There were no visible rank stripes, but his uniform was definitely a cut or two above the others. He was followed by a stocky man—no, a *woman*. Rachel was mildly surprised, even though one of her captors had reminded his fellows that their sergeant was female. She eyed the woman thoughtfully, knowing better than to expert any mercy from her. Female soldiers were rare, even in the corps. They had to be tough to keep up with the men. And a sergeant wouldn't command the respect of her men unless she could do everything they could do and more besides.

"She's a woman, sir," her captor said, tightly. He'd kept his pistol pointed firmly at Rachel's head. Damn. He was going to be a problem. "And a sniper."

"And now a prisoner," the officer said. His voice was faintly aristocratic, although he sounded as if he was losing the accent. Close contact with soldiers would do that. He'd probably led from the front, bedding down with the men instead of retreating to a proper bedroom each night. It was almost admirable. "Who are you?"

Rachel studied him as his men helped her to her feet. Young, but...experienced *and* at the very end of his tether. She would have felt sorry for him, if he hadn't been on the other side. She knew what it was like to be pushed closer and closer to breaking point...the Slaughterhouse had prepared her for heavy combat, training her to keep going. The enemy probably didn't have anything like it. Their officers wouldn't understand what they were facing until they went into combat for the first time.

"Rifleman Opel Moonchild, Oliver's Own," she lied, smoothly. She hadn't been carrying anything that'd mark her out as anything more than a common or garden marine. Marines were hardly common...hopefully, they'd assume she'd been caught behind enemy lines and tried to set up an ambush instead of making her way to friendly territory. "I got a little lost."

"A likely story," the female sergeant sneered. Her accent was much like her soldiers, but there was a faint hint of something familiar in her tone. Terra Nova? Could she be a retired marine? It didn't seem likely, but it wouldn't be the first time a retired marine had found employment with the corprats. "You're not lost."

"No," Rachel agreed. There was no point in pretending otherwise. "I know precisely where I am."

She glanced from face to face, assessing them again. The sergeant was the greatest threat, if only because she probably wouldn't underestimate Rachel. A female marine was nothing to sneer at, even without enhancements. She'd probably start suggesting shackles in a moment, making escape difficult if not impossible. Rachel's head ached as she leaned forward, trying to pack as much malice into her next words as she could. If they cooperated...

"I killed your trucks," she sneered. "How many of your people died?"

The man beside her drove his fist into her chest. It hurt, but helped. She bent over, pretending to gasp for breath. For a moment, the pistol wasn't pointed at her chest. She boosted, snapping the zip-tie effortlessly and lashing out at the armed man. The gun went off as his ribs shattered under her blow, the bullet going wide. Rachel smiled, then pulled herself up...

...And smashed her fist, as hard as she could, into the sergeant's throat.

CHAPTER THIRTY-ONE

And, if it is the defender, it may be surprised because the troops along the border have not reported enemy forces massing on the far side, either because the troops themselves didn't dare send the message or it vanished somewhere between the border and the government itself. By the time reality crashes in, it may be too late.
—**Professor Leo Caesius**
The Right to be Wrong: How Silencing People Hurts You

GARFIELD COULDN'T MOVE.

He hadn't been quite sure what to do, when it turned out they'd captured a woman. He wouldn't have hesitated to shoot a man—he was damned if he'd risk lives capturing a sniper—but a woman? It had been hard to believe the marine even *was* a woman. She looked like a man, if a slightly effeminate one. And yet...

She moved with blinding speed, impossible speed. The soldier guarding her tumbled to the ground. Garfield heard the sound of breaking bones as the marine spun around, bringing her fist up to hit Janelle in the throat. Janelle's head snapped back, so hard Garfield *knew* she was dead. The impact had broken her neck as well as crushed her throat. He stumbled back in utter shock, so stunned he couldn't bring himself to draw his weapon.

The marine spun again and ran, moving like the wind. She was out of sight before he could so much as bring himself to do anything.

"Fuck!" Garfield shook himself, violently. "Janelle!"

The sergeant was lying on the ground, quite dead. Garfield knelt beside her, half-remembered medical training surfacing in his head as he searched desperately for a pulse. It was pointless. Her neck was broken, twisted out of shape. She looked so still, so small, as if something had vanished the moment she'd died. Garfield felt tears prickling at the corner of his eyes. Janelle had taught him everything he knew, from how to respond to enemy fire to how to lead men in combat. And now she was dead, killed by a treacherous bitch who'd pretended to surrender until she'd had a clear shot. Raw hatred washed through him. The bitch was going to die!

He tapped his communicator, snapping orders to the mortar crew. The odds of hitting anything were very low—the marine had run like the wind, quite literally—but he didn't care. The bitch might just be hit…he felt a wave of bitter remorse. If he'd shot the captive at once, if he'd ordered her killed before he knew she was a woman, Janelle would be alive. She wouldn't be happy with shooting surrendering men out of hand—and she'd tell him so, when they were alone—but at least she'd be alive. She hadn't deserved to die. Not like that. Not…

The ground shook as mortar shells plunged down to the north. Garfield forced himself to stand, picking up Janelle's body and slinging it over his shoulder. She was surprisingly light, for such a stocky woman. She felt empty, as if she'd already gone…she *had* already gone. Garfield had thought he'd grown used to losing men, but…Janelle had been a friend. He'd known her. Her death meant more to him than losing a dozen men he didn't know.

"Back to the convoy," he growled. "Hurry."

The shells continued to fall, pounding the hillside. Garfield hesitated, then reluctantly ordered the gunners to stop firing. There was no time to search for the marine's body, even if he'd been inclined to take the risk. Garfield knew himself to be in good health—his genetic enhancements had seen to that, even before he'd joined the army—and yet, he doubted *he* could have snapped Janelle's neck with a single blow. What *was* the bitch? Opel Moonchild, she'd called herself. A RockRat name? He'd never heard of any RockRats joining the military, but every society had dissidents. Or... she might not have given them her real name at all.

He felt Janelle's absence like a physical blow as he walked back to the convoy. The supply trucks were burnt-out ruins, along with one of the troop transports. The remainder of the convoy was intact, for what it was worth. He lowered the body into the nearest transport, then ordered his remaining men to mount up. Space was going to be tight, but they'd have to deal with it. They didn't dare stay near the hills any longer. There could be other marines out there, watching them.

"Sir." The driver looked wary, as if he expected to have his head bitten off. "HQ is demanding an update."

Captain Lopez is going to kill me, Garfield thought numbly. *And then I'll be resurrected so Colonel Asshole can kill me. And then General Rask will want his turn to kill me.*

The thought mocked him as he took the headset and reported, as clearly and concisely as he could. HQ would be shocked, then...then what? Would he be blamed? Or would his superiors try to pin the blame on someone else? His fists clenched as he realised they might try to blame everything on *Janelle*. He'd kill them if they tried. Damn it, he really *would* kill them.

He expected someone to shout at him, but—instead—he was merely ordered to reach the FOB as quickly as possible. Garfield sat back down, resting his back against the hard metal bulkhead. Janelle's body lay at the rear, accusingly. He wondered, suddenly, what would happen to her. Some bodies were shipped home, but others...he promised himself he'd make sure her body was treated well. If she had any last wishes, he'd carry them out. It wasn't as if he couldn't afford it. His trust fund had enough money to purchase an entire starship, if there was one available. The last he'd heard, there were no starships on sale for love or money.

Night fell rapidly as they drove into the FOB. Captain Lopez stood just inside the gates, looking grim. Garfield passed command to a newly-minted corporal he barely knew—hopefully, he'd be able to get the men bedded down without any problems—and jumped to the ground. Lopez nodded to him, then jerked his head towards the distant command post. Garfield followed him. The captain didn't stop until they were well out of earshot.

"What the fuck happened?"

Garfield took a breath. "We were ambushed, sir," he said. He didn't want to talk about it, but there was no choice. "They lured us into a trap and fucked us."

He found himself replaying the whole scene in his mind, time and time again. What could he have done differently? Spotted the IED ahead of time? Not tried to chase the marine? Shot her, the moment they caught her? Or...it didn't matter. There was no escaping the simple fact Janelle was dead. He'd killed her, as surely as if he'd put his gun to her head and pulled the trigger. He'd killed her.

"I see," Lopez said, when Garfield had finished. "You should count yourself lucky. If you weren't *you*..."

His voice trailed off. Garfield gritted his teeth. He knew what Lopez meant. If he hadn't been an Onge, they would have thrown the book at him. They *should* throw the book at him. He was a failure. He'd gotten his sergeant killed...he'd thought Janelle was damn near impossible to kill. But it had only taken one mistake to take her life...

"I know, sir," he said, miserably. "I'm sorry, sir."

"Sorry won't bring any of the destroyed supplies back." Lopez pointed at Garfield's shoulder, where his stripes should be. "If you were anyone else, you'd have lost those stripes a thousand times over."

He snorted, rudely. "They've been putting together a new order of battle. It looks like we're going to be folded into another company or two. Fuck knows which of us is going to be in command. Captain Higgs is dead, I've been told, but Lieutenant Rawlings is pretty senior and we're in disgrace"—he shrugged—"we'll see how it goes. For now, get some rest. I'll see you in the morning for your very public ass-chewing."

"Yes, sir," Garfield said. "What'll happen to Janelle's body?"

"She'll be buried with the others, I imagine," Lopez said. "Bed. Now."

Garfield nodded—he was too angry to salute—and headed back to the makeshift barracks. They looked chaotic, dozens of newcomers added to the mix until there was barely any room for him and his men. He gritted his teeth as he recovered Janelle's rucksack and put it to one side. By tradition, anything of hers that wasn't specifically mentioned in her will was to be divided amongst the company. He doubted she had anything worth the effort. A pack of cigarettes—he'd never actually seen her smoke—a change of clothes and little else. No family photographs, no letters from friends or lovers, no nothing. He felt his heart twist again as he put the supplies out for whoever wanted them. Janelle had deserved better...

...And she hadn't deserved to die.

• • •

Rachel gritted her teeth as the drugs started to wear off. Her entire body ached, as if she'd tried to go into the ring and fight three very aggressive men at the same time. The booster drugs hadn't combined well with the painkillers, she realised dully. Her leg hurt so badly she was half-convinced it was broken, even though cold logic assured her it wasn't. She stumbled, then tumbled to the ground. There was no sign of pursuit, but that was meaningless. They'd done their level best to kill her with mortars.

They must have really been pissed, she thought, as she rolled over and lay on her back. *I killed their fucking sergeant.*

She felt a twinge of sympathy, even though she knew she'd done the right thing. A sergeant she'd met once had told her that sergeants protected troops from their officers, from aristocratic fools who thought their troops were servants to incompetents who thought standing up and marching very slowly towards the enemy was the height of military brilliance. A good sergeant was worth his—or her—weight in just about anything. And she'd killed one...

It doesn't matter, she told herself, as she sat up. Her leg was sore—it was probably bruised—but it was definitely not broken. *I have to keep moving.*

She forced herself to her feet, staggering forward as darkness fell across the land. It was hard to tell if the enemy was watching for her, if indeed *anyone* was watching for her. She'd have to keep moving until she reached the pickup, then call for a Raptor to pull her out. She groaned inwardly, cursing under her breath. She'd hoped to spend longer harassing the enemy before she'd had to flee. But things hadn't gone the way she'd hoped.

I took out their supply trucks, she thought. She wasn't fool enough to believe she'd taken out *all* the supplies, but she was pretty sure she'd put a crimp in their plans. *That'll slow them down. A little.*

Gritting her teeth, she kept walking.

• • •

"They've definitely made their way across the river, sir," Lieutenant Yen reported. "Our scouts report they've started to establish a secure lodgement."

"I noticed," Gerald growled. A lodgement—particularly there—wouldn't be anything like as useful as the bridges, but the bridges were no longer an option. His men had ensured they fell completely, to the point they couldn't be repaired in less than a month. "And there's not much we can do about it, is there?"

He pushed his irritation aside as he studied the map. He'd expected the enemy to find another way to cross the river—they had no choice, if they wanted to win—but it was still annoying. And worrying. They'd have problems developing the lodgement as long as they needed to use tanks and sealed transports to move men across the river, but that would change the moment they built a bridge. Their replacement bridge wouldn't last very long, depending on what they used to build it, yet...it didn't *have* to last very long. The bridge just needed to endure long enough to let them transfer their army from one side of the river to the other.

"Lieutenant," he said. "Have the gunners had a chance to change position?"

"Yes, sir," Lieutenant Yen said. "They've also rearmed, but they're short on ammunition and other supplies."

Gerald nodded. They'd captured plenty of enemy supplies during the invasion, and the planners had assumed—as always—that consumption would be an order of magnitude more than expected, but it they were still burning through their supplies at a terrifying rate. They certainly weren't getting any more supplies, at least for the moment. Gerald had tried to think of a way to drop supplies from orbit, but it was impossible. The enemy fleet would blast them out of space before they reached the surface.

He frowned as he studied the map. It would be easy enough to send a flying column around the enemy positions and drive directly on the landing zone, but the enemy fleet would turn them into scrap. He'd already lost two Raptors, and a dozen drones, because they strayed too close to the fleet's weapons. It was something to bear in mind, if Captain Stumbaugh's plan worked. And if he didn't...

"Order the gunners to shell the enemy lodgement, then fall back as planned," he said, after a moment. "Did the recon team report back?"

"Yes, sir," Yen said. "The sappers say it should be doable."

"Let's hope they're right." Gerald let out a breath. There was little hope of stopping the enemy before they reached the mountains. The land was ideal for tanks, unless...his wild plan actually worked. It would require some careful timing, and coordination with the fleet, and probably end with him getting put in front of a court-martial. "Tell them to start preparations at once."

And hope to hell, he added silently, *that the enemy doesn't realise what we're doing ahead of time.*

• • •

"Rachel!"

Rachel tensed, half-expecting to see enemy soldiers waiting for her. It took longer than it should have done—her head was still filled with mush—to realise enemy soldiers wouldn't know her name. Phelps was running towards her, Perkins keeping his distance by the pickup point. Rachel almost fell as she forced herself to stand up straight. She'd been told it was important to make sure her fellows knew if she was injured, but she had her pride. Rachel had worked too hard for respect to let them down now.

"What happened?" Phelps looked her up and down, frowning. "Are you alright?"

"Nearly got caught." Rachel ran through a brief explanation. "They came pretty close to killing me."

"It looks like they *did* kill you," Phelps said. "You look like a zombie from that stupid flick we watched when we went on leave."

"And promptly got thrown out of the cinema," Rachel reminded him. She knew what he was doing. He wanted to make sure she was thinking straight, that there was nothing wrong with her memory. "We probably shouldn't have laughed so much."

"No." Phelps snorted. "But it really *was* a stupid movie."

Rachel nodded as they made their way towards the pickup point. Whoever had written the script had known absolutely nothing about the military. She could forgive that—maybe—but not the untalented actress who'd dangled her boobs across the screen when Rachel had wanted to watch death and destruction. Not that there'd been much of that, she recalled. The producers hadn't realised the military would simply drive its tanks into—and *through*—the zombie horde. The threat would have lasted as long as it took to crush the zombies into a bloody stain on the floor.

"Let me check you," Perkins said. "I've already called for the Raptor."

"What about Mike?" Rachel frowned. Bonkowski hadn't reached the pickup point yet. She had no idea if he would. He'd planned to do something that was either brilliant or stupid, depending on whether or not it worked. "What happened to him?"

"I don't know," Perkins said. He rolled up her trousers and examined her leg. "You're bruised and battered, but otherwise fine. I'd tell you not to put any weight on that leg, but I don't think you'd listen to me."

"I'd just have to requalify before returning to the team," Rachel said. Perkins could, technically, order her to go on medical leave, but it was a little pointless when there was no safe rear area. "Give me a day or two and I'll be back to normal."

Perkins looked displeased. "If it gets any worse, I expect you to tell me," he said. "Or a medic, if you don't want to confess your sins to me."

Rachel made a rude gesture. "I think you know I'm honest enough to tell you if I was having real problems."

"Hah." Perkins rolled his eyes, dramatically. "And the next SF soldier I meet who admits to being wounded, and unfit for duty, will be the first. If I had a credit for everyone who insisted that a serious wound was just a mere scratch…"

"Look sharp," Phelps said. "Here comes the boss."

Bonkowski strode into the clearing, just as the Raptor appeared in the distance. "How did it go?"

"Well, Rachel nearly got caught," Perkins said, ignoring the sharp look Rachel sent him. "But otherwise, we did well."

"I nearly got caught too," Bonkowski said. "Luckily, I managed to put them off the scent by running away very quickly."

He grinned. "Between us, we probably gave them a shock. And we might even have slowed them down too."

CHAPTER THIRTY-TWO

It is not just governments that fall prey to this kind of disaster. Corporations, religions and all other forms of human organisation tend to encounter the same problem. If they regard dissent as treason, they will find themselves caught by surprise, by anything between a superior product from a rival firm to a sudden shift in government policy.
—**Professor Leo Caesius**
The Right to be Wrong: How Silencing People Hurts You

"DON'T TRY TO BE CLEVER," DEREK WARNED, as they walked down the street arm in arm. "Remember, you have to look harmless until you're not."

"I got it," Jenny said. There was a hint of irritation in her tone. "I listened to you."

I hope so, Derek thought. *If you're wrong to listen to me...*

He let out a breath. They *had* to look innocent, just another upper-class couple out for a walk. They'd changed their appearance as much as possible, using wigs and padding in a bid to fool prying eyes, but he was uncomfortably aware they were all too exposed. A watching surveillance system might note their similarities to a pair of wanted insurgents and sound the alarm. Derek had read the documents the marines had salvaged, before they'd taken the old system down. The cameras were just the tip of an ever-watching iceberg.

A line of enemy soldiers marched past them, eyes flickering from left to right as they moved. They kept a wary distance from a handful of parked groundcars, as if they feared the vehicles had been used to hide IEDs. Derek smiled inwardly, despite the certain knowledge they could expect no mercy if they were caught. That was *his* work. The enemy knew they weren't welcome within the city. They didn't feel safe anywhere.

Particularly as someone shelled the government complex last night, he mused, as they turned into the shopping district. *They have to feel really unsure of themselves.*

He looked around with interest, noting how a handful of shops had reopened despite the chaos. The invaders were doing their level best to introduce a new currency, ensuring—deliberately or not—that pre-invasion bank accounts were effectively useless. Derek wondered how the rich—the former rich—would cope when they realised most of their wealth had vanished at the touch of a button. They'd have to *work* to earn enough to buy their daily bread. The invaders were still handing out ration bars, but feeding the entire city was a monumental commitment. It was only a matter of time before they put the entire population to work.

His eyes narrowed as he spotted the brothel. It would never have been established before the war. Derek had heard rumours, but he'd always assumed they were nothing more than locker room talk. Now…a pair of enemy guards stood outside, either protecting the girls or keeping them prisoner. The girls probably hadn't volunteered for the duty, Jenny had said. There'd been no arguing with her about it. Derek hoped she was right. He'd have hated to have to execute the girls for collaboration after the war.

Although they're probably getting more than enough punishment right now, he thought, as he saw a line of enemy soldiers form outside the building. They were joined by a handful of men in civilian clothes, workers just like he'd been a few days ago. He felt a stab of irritation, mingled with the grim awareness the workers probably hadn't had much choice either. *If they told me I had a choice between working or starving, they probably told everyone else the same thing.*

He put the thought aside as they reached the bottom of the street. He had every intention of executing *real* collaborators, but he didn't want to hurt people who'd had no choice. It would give the invaders a chance to rally the locals against the invaders, particularly if the invaders managed to start the planet on the route back to normality. Derek knew there was no going back for *him*, and probably his comrades as well, but he could understand the attraction for people who *hadn't* committed outright treason. The war had thrown the entire world into chaos. Going back to the days before the invasion sounded very tempting.

"There," Jenny muttered. "That's the place, right?"

Derek nodded as his eyes took in the recruiting office. It was smaller than he'd expected, with only one guard standing outside. He'd heard the enemy was having problems meeting all their manpower requirements, but it was the first time he'd *seen* it. The guard probably assumed the soldiers had checked and rechecked everyone coming in and out of the shopping district. It didn't look as if he was taking the job very seriously. A combat infantryman would have known better.

He's more of a clerk with a gun, Derek thought. He knew bureaucracy was important, if one wanted to keep an army running, but experience had taught him bureaucracy could become a cancer very quickly. *That idiot shouldn't be allowed anywhere near the front lines.*

He tensed as they walked towards the office, keeping a wary eye out for watchdogs. It *could* be a trap, after all. He spotted a handful of sensors scattered near the door, watching and waiting…it didn't look as if they had sniffers, but the devices were so tiny they were practically invisible. The enemy might have decided they were useless. Derek and the others had set off so many false positives, over the last few weeks, that the enemy *had* to have stopped taking the alerts entirely seriously. They were going to bitterly regret it.

The guard looked them up and down, his eyes lingering on Jenny's cleavage for just a second too long. Derek felt a hot flash of rage, even though he knew he should be grateful. If the guard was paying attention to an obvious distraction, he might not be paying attention to the real threat. He kept walking, pushing the door open and stepping into the shop. The guard made no move to stop him. Inside, the air was surprisingly cool. A recruiting officer who might as well have stepped off a recruiting poster sat behind a desk, studying them with gimlet eyes. Derek wasn't impressed. It hadn't taken him longer than a week to realise that soldiers could either look good or *be* good. The recruiter was dressed to impress, not to kill.

"Hello," he said, trying to sound nervous. "I was wondering if you had any work for me."

The recruiter shrugged. "And what qualifications do you have?"

Derek babbled out a string of useless answers, all the while looking around to make sure there was only one person in the office. There was a second room behind the first, but he couldn't hear anyone inside. It certainly sounded as though they were alone…save for the guard outside, of course. The office looked like someone had crammed a bunch of cheap furniture inside in a hurry. He couldn't spot any emergency alarms or anything else that should worry him. The contempt in the recruiter's eyes would have annoyed him, if it hadn't been what he wanted. They'd gone to some trouble to draw up the most useless resume they could.

The recruiter looked thoroughly displeased when he'd finished. "I think we'll be sending you to training," he said. His eyes flickered to Jenny. "And you?"

Derek reached into his pocket and drew his pistol. "Keep your hands where I can see them, please," he said. "Do as I tell you and you won't be hurt."

"You…" The recruiter looked shocked. "You can't…"

"Stand up," Derek ordered. "Keep your hands in the air. One false move and I blast you."

He searched the recruiter quickly, removing a terminal, a pistol and a small knife. It wasn't army-issue, somewhat to his surprise. He pocketed the pistol, then ordered the recruiter into the corner. The moment the man's back was turned, Derek cut the recruiter's throat with his own knife.

"Shit," Jenny said. "I..."

Derek shot her a warning look as he lowered the body to the floor, then peered into the next room. It was a small kitchen, rather than the office he'd expected. A pile of paperwork sat on the table, mocking testament to the destroyed planetary datanet. Derek glanced at the documents, then stuffed them into his bag. They'd be time to go through them later, when they got back home. He picked up a handful of passes and pocketed them too—they might come in handy, if they could be altered later—before sweeping the rest of the room. The office was almost a disappointment. It looked as if the invaders hadn't anticipated hordes of recruits.

Even with them tightening the screws, people are still waiting to see who comes out on top, Derek thought. There were hundreds of rumours about the war, ranging from the marines being utterly defeated to the marines winning effortlessly. The official bulletins were so bland they were completely uninformative. Derek hoped that was a good sign. *If the marines are defeated, countless fence-sitters will swear blind they were on the other side all along.*

He checked the desk as he stepped back into the outer office, then looked at Jenny. "When I give the word," he said as he rigged the IED under the chair, "call your admirer in."

Jenny gave him a dirty look, but did as she was told. The guard stepped into the office, blinking in confusion. Derek shot him in the head, then stepped over the body and peered outside. There were no prospective recruits waiting to be seen. Derek went back to the chair, armed the IED and led Jenny back out. The surveillance devices would see them come and go, but hopefully they wouldn't be able to follow them all the way back to their lair. Hopefully. Derek looked up, all too aware he wouldn't be able to see a drone holding position in the clear blue sky. There was no way to *know* they weren't being watched.

"Stay calm," he ordered, as they made their way down the street. "As far as they know, we're just a pair of upper-class twits."

"Got it." Jenny sounded excited, not fearful. "How long do you think we have?"

Derek shrugged. The recruiting office was in the shopping district. The enemy ran patrols through the sector all the time, randomly shifting their timetables to make it harder for the insurgents to plot an ambush. It wouldn't take long for them to notice the guard was missing, even if the office *wasn't* supposed to check in every so often. *Derek* would have been a little more careful, if he'd been on the opposing side. He supposed it really *was* a sign the enemy were having manpower problems.

Or that they didn't face any real threats until the marines invaded, he thought. He was proud of his service, but he had to admit *he* hadn't faced any real threats until the war began either. He'd had to learn everything the instructors hadn't taught him, everything they hadn't known themselves, on the job. *They might not have realised the risks either.*

He tensed as they passed another platoon of enemy soldiers. They looked surprisingly unconcerned, for troops who knew they were in a war zone. Perhaps they'd just come off their patrol route, he mused; perhaps they'd already slipped into post-patrol mode when they should have been keeping an eye open for trouble. He wondered, idly, where they'd been patrolling. The other side of the river? It was supposed to be bad. The enemy had actually conceded large swathes of the districts to the gangs. If they won the war, they'd deal with the gangs afterwards.

"So." Jenny held his hand tightly. "What now?"

Derek started to answer, but stopped when he heard an explosion behind him. Someone had just tried to go into the recruiting office, triggering the bomb. The locals hit the ground, cowering as if they expected incoming shellfire. Derek dropped too—it wouldn't do to stand out, not now—and crawled forward. Jenny followed him, glancing behind nervously. The enemy patrol was no longer in view, but if they'd checked the records and realised they'd passed the bombers...

"This way," he said. He scrambled to his feet and led her into an alley. "Get your wig off and jumper on."

"Are you well?" Jenny grinned as she yanked the jumper over her shirt. "You normally want me to take my top *off*."

"They're going to be looking for a redhead with a low-cut top," Derek reminded her, before realising he was being teased. "Don't forget to take off the padding too."

"Just think how disappointed they'd be if they caught me," Jenny said. "I think…"

"You'd wind up in the brothel if they caught you," Derek said, sharply. He changed into a different outfit, a lowly worker's uniform, then hurried down the alleyway. "And you don't want that, do you?"

Jenny said nothing as they emerged onto the street and headed down towards the riverside. Derek hoped she wasn't sulking again, even though she was finally getting a chance to do something more useful than sitting around. And…he put the thought out of his head, concentrating on looking like a young man out for a stroll with his girlfriend as they passed another enemy patrol. They shouldn't notice anything, unless they really *were* being tracked. The patrol could have strict orders to let them pass, seemingly unmolested. Derek wished, suddenly, for the simplicity of a battlefield. There'd be no doubt who was on what side.

He breathed a sigh of relief as they kept moving, slipping through streets empty of both enemy soldiers and civilians. If they were being watched, the watchers were keeping their distance. A handful of homeless men eyed them warily, but did nothing. Derek was surprised they were still on the streets. The invaders hadn't done *much* for them, but they had opened a handful of abandoned homes for the homeless. He wouldn't have blamed the homeless guys for taking the homes. They didn't have anything else.

Roger stepped out of the shadows as they reached the safehouse, one finger touching his lip. Derek nodded and stood still long enough for Roger to check them both for bugs. They appeared untouched…Derek breathed a sigh of relief as he followed Roger into the safehouse, Jenny bringing up the rear. Gayle sat at the table, putting together an IED. There seemed little point in trying to conceal what they were doing from anyone who entered the safehouse. The enemy already knew who they were.

Or at least they have clear proof we were mixed up with the insurgency, Derek thought. *And they could have scraped our DNA out of the old house.*

Roger grinned at them. "Success?"

"It was awesome," Jenny said. "We totally caught them by surprise!"

"Glad to hear it." Roger sounded a little surprised. "How many did you kill?"

Derek smiled. *He* wasn't surprised. Jenny might have been a spoilt brat several months ago, but now…she'd learnt hard lessons, first as a medical assistant and then as an insurgent. She might not have been on the front lines, yet that hadn't kept her from seeing her fair share of horror. It had been a long time since she'd fainted at the sight of blood.

"Two for sure," he said, calmly. "And whoever entered the office got a nasty surprise."

"I bet they did," Roger said. "Do we know who?"

"No," Derek said. "It *could* have been someone who genuinely wanted to join. But there wasn't a long line outside when we arrived. The guard didn't look very alert either. A smart bastard would have insisted on searching us before opening the door."

"I bet he regrets it now," Roger said. "A couple of our contacts suggested volunteering, so we'd have people on the inside."

"They'd be taking a hell of a risk," Derek pointed out. "If they get taken for real quislings, they might wind up dead. And if they get checked under lie detectors…"

"I've pointed the risks out to them," Roger said. "But you know how people can get set on doing something and then refuse to listen to common sense."

"I have no idea who you're talking about," Derek said, primly. "Really, I don't."

Jenny wrapped her arms around him. "What now?"

"We plan the next attack," Roger said. "And keep training the newcomers."

"And hope they're not biding their time before they wipe us out," Derek added. "They know who to watch for now."

"They'll have to start checking people at random," Roger said. "And they don't have the manpower."

"Not until they finish the war," Derek agreed. "Have we heard anything reliable from the front?"

"One of our listeners overheard some chatter about a town being *finally* taken," Roger said, "but I don't know anything else. It could be completely true or utter bullshit."

"And useless, as we don't know which town," Gayle pointed out. She finished building the IED and placed the detonator beside it, ready to be slotted into position. "There're thousands of towns that could be under attack."

"True," Derek agreed. "We'll just press on. It isn't as if we can do anything else."

"No," Roger said. "Did you hear what happened last night?"

Derek's eyes narrowed. "What?"

"A bunch of people tried to flee the city," Roger said. "They made the mistake of crossing the motorway and got gunned down. They weren't insurgents, just...people who'd had enough of living in fear. And they were killed."

"Shit." Derek shook his head. Civilians. The invaders had gunned down civilians. He wished he was surprised. "And there's nothing we can do about it, is there?"

"Just keep fighting," Roger said. He smiled, humourlessly. "And use the whole incident for black propaganda."

"Yeah," Derek agreed. "Right now, people will believe anything."

CHAPTER THIRTY-THREE

Those who fail to realise that this happens are inevitably doomed. It should be no great mystery why the Catholic Church ran into so many problems (and successive attempts at reformation) after the post of Devil's Advocate fell into disuse. The church—and nearly everyone else—was no longer capable of grasping that one might argue for a cause, or a point of view, without actually sharing that point of view.
—**Professor Leo Caesius**
The Right to be Wrong: How Silencing People Hurts You

THE BRIDGE LOOKED LIKE A DISASTER waiting to happen.

It was, Garfield had to admit, an impressive piece of work given how quickly the engineers had had to put it together. The fleet hadn't brought pontoons and bridging equipment when they'd departed, if only because no one had realised they would be needed. Instead, the engineers had snatched up every boat for miles up and down the river and welded them together into a giant floating bridge. They swore blind it was safe, and easy to repair if the marines managed to drop a shell onto the bridge, but he couldn't help noticing they'd also insisted that trucks and other vehicles—the ones that couldn't simply be driven across the riverbed—crossed one at a time. Garfield was *sure* it was just a matter of time before something broke, throwing whoever was crossing it into the churning waters. He'd never been so glad to be in the infantry.

The bridge shifted uncomfortably under his feet as he walked across the river, followed by what remained of his company. He'd been mildly surprised not to be immediately relieved of duty and placed under arrest, but...he supposed the higher-ups had noticed he wasn't the only officer to have lost a convoy to enemy attacks. And he was one of their more experienced officers...Garfield shook his head. They'd won the last engagement, only to have the victory snatched from their grasp. The destroyed bridges had added weeks, if not months, to the timetable.

He felt a pang of bitterness as he peered towards the distant mountains. The terrain between rivers was surprisingly flat, ideal for tanks, although there was a great deal of foliage to provide cover for enemy snipers. A cluster of tanks and self-propelled guns sat on the far side, providing support to ramparts manned by heavily-armed soldiers. The enemy hadn't mounted a counter-offensive yet, but it was just a matter of time—everyone agreed—before they tried. They *had* to smash the bridge before the offensive continued, driving west towards the PDCs. Garfield allowed himself a grim smile as he reached the far side of the bridge and stepped onto solid ground. Janelle would get the men in line...

She's gone. Garfield still couldn't believe it. *She's gone.*

He gritted his teeth in rage. There would be no more prisoners, no more attempts to take enemy soldiers alive. If the marine had been shot, the moment she'd been caught, Janelle would still be alive. The thought nagged at him, tormenting him, as he ordered the men to advance towards their jump-off positions. He was not going to let them get away with murdering his sergeant. If he saw that marine again...

The air filled with sound as the tanks started to move, advancing forward like a mailed fist being driven into an enemy's gut. Lopez caught his eye and waved towards an AFV, moving forward in support. Garfield nodded and led the first squad—he couldn't remember their names, if he'd known them in the first place—onto the vehicle. The AFV would carry them into battle, hopefully covering them long enough to dismount the moment they encountered the enemy. Garfield hoped the tanks would draw fire. If the enemy could put an antitank weapon through a heavily-armoured tank, they'd have no trouble taking out a thin-skinned AFV. He promised himself he'd ensure the design was improved, if—when—he returned home. The combination of family connections and combat experience should give him enough clout to see the changes through.

He felt his head starting to pound as the AFV rattled forward. It felt uncomfortable inside the vehicle, even though it was safer than exposing himself to enemy snipers. The compartment was cramped, too hot for his comfort. Sweat trickled down his back, pooling in his pants and boots. The air started to smell of burning rubber and things he didn't want to think about. He wished he could see outside, despite the risk. It was quite possible the AFV—and its passengers—would be blown to hell before they even knew what had hit them.

It felt like hours before he heard a bullet pinging off the armour. A sniper? It didn't seem likely. The marines would know there was no point in wasting ammo trying to shoot through the armour. The AFV wasn't *that* thin-skinned. Maybe it was just an attempt to keep them on the alert, to force them to wear themselves down before they encountered the *real* threat. It might have worked, too, if the men hadn't been fighting for the last few weeks. They knew not to panic, even if they were on the verge of being blown away.

His headset buzzed. "Enemy positions, directly ahead..."

The intercom screamed an alert before he could react. "DISMOUNT! DISMOUNT!"

Garfield stood as the hatches banged open, diving through the hatch and taking cover behind the AFV as bullets pinged through the air. They were in the middle of what looked like a giant quarry—he'd been assured that all planets looked like giant quarries, although he was fairly sure it was a joke—with enemy troops pouring fire towards them. One of the tanks was burning, the others laying down covering fire as the infantrymen rallied.

Garfield felt a hot flash of contempt, mingled with grim understanding. Tankers tended to get nervous when asked to go up against antitank weapons, but...he understood their concern. If their armour was compromised, their vehicles would become fireballs so quickly there'd be almost no hope of escape. Armouring a tank so completely as to make it invulnerable would also have made it completely immobile.

He snapped orders as the troops rallied behind him, advancing forward as bullets snapped over his head. The tanks were raising their fire, aiming upwards so the bullets didn't hit his men in the back. Garfield was surprised they were showing that much consideration, although they'd be in deep shit if they accidentally sprayed his men with machine gun fire. They'd be dead in a heartbeat if they *did*. He hoped they understood that a spray of bullets that wouldn't even scratch their hulls would literally vaporise his men.

The ground heaved. He threw himself down, instinctively, as pieces of rocks and debris flew over his head. The sound of shooting stopped abruptly. He rolled over and peered towards a cloud of smoke, rising from the enemy position. Had one of the tanks gotten lucky and scored a direct hit? Or...a chill ran down his spine as he realised what had happened. The enemy had rigged the area to blow, then retreated and triggered the explosion as soon as they were clear of the blast radius. He rose, keeping low as he inched towards what remained of the enemy position. It was nothing more than a smoking crater. If any of the marines had been killed, there was no trace of it. Garfield suspected *none* of them had been killed.

His headset buzzed. "Report!"

"The enemy appears to have retreated, sir," Garfield said. "We'll have to resume the advance."

"Understood," Lopez said. "Return to your vehicle."

Garfield nodded, taking a moment to look east. The river was eastwards, but he saw no sign of it. They'd moved fast, very fast. And...he'd known the terrain was vast, yet he hadn't grasped *how* vast until he'd seen it with his own eyes. The armoured force was tiny, compared to the terrain it had to cover. Smoke rose in the distance, suggesting other units were encountering their own challenges. He forced himself to walk back to the AFVs as the tanks moved forward, their machine guns swinging from side to side as they searched for targets. Garfield suspected it was too late. The marines were well on their way to the next ambush point. They could keep harassing the invaders until they finally reached the *real* defence line. By then, they'd be so weak that taking the line would become impossible.

He frowned as he clambered into the AFV. Something was nagging at his mind, something from class…he shook his head. It couldn't be important, not compared to the task of staying alive. And killing as many marines as possible.

The AFV rumbled into life. Garfield leaned back against the bulkhead and closed his eyes.

• • •

"Here they come," Phelps muttered. "Drone picked them up hours ago."

"Watch your flanks," Bonkowski reminded him. The team had found the perfect spot for an ambush, if the enemy didn't know they were there. "They might know the drone is up there, watching them."

Rachel nodded. She was surprised—and worried—the enemy hadn't shot the drone out of the sky. The vehicle was tiny, but hardly immune to an HVM or point-defence laser. Hell, a sniper with a high-power rifle could do a lot of damage if he hit the wrong—or rather the right—spot. She gritted her teeth as the enemy vehicles came into view, slipping and sliding across the tundra. General Anderson had talked about luring the enemy into a trap, but she wasn't so sure his idea was going to work. There were too many things that could go wrong.

Luckily, we only need part of the plan to work to win, she told herself. *And it should be possible…*

"Choose your targets," Bonkowski ordered. "Hit the tanks."

"Yes, sir," Rachel said. She'd argued for hitting the AFVs instead, but she'd been overruled. She understood the logic. She just didn't agree with it. "Weapon…locked."

The antitank launcher bleeped, once, as she counted down the seconds. The enemy had been harassed constantly since they'd started driving west. They'd be on alert, firing at anything that even *looked* like a threat. The drone had picked them shooting holes in perfectly innocent bushes, clearly under the belief they hid heavily-armed marines. Rachel smiled, knowing the enemy might have had a point. The Pathfinders were trained to hide anywhere.

She felt her heart sink as the seemingly endless row of tanks, AFVs and other vehicles advanced. The enemy offensive looked a little ramshackle, but she had to admit it was working. They were advancing across a broad front, yet bringing immense firepower to bear on each of the strongpoints as they stumbled across them. And they were doing their own harassing, firing shells into marine positions and trying to interdict supply lines. Given time, they'd win. There was no way to do anything more than delay the inevitable.

Or change the rules, Rachel thought. It was what she'd been taught to do. *If you can't win by fair means, win by foul. And if you can't win by foul means, cheat.*

"Fire," Bonkowski snapped.

Rachel pulled the trigger. The missile launched itself from the tube, picking up speed rapidly as it lunged towards the enemy tank. The tank crew were sharp, altering course so quickly they nearly managed to dodge the missile. They *would* have succeeded if the seeker hadn't guided the missile into the enemy tank, punching through its side armour and detonating inside the hull. The tank skidded to a halt, smoke pouring from the gash in the hull. The crew were already dead.

The remaining enemy tanks opened fire. Rachel felt a flash of *déjà vu* as bullets tore through their position, passing bare inches above their heads. She thought she heard shouts behind her as the enemy infantry dismounted, although it was hard to be sure. Would they advance on their position or try to flank it? Or would the tankers drive forward themselves, gambling they wouldn't be impaling their vehicles on her weapons? The rumbling behind her suggested the latter. She boosted, running for her life. They had to reach cover before they were spotted. Their suits were supposed to hide them from prying eyes, but she didn't dare count on it.

She jumped over a hummock and ducked down as the rumbling grew louder. The enemy tanks were charging forward, crunching over the firing position without ever realising how close they'd come to certain death. The IED exploded, too late. She thought she saw an AFV picked up and thrown backward by the force of the blast, but it was hard to be sure. In hindsight, using explosives *designed* to produce as much smoke and confusion as possible might have been a mistake. The IED might have confused the enemy, but it had definitely confused *her*.

"Stay down," Bonkowski shouted. His voice was almost lost behind the whistling of incoming shells. "Incoming!"

Rachel hit the ground as shells rocketed over her head, striking dangerously close to their position. The ground shook violently, the enemy offensive spluttering to a halt as two or three AFVs were hit and destroyed. She picked herself up and ran as the bombardment continued, shells and missiles streaking to stop the enemy column in its tracks. A handful of shots rang out behind, none coming remotely close to actually hitting her. She grinned as she ducked into the trench and kept running. They didn't know it, but they'd already lost their best chance at capturing or killing the marines. They'd have to be reluctant to give chase. The marines might have left a surprise or two behind.

She kept running until they reached the next strongpoint. A handful of marines were already there, half laying mines while the other half readied firing positions. They wouldn't slow the enemy for long, but it would wear them down. And, beyond them, lay the mountains. And the trap.

And if this doesn't work, she thought morbidly, *we might wind up being trapped instead.*

• • •

Garfield unhooked a grenade from his belt and hurled it over the rock, then scrambled forward as soon as it detonated. It had felt like a hundred marines were hiding on the far side—they'd certainly fired thousands of shots in his general direction—but he only saw three as he fell into the enemy position. One was dead; he'd taken the full brunt of the blast. The other two were badly wounded, barely able to move. And yet...one of them started to raise a gun. Garfield kicked it out of his hand, then slammed his rifle into the marine's face. The man didn't make a sound as he died.

He stared at the other marine for a long moment. He'd been told the marines were different, yet...the marine didn't look too different to *him*. Blood was leaking from his chest—the blast looked to have shattered his body armour, driving fragments into his bare skin—yet his face was surprisingly intact. He couldn't be much older than Garfield himself, if only because it was unlikely he had any genetic enhancements spliced into his DNA. They might have been friends, if they'd met under other circumstances. And yet...

A surge of hatred rose up within him. The marines had attacked his people...they'd *killed* his people. His first platoon was gone, as far as he knew; *Janelle* was gone. He lifted his rifle, pointing it between the marine's eyes. The bastard had invaded a world and killed uncounted and uncountable numbers of people for...for what? Rumour had offered all sorts of answers, but even *his* connections hadn't been able to get him any solid answers. The marines might as well have invaded on a lark. It wasn't right. Why?

He wanted to ask, to demand answers, but the marine was in no state to offer them. Even if he was...rumour insisted the marines were immune to everything from simple torture to direct brain simulation. He wouldn't talk, unless he wanted to talk. And besides...Garfield didn't *want* to take him prisoner. He wanted the man to *die*. He pulled the trigger, watching emotionlessly as the marine went limp. His skull was a broken mess. It was impossible to believe anything could survive.

"Fuck you," he whispered. He had orders to take prisoners. Orders were orders...*fuck* orders. Fuck prisoners. The marines didn't deserve to be taken prisoner. "Fuck the lot of you."

He turned and headed back to the AFVs. The offensive had continued, pushing back the marines by sheer weight of numbers. They'd run out of room soon enough and then they'd have to make a stand, even though they *knew* a vast force was heading straight towards them. If they ran, the PDC would be invaded or destroyed. And that would be the end.

His eyes swept the distant mountains. The river came from a lake up there, if he recalled correctly. Hameau really *was* a beautiful planet. He'd like to go up there, after the war, and explore. He'd always liked mountain climbing. Perhaps Janelle would like to go with him…he remembered, suddenly, that she was dead. Dead and gone and…

He scrambled into the AFV. "Drive on," he ordered, putting his grief aside. "Take us to the next ambush."

"Aye, sir," the driver called. The vehicle rumbled into life once again, following the tanks as they surged forward. "I'm sure we'll find one if we just keep going."

And then we'll kill a few more marines, Garfield thought. The thought cheered him as he tried to get some sleep. It didn't work. *And a few more. And a few more, until they're all dead and gone.*

CHAPTER THIRTY-FOUR

This caused the decline and fall of many great institutions, including Imperial University. There could be no more provocative or challenging questions, no more disagreement with orthodoxy; those who refused to toe the official line, whatever it was, were punished for their heresy.
—**Professor Leo Caesius**
The Right to be Wrong: How Silencing People Hurts You

"THEY'RE ENTERING THE DANGER ZONE," Lieutenant Yen reported. "And they're bringing their guns to bear on the PDC."

Gerald nodded as he studied the display. One very definite advantage of the current position, he supposed, was that he had a live feed from the PDC itself as well as the handful of drones holding position over the battlefield. The realtime information at his fingertips was more comprehensive than anything he'd had following Earthfall, although even *that* wasn't completely a good thing. He could watch disaster unfolding in perfect detail, without being able to do anything to stop it.

Clever of them, he acknowledged sourly. *They might damage the PDC enough to let their starships finish the job.*

"Contact the engineers," he ordered. "Tell them to detonate the charges as soon as possible."

"Aye, sir," Lieutenant Yen said. "And our troops?"

"Order them to stand ready," Gerald said. "And be ready to move to high ground."

He leaned forward as more and more enemy units appeared on the display. It was a scene out of nightmares, a scene no one had seen since humanity had learnt how to base weapons in orbit…unless, of course, one lived on a world so primitive it had no way to turn space itself into a weapon. Hundreds of tanks and thousands of transports and supply trucks were flowing across the tundra, transporting men and supplies for the final offensive. They'd done a pretty good job of securing their rear area too, he admitted sourly. The Pathfinders and other units, cut off by the sheer speed of the enemy advance, had done their best, but they hadn't managed to do more than annoy the enemy. They were gathering themselves for a final push at the PDC. If they won…

"Sir," Lieutenant Yen said. "The combat engineers are ready."

Gerald looked at the map. If something went wrong…

"Send the command," he ordered. "Tell them to detonate now."

"Aye, sir."

...

Garfield watched, coldly, as the enemy town burned.

He didn't feel anything, even as a pair of shapes tried to escape the town, only to be shot before it was too late. It didn't bother him, not any longer, that the town had belonged to locals, to the people he was supposed to protect. The marines were just too good at turning towns into strongpoints, forcing the invaders to fight their way through an endless series of ambushes, IEDs and other nasty surprises. No one took chances any longer, not when they didn't have a good reason to take the town intact. The troops had surrounded the town, then smashed it to pieces with long-range fire. The handful of incendiary shells mixed with the high explosive had started a fire, burning the town to the ground. If there were any marines still inside, they were roasting. They'd never get out alive.

His communicator buzzed. "You'll be holding position, keeping the roads open until the next wave arrives."

"Understood." Garfield took a long drag on his cigarette. "We'll be ready."

He rubbed his eyes as he watched the town burn down. It felt as if the offensive had been going on for years, endless hours of boredom followed by brief and violent encounters with the enemy or attempts to catch some sleep before the offensive resumed. They were drawing closer to their target, to the point where the marines would have to either stand and fight or give up and admit defeat. He studied the mountains, drawing ever closer. The PDC was wrapped in smoke as the guns pounded it, trying to turn its giant weapons into scrap. If they succeeded...

No, he told himself, as the next set of tanks arrived. He'd lost count of how many had passed him, or been destroyed, or simply damaged to the point they'd had to be abandoned until the engineers managed to put them back into service. *I'll have my chance to kill them.*

The flames finally started to die down. Garfield stood, donned his mask and ordered the platoon forward. They moved carefully, inspecting the ruins for survivors or traps. For once, there were no IEDs. Garfield suspected they'd been set off by the shelling, although it was hard to be sure. The marines had been slacking over the last few days, as if they were on the verge of running out of ammunition. It was quite possible. They presumably hadn't anticipated having to fight two full-scale wars in quick succession. There had to be limits to what they'd shipped to the surface or been able to capture during the earlier war. And they might be reaching those limits.

Once we take the PDC, we can break them, he told himself, as they reached the edge of the village. The AFVs were already there, waiting to take them to the next engagement. *And that will be the end.*

And then he felt the ground start to shake.

・・・

Captain Nicolas Lang, Terran Marine Corps Combat Engineers, felt oddly guilty as he surveyed the landscape around him. Hameau was *odd*, certainly by the standards of any normal world, yet there was no denying that it was also a beautiful place. Nicolas wouldn't have expected a planet that suffered regular asteroid impacts to be stunning, and yet it was. The combination of hardy native wildlife and the standard terraforming package—and the battered landscape—had produced a pearl in humanity's crown. And yet...he and his men had spent the last week surveying the giant lake and emplacing charges, explosive and thermal, right where they'd do the most damage. He was about to destroy a natural landmark in order to save it.

He put the thought out of his mind, sharply. The lake was immense, linked to underground reservoirs and giant strata of frozen ice. Only the combination of solid rock and metallic ore—and a single giant river—had kept the lake from bursting its banks centuries ago. Nicolas had a feeling that was going to change, as the planet steadily grew warmer. The terraforming effect had triggered off a greenhouse effect that would eventually, inevitably, melt most of the frozen ice. And who knew what would happen then?

"Get everyone to higher ground," he ordered, as he picked up the detonator and checked the display. They were about to speed things up a little. "The charges will detonate in five minutes."

He let out a breath as he forced himself to stroll to what was—he thought—safe ground. It was hard to be sure. They'd done their best to model the impact, but there were too many complicating factors to say anything for certain. There hadn't been time to carry out more than a basic geological survey, forcing them to rely on enemy data as they laid their plans. He hoped the newcomers hadn't bothered to study the data or consult with locals who had. There was nothing as blindingly obvious as a dam in the vicinity, but someone who considered the landscape with an eye to tactical possibilities—and a complete lack of scruples when it came to radically reshaping the terrain—would see it at once.

The timer bleeped. He checked his team were all above him, hopefully safe, then pushed the button. For a moment, nothing happened. It was just long enough to make him wonder if something had gone wrong...

...And then the rocky lakeside, the crater edge holding the water trapped, collapsed outwards with a roar. A giant sucking sound echoed through the air as the lake emptied, thousands upon thousands of tons of water heading down towards the sea. It was hard to be sure, but by his estimate there were—they'd been—over eight cubic kilometres of water within the lake, all now rushing towards the enemy lines. The second set of charges detonated moments later, followed by a series of smaller explosions as ice—suddenly flashed to steam—sought the quickest way out. He watched in awe as more and more water surged through the lake and down through the hole. Anything in the way was completely and comprehensively fucked.

There seemed to be no end to it, no end to the waves upon waves of water. He knew there had to be a limit, but...where was it? The surge seemed to be growing more powerful with every second, as if they'd tapped into more water and ice than they'd thought. Perhaps they had. The enemy surveyors hadn't done a very comprehensive job. It wouldn't be the first time a corprat had skimped on the survey, although he was surprised to see it here. The Onge Corporation had considered the planet a private fiefdom.

The ground rumbled under his feet. He wanted to stare, to watch the waters run, but he knew he had to move. They scrambled up, the ground shaking so badly he wondered if he'd accidentally triggered an earthquake—or a volcano. It was awesome, yet terrifying. He'd never done anything like it. He'd built defences and schools, fixed vehicles and guns, but never played with the land itself. And to think he'd considered joining the Terraforming Corps! They'd never authorised anything so dramatic...

Not on a populated world, at least, he thought. Bombarding planets with ice asteroids to increase the native water was best done before thousands of settlers were landed. *The risk would be far too high.*

"I have become death," he muttered, as he caught up with the others. How many men had he sentenced to death? He would never know. "The destroyer of worlds."

...

"What the fuck...?"

Garfield looked north, just in time to see a giant cloud of smoke appear above the distant mountains. Light glinted...he stared, unable to make sense of what he was seeing. There was no PDC up there, was there? He didn't *think* there were any settlements on the mountains and, even if there were, they weren't important. But the ground was shaking and a dark mass was rushing towards him...

He swore and dived into the AFV, screaming for his men to buckle up and slam the hatches closed. It was just in time. The hand of God Himself reached down and slapped the AFV, throwing it over and over and over... Garfield heard someone being violently sick, the stench so awful he threw up too. The vehicle kept moving, the gravity spinning so madly he half-thought they'd been thrown into orbit. A series of deafening crashes ran through the AFV as it smashed into...*something*, an endless series of objects. The tanks? He thought the tanks were too heavy to be picked up by a tidal wave, but no one had anticipated a tidal wave in the first place. His blood ran cold as he realised that everything, from the supply trucks to the bridges and garrisons, had probably been caught by the wave. If the river had suddenly swelled, bursting its banks, the makeshift bridge had been smashed to rubble, if it hadn't been thrown halfway to the sea. The AFV finally hit something too hard and crashed to a halt. Garfield was so unsteady he wasn't sure it had finally stopped at first. His head was too sore.

It was hard, so hard, to grasp what had happened. He was hanging upside down, so dazed it took him several minutes to work out how to get down. His buckles should have been released instantly, but his fingers refused to work properly. It was all he could do to free one of his arms and get to his knife, then use it to cut the remainder of the buckles. He fell, banging his head against the metal as he hit the roof. His head was too sore to realise that down was now up and vice versa as he stumbled to the hatch. It was hard to open. Mud poured in as soon as he forced it to move.

"This way," he managed. He was in no state to give orders. Half of his men were in no state to take them. Two were hanging awkwardly, their buckles caught around the necks. The others were alive, if badly injured. "Quickly."

He helped them out of the AFV, then looked around in horror. The AFV was half-buried in a sea of churning mud, bubbling and boiling as if the water was somehow hot and cold at the same time. The landscape had been devastated, the tundra covered with a layer of mud that covered the remnants of trees, buildings and military vehicles. An AFV lay nearby, smashed open as if it had been hit by a giant hammer. Two more trucks lay on their sides, smoking lightly. There didn't seem to be any survivors.

And it was quiet...

He glanced eastwards. The guns had fallen silent. The constant pounding that had echoed in his ears ever since the offensive had begun, from morning till night and then till morning again, was gone. No birds flew through the air, no aircraft or drones swept high overhead...a sense of desolation, of abandonment, washed over him. They were alone. Tears prickled at the corner of his eyes. He blinked them away, angrily. They'd taken a beating—he couldn't deny it—but they were alive. He just wished he knew where the rest of the army was.

Down there, drowning, a little voice whispered at the back of his head. *How far are you from the front lines?*

He ignored the voice as he helped the wounded out of the AFV, then inspected his men. Seven survivors, three too badly wounded to walk. The remainder were dead. He ignored the twist in his heart as he keyed his communicator, hoping for a medical evacuation. But there was no answer. He shuddered, realising—for the first time—the true extent of the devastation. The marines might have hit the FOB, hit the garrisons...there might be no one left in charge. General Rask might be dead. Or worse. Admiral

Nelson Agate was meant to be in overall charge—Garfield had met the admiral once, during a tedious dinner party—but where the hell was he? If Agate was in orbit, he wouldn't be able to do anything. The men on the ground would have to save themselves.

"We'll head back to the bridges," he said. It wouldn't be easy—they'd have to march over ninety miles, carrying stretchers—but surrender wasn't an option. Hell, for all he knew, the marines had taken a beating too. The flood might have been a genuine accident, a completely unexpected natural event. "Hopefully, we'll meet others along the way."

There was no argument. He ordered the wounded injected with painkillers, then helped them onto the makeshift stretchers. Carrying them even a short distance wasn't going to be easy, but there was nothing else they could do. Surrender wasn't an option, leaving them with the ruined AFV wasn't an option...they collected what little supplies and ammunition they had left, then started to march east. He thought he heard an aircraft in the distance, but it didn't come close enough to see which side it was on. He told himself to be grateful. They were in the open, easy targets for when—if—the enemy decided to strafe his platoon. He couldn't believe they'd be allowed to leave easily. God knew they'd gunned down retreating marines too.

He felt his sense of being abandoned, of being *alone*, grow stronger as they walked on, through a scene of unparalleled devastation. The spooks had confidently claimed the marines wouldn't use nukes—or some other form of WMD—but they'd been wrong. Disastrously wrong. Garfield had no idea what the marines had done, but he was sure they'd used WMD *somehow*. Everyone had claimed nukes would never be used on a planet's surface again, not since humanity had developed much better weapons that didn't have so many downsides, yet...what had they done? He felt worse and worse with every passing hour, as they stumbled over shattered trees or passed destroyed vehicles. A town that had—somehow—avoided being destroyed during the offensive had been damaged beyond repair, the nice-looking homes and shops reduced to a sodden mass. He forced himself to keep walking, feeling eyes following them from a distance. The marines were coming out to clear up the mess.

Janelle would have seen the danger, he told himself. The thought plagued his mind, even though cold logic told him it wasn't true. None of them had seen it coming, not even the oh-so-confident spooks. *She would have known what to do.*

Garfield kept walking, even as the sun started to descend behind the distant mountains. There was nothing else to do. The offensive had been shattered. Every time he checked his communicator, he got static. The flood couldn't have killed everyone, could it? He didn't think so, but…he couldn't be sure. Someone would have taken command, if General Rask was dead. Right? He told himself that *yes*, someone would be in command. But…but what if it was *him*. As far as he knew, *he* was the senior survivor. *He* might be in command.

The Admiral will still be alive, he told himself, firmly. *The flood cannot have reached all the way to Haverford. Or the landing zone.*

Sure, his thoughts mocked him. *And what if you're wrong?*

CHAPTER THIRTY-FIVE

These punishments tended to be either formal or informal. Corporations could—and did—simply fire people who questioned the official line. Universities found it harder to sack people, but they could find all sorts of ways to pressure dissidents.
—**Professor Leo Caesius**
The Right to be Wrong: How Silencing People Hurts You

"WE'RE DONE," JULIA SAID.

Nelson couldn't disagree. The offensive hadn't just failed. It had been *smashed*, caught in a trap that—in hindsight—had been brutally obvious. It should have been...his soldiers hadn't done something as foolish as driving beneath a dam, but...the lake was there. The marines had smashed the crater edge and drenched the offensive, drowning thousands of men and smashing all hope of a quick victory. He felt a yawning emptiness in his soul as he tried to assess the scale of the disaster. It wasn't possible. They'd been beaten.

He clenched his fist until his nails were digging into his palm. He needed to think clearly. He needed to come up with a brilliant tactic that would save them all from exile—or execution. He needed...he thought desperately, but nothing came to mind. The war had stalemated, at least until reinforcements arrived. The marines couldn't win outright, but neither could he. And yet...they had the edge. He'd committed nearly all of his mobile forces to the offensive.

The insurgents will make us pay a bitter price, even if the marines don't venture out from under the PDC umbrella, he thought. *And now we've been beaten, they'll take heart.*

He calmed himself with an effort. It was bad. It was very bad. And yet, it wasn't complete disaster. They'd lost the battle, but they hadn't lost the war. That was how he'd spin it. They could still win, once reinforcements arrived. And if he laid the groundwork properly, they might just survive. Might. They'd have to convince their superiors that they did all they could. He keyed his console, opening a link to General Rask. He'd have to be the scapegoat, when all was said and done, but there was nothing to be gained by telling him that *now*. The general would need to cooperate.

"What do we do?" Julia sounded as if she was panicking. "What do we do?"

"For starters, we know when to fold them," Nelson said, calmly. "Let me handle it."

Julia gave him a sharp look as General Rask's face appeared in front of them. The general looked as if he'd aged ten years overnight, his pristine uniform oddly contrasting with his haggard appearance. He hadn't led from the front, something Nelson had always found a little odd. Naval officers rode their flagships into the teeth of enemy fire. But then, a flagship *was* surrounded by layer upon layer of hullmetal. A single enemy shell might be enough to take out a general and his entire staff.

"General," Nelson said. "How bad is it?"

"Bad." General Rask's voice suggested he was on the verge of eating his own gun. "They've stopped us in our tracks. Thousands are reported dead or missing, along with most of our vehicles. Given time, we can probably recover the tanks..."

"But they won't give us time." Nelson cut him off. "The offensive has failed, correct?"

General Rask nodded, curtly. "Yes, sir. There's no way we can resume operations in less than a week. More like a month. The entire army has been shattered. It'll be hours, at least, before we patch together a command network. Right now, there are so many missing links..."

"I understand entirely," Nelson said. The marines would move to take advantage of their success, once the water had finished draining away. The only good news, he supposed, was that the tundra had turned into a bog. The marines would have trouble moving their armour across it too. "General, we need to pull back."

"I've already got staff working on establishing a fallback position," General Rask said. "We can build on the old defence line, the one we used as a jump-off point. That should..."

"No." Nelson shook his head. "I want you to pull all the way back to Haverford. Hold the capital, hold the landing zone and *wait*. The reinforcements will arrive shortly. That'll give us a chance to plan our *next* offensive. The fleet will provide fire support if the marines attack first."

"Yes, sir." General Rask didn't sound unhappy. It sounded as if he'd considered something similar himself. "It won't be easy to get so many men back to the city. They may have to walk."

"They can cope," Nelson said. It really *wasn't* going to be easy, but it was the only hope of salvaging *something* from the disaster. "Get yourself back there too. And start looking for other unconventional ways the marines can hurt us. Look for ways to do the same to them, while you're at it. Maybe we can turn a mountain into a volcano."

"A mountain with a PDC on top?" General Rask shook his head. "I'd be very surprised if we could, sir. I doubt the designers skimped on the survey. We'd have better luck adapting a laser warhead to take one down."

"That'll give us an edge," Nelson agreed. It would also be hideously dangerous, but he found it hard to care. Desperate times demanded desperate measures. They could clean up the mess later, if they won. If they lost, it would be someone else's problem. "Look for other ideas along those lines."

"Aye, sir." General Rask saluted. "I'll get right on it."

Nelson winced as the general's image vanished. He'd have problems coordinating a withdrawal at the best of times, even if the marines didn't try to interfere. It was never easy to retreat under enemy fire. And the once-proud army was shattered, each unit isolated from the others. It would take time, time they didn't have, to rebuild the individual pieces into a united force. The marines wouldn't give them the time.

Julia caught his arm. "You're conceding defeat?"

"We lost the battle, but not the war," Nelson said. He had a feeling he was going to be saying it again and again, over the weeks and months to come. There was no way to avoid at least *some* shit landing on their heads, no matter what they did. General Rask would get most of the blame, but… he'd been supervising the poor bastard. And the corprats might not be too impressed if he tried to duck responsibility. "Right now, we preserve what we can."

Julia snorted. "And then what?"

Nelson pulled back the map, showing her the PDC umbrella. "Right now, we have a stalemate. We can't get to them, but they can't get to us either. If they poke their noses out from under the umbrella, we'll smash them from orbit. So we pull back and wait. When our reinforcements arrive, we retake the offensive. It'll give us time to reorganise, produce *more* KEWs and generally do everything we need to do to ensure success next time."

He allowed himself a tight smile. "Their forces were already running short on ammunition," he assured her. "Next time, they'll run dry in the middle of a battle."

"Really." Julia didn't sound convinced. "And what if they find a way to fuck us anyway?"

Nelson kept his face under tight control. Julia was growing desperate. It was easy to understand why. She'd staked everything—her career, her reputation, her life—on him. If he failed her…he made a mental bet with himself that Julia was already trying to figure out a way to distance herself from him. He couldn't really blame her. Her connections meant she couldn't be cast out entirely, but she sure as hell could be sent well away from *real* power. A life of luxury would mean nothing to her, if she couldn't wield power or influence...

"They don't have many options," Nelson said. The greatest danger lay with the insurgents, unless the marine reinforcements arrived first. He kept *that* thought to himself. "They can't drown Haverford. There are no convenient lakes nearby."

He scowled. A year ago, doing so much damage to the local scenery would have been completely out of the question. The environmentalist factions would have blown a fuse if they'd watched the marines—or anyone—devastate the landscape. They'd throw several different kinds of fit, insisting the marines had destroyed a unique ecology and slaughtered untold billions of animals. Even destroying a *dam* would have earned their censure, which had always struck him as odd. But now...there was no one left to restrain the marines. Or him. He could use WMD if he wished...

"We took a beating, no denying that," he said, as reassuringly as he could. "But we haven't lost. Not yet."

...

Garfield had quite lost track of time as the platoon trudged east, taking turns to help carry the stretcher. The landscape was utterly unrecognisable, even though they'd spent the last few days fighting their way through it. Water dripped everywhere, a mocking reminder of the flood that had stopped them in their tracks. Trees lay on the ground, shattered beyond reason; towns and villages had practically been washed off the face of the planet. The sky looked gloomy and overcast, the clouds heavily pregnant with rain. He wondered, morbidly, just what the marines had done to start the flood. If they'd blown vast amounts of steam into the atmosphere, it would probably start turning into rain...

He gritted his teeth as the downpour finally started, growing so rapidly that visibility shrank to almost nothing. He would have preferred to stop, if only long enough for the rain to come to an end, but the ground was already turning into a swamp. There was no hope of finding shelter, let alone safety.

He forced himself to keep going, trying to encourage the soldiers as they were drenched again. His uniform clung to him, utterly waterlogged. He slipped and slid as he clambered up what had once—he thought—been a road. It was now steadily turning into a boggy mire.

Janelle would have known what to do, he thought. Light flashed in the distance. *She wouldn't have let it come to this.*

Thunder roared, high overhead. Garfield flinched, half-convinced the marines were raining shells on them. They were probably snug in their trenches, laughing...he tried to tell himself their trenches were probably filling with water too. They'd known the flood was coming, they'd known they needed to protect themselves, but the rain? Gallons upon gallons of water were crashing down, soaking everyone. Even tanks would have trouble advancing across the battlefield. The marines would be—he hoped—taking shelter and waiting for the downpour to stop. If they were advancing instead...

They'll be bogged down too, he told himself, as they walked around a rapidly-growing piece of marshland. *They can't advance through the mire.*

It felt like hours before they finally reached the river. The bridges were gone...he tried to convince himself they were below the bridges, but the river had already burst its banks. The bridges hadn't been very secure, he recalled. The torrent had probably smashed the boats and carried the wreckage down to the sea. Garfield looked around, staring into the churning muddy waters. He was a good swimmer, but there was no way anyone could get across the river without being swept away. He'd be carried straight down to the sea.

"Fuck," he said, numbly. "How the hell do we get across?"

He heard a dull rumbling on the other side of the river. An AFV was making its way forward, slipping and sliding as it drove into the water. Garfield's heart clenched, suddenly very aware the vehicle could bog down in the riverbed and wind up trapped. Or simply be swept away, like his AFV. The crew would be very lucky to escape, if they wound up trapped. His eyes narrowed as he spotted movement on the far side. Troops—combat engineers—were doing *something*. He couldn't see what...

The AFV burst out of the water and struggled up the far side. It was dragging a cable behind it, lashing in the river as it was pulled inexorably forward. Garfield waved as the AFV came to a halt, the rope snapping taut. The troops on the far side had fixed the other end to another AFV. Garfield hurried forward as the combat engineers vacated their vehicle. They looked as if they'd been through hell.

"Sir," Garfield said. "I...what happened?"

"We have orders to get as many men out of the trap as possible," the combat engineer said, briskly. "We're falling back to Haverford."

"Haverford?" Garfield didn't believe it. "Really?"

"Yeah." The engineer started to hook up the sling. "There's no hope of establishing a defence line short of the city itself. Or so I've been told. Half the command staff are dead and the rest are in a paddy. No one knows how many people survived."

"Shit," Garfield said. How were they even going to *get* to the city? Walk? He didn't think there were many trucks left. "We get back to the city...what then?"

"Fucked if I know," the engineer said. "But if you stay here, you'll die."

"Yes, sir," Garfield said. It wouldn't be fun crossing the water on a wire, but there was no other choice. "Let's move."

He'd half-hoped there'd be transports on the far side, waiting to take them home. But there were no vehicles, save for a pair of engineering units trying to assemble a pair of shelters and replacement bridge. He gritted his teeth as they started to walk, leaving the wounded with the medics. Their chances weren't good, he thought, but—again—there was no choice. He hoped the marines wouldn't kill them, if they overran the medic station. But...

Rage built within him as they linked up with other soldiers, looking as helpless and drenched as themselves. The army had been broken, its morale shattered beyond repair. Garfield forced himself to keep moving, despite a growing desire to sit down and die. A handful of soldiers staggered out of line, collapsing by the roadside. No one moved to help them, or to kick them back into movement. It was every man for himself.

It felt very much like hell.

...

"It looks like hell," Lieutenant Yen breathed.

Gerald nodded in grim agreement. The live feed from the drone was jerky—the operator couldn't hold it steady—but he could see enough. The tundra had been devastated by the flood. Entire settlements—or what remained of them—had been swept away, the wreckage scattered across the land or carried down to the sea. The forests had been washed away, thousands of trees uprooted and tossed across the broken landscape. And the enemy offensive had been stopped in its tracks. Here and there, he saw soldiers wandering around or trying to make their way east. Their mobile forces had been shattered. A number of tanks looked to have survived, but their AFVs and trucks had been broken. It would take a long time for them to regroup, let alone patch up the damage.

"Yes," he said. It was the sort of thing they'd never have been allowed to do, before Earthfall. He wondered, absently, just what his superiors would make of it. Would they see it as a reasonable tactic, or vandalism on a planetary scale? Would they understand he'd had no choice, or would they come up with a tactic he could have used instead? "It does."

He clasped his hands behind his back as he considered his options. The enemy seemed to be withdrawing as quickly as possible, although it was hard to be sure. The enemy themselves probably weren't sure what they were doing. Gerald's sensors weren't picking up many enemy transmissions. It was quite possible the flood had either killed or isolated the enemy commanding officers. Gerald couldn't allow himself to believe it, but...it was possible. It gave him an opening.

And yet, there were limits to what he could do.

He glanced at Yen. "Is the pursuit force ready to go?"

"Yes, sir," Yen said. "However, the terrain isn't good..."

Gerald nodded. The terrain had been ideal for tanks, before the marines had turned it into marshland. The heavy tanks would probably be fine, but the lighter vehicles would get bogged down...just like the enemy tanks. And yet, he *had* to force the enemy to keep moving. The more they managed to salvage from the disaster, the more they could throw at him when he mounted his counteroffensive. And...

"Prepare to record a message," he ordered. "I need to signal the fleet."

"Aye, sir," Yen said. "It'll take hours for a signal to reach..."

"I know," Gerald said, more sharply than he'd intended. He'd been struggling with the realities of interplanetary and interstellar communications when Yen had been in diapers...if he'd even been born at all. "As long as it reaches the fleet, I don't much care."

He took a moment to gather his thoughts, then waited for the nod. "Commodore. As you can see from the attached files, we have shattered the enemy army. They're currently falling back. I believe they're trying to get out of the PDC umbrella before we manage to mount a pursuit. We will not have a better opportunity to put your plan into action.

"If you believe Downfall can be launched successfully, do so. We'll move to take advantage of the opening as soon as we see it. If not, hold your position. Either way, inform me as quickly as possible."

He nodded to Yen. "Send the message, then inform the Pathfinders I have a job for them," he ordered. "I want them heading back to the city. Now."

"Yes, sir," Yen said.

CHAPTER THIRTY-SIX

And, of course, there was no shortage of idiotic students who could be directed against dissidents. It was very easy to manipulate them by offering rewards in exchange for serving the cause.
—**Professor Leo Caesius**
The Right to be Wrong: How Silencing People Hurts You

"CAPTAIN," TOMAS SAID, as Captain Kerri Stumbaugh stepped onto the bridge. "The drones are in position. The marines are ready to deploy. And the squadron is standing by."

Kerri nodded, adjusting her tunic as she sat on the command chair. She felt a thrill of anticipation, mixed with the grim awareness the plan could go horribly wrong. She'd always wanted to fight a *real* engagement in space, to test herself and her crew against an enemy warship, even though she'd known she could lose. The Imperial Navy's exercises hadn't been worthy of the name—everyone had known the winners and losers in advance—and even the Marine Corps exercises had their limits. Now...now she was going to do or die.

She studied the display for a long moment. The enemy fleet was still holding position near the planet, ready to provide fire support to the troops on the ground. It wasn't clear how many KEWs they had, but Kerri doubted they'd shot themselves dry. Smart officers knew to keep a reserve for unexpected contingencies. And besides, it wouldn't be *that* hard to start producing more KEWs. They could do it manually if they had the manpower. There was enough junk orbiting the planet to ensure they never ran out.

"Signal the squadron," she ordered. "We move in five minutes."

"Aye, Captain."

Kerri ran through the plan again, silently praying everything went as she hoped. She'd worked as many contingencies into the planning as possible, but she was all too aware they were going to be overcommitting themselves. If something went wrong, they would be committed to a close-range engagement against massively superior firepower. The sheer audacity of the plan should keep the enemy from looking for out-of-the-box tactics, but...she shook her head. There was no point in worrying about it now. She'd drawn up contingencies for total disaster, as well as total success. And if they needed them...

She felt a twinge of guilt. If she failed, if the plan failed, she would have sent hundreds of men to their deaths.

"Bring up the drives," she ordered. "On my command, activate the drones."

"Aye, Captain," Commander Joaquin said. A dull quiver ran through the ship. "Drives online...now."

Kerri nodded. The enemy probably wouldn't be able to detect them yet—unless they'd scattered sensor platforms all over the system—but that was about to change. She braced herself as the gravity field flickered, the drives slowly powering *Havoc* away from the asteroids. The remainder of the squadron fell into formation around her, readying their weapons and defences for the coming engagement. She reminded herself, again, that she had a formidable force under her command. Her subordinates had worked with her to develop the plan...

And yet, none of them raised serious objections, she thought. *Is the plan that good? Or did they just want to go into action?*

She scowled as the drive hum grew louder. Playing Devil's Advocate was never a popular move, even though it was important. Someone who argued against everything could easily find themselves unpopular, or charged with cowardice in the face of the enemy. She gritted her teeth at the thought. No one who'd gone through the Slaughterhouse could possibly be considered a coward, but many of the auxiliaries had never even started. It was all too easy to confuse caution with cowardice, if one didn't know what courage *was*...

"Activate the drones," she ordered. "And then set course for the enemy fleet."

"Aye, Captain," Tomas said. "They'll see us in roughly fifty minutes."

"Good," Kerri said. "Keep us on course."

She let out a breath. The drones were top of the line, but...it was quite possible the enemy would realise the squadron was largely composed of sensor ghosts. She'd been tempted to overdo it, just to make sure they *knew* two-thirds of the fleet coming towards them simply didn't exist, yet... she hadn't dared. The key to deception was not appearing deceptive. One couldn't lie successfully if one told an insultingly obvious lie. It was too much to hope the mark thought the liar was too stupid to realise the mark wouldn't believe the lie.

So they have reason to think we're weak, she mused. *But not weak enough to make them wonder why we're doing something that looks stupid.*

She leaned back in her chair. There was no point in worrying about it now. They were committed. Technically, she supposed, she could back off, break contact and leave the enemy wondering what the fuck she'd been trying to do, but—practically speaking—she was committed. She had no idea when the enemy reinforcements would arrive, yet...they would arrive. She was sure of it. And her own reinforcements were still weeks away.

"Deploy recon probes," she ordered. "I want to know the moment they see us."

"Aye, Captain."

...

Nelson lay in bed, staring up at the ceiling. It hadn't been easy to arrange matters so General Rask would take the fall, not when he had to work with the general to pull the surviving troops back to the city. The army had been shattered beyond easy repair. They'd had to put captured civilian groundcars into service, just to transport the wounded back to the city. It was starting to look as if they'd lost nearly two-thirds of their forces.

The intercom bleeped. "Admiral?"

Nelson sat up. His staff knew better than to wake him unless it was *important*. "Go ahead."

"Admiral," Commander Davis said. "Long-range sensors are picking up enemy ships, on a least-time course for the planet. They'll intersect with our position in just over ninety minutes."

"So they're coming at us like bats out of hell," Nelson said. He reached for his terminal and brought up the live feed. The enemy fleet—nineteen cruisers, twenty-seven smaller ships—was advancing towards his fleet with murderous intent. He'd take a bite out of them—they didn't have anything capable of matching his battlecruiser's firepower—but they'd overwhelm him by sheer weight of numbers. "Alert the fleet. Prepare for redeployment."

"Aye, sir," Davis said.

"And I'll be on the CIC in ten minutes," Nelson added. "Have a cup of coffee ready for me."

Julia stirred as Nelson closed the connection. "What's happening?"

"The enemy reinforcements have arrived," Nelson said, although he wasn't sure it was true. There was something odd about the enemy deployment. "Or...they might be trying something clever."

He stood and hurried into the washroom, showering before emerging and dressing with breakneck speed. Julia watched, clutching the duvet to her breasts and looking as if she hadn't had any more sleep than he had. Nelson grinned at her, then studied the display for a long moment. The enemy could have sneaked a lot closer without setting off any alarms, practically getting into missile range...if, of course, they'd *wanted* to pound his ships into scrap. An idea was gnawing at the back of his mind, nagging at him. Either the enemy commander was an idiot or...

"They're trying to be clever," he said. Cleverness, in his experience, worked better in the simulators than on the battlefield. People remembered the successful tricks, ignoring the simple fact they rarely worked twice. "I bet you half of those ships aren't real."

Julia stood, dropping the duvet. "How do you know?"

Nelson felt his grin turn predatory. "If you had an overwhelming advantage, would you throw it away? Of course not. But they did, which suggests they're either stupid or trying to be clever. And we know they're not stupid."

He watched her dress, then turned to the hatch. "They're trying to scare us," he said. "And I don't intend to let them."

"I hope you're right," Julia said.

Nelson hoped he was right too, as they made their way into the CIC. The theory sounded good in his head, but...was he *right?* Cold logic insisted a superior enemy fleet, particularly one that would take a pounding if it tried to fight fair, would sneak up on his formation and try to blow hell out of it before the sensors realised they were under attack. They lost nothing by trying, even if they *were* detected before it was too late. No, the enemy ships were trying to be clever. They thought they could scare him into retreating. But they'd overplayed their hand.

"Launch probes," he ordered, as he took his seat. "Prepare to leave orbit."

The enemy fleet was still advancing, on a course that was surprisingly leisurely for a fleet that knew it had the edge. Nelson smiled as he sipped his coffee. More proof, as if he'd needed it, that the enemy were trying to be clever. He studied the live feed from the probes, nodding to himself as a number of enemy ships were revealed to be illusions. At least a third of the enemy fleet simply didn't exist. It would have fooled civilian-grade sensors, perhaps even military-grade systems with incompetent operators, but *his* crews knew what they were doing. The sensor ghosts had been noted and logged before they had a chance to draw his fire.

"Admiral," Davis said. "We've identified twenty sensor ghosts amongst the enemy fleet."

"Well, let's pretend to be fooled." Nelson grinned at Julia, then raised his voice as he drew out a line on the console. "Prepare to leave orbit. Let them think we're going to fire a salvo for the honour of the flag."

"Aye, sir."

Julia caught his eye. "What do you have in mind?"

"They're trying to scare us, but we've seen through their deception," Nelson said. "If we charge straight at them, they'll know and alter course themselves. If we look like we're going to try to take a bite out of them as we run, they'll think we're fooled until we alter course to bring our guns into range. And by then it will be too late."

"The fleet is ready to depart, sir," Davis said.

"Then pass the word," Nelson ordered. "Take us out."

He settled back in his seat, feeling the battlecruiser start to leave orbit. Let the enemy think he was fooled. Let them think he intended to fire one shot and then run for his life. Let them think he was an idiot, if they wished. He'd make them pay, once he got within weapons range. They wouldn't be able to run if he caught them by surprise, if he managed to turn *their* surprise against them. He'd tear them to ribbons, then declare victory. The previous defeat would be forgotten, if he managed to produce victory now. There would be no more need to worry about losing everything...

"Admiral," Davis said. "We'll be within weapons range in fifty minutes."

"Good," Nelson said. "Keep active sensors unfocused. No need to give away the surprise too soon."

"Aye, Admiral."

• • •

"I think they know," Tomas said. He was studying his console. "Captain, they're not doing a sensor focus. And they really should."

"Which means they're sure they already have locks on our hulls or they've seen through our trick and are doing their level best to keep us from realising," Kerri said. She felt another thrill of excitement. They knew. She knew they knew. Did they know she knew they knew? It didn't look like it, not yet. Their tactics suggested they were trying to lure her into point-blank range before they revealed their surprise. "Did they sneak a drone through our formation?"

"They might have done," Tomas said. He glanced up, his face grim. "If they flew the drone through on ballistic, we might not have noticed."

Kerri nodded. Drones, particularly top-of-the-line drones, were designed to be hard to track. Not impossible, if the sensor techs were to be believed, but the next best thing. And the enemy crews knew what they were doing. It was quite likely they'd managed to get a good look up her skirts, despite everything she'd done to prevent it. She smiled at the thought. It hadn't been easy to do everything she'd needed to do to keep them from doing just that, without letting them wonder if that was precisely what she wanted them to do. She wanted—she needed—them to think she thought she was fooling them.

This battle will confuse the kids in school, when they read about it, she thought, with a flicker of amusement. *One of us is going to go down in history as an idiot who didn't understand what she was seeing until it was too late.*

She watched, calmly, as the range steadily closed. The enemy fleet wasn't making any attempt to deceive her, as far as she could tell. They seemed bent on firing at long range, before turning and retreating...a wise tactic, if her sensor ghosts had been real. She made a bet with herself that the enemy ships would alter course within twenty minutes, ramping up their speed to close the range as much as possible. It was their best chance to inflict real damage. Even if she turned and fled herself, it would be difficult to get out of range before it was too late.

"Captain," Tomas said. "I just picked up a sensor ghost. I think they flew a second drone though our formation."

"And they definitely know we're faking it," Kerri said. She believed the drone was real. The enemy fleet hadn't focused their sensors, suggesting they felt they didn't *need* to. "Prepare to alter course."

"Aye, Captain."

Nelson could taste Julia's impatience as the two fleets slowly converged, but said nothing. It was difficult to explain to civilians how starships could both travel at unimaginable speeds and yet—also—take so long to come into weapons range. The distances they were travelling were also unimaginable, he supposed. It was difficult to move from living on a planet, where nowhere was more than a few hours away, to living in interplanetary space. It could take days to travel from planet to planet, weeks or months to travel from star to star...it took over three months to travel from the Core to the Rim. He wondered, suddenly, just what was happening along the Rim. Cut off from the Empire, even before Earthfall, who knew what would happen to all the colonies...

"On my mark, swing us into a least-time intercept course and open fire," he ordered, putting the thought aside. The corprats intended to sweep up the colonies, sooner or later, but right now they weren't important. A few decades without help from the outside universe might leave them more inclined to obey their superiors when contact was finally re-established. "On my mark..."

"Aye, Admiral," Davis said. The range steadily ticked down. "The fleet is ready."

"Mark," Nelson said. "Fire!"

The battlecruiser shuddered, altering course as she fired her first salvo. The range was still longer than Nelson would have preferred, but there were limits to how close they could get before the enemy smelled a rat. Besides, if they altered course too late, there was a prospect of the enemy being able to ramp up their own drives and flee *towards* the planet. *That* would be awkward, particularly if they had a chance to hurl missiles or KEWs at the remaining forces on the ground. It would be embarrassing as hell if they managed to nuke Haverford before he caught up with them.

"The enemy fleet is deploying ECM drones," Davis said. "They're trying to spoof our sensors."

"Too late," Nelson said. The display was starting to fill with bursts of static, but it was far too late. He had solid locks on the enemy hulls, on the *real* hulls. The sensor ghosts no longer mattered. They'd be ignored, at least until the real starships were blown away. "Fire at will."

He grinned, savagely, as the enemy fleet seemed to flinch. The range was still too wide, but they'd been caught with their pants down. They wouldn't be able to either stop or outrun his missiles before they slammed into their hulls. The only upside, for them, was that they'd have plenty of time to plot their point defence solutions. Nelson smirked at the thought. He'd run simulations. The marines would have to get outrageously lucky to stop more than two-thirds of his missiles. The remainder would do enough damage to seriously weaken their fleet.

And then the stain of defeat will be washed away, he promised himself. *And we can resume our climb to the top.*

・・・

"Captain," Tomas said. "They've definitely seen through the sensor ghosts."

"I'd be more surprised if they hadn't," Kerri commented. The enemy fleet had altered course with surprising speed—they *were* well-drilled, she conceded sourly—and belched a massive volley of missiles towards her formation. They'd timed it well, too. She couldn't reverse course or race for the planet without getting her butt kicked. "Alter course, as planned."

"Aye, Captain," Commander Joaquin said. "They're ramping up their drives."

"Bring ours to max too," Kerri ordered. She wouldn't have dared on a regular naval ship—there was no way to know who'd skimped on the maintenance, or which component was going to fail spectacularly when the ship went to full military power—but her crew knew the importance of good maintenance. "And then signal Steel. He's to deploy at will."

"Aye, Captain."

Kerri nodded, curtly. The games were over. Now, the enemy fleet was breathing down her neck, trying to destroy or cripple as many of her ships as possible before the range started to widen again. And it was going to end very badly...

...And now it was time to change the rules.

CHAPTER THIRTY-SEVEN

This produced quiet, but not mental surrender.
—Professor Leo Caesius
The Right to be Wrong: How Silencing People Hurts You

IF THIS WORKS, WE WIN, Captain Haydn Steel thought, as the marines drifted through interplanetary space. *And if this fails, we die.*

He put the thought aside as the enemy fleet glided towards them. The marines were too small to detect, if only because they weren't radiating any betraying emissions. Kerri—Captain Stumbaugh, he reminded himself sharply—had promised to deploy ECM drones to ensure the marines were even harder to detect, but Haydn knew better than to assume they'd be totally safe. The enemy might suspect a trap, if they'd realised Kerri was trying to bluff them. They might even work out what she *really* had in mind.

His helmet flickered up alerts as missiles roared past them, heading towards the fleet. The marine ships weren't returning fire as enthusiastically as they should, something else that might tip off the enemy. Their one edge was that the enemy ships *had* to impale themselves on their weapons, if they wanted to keep closing the range. That they were throwing that away…sure it might look like panic, but it might *also* look like a plan. He understood Kerri's logic—the plan would fail if her ships accidentally killed the marines—yet he also saw the weaknesses. They couldn't risk being rumbled until it was far too late to be stopped.

He let out a breath as the enemy battlecruiser came into view. It was a monstrously ugly vessel, a solid cylinder bristling with weapons, sensor nodes and—at the rear—drives. He thought he saw flickers of light on the dark hullmetal as she roared towards them, seemingly unaware of their presence. Haydn flinched, a sudden image of a bug on a windshield nearly overwhelming him as his suit matched course and speed. The enemy ship could swat them, if it realised they were there. It grew and grew until it dominated the horizon.

His perspective shifted rapidly as he crashed onto the hull. The impact was so rough he was *sure* the crew would have heard it, even though cold logic insisted it was unlikely. The engineers had sworn blind the drive units embedded in the suit would be able to merge with the starship's drive field, yet *they* weren't the ones taking the suits into battle…he shook his head as the rest of the company landed. He wished he had more men—he'd had to scatter his force over the enemy capital ships—but he'd have to make do with what he had. He glanced around, checking there were no visible enemy soldiers on the hull, then nodded to the demolitions crew. They unstrapped the makeshift burners from their backs, placed them against the hull and hurried backwards. A moment later, the burners glowed with light. The hullmetal melted, tearing a breach in the hull.

Hurry, he told himself. The gash was already cooling. Superheated air boiled out, dwindling rapidly as airlocks and emergency hatches slammed closed. Anyone in the compartments below would have been killed instantly. *They know we're here now.*

He hurled himself into the gap. The gravity twisted again as he landed in a corridor, yanking him down. Haydn caught himself and hurried forward, pushing through gashes in the inner hull and bulkheads. There were internal layers of armour that could catch and redirect nuclear blasts, but none of them had been designed to deal with a burner. It was just possible they could hack their way out of the bridgehead before it was too late.

And hope they haven't got many armed men on deck, Haydn thought, as he directed his men into four teams. Three would move to secure vital locations, while the fourth would head as far as they could into the ship. If all else failed, they'd detonate their backpack nukes and blow the ship to hell. It wasn't a perfect tactic—Haydn disliked the idea of suicide tactics, even if no one was entirely sure the backpack nukes would do *enough* damage—but there were no alternatives. *They could block us if they move fast.*

• • •

Nelson recoiled in shock. "What the fuck?"

"We've been boarded," Davis said. Alarms—alarms Nelson had never heard, outside training exercises—howled through the giant ship. "They've landed troops on our hull!"

Red icons flashed on the display. "They've burnt their way into the hull," Davis added. "Internal sensors are down!"

Nelson glanced at the display. Captain Allan Barras looked back at him. "Captain?"

"I'm deploying guardsmen now," Barras said. "My crew is trying to keep the marines from breaking into the rest of the ship. But…they don't have many weapons."

"Shit." Nelson cursed out loud. The Imperial Navy rarely allowed its crews to carry weapons. Officially, it wasn't safe to put loaded weapons in the hands of untrained crewmen; unofficially, it was to prevent mutiny. He'd never thought to change that policy, even when he'd offloaded two-thirds of the battlecruiser's security troops to reinforce the army on the ground. "That's not good."

His eyes swung back to the display. The enemy ships had lured him into a trap. That was clear now, too late. They'd let him think they were trying to bluff him…he scowled, realising the enemy would have come out ahead no matter *what* he did. If he'd fled, they'd have retaken the planet; if he'd made a beeline for them, they'd have fled well before he got into weapons range…whatever he did, the enemy would have come out ahead. And yet…

"Continue firing," he ordered, shortly. The enemy fleet was *still* within range. "And isolate the datanet. Switch to manual, where possible. I *don't* want them taking the datanet down."

"Aye, sir," Davis said.

Nelson gritted his teeth as Captain Barras issued further orders, ordering his crew to pick up weapons and repel boarders. Nelson had stood on the captain's toes rather badly…he'd apologise later, if there was a later. More alerts flashed up, warning him that nine of his capital ships had been boarded. The remainder were drawing fire from the enemy fleet. It was nice to know the marines hadn't managed to board *all* his ships…they'd probably thrown the plan together on the fly. Given enough time, they could probably have landed several hundred men on *each* ship.

Julia stared at him. "What now?"

"We repel boarders," Nelson said. The battle wasn't over yet. He couldn't extract himself, not without eliminating the marines who'd invaded his ships, but he sure as hell could make them pay a price for victory. "And we continue to fight."

...

Haydn smiled as he reached an airlock that looked bent and twisted out of shape, then unhooked a charge from his belt and placed it against the hinges before stepping back and hitting the detonator. The hatch exploded inwards, a rush of air flashing past him and out into the vacuum of space. Haydn thrust himself forward, feeling a twinge of guilt as a crewman started to suffocate. There was no time to repair the hatch. It had already been damaged before he'd punched through it.

Sorry, he thought, as he oriented himself. The battlecruiser's design was supposed to be standardised, but it was impossible to be certain the builders hadn't changed the interior design at some point. The ship might have gone through a dozen refits before it was pressed into corprat service. *There isn't time to help.*

His intercom bleeped. "Captain," Lieutenant Frost said. "I found a datanet node, but I can't hack the system."

"Understood." Haydn hadn't expected the hacking attempt to work. A military crew would know better than to allow a boarding party to compromise their systems as soon as they captured a node. "Join Team Four. You can invade the system once we secure the ship."

He glanced back as they reached another hatch. It was sealed, but they had no trouble fiddling with the override and sliding the hatch open. Air rushed out, heading towards the breach in the hull. Haydn frowned, wondering if they'd just walked into a trap. The hatch should have been harder to open, particularly given the vacuum on the far side. And yet, the enemy hadn't sealed it…a hail of bullets snapped towards him, coming from firing positions further down the corridor. Haydn noted the enemy wore masks as they pushed forward, trying to drive the marines back into space. Someone was clearly thinking ahead.

Sergeant Mayberry hurled a set of grenades down the corridor. They detonated seconds later, catching most of the enemy defenders in the blast. Haydn led the way forward, throwing grenades into each of the side cabins as they made their way towards the CIC. The enemy commander *should* be there, he'd been told. It was quite possible the bastard was trying to flee—they'd considered the possibility, back when they'd planned the operation—but it wouldn't be easy to make it out in the middle of a battle. Haydn wouldn't care to fly a shuttle though the battle outside. And even hiding within the hull would cut the enemy commander's communications. Killing a commander was good, isolating him so he couldn't give orders would be even better.

"I've sealed the hatch," Rifleman Kent snapped. "The atmosphere is starting to regenerate."

"Keep your helmets on," Haydn ordered. "We don't want them pumping poison gas into the air and killing us, do we?"

He smiled coldly as they punched through another airlock. It was growing increasingly obvious the defenders weren't trained combat troops. They barely knew how to handle their weapons, let alone think tactically. There were a dozen ways they could have slowed down the marines, if only by setting traps. Haydn almost felt sorry for them. The enemy could at least have given the crew some proper combat training if they were going to throw them at the boarding party.

They probably didn't think they needed to bother, Haydn thought, as he picked off an enemy crewman with a single shot. *And they worried about who the crewmen would want to shoot.*

He smiled, then kept moving. It wasn't over yet.

• • •

"Sir," Davis said. "*Hawking* just exploded. I think the captain triggered the self-destruct."

"Perhaps," Nelson said. He doubted it. Captain Fisher had never been particularly self-sacrificial. *And* her crew had been doing a better job at containing the boarding party. It was far more likely one of the marines had triggered a nuclear bomb inside the cruiser's hull. "Any survivors?"

"No lifepods detected, sir," Davis said. "They might have their beacons switched off."

"They might," Nelson said. He hoped it was true, but he feared it wasn't. "Continue firing."

He gritted his teeth as he studied the display. They *were* hurting the enemy ships. Their point defence was better than he'd expected, but they were still being hurt. And yet, his ships were being invaded. The enemy marines were hacking their way towards the bridge, the CIC and main engineering, slaughtering everyone who got in their way. Nelson shuddered, unable to avoid thinking of cancer cells tearing a human body apart. In hindsight, it was all too clear he'd screwed the pooch.

"Fuck." Julia sounded numb, as if she couldn't muster the energy to feel anything. "I…what do we do?"

"We keep fighting," Nelson said. "We still have the edge."

His mind raced, desperately seeking a way out. If one boarding party carried nuclear bombs, the others would do so too. *Hammerblow* was the biggest ship in his fleet. It was impossible to believe the marines wouldn't have brought nukes with them, when they'd targeted his flagship. And that meant…even if he won the battle, he might be blown to atoms anyway. *Hammerblow* had far more armour than *Hawking*, but the nuke—or nukes—would be exploding inside the hull. In theory, the blast would be survivable. In practice…he didn't want to be anywhere near a nuke when it went off. There was no way to be *sure* they'd survive.

And no way to keep them from detonating the nukes, he thought. Even shooting the marines wouldn't be enough to stop them, not if the weapons had a dead man's switch. *We're doomed whatever we do.*

"Increase speed, run the drives into the red if you must," he ordered. Oddly, the certain knowledge his career was now doomed made it easier to give the right orders. "The ships which do *not* have boarding parties are to take up the rear. Ready a flight of shuttlecraft to take off essential personnel."

Davis hesitated. "Yes, sir."

Nelson winced. "And order the non-alpha crews to break off and head for the lifepods," he said, feeling a twinge of conscience. He could at least *try* to save his crew. "And continue firing."

"Aye, sir." Davis didn't sound happy. "Drives ramping up…now."

"Good." Nelson stood. He didn't really blame his subordinate for having doubts. He was effectively saving his own skin, doing as little as he could for his crew to salve his conscience. "Once the shuttles are ready, we'll take our leave."

. . .

Haydn dropped back as the next hatch exploded, revealing empty corridor. A faint mist hung in the air. His sensors poked at it, then concluded it was harmless. Haydn frowned, wondering if the enemy was trying to bluff him. There were plenty of stories of people filling the air with something misty and then claiming it was actually rocket fuel or something else that would explode the moment someone struck a light. He'd seen something like it happen once, although the bastard hadn't been bluffing. That hadn't ended well.

He inched forward, feeling a dull vibration echoing though the hull. The battlecruiser was picking up speed, running its drives up to the point where catastrophic failure was just a matter of time. Haydn suspected that wasn't good news. If the ship's crew had realised they were doomed no matter what they did, they might just have decided to try to ram their ship into *Havoc* or one of the other cruisers. The squadron was flying in such a tight formation that the explosion might take out more than one ship.

Sergeant Mayberry caught his arm. "Sir, the CIC's down there," he said, jabbing an armoured finger down the corridor. "We have to move!"

Haydn nodded. "Understood," he said. Time wasn't on their side. "Hurry!"

• • •

"Admiral, I'm picking up a signal from the surface," Davis reported. "The marine tanks are on the move. General Rask is requesting fire support."

Nelson let out a harsh laugh. "Does the general know where we are? What we're doing?"

He silently tipped his hat to the marine commanders. They'd timed it well, very well. Even if he regained control of his ship without further ado, even if he managed to break contact with the enemy fleet—or destroy it—even if…he'd never get back to the planet in time to save the landing force. General Rask was on his own. The marines wouldn't have the advantage of orbital fire, but neither would he. They were both well and truly fucked.

And to think I was going to make him the scapegoat, he thought. *There's going to be enough shit coming our way to bury all of us.*

Alarms howled. "Sir," Davis said. "They're outside! Outside the hatch!"

Julia turned towards the hatch, as if she intended to jump right through it. Nelson didn't stop her. There were no other ways to leave the compartment. And even if they could, where would they go? The marines were already breaking into main engineering, where they could shut down the drives and depower the entire ship. Two other ships had already dropped out of the command network. Surrendered? Or merely turned into powerless hulks? It didn't really matter. The battle was over.

"It's over," Nelson said. The words hung in the air. "It's over."

The hatch exploded inwards. Nelson caught himself before he could draw his pistol as a pair of armoured forms crashed into the chamber. They looked ready to fight, ready to gun the entire command crew down if they so much as made one false move. Nelson forced himself to raise his hands, trying to look as harmless as possible. Julia and he had *something* to negotiate with, if they lived long enough to speak to their counterparts. But they had to live.

"Shut down your drives and weapons," the marine grated. "And tell your fleet to surrender."

"As you wish." Nelson glanced at Davis. "Do it."

Julia started to mutter to herself, shaking as she fell to the deck. The marines glanced at her, then turned back to Nelson. Nelson stared back at them, wishing—inanely—that he could see their faces. Their blank helms were hellishly intimidating. It was suddenly easy to believe they lived up to their reputation.

"Signal sent, sir," Davis said. "The fleet is surrendering now."

"Good," the marine said. He motioned the captured staff into a corner as his comrades took the consoles, hacking into the datacores with practiced ease. "And now we wait."

And see, Nelson thought. There were no other options. *And hope we can find a way to come out ahead.*

He shook his head as he pulled Julia against him. There wasn't a way to come out ahead, not now. The best they could hope for was striking a deal...

• • •

"Captain," Tomas said. "The enemy fleet is powering down."

Kerri breathed a sigh of relief. "Detail two ships to watch over the enemy fleet, then reassemble the remainder of the squadron," she ordered. It wasn't over yet. Not quite. "And then set course for the planet. Best possible speed."

"Aye, Captain."

CHAPTER THIRTY-EIGHT

Indeed, given the simple fact that living in such an environment provokes both resentment and fear, someone may simply keep their mouth shut—or deny knowing anything—when they could speak up and stop the disaster from ever happening.
—**Professor Leo Caesius**
The Right to be Wrong: How Silencing People Hurts You

"DEREK! DEREK!"

Derek woke, disentangling himself from Jenny as Roger crashed into the makeshift bedroom. There was very little privacy, but it hadn't stopped them from celebrating their survival every time they returned from a mission. The enemy was bringing in more troops from somewhere, making it harder and harder to carry out an attack successfully. They'd had to call off one attack when they'd realised the enemy was ready and waiting for them.

Roger waved a communicator under Derek's nose. "They're coming!"

"Fuck!" Derek jumped up, heedless of his nakedness. "Who's coming!"

"The marines!" Roger shoved the communicator into Derek's hand. "They're coming back!"

"What happened?" Derek glanced down at the communicator. "They won?"

"They smashed the enemy army," Roger said. "And they've drawn the fleet out of place. We have a window—if we move now!"

Derek grabbed for his trousers and pulled them on. "Go alert the others, tell them to spread the word," he ordered. He glanced at the clock. It was early morning. "How long until the marines arrive."

"Their tanks will be here in a few hours, I'm told," Roger said. "There might be others here sooner."

"Got it," Derek said. It was *important* that the insurgents liberated the city before the marines arrived, if at all possible. God knew what sort of future the planet would have, but it would have a better chance of a *decent* future if it saved itself. "Go tell the others. I'll be along in a moment."

He yanked on his shirt as Roger hurried away. They'd spent the last week building up and arming more insurgent cells, knowing it was only a matter of time before the enemy brought troops back to Haverford. They might have lost control of entire swathes of the city, but there was no way they'd let that stand. They wanted—they needed—to seem invincible. They wanted people to believe resistance was futile. They couldn't do *that* if half the city was firmly outside their control.

Jenny sat up and reached for her clothes. "You think this is it?"

"Let's hope so." Derek wanted to tell her to go hide somewhere, but he knew she'd never agree. "Are you ready?"

"Yeah." Jenny dressed quickly, then picked up and checked the pistol he'd given her. "I think so."

Derek nodded as he checked his own weapons. It wasn't going to be easy, no matter what happened. The enemy had managed—somehow—to keep word of the defeat from getting out too early. Derek and the others had planned for a long-term insurgency, a steady series of pinpricks rather than a single massive explosion. It would take time, time they didn't have, to craft a full uprising. Their planning barely touched upon seizing the city and holding it until the marines arrived. He hastily reviewed what little they knew of the enemy dispositions. In theory, the insurgents could take the city and hold it. In practice, it would depend upon how quickly—and brutally—the enemy reacted.

He smiled at Jenny, feeling a surge of emotions he didn't dare look at too closely. Love and protectiveness and worry and fear and...he wondered, suddenly, just what sort of future they had. If indeed there was a future... the enemy wouldn't hold back, if they realised they'd switched from holding Haverford to fighting for their lives. They might call down fire from outside the city, smashing the insurgency strongpoint by strongpoint. Or they might just seal themselves up and wait, praying desperately their reinforcements arrived before the marines dug them out. Why not? It had happened once before.

Derek met her eyes. "When this is over...want to get married?"

Jenny laughed. "I think that's bad luck," she said. "How many flicks have you watched where the engaged couple is the first to die?"

"Those are *flicks*," Derek pointed out. "Not real life."

"True." Jenny leaned forward and kissed him. "Ask me afterwards, if there is an afterwards."

"Understood." Derek kissed her back, then turned and headed for the door. The remainder of the cells would already be gathering, readying themselves to do or die. "Let's move."

...

"Got some air-search sensors ahead of us," the pilot called. "I'm staying as low as possible."

"Don't let the ground come up and hit you," Phelps called back. "It would be pretty damn awkward if we had to wait for the tankers."

Rachel nodded as she checked and rechecked their weapons. The Raptor was designed to be stealthy, but they'd learned too much about the enemy's air defences to be sanguine about their chances if they flew too close to a sensor node. She would have preferred to sneak through the enemy lines, counting on the fact they weren't *trying* to hit their positions to provide an extra degree of protection. But they didn't have time. The enemy troops had been flooding back to the city, ever since the wave had smashed their vehicles and halted their advance in its tracks. The marine tankers were driving on the city themselves, but they were trying to circumvent the enemy positions. It was quite likely they wouldn't reach the city in time to prevent a massacre.

"We'll be crossing the motorway in five minutes," the pilot said. "And I'll drop you a minute afterwards."

"Got it." Bonkowski grinned at his team. "Any of you want to back out now?"

"I forgot to write a will," Perkins said. "Can I do it now?"

"Just remember to leave everything to me," Rachel said. The joke helped defuse the growing tension. She'd made drops into hostile territory before, but this was the first time they'd flown through a modern air defence network. It was quite possible they'd be blown out of the sky before they even knew they'd been detected. "In fact, why don't you let me write the will for you?"

"I'll remember you in my will," Perkins said. "No money. I'll just say I remembered you."

Bonkowski laughed, then sobered. "Brace yourselves," he ordered. "We'll only get one shot at this."

Rachel nodded, silently counting down the seconds as unexploited forests and valleys became increasingly developed and populated—and abandoned—farms. She spotted a handful of burnt-out buildings, destroyed during the first or second invasion. There was no one in view, as far as she could tell. She hoped the farmers had managed to make it out before it was too late. They'd be needed, after the fighting was over. Man couldn't live on ration bars alone.

Well, technically they can, she mused, as the pilot started to count down to zero. *They just hate it.*

The Raptor flashed over the motorway, guns and rocket launchers yammering as they spotted targets of opportunity. Explosions shook the air, shaking the aircraft violently. They'd been no way to predict what they'd encounter, no way to turn on active sensors to sweep the area without inviting the enemy to kill them. She gritted her teeth as the aircraft raced over the city, potting a handful of missiles towards known enemy positions as it crossed the river. There was no point in trying to hide now. The enemy would have seen them with the naked eye.

"Two seconds," the pilot said. The Raptor came to a stop, hovering above a—hopefully—abandoned building. "And go!"

The hatches slammed open. Rachel stood, grabbed hold of the rope and hurled herself into space. The building seemed to rise towards her—she thought she saw someone staring at her in horror—as she twisted through the air, yanking on the rope hard enough to slow her fall before she hit the rooftop. Behind her, the rest of the squad dropped down and headed straight for the pipes. Scrambling down to the ground was hardly the safest thing to do, even if the city's builders had been neurotic about making sure the pipes were securely fixed to the walls. They had to move fast. The enemy might already be calling in mortar shots on their position. They'd never have a better chance to hit the Raptor—and the Pathfinders—before they were gone.

She breathed a sigh of relief as she touched down. The streets were empty, surprisingly so. The briefing had stated the enemy had ordered everyone to stay off the streets, but there'd been no guarantee the civilians would actually follow orders. Haverford felt odd, compared to the last time she'd visited. The vast majority of the groundcars and aircars she'd seen were gone. The remainder were burnt-out wrecks. A handful of buildings were scarred, or covered with pockmarks. The insurgency hadn't had much time to prepare, but it had clearly given the enemy a decent fight. Rachel smiled, coldly, as they started to lope down the street. Given a little help, they'd take the city before the tankers arrived.

Unless the enemy fleet surrenders, she thought. The briefing had been grim. The fleet had been drawn away, as planned, but it hadn't been beaten. Rachel had every confidence in her comrades, yet she had to admit they might lose the engagement. And if that happened...she shook her head.

There was no point in worrying about it now. *We have to take the city before the fleet gets back.*

"This way," Bonkowski said. "I have a beacon."

"Great," Phelps said. "We're doomed."

Bonkowski made a rude gesture, then led them further into the city.

...

"Sir! Sir!"

Garfield jerked awake, so dazed and confused he honestly wasn't sure if he were still dreaming. The journey back to the city had been nightmarish, yet...his dreams had tormented him ever since he'd closed his eyes. He'd watched Janelle die, time and time again; he'd watched his hopes and dreams die when the tidal wave had washed across his forces. Hundreds of men—men he should know, but didn't—had died in his nightmares. He reached into his pouch, trying desperately to find a stimulant. They were frowned upon in combat, but he saw no choice. He'd only slept for an hour or two.

He pressed the tab against his skin, then scowled at the messenger. "Report!"

"The streets are full of protestors," the messenger said. "And they're coming here!"

Garfield stood on wobbly legs, barking orders at his men as they woke. They *were* his men, although two-thirds of them came from different units. The unit had been put together out of refugees and left under his command...Lopez was gone. It was impossible to tell if he was alive or dead, if he was struggling back to the city or languishing in an enemy POW camp or...or what? Garfield promised Janelle's ghost he'd take care of them. He'd make sure they wouldn't be thrown away, this time. A soldier brought him a mug of coffee and he drank it automatically, barely noticing the taste. It rested heavily in his stomach, mingling awkwardly with the stimulant. Garfield didn't have time to worry about it.

The messenger hurried away. Garfield keyed his terminal, hoping for orders, but there was nothing. The communication channels were full of shouting, of endless panicky reports that were retracted bare seconds after they were made...the enemy was at the gates, the enemy was inside the city...no, the enemy was thousands of miles away. He couldn't tell who was in command...he couldn't tell if *anyone* was in command. General Rask seemed to have dropped out of sight. Garfield waved at Corporal Psaltery, who seemed to be the second in command by default, and ordered him to get the men ready to deploy. Thankfully, the government complex didn't seem to be under immediate attack.

Garfield stumbled outside, catching sight of a colonel running into the next room. He followed, even though—normally—he wouldn't be allowed anywhere near the complex's nerve centre. Corporate royalty or not, he was only a mere lieutenant. He was tempted to ask if he could get a promotion—he was effectively commanding a company now—but swallowed the urge before it could get him into shit. The higher-ups were probably hunting desperately for a whipping boy. He doubted his connections would save him if the shit really hit the fan.

General Rask was standing by the big display, looking grim. Entire swathes of the city were faded, hidden under the fog of war. Red icons were scattered everywhere, each one marking a bomb or shooting or...it was hard to be sure. The occupation force was no longer in control. The insurgents were growing bolder by the second, overrunning small bases while isolating larger strongpoints. And they were taking control of the streets leading to the motorway. The government complex itself was growing increasingly isolated. Garfield winced as a staff officer started shouting about enemy HVM teams. The airspace was no longer safe either.

He saluted as General Rask looked at him. "Sir."

"You have a company under your command," General Rask said. He went on before Garfield could answer the question, if indeed it *was* a question. "Take them here"—he tapped a spot on the map—"and clear the streets. I want the route to the motorway and the landing zone cleared, by all means necessary. Do you understand me?"

"Yes, sir," Garfield said. It was their only hope of extracting men and materiel from the city before it was too late. "I understand."

"Consider yourself promoted," General Rask added. "Congratulations, Captain."

He probably doesn't know my name, Garfield thought. He'd been told, more than once, that a captaincy would be the very peak of his career. He might rise further, but he'd never enjoy direct command again. And yet... right now, the promotion felt more like a poisoned chalice than a reward for good service. *Fuck.*

His veins burned as he headed outside, barking commands at everyone within earshot. A pair of AFVs sat in the courtyard, their drivers looking for orders. Garfield snapped them up, adding them to his command before they could muster a protest. They probably didn't *know* he was a captain, not yet—he still had an LT's rank bars—but no one seemed to be in command. He felt a flicker of grim amusement as the company rallied, readying itself to march out and clear the streets. There was so much chaos in the complex that *anyone* could start issuing orders, as long as they sounded as though they had a plan.

He ordered Corporal Psaltery to bring up the rear—Garfield intended to lead from the front, even though he knew he could be shot at any moment—then led the company onto the streets. The sound of distant explosions and gunfire and shouting was deafening, echoing off the buildings and blurring into a single giant crescendo of noise. Garfield clenched his teeth as his head started to pound, trying to ignore the ever-growing hammering battering its way into his brain. It was hard, so hard, to remain focused. The ground shook, repeatedly, as IEDs or shells detonated. He could no longer tell the difference.

They reached the edge of the complex and headed into the unknown. The giant buildings seemed harmless, but who could tell? The road might be big, on a human scale, but it was a pathetically-cramped battlefield. The work crews had cleared away the abandoned vehicles, and everything else that could be used as cover, yet...he found himself eyeing the buildings with concern. Anyone could be in there, anyone at all. The shops could become strongpoints at a moment's notice. He winced as he saw a series of explosions overhead, shells intercepted before they could fall on the government complex. And...

His heart clenched as a row of people emerged from the distant buildings, flooding onto the streets. It was a protest march, spearheaded by armed men...insurgents. They *had* to be insurgents. He felt a surge of hatred for the bastards, for the ungrateful assholes who'd betrayed his family and turned on them...didn't they know they'd been saved? Didn't they know they would have died—or worse—if they'd stayed on Earth? Their sons would have gone into gangs, their daughters trapped in an endless cycle of rape and pregnancy and early death...he lifted his rifle, snapping orders as the protesters grew closer. They were clogging the roads...how *dare* they?

"Take aim," he ordered, coldly. Rage built within him. The security troops should have cleared the streets, but the bastards were nowhere to be seen. Typical! They'd happily harass women and little girls and everyone else who couldn't fight back, but whenever *real* danger was looming they ran for their lives. "Prepare to fire."

The protestors moved closer. They looked...normal. They'd been biding their time, waiting to see who won before they chose a side. He cursed them mentally, as savagely as he could. Janelle had *died* for them. Countless men he didn't know—men who'd been under his command, yet strangers—had died for them. And they were rejecting him. And now...now the fighting was over, they were trying to show their loyalty to the marines, to the ones who'd plunged their world into war. And they were clogging the streets...

It isn't over yet, he thought coldly. The protesters were marching right towards armed men, driven by self-righteousness and stupidity. *Not yet.*

His finger tightened on the trigger. "Fire."

CHAPTER THIRTY-NINE

Some of them will do it because they are too scared to speak, even when they know they're in the right; some of them will do it—or not do it—because it's the only sort of revenge they'll ever be allowed to take. Petty? Yes. Human? Yes.
—**Professor Leo Caesius**
The Right to be Wrong: How Silencing People Hurts You

"SHIT."

Derek watched in horror as the enemy troops opened fire, bullets tearing through the crowd like knives through butter. It wasn't the first time he'd seen innocent civilians killed, but...it was the first time he'd seen them mown down like...his mind refused to process what he'd seen, as if by ignoring the massacre he could cause it not to be. Not to have happened... he caught himself as the crowd wavered and broke, the survivors running for their lives. He'd never thought, when he'd arranged the protest, that the enemy would gun them down. He'd never thought...

His brain spun in circles. How many people had just died? How many people were lying on the street, bleeding to death? The enemy troops didn't seem concerned by what they'd done. They were already pushing forward, putting the wounded out of their misery as they advanced. Derek saw a young man, barely into his teens, shot as he tried to crawl away. The streets were drenched in blood.

He bit his lip, hard. "Hit them. Hard."

The shooting started, immediately. Derek gritted his teeth, taking aim as the enemy troops scattered for cover. He'd never imagined...he wondered, in hindsight, how he could have been so stupid. He'd assumed the enemy would hesitate to blow away the experienced men they needed to rebuild the planet, never realising the enemy knew they were already screwed. Even if they won the war, without further ado, things would never be the same again. The planet had found its voice. The population wouldn't be content to be corprat slaves again.

Jenny looked pale, but grimly determined. "They killed..."

"Keep firing," Derek said. He keyed his communicator. "Assault teams, go."

...

Rachel was no stranger to atrocity. She'd seen everything from villages being attacked—their menfolk killed, their womenfolk raped and then killed, their children stolen to replenish enemy ranks—to horrors on a planetary scale, but even *she* felt numb horror at the scene unfolding beneath her. Insurgencies were never clean—she'd played both the insurgent and the counter-insurgent—yet slaughtering so many people so casually was a new horror. She couldn't count how many people had been killed in the last few seconds.

She lifted her rifle and swept the enemy force for targets as mortars started thudding in the distance. The insurgents had intended to lay siege to the government complex, rather than try to take it by force, but now...now they intended to storm the buildings and kill everyone inside. Lasers swept through the air, trying to swat the shells before they fell into the enemy complex; counterbattery guns fired, trying to take out the mortar crews before they relocated and fired again. Rachel prayed the tankers would stop arsing around and get to the city before it was too late. Whoever won, there was going to be a dreadful slaughter if the tankers didn't get there on time.

"Find their commanders," Phelps said. "They have to be there somewhere."

Rachel wasn't so sure. The enemy force was acting more like a mob than an organised and directed military unit. Disciplined units didn't carry out atrocities...usually. They certainly didn't *look* like the green-tabbed security troops she'd witnessed pushing unarmed and helpless people around. The force in her scope was advancing forward, a strange combination of disciplined and undisciplined manoeuvre. She wasn't sure there was anyone in command any longer.

She selected a target and fired, once. The target dropped. The enemy troops normally swung their weapons around and unloaded everything on the sniper, but *these* troops didn't seem to notice they'd lost an officer. They just kept firing in all directions. Rachel had heard all the jokes about unit efficiency doubling when their officers were shot, but—in the real world—that wasn't actually true. Were they *really* a mob? Or had she missed the commander? A smart commander wouldn't wear a nice sharp uniform where a sniper could see him. Her lips quirked as she picked off another possible candidate. The nice girls wouldn't like a man in uniform if his brains were on the floor.

"The tankers are picking up speed," Bonkowski yelled. "But they're not going to be here for an hour, even if they don't run into any opposition!"

"Fuck," Rachel said. The plan had gone haywire the moment it had encountered the enemy. "What now?"

"Keep firing," Bonkowski said. An explosion, closer than most, shook the city. "And hope we can help the insurgents win."

Rachel gritted her teeth as a skyscraper started to tumble into a pile of debris. Smoke and dust drifted across the city. She could see mobs in the streets, attacking enemy troops and collaborators with their bare hands. Whoever won, Haverford was never going to return to normal. The population wanted blood. Anyone who'd so much as *smiled* at the enemy troops was going to be brutally murdered. And there was no one who could stop it.

She shot another man, then another. But it wasn't enough.

...

Garfield laughed as he splashed through the blood, finally feeling as if he was coming to grips with the enemy. He shot three men who were wounded, then hurled a pair of grenades into a shop that had concealed a pair of shooters. An insurgent tried to run, only to be gunned down as the AFVs advanced forward. Garfield snapped commands, telling the crews to put shells into the nearest enemy strongpoints. There wouldn't be anything left of the city by the time they were done, but it didn't matter. He intended to clear a path out if it meant flattening the entire city.

He watched as they ground their way to an intersection, barking orders for more troops to come forward and hold the territory. Their bloodlust was up, discipline fading as they finally got a chance to wrap their arms around the enemy's neck and squeeze. Garfield smiled in cold delight as he gunned down another insurgent, kicking the man's corpse as he kept moving. He knew, on some level, that he'd lost it completely, but he no longer cared. The insurgency was doomed. There would be no attempt to win hearts and minds any longer. Dead bodies were much less trouble. They wouldn't kill good soldiers in treacherous ambushes...

Smoke drifted across the battlefield, the enemy trying desperately to use it for cover. He wasn't deterred, even as IEDs started to explode. He keyed his communicator, calling down shellfire on enemy strongpoints. The command network was fading, as if it were being jammed. Garfield was almost relieved. The commanders—even General Rask—had screwed the dickhead one too many times. This time, *he'd* be in command. They'd be glad afterwards, when he'd finished. They could abandon the city and nuke what remained of it, then bring in a new population from Earth and the other Core Worlds. *They'd* be properly grateful. Earthfall should have taught them a lesson.

His headset bleeped. "Return to the FOB. Immediately."

Garfield blinked. "What? Say again?"

"Return to the FOB." General Rask sounded tired. Beaten. "Admiral Agate has been defeated. We have orders to surrender and prepare for a peaceful transfer of power. That is a direct order..."

"No." Garfield spoke before he could think better of it. But he didn't *want* to think better of it. They'd done too much, sacrificed too much, to *surrender*. The cowards in orbit had probably taken one look at the enemy fleet and soiled themselves. They'd never been within a kilometre of *real* danger. They didn't know they *couldn't* surrender. "I..."

"That is a direct order," General Rask repeated. "You are to withdraw..."

Garfield tore the headset from his helmet and threw it away. General Rask would be grateful, afterwards. Garfield would be rewarded, once he brought the general victory. Admiral Agate probably hadn't surrendered, not really. Garfield knew his commissioner. *She* would never have signed off on surrender, not as long as the Onge remained alive. A retreat, yes. A surrender? No. Never.

A shot cracked through the air. Garfield turned and saw a building occupied by insurgents. It looked tougher than most, bullets leaving pockmarks on the walls rather than bursting through and doing *real* damage. Garfield was tempted to call the AFVs to take the building down—the gunners had probably already been told to stand down, the cowards—but he wanted to wrap his hands around the enemy's throat. He snapped orders, a platoon forming around him as he headed to the strongpoint. They wouldn't get away, not this time.

Smiling, Garfield yanked a grenade from his belt and hurled it through the window.

• • •

"Grenade," Roger shouted.

Derek winced as the building shook, pieces of plaster and sawdust falling from the ceiling. They'd picked the building because it had been over-designed—he wasn't sure why, although he had a couple of private theories—but, in some ways, it was a weakness as much as a strength. The enemy had just broken through the walls and was heading upstairs. And Derek was on the second floor. It had made a good sniper nest, but now... There was little hope of getting out before it was too late.

"Jenny, get out of here," he ordered. He cursed himself for stupidity. He should never have let her come with them, even if she *was* a good shot. He should have tied her up and left her in the safehouse. She'd have hated him afterwards, but at least she'd be alive. He'd have happily lived with her hatred if it meant she was alive to hate him. "Go down the pipe outside and *run*."

"But..."

"Go," Derek snapped. "Move!"

Roger took a grenade of his own and hurled it down the stairs. Hopefully, the enemy would take the brunt of the impact. Even if they didn't...the building shook again, a distant crash suggesting the ceiling below had caved in. Derek glared at Jenny until she turned and left...he prayed, silently, she'd survive her flight. The enemy had gone mad, gunning down everyone they saw. Derek thought they were trying to kill *everyone*. There was no looting, no raping...just death. They'd lost it completely.

The floor heaved. Derek found himself being thrown across the room. Roger yelled—in pain or shock or...Derek couldn't tell—and threw himself down the stairs. There was a yell and a bang, then the sound of running footsteps. Derek hit the ground, one hand scrambling desperately for a pistol. Someone was coming up the stairs...

...

Garfield ducked as a grenade shot past him, hitting the ground as it exploded. Pieces of debris flew through the air, none of them coming *close* to hitting him. He giggled as he picked himself up and hurried for the stairs. He was invincible, unbeatable. He'd walked through clouds of bullets and never so much as been scratched. Janelle had died to turn him into an unstoppable warrior, a killing machine that could not be halted. He could not even be slowed down. A shape flew at him, a dark man wearing a black outfit. Garfield shot the insurgent in the chest, then stood aside and watched the man fall to the floor. He might not be dead, but it didn't matter. The wound would kill him slowly if it didn't kill him quickly.

He kept moving, ignoring the growing pain in his chest. He'd lost count of how many stimulants he'd taken, but it didn't matter. He needed to keep moving, he needed to produce victory...he needed it to be for something. He couldn't stand the thought of it all being for nothing. Someone was shouting outside, something about...surrender? Garfield ground his teeth in rage. He was going to hang the traitor himself, be he a mere private or a general...perhaps it was time for General Rask to meet the hangman's noose. He'd betrayed his oath when he'd tried to order a surrender. No wonder the troops weren't listening to him.

A shape moved, behind him. Garfield turned, too late, as the insurgent slammed into him.

...

Derek crashed into the enemy soldier, sending them both crashing to the ground. The man was strong, stronger than he'd thought. He didn't seem to notice Derek's blows, even though they were hitting soft flesh. His eyes burnt with madness, his mouth drooling...Derek realised, to his horror, that the man was drugged to the gills. Blood spilled, gushing from a wound on cheek. And yet he kept fighting, hitting out and trying to wrap his hands around Derek's neck. And...

"Die," the man snarled. Outside, the shooting was gradually dying away. Someone was shouting orders, commanding the troops to stand down. "Die, you..."

He bumped Derek's arm. Derek felt the knife on his opponent's belt, an instant before the man wrapped his hands around Derek's neck and started to squeeze. Derek grabbed the knife and drove it, as hard as he could, into his opponent's chest. He let out a gurgle, his mouth opening to spit blood...his entire body convulsing in shock. Derek pulled himself free, then stabbed the man in the throat. He shuddered, then lay still.

"Fuck," Derek said, numbly. His neck hurt. His body hurt. "What were you on?"

He forced himself to stand, somehow. The streets seemed to have fallen quiet, but...Roger and Jenny were still out there. His legs felt unsteady, but he managed to half-walk, half-crawl down the stairs. Roger was lying on the bottom floor, his body resting in a pool of blood. Derek checked his pulse, but he knew it was only a formality. Roger was dead. He wished, suddenly, he'd known more about the other man. They might have fought together, but they hadn't shared any real confidences. Now...

His hand dropped to his pistol as he heard someone entering the house. "Derek?"

Derek blinked. "Jenny?"

"They're surrendering." Jenny looked at Roger's body and winced. She hadn't known Roger any better than Derek himself, but...they'd shared so much together. "It's over."

"Is it?" Derek took her hand and held it, gently. He knew he should tell her off for coming back, but—right now—he just wanted to hold her. "It feels as though it will never be over."

...

"The tankers will be here in twenty minutes," Phelps reported. "The enemy defences have gone silent."

Rachel didn't feel very reassured as the squad made its way towards the government complex. They were terrifyingly exposed, something she'd been taught to shun if at all possible. If the enemy was planning an ambush, they'd take the brunt of it. She braced herself as the makeshift defences came into view. The government complex hadn't been designed for a long siege. *She* would have installed a hell of a lot more defences if *she'd* been in charge.

But it would have taken time to build an invincible fortress, she reminded herself. *They simply didn't have the time.*

General Rask met them at the gates, looking a broken man. Rachel wasn't too surprised. He'd failed his superiors—bad enough, as far as the corprats were concerned—and forces under his command had committed atrocities. Bad things happened in war, but there were limits. General Rask was looking at a firing squad, if it turned out he'd ordered the atrocities or simply done nothing to stop them. A WARCAT team was already on the way. It might be victor's justice, Rachel thought savagely, but it would be all they'd get. And if it turned out the person who'd ordered the atrocity was already dead...

"Order your troops to put down their weapons," Bonkowski said, as he collected General Rask's firearm. It was more symbolic than anything else, but everyone in uniform would understand. "They'll be held until the WARCAT team has finished its work."

General Rask scowled, but nodded. He looked too tired to argue. Rachel found it hard to feel anything for him, beyond a grim determination to make sure he paid for his crimes. If, indeed, they had been *his* crimes. There'd be people in the city—people with weapons—who'd feel Rask was responsible, even if he hadn't issued the orders. It might be safer to transport him off-world as quickly as possible. The insurgents would have no other way of taking revenge.

Silence fell, broken only by the Raptors as they hastily ferried occupation troops to the government complex. There was no provisional government, no civilian entity willing and able to take control. God alone knew what was going to happen, once the insurgents got over their shock and the civilians realised what had happened. Their city had been devastated. Thousands were dead, thousands more were wounded...supplies of power, water and food had been cut off. And it wasn't going to be easy to get everything back online. The marines were going to take the brunt of their rage, damn it. She didn't blame them. The planet had been a nice place—if creepy—before the first invasion had begun.

And it isn't over yet, she told herself, numbly. The vast majority of the enemy troops had surrendered, but some seemed more inclined to go underground and continue the fight. They would have to be dealt with, quickly. *The enemy reinforcements could arrive at any moment. Again.*

CHAPTER FORTY

And this is, in a very real sense, a major factor in the decline and fall of the Empire itself. Speaking truth to power was no longer permitted. And so 'power' no longer knew when matters were sliding out of control.
—**Professor Leo Caesius**
The Right to be Wrong: How Silencing People Hurts You

"**The only thing costlier than a battle lost,**" General Anderson said quietly, "is a battle won."

Derek scowled. It had been a week since the Second Battle of Haverford, a week spent burying the dead, clearing up the damage and trying to plan for a future that looked as much in doubt as ever. The planet had taken a beating, the population was badly traumatised, there were thousands of enemy POWs to deal with and…the list of problems seemed never-ending. He'd barely even had a moment to catch his breath before being plunged back into the fray.

"That makes no sense," he said, as they stood in Gabe Alyson's office. Jenny's father had become the head of the provisional government, at least partly because there weren't many other prospective candidates. "At least you *won*."

"Perhaps," General Anderson said. "But we also have to deal with the aftermath."

Derek resisted the urge to point out that the marines had *started* the war. He understood their logic—he understood what the corprats were doing, and what they *would* have done if they'd been left alone—but too many people had died in the past few months for him to be *pleased*. Roger was dead, Jock was dead…Gayle was dead. He wasn't sure when and where she'd died, or what had happened to her in the moments before her death. He couldn't help feeling guilty. She'd been cut down and…and he hadn't even *known* until her body had been found among the dead.

"Yeah," he said. "I know."

He felt tired, tired and worn. His family was scattered. Too many of his friends and comrades were dead. It felt as if everyone he'd ever known was dead or wounded or simply confined to a refugee or detention camp until they could be sorted out. Jenny's father had a hard task ahead of him, preparing the planet for its first free elections. Derek wasn't sure just how *free* they'd be. Jenny's father wouldn't want to give up power in a hurry. And the marines would be more interested in installing a friendly government than a decent one.

"It doesn't get easier," General Anderson said. "Have you thought about my offer?"

Derek nodded. "You want me to be a general," he said. "Why…why *me*?"

"You fought well," General Anderson said. "And you're a bridge between the old and the new."

"And you have a lot of admirers," Gabe Alyson pointed out. "Including my daughter."

Which can't be too pleasant for you, Derek thought. *You wanted Jenny to marry someone powerful, not…*

He put the thought aside. "If I do this, I will be my own man," he said. "I won't be a puppet."

"Good," General Anderson said. "That's what we want."

Derek lifted his eyebrows, ignoring the sharp intake of breath from Gabe Alyson. "Why? I mean...why *don't* you want a puppet?"

"In the short term, puppets are always useful," General Anderson said. "But, in the long term, they're more trouble than they're worth. Their own people grow to resent them, even if the puppets themselves don't resent being *treated* as puppets. And then they get overthrown or rebellious or..."

He shrugged. "We're interested in rebuilding the empire," he added. "But we don't want to repeat the mistakes of the past."

"I understand," Derek said. He wasn't entirely blind to the politics. Jenny and he had discussed them, late into the night. Derek *couldn't* go back to the corprats. He'd be loyal to the planet, if not to the marines. And his role would make it easier for Gabe Alyson to surrender power, if—when—he was voted out of office. "What do you think will happen now?"

"Right now, you rebuild the planet and prepare for the worst," General Anderson said. "And we'll look for ways to keep the worst from happening."

"Good," Derek said. "But it seems to me the worst has already happened."

"It isn't over yet," General Anderson said. "Just ask the folks on Earth."

• • •

The city felt uneasily quiet as Gerald travelled from the government complex to the shuttleport, then clambered into a shuttle for the brief trip to orbit. Haverford was still trying to come to terms with everything that had happened, from the massacre to the final desperate battle in the streets. It didn't help, Gerald supposed, that the WARCAT team had proved General Rask hadn't ordered the slaughter. Hanging him in public might *just* have put a dampener on their rage.

He checked the reports as the shuttle headed straight for *Havoc*. The enemy fleet had surrendered, although it was hard to tell if the enemy *government* knew the fighting was over. Gerald hadn't been too surprised to discover the presence of political commissioners, watchdogs keeping a wary eye on the starship commanders and crew; it wasn't *that* unlikely there were also stealth ships keeping a watch on the fleet from a safe distance.

The enemy HQ might know, soon enough, that the marines had won the war. Unless, of course, their reinforcements arrived. Again.

His communicator bleeped as the shuttle docked. "General," Captain Kerri Stumbaugh said. "Colonel Steel, Major-General Foxtrot and myself are waiting in the briefing room."

"On my way," Gerald said. He concealed his amusement with an effort. Foxtrot and his reinforcements had arrived only two days ago, after the fighting was over. "I'll be there in a moment."

He allowed himself a sigh of relief as he made his way to the compartment. It had been a close-run thing, as much as he would have liked to believe otherwise. The marines had been caught by surprise, accidentally lured into an engagement that could easily have gone the other way. It would have been maddening if the corprats had done it on purpose, but... he snorted in amusement. Doing it to *themselves* was just as maddening. In hindsight, they really should have wondered if Hameau was truly alone.

"Thank you for coming," he said. His eyes swept the room, noting that Kerri and Captain—Colonel—Steel were just a *little* too close to one another. "It's good to see you all again."

"And you," Foxtrot said. "Next time, leave some of them for us."

"If I'd known you were coming, I'd have made sure of it," Gerald said. He took his seat and leaned forward. "I take it you've read the interrogation reports?"

"Yes, sir," Kerri said. "Admiral Agate proved quite talkative, once we came to terms."

Gerald nodded, stiffly. He didn't like the idea of someone casually betraying his former allies—if nothing else, turning one's coat tended to be habit-forming—but he had to admit the enemy admiral had nowhere else to go. *Someone* would have to be blamed for the disaster, someone who wasn't closely linked to corporate royalty. And it was fairly certain Admiral Agate hadn't ordered any atrocities. Gerald found it easier to dicker with him than the troops on the ground.

"We know what they're doing," he said. He shook his head in irritation. In hindsight, they really should have wondered who *else* had been making plans for Earthfall. It was growing increasingly clear the Onge Corporation had helped to *trigger* Earthfall. They might even have destroyed the Slaughterhouse. "They're trying to establish themselves as the new ruling power."

He had to admit, sourly, that they'd done a good job. They'd recruited discontented, but competent military personnel; they'd hired experienced designers and engineers and technicians...they'd even given them their head, as long as they didn't turn political. And they'd been doing everything in their power to keep the fires burning through the Core Worlds. The Onge Navy—or whatever it was called—was nowhere near powerful enough to stand up to the Imperial Navy. But the Imperial Navy was steadily destroying itself.

And that's something that's going to have to be dealt with too, he thought. *Sooner or later, some of the new warlords will get established, stabilise their territories and start seeking out new conquests.*

"We have two options," he said. The real decision rested with the Commandant, but he had to lay the groundwork now. "We can talk to them, open up lines of communication and try to come to terms. There might be something to be said for dividing the galaxy between us. The Empire is burning, the Core Worlds are in ruins...civilisation itself is under threat. Or..."

He took a breath. "We take the war to them, now. We hit their homeworld quickly, get troops on the ground and put an end to their ambitions. We cannot afford a long, drawn-out engagement. Nor can they, really."

"You're proposing widening the war," Kerri said, quietly. "We don't even know what we'll be facing."

"No," Gerald agreed. "But neither do they."

"Yet." Foxtrot leaned forward, resting his hands on the table. "We don't know what they know. They may assume we'll come knocking at their door tomorrow. Or they may assume we don't have the slightest idea where to look."

"We have their datacores," Kerri said. "We know where to find them."

"Yes." Gerald nodded, briskly. "And we have to move."

Kerri made a face. "If the datacores are accurate, their homeworld is heavily defended," she said. "We might bleed ourselves white trying to crack them."

"Leaving them alone isn't an option either," Steel said. He was the lowest-ranking marine at the table, but he didn't seem intimidated. "I was down there"—he jabbed a finger at the bulkhead—"during the first round of fighting. It was creepy, an entire population held in a grip that was both very subtle and nearly impossible to escape. There is no way anyone could have dropped off the grid, unless they wanted to escape into the countryside and try to live there. They tagged people like animals and watched them constantly. And all the little abuses of the system pale in comparison to the *big* abuse. The entire population was steadily going mad."

He paused, as if he was trying to decide what to say. "They weren't taking any chances. Every move the population made was filmed. Every word they said was recorded. Every message they sent over the datanet was scanned before it was forwarded to its destination, if it didn't get trapped in the filters. Anyone who even *thought* about resistance, anyone who looked likely to become a troublemaker, was removed before they could become remotely dangerous. The system was not a common or garden tyranny, a communist or fascist or theocratic hellhole. It was complete control, from birth to death. And it was taking a toll.

"The population could *not* cope. They knew they had no freedom. It was just a matter of time before something went seriously wrong, before there was an explosion of pent-up rage or a steady collapse into stasis and inevitable decay. I talked to them, sir; I know what was going through their heads. And the corprats wish to export their system to the rest of the galaxy. They have to be stopped. They'll crush us, they'll crush every star system that fails to fall in line…"

"They cannot hope to impose their system everywhere." Foxtrot sounded disturbed. "It would take years, centuries, to build the infrastructure."

"They'll have time," Steel said. "Who's going to stand in their way?"

His words hung in the air. "If not us, then who?"

Gerald kept his face under tight control. Steel had a point, damn it. The corprat system could not hope to survive in the free marketplace of ideas. They'd be sure to take down everyone else, before the natural advantages of a *free* system came into play. The spooks had speculated the corprats—or someone—were involved with triggering off the post-Earthfall wars. *Someone* had certainly destroyed the Slaughterhouse. He gritted his teeth in bitter frustration. If it was them, they'd pay in blood. He'd make sure of it.

"We'll prepare to take the offensive, again," he said. It would take time to embark the marines, rearm the troops, reconfigure the logistics, study the interrogation reports and do everything else they'd need to do to ensure a successful mission. "And we'll be ready to go, when—if—the Commandant gives the order."

The fate of the galaxy is still very much in the balance, he thought. *This could go horrifically wrong. And that would be the end.*

• • •

TO BE CONTINUED IN
The Halls of Montezuma
COMING SOON.

AFTERWORD

But anything can happen, things can go wrong;
One minute you're up then you're down and you're gone.
—Huw and Tony Williams

IT IS A CURIOUS HISTORICAL FACT that Osama Bin Laden was on the verge of moving from one hideout to another when SEAL TEAM SIX came calling. Bin Laden—through a combination of selfishness, arrogance and simple idiocy—had managed to alienate his keepers, a serious misstep when they were all that was standing between him and a weighty helping of justice for a tiny fraction of his misdeeds. After he pushed them too far, they snapped and ordered him to leave…unaware that time was already running out. The hunters were already closing in. If Bin Laden had left a week earlier, the SEALs would have crashed into an empty home that—on the surface, at least—would have appeared to belong to a perfectly innocent family. Instead of a glorious victory, the US would have wound up with egg on its face and further cross-border raids would have been strongly discouraged.

The American hunters, of course, had no way to know what was actually happening inside the Bin Laden household (although it has been strongly suggested that Bin Laden was betrayed by one of his minders, or more distant partners in terror.) They had no way to know that Bin Laden was on the verge of leaving. Nor, for that matter, did Bin Laden have any way to know the Americans were closing in. If either party had known that time was running out, they would have moved quicker. The US got very lucky. The raid could easily have turned into a minor disaster.

It is difficult to exaggerate the role that simple random chance plays in human affairs. If the weather had worsened early, during the invasion of Normandy, D-Day would probably have failed. If General Lee hadn't lost a copy of his orders prior to the Battle of Antietam, it's possible the Confederate States could have won the day. If Benedict Arnold's plot to surrender West Point hadn't been uncovered, he might have delivered a fatal blow to the American cause. If…I could give an endless list of battles and wars that were decided by sheer random chance, by the weather or a single incident that could easily have gone in the opposite direction. The blunt truth is this: things can and do go wrong.

It's easy to say, as we have been increasingly wont to do over the past few decades, that there must be *someone* to blame. That person screwed up, either by accident or through cold-blooded malice. We have given birth to a culture that makes endless recriminations and files lawsuits—some sensible, some absurd, some *seemingly* absurd—in response to things that don't go our way. And yet, this is growing increasingly dangerous. The sad fact is that, sometimes, you can do everything right and still lose.

In 2003, for example, it was commonly believed that Iraq possessed weapons of mass destruction. This was an entirely reasonable belief, based on a decade of Iraqi lies, misinformation, reluctant confessions and a humanitarian crisis that was created and exploited for political ends. There was a strong tendency for analysts to assume the worst, because experience had *taught* them to assume the worst. The US Government wasn't inclined to listen to analysts who suggested otherwise because they'd noted a pattern of behaviour that suggested that nothing that came out of Iraq could be trusted. It was a mistake to base the rationale for invasion on a cause that demanded the US uncover a massive stockpile of WMD (instead of a dismantled WMD program that could easily be rebuilt), but it was an *understandable* mistake.

If something—a military operation, a new product rollout, a political campaign—succeeds, people will generally overlook its flaws. It isn't commonly understood that Donald Trump make mistakes during the 2016 campaign, at least partly because Trump *won*. The victory overshadows the errors. Hillary Clinton's mistakes loom large because she *lost*. And indeed, part of the problem facing the Democratic Party—as we move towards the November 2020 election—is that the party is reluctant to face up to its mistakes, let alone point the finger at the guilty people.

But why should it? We live in a society where admitting a mistake is tantamount to confessing guilt. Who wants to be the scapegoat? Who wants to have their life destroyed by a simple mistake? If the price of admitting fault is utter (personal) disaster, who in their right mind will admit fault? There is a strong case to be made that the last politician to admit responsibility for a mistake and resign was Lord Peter Carington, who took responsibility for the Foreign Office's failure to foresee the 1982 Falklands War. How many modern-day politicians would make the same decision?

And yet...Carington was lucky. He would go on to serve as Secretary General of NATO and play a major role in the diplomacy surrounding the Balkan Wars. Would this happen today? I doubt it. Someone who made a serious error would be lucky if they were ever entrusted with a sensitive role again.

The problem has been growing steadily worse, in matters military, social and political. In 2020, the Iowa Democratic Party spent a considerable sum of money on developing an app to manage the caucus and report the results. The app was a disaster, which sparked conspiracy theories and suggestions the party had rigged the results. (It didn't help that several candidates declared victory prior to any official results.) There was, it seemed, a great deal of evidence to suggest the developer wasn't unbiased.

Was it a mistake? It could have been. The app was rolled out too quickly for proper stress tests. Coding errors and other problems that should have been noted and solved in beta-testing weren't noticed until they tried to use the app. It's the sort of issue one gets when one tries to do something too quickly. A mistake creeps in and passes unnoticed until it's too late to easily resolve.

But was it a conspiracy?

The problem with our 'someone must be blamed' mentality is that it is very easy to believe that yes, it *was* a conspiracy. If you don't accept that mistakes happen, and some of them can have awful consequences, you'll start looking for someone to blame. (It didn't help that this wasn't the first time the DNC was accused of rigging the nomination process.) Instead of learning from the mistake—next time, stress-test the app *before* you rely on it—it's easy to start looking for a scapegoat. And then everyone in your sights switches to full cover-your-ass mode and any prospect of genuinely learning from the mistake is lost.

Things can and do go wrong. Sometimes, like I said above, victory or defeat hinges on sheer random chance. Sometimes, the intelligence is faulty or misinterpreted (in 1979, the CIA missed the Russian plan to intervene in Afghanistan because the Russians themselves didn't know they were planning to do it until they felt themselves pushed into a decision). Sometimes, what works on a small scale fails badly when tried on a larger scale (communism can only work on a small scale, when everyone knows everyone else). Sometimes, the story is simply too good *not* to be true, thus due diligence is left undone (*A Rape on Campus*, a thoroughly-discredited story published in *Rolling Stone*). And sometimes, yes, you can do everything right and still lose.

Mistakes happen. There were *hundreds* of mistakes made during the lead-up to World War Two. Some of those mistakes occurred because of stupidity, some because politicians feared the consequences of fighting another war, some because of sheer random chance. (Somewhat akin to Lee's Lost Order, the 1940 Mechelen Incident may have forced the Germans to change their invasion plans for France.) And yet, it isn't *just* the mistakes that matter. The outcome matters more.

I've been accused of saying this too often, but it's true. War is a democracy. The enemy, that dirty dog, gets a vote. And his vote may be enough to counteract yours.

We can learn from our mistakes. We can work to overcome them while keeping our eyes on the prize. Or we can allow ourselves to get bogged down in bitter, useless and ultimately destructive recriminations.

Christopher G. Nuttall
Edinburgh, 2020

PS.
And now you've read the book, I have a favour to ask.
It's getting harder to earn a living through indie writing these days, for a number of reasons (my health is one of them, unfortunately). If you liked this book, please post a review wherever you bought it; the more reviews a book gets, the more promotion.

CGN.

If You Enjoyed This Book, You Might Enjoy *Debt of Honor*...
KAT FALCONE RETURNS!

A year ago, the war against the Theocracy ended. But it didn't bring peace.

Admiral Kat Falcone was lucky—her side won the war. But without an external threat, Kat's homeworld government, the Commonwealth, begins to burst. The galactic war may be over, but there is a civil war on the horizon.

The king and parliament disagree over the Commonwealth's future. The Commonwealth's first recession is plaguing corporations. Hundreds of thousands of people have lost their jobs. And the colonies are demanding their share of power. The Commonwealth has become a ticking time bomb, just waiting to explode.

Meanwhile, the Theocracy is making one final, desperate bid for power. As the external threat looms and the internal threat grows ever larger, Kat and William will need to join forces in order to save the Commonwealth. But it may already be too late.

PROLOGUE

"That's all you could find?"

The two officers winced in unison, as if they expected to be marched to the airlock and unceremoniously thrown into space for failing to accomplish the impossible. Once, Admiral Zaskar acknowledged ruefully, they might have been right. Failure was a sign of God's displeasure, a proof that the failure—the failed—deserved to be punished. But if that was true, and he no longer believed it was so, what did that say about the Theocracy?

He studied the manifest on the datapad for a long moment, trying to hold back a tidal wave of depression. A few crates of starship components, some so old they probably dated all the way back to the early days of spaceflight; boxes of ration bars that were older than most of the men who were going to eat them... It was a far cry from the supplies they *needed* to keep the fleet alive. The fleet—the squadron, really—was on the verge of breaking down completely. In truth, he'd started to lose faith in his ability to keep his ships and men together long enough for the enemy to give up the pursuit.

"And the asteroid base?" He looked up at the officers. "Were there any people who might be interested in joining us?"

"No, Admiral," the older officer said. "They refused our offers."

And we can't make them a little more compulsory, Zaskar told himself. *We'd be betrayed within the week.*

He cursed his former masters under his breath. His crew was composed of the ignorant and the fanatics, neither of whom could do maintenance work worth a damn. The only thing they could do was remove a broken component and slot in a replacement, which had worked fine until their supply lines were destroyed once and for all. Even the finest engineers in the fleet couldn't repair *everything*, let alone build new components from scratch. He'd had to cannibalize and abandon a dozen ships just to keep the rest of the squadron going. And he was all too aware that their time was running out.

"Go see the cleric for ritual cleansing," he ordered shortly. "And then return to your duties."

The two officers bowed, then retreated. Zaskar watched them go and tapped a command into his terminal. A holographic image snapped into existence, flickering slightly. Zaskar's eyes narrowed as he studied his fleet. The flicker was tiny, but it shouldn't have been there at all. A grim reminder of their predicament. The onboard datanet was glitched, and no one, not even their sole computer expert, had been able to fix it. His entire ship was breaking down.

He wanted to believe that the handful of light codes in the display represented a powerful force. Four superdreadnoughts, nine cruisers, twelve destroyers, and a pair of courier boats... On paper, it *was* a powerful force. But one superdreadnought could neither fire missiles nor energize a beam, and ammunition was in short supply in any case, and five of the smaller ships were on their last legs. Each failure, small in itself, led to a cascading series of failures that simply could not be fixed. Zaskar rather suspected that the Commonwealth wouldn't need an entire superdreadnought squadron to wipe out his fleet in a stand-up battle. A single superdreadnought would be more than enough.

Which is why we are here, he thought, switching to the near-space display. *They won't come looking for us here, not until we are betrayed.*

He gritted his teeth in bitter rage. The asteroid settlement was the sort of place he would have destroyed, if he'd stumbled across it before the war. Smugglers weren't allowed to operate within the Theocracy, which hadn't stopped a number of high-ranking personnel from trading safety and political cover for items that they simply couldn't obtain anywhere else. And now... He swore, angrily. The smugglers might be their only hope, if they could find something to trade. But the squadron had very little to offer the scum of the galaxy.

Except ships, he reminded himself. *And we're not that desperate, are we?*

Zaskar tapped the console, shutting off the display. He didn't want to admit it, even to himself, but perhaps they *were* that desperate. His fleet was dying. And its crew was dying too. Discipline was steadily breaking down—internal security had logged everything from fights to a handful of unpopular officers being murdered in their bunks—and he didn't dare try to crack down. His crewmen were too ignorant for now to realize just how bad things really were, but he knew it was only a matter of time. The squadron was well on its way to collapsing into irrelevance. The Commonwealth wouldn't have to lift a finger to destroy them. They'd do that for themselves.

He took a breath, tasting something faintly unpleasant in the air. The air circulation system was starting to break down too. He'd had men cleaning the vents and checking—and rechecking—the recycling plants, but if their air suddenly turned poisonous...that would be the end. It wouldn't even have to be *that* poisonous. An atmospheric imbalance, perhaps an excess of oxygen, would be just as bad. A spark would cause an explosion. Hell, merely breathing in excess oxygen would cause problems too.

The hatch hissed open. Zaskar looked up, already knowing who he'd see. There was only one person who would come into his ready room without ringing the buzzer and waiting for permission to enter. Lord Cleric Moses stood there, his beard as unkempt as ever. Zaskar couldn't help thinking there were more flecks of gray in his hair than there'd been yesterday. Moses was nearly two decades older than Zaskar himself and hadn't had the benefit of a military career.

And he isn't even the Lord Cleric, Zaskar reminded himself, dryly. *He just took the title on the assumption that he was the senior surviving cleric.*

The thought brought another wave of depression. Ahura Mazda had fallen. The Tabernacle had been destroyed, and the planet had been occupied... if the wretched smugglers were to be believed. Zaskar wanted to believe that the smugglers had lied, but... he'd been there, during the final battle. He was all too aware that the Royal Tyre Navy had won. And his fleet, the one that should have fought to the bitter end, had been all that remained of the Theocratic Navy. He sometimes wondered, in the dead of night, if it would have been better to stay and die in defense of his homeworld and his religion. At least he wouldn't have lived to see his fleet slowly starting to die.

"They found nothing, it seems," Moses said, taking a seat. "They didn't even find any worthy women."

Zaskar snorted. Some of his officers had suggested, quite seriously, that they leave Theocratic Space entirely and set out to find a new home somewhere far from explored space. But his fleet's crew consisted solely of men. Kidnapping women was about the only real solution to their problem, but where could they hope to find nearly a hundred thousand women? Raiding a midsized planet might work—and he'd seriously considered it—yet he doubted they could withdraw before the occupiers responded. Come to think of it, he wasn't even sure he could punch through the planet's defenses. His fleet was in a *terrible* state.

"No," he said.

"And they heard more rumors," Moses added. "More worlds have slipped from our control."

"Yes," Zaskar said. "Are you surprised?"

The cleric gave him a sharp look. Zaskar looked back, evenly. The days when a cleric could have a captain, or even an admiral, hauled off his command deck and scourged were long gone. Moses had little real power, and they both knew it. Speaking truth to power was no longer a dangerous game. And the blunt truth was that the Theocracy had alienated so many locals on every world they'd occupied that the locals had revolted almost as soon as the orbital bombardment systems were destroyed.

Moses looked down. "God will provide."

Hah, Zaskar thought. God had turned His back. *We need a miracle.*

His console bleeped. "Admiral?"

Zaskar stabbed his finger at the button. "Yes?"

"Admiral, we just picked up a small scout ship dropping out of hyperspace," Captain Geris said. "They're broadcasting an old code, sir, and requesting permission to come aboard."

"An old code?" Zaskar leaned forward. "How old?"

"It's a priority-one code from four years ago," Captain Geris informed him. "I'm surprised it's still in our database."

Moses met Zaskar's eyes. "A trick?"

Zaskar shrugged. "Captain, are we picking up any other ships?"

"Negative, sir."

"Then invite the scout to dock at our forward airlock," Zaskar ordered. "And have its occupant brought to my ready room."

"Aye, Admiral."

Zaskar leaned back in his chair as the connection broke. A priority-one code from *four* years ago? It could be a trap, but outdated codes were generally rejected once everyone had been notified that they were outdated. The Theocracy had been so large that it had been incredibly difficult to keep everyone current. And yet, four years was *too* long. It made little sense. The code dated all the way back to the Battle of Cadiz.

"They wouldn't need to play games if they'd found us," he said, more to himself than to Moses. The scout could be crammed to the gunnels with antimatter, but the worst they could do was take out the *Righteous Revenge*. "They'd bring in a superdreadnought squadron and finish us off."

"Unless they want to be sure they've caught all of us," Moses said. "The Inquisition often watched heretics for weeks, just to be certain that *all* their friends and fellow unbelievers were identified."

Zaskar smiled. "We'll see."

He couldn't help feeling a flicker of shame as the guest—the sole person on the scout, according to the search party—was shown into his ready room.

Once, it would have taken a mere five minutes to bring someone aboard; now, it had taken twenty. He dreaded to think of what would happen if they had to go into battle. A delay in raising their shields and activating their point defense would prove fatal.

Their guest didn't seem perturbed by the delay, or by the armed Janissaries following his every move, or even by the obvious fact that *Righteous Revenge* was on her last legs. He merely looked around with polite interest. Zaskar studied him back, noting the hawk-nosed face, tinted skin, and neatly trimmed beard. The man had gone to some lengths to present himself as a citizen of Ahura Mazda. Even his brown tunic suggested he'd grown up on Zaskar's homeworld.

And he has a dozen implants, Zaskar thought, studying the report from the security scan. The visitor was practically a cyborg. *And that means he's from...?*

"Please, be seated," Zaskar said. He kept his voice polite. Advanced implants meant that their guest was from one of the major powers. The Commonwealth was right out, of course, but there were others. Some of them might even see advantage in backing his fleet. "I'm Admiral Zaskar, commander of this fleet."

"A pleasure," the man said. He inclined his head in a formal bow. "I'm Simon Askew."

"A pleasure," Zaskar echoed. The name meant nothing to him, but he rather suspected it wasn't the man's real name. "You seem to have come looking for us."

"Correct," Askew said. He leaned forward. "My... superiors would like to offer you a certain degree of support in your operations."

"Indeed?" Zaskar wasn't sure whether he believed it or not. Keeping his fleet going would require an immense investment. "And the price would be?"

"We want you to keep the Commonwealth busy," Askew said. "It is in our interests to see them get bogged down."

"Is it now?" Zaskar frowned. "And who would be interested in seeing them bogged down?"

"My superiors wish to remain unnamed," Askew informed him. He reached into his pocket and removed a datapad. "But they are prepared to be quite generous."

He held the datapad out. Zaskar took it and scanned the open document rapidly. It was a list of everything the fleet needed to keep functioning, everything from starship components to missiles and ration bars. It was... it was unbelievable. It had to be a trap. And yet... and yet, he *wanted* to believe. If the offer was genuine, they could keep wearing away at the Commonwealth until it withdrew from Theocratic Space. They could *win*!

Moses reached out his hand for the datapad. Zaskar barely noticed.

"You want us to keep the Commonwealth busy," he said. It was suddenly very hard to speak clearly. "It seems a reasonable price."

His mind raced. No smuggler could transship so much material into a war zone, not without running unacceptable risks. And no smuggler would have access to cyborg technology. Only a great power could supply the weapons and equipment... and only a great power would benefit from keeping the Commonwealth tied down. The list of suspects was relatively short.

And it doesn't matter, he told himself. They'd have to be alert for the prospect of betrayal, but that was a given anyway. The Theocracy had been the least popular galactic government for decades, even before the war. *We could win!*

"Very well," he said. "Let's talk."

CHAPTER ONE

AHURA MAZDA

The sound of a distant explosion, muffled by the forcefield surrounding Commonwealth House, woke Kat Falcone as she lay in her bed. Others followed, flickers of multicolored light dancing through the window as homemade rockets or mortar shells crashed into the forcefield and exploded harmlessly. She rolled over and sat upright, blinking as the lights automatically brightened. Her bedside terminal was flashing green. Pointless attacks had been so common over the last year that hardly anyone bothered to sound the alert any longer. The insurgents had yet to realize that no amount of makeshift rocketry would pose a threat to the Commonwealth HQ. Even without the forcefield, Commonwealth House could take the blow and shrug it off. The blasts wouldn't even scratch the paint.

Not that we're going to turn off the forcefield to let them try, she thought morbidly as she crossed her arms. *That would be pushing fate too far.*

She snorted at the thought as she forced herself to key her terminal to bring up the latest set of reports. There was no change, she noted wryly: an endless liturgy of shootings, bombings, gang rapes, robberies, and other horrors undreamed of on Tyre. But Ahura Mazda's population had been kept under tight control for decades, centuries even. The sudden collapse of everything they'd once taken for granted had unleashed *years* of pent-up frustrations. She sometimes thought that the insurgency was really a civil war, with Commonwealth troops being engaged only when they got in the way. Ahura Mazda seemed to have gone completely mad.

Damn them, she thought. A final spread of makeshift rockets struck the forcefield outside, then faded away. *And damn their dead leaders too.*

She looked down at her hands, feeling as if she simply wanted to stay in bed. She'd had plans for the future, once. She was going to get married and see the universe, perhaps by purchasing a freighter and traveling from system to system, doing a little trading along the way. Instead, her fiancé was dead, and she was still in the navy, technically. She hadn't stood on a command deck for nearly a year. Instead, she was chained to a desk on an occupied world, trying to govern a sector of forty inhabited star systems that had just been liberated from one of the worst tyrannies humanity had the misfortune to invent. The chaos was beyond belief. Ahura Mazda wasn't the only world going through a nervous breakdown. She'd read reports of everything from mass slaughter to forced deportation of everyone who'd converted to the True Faith.

Years of pent-up frustrations, she reminded herself. She'd been lucky. She hadn't grown up in a world where saying the wrong thing could get her beheaded. *And they have all been released at once.*

There was a sharp knock at the door. Kat glared at it, resisting the urge to order the visitor to go away. There was only one person who could come through that door. It opened a moment later, allowing Lucy Yangtze to step into the bedroom. The middle-aged woman studied Kat with a surprisingly maternal eye as she carried the breakfast tray over to the bedside table. Kat had to fight to keep from snapping at her to get out. Lucy was a steward. Looking after Kat was her job.

"Good morning, Admiral," Lucy said. She managed to sound disapproving without making it obvious. "How are you today?"

Kat swallowed a number of remarks she knew would be petty and childish. "I didn't sleep well," she said as Lucy uncovered the tray. "And then they woke me up."

"You need to go to bed earlier," Lucy said, dryly.

"Hah," Kat muttered. She forced herself to stand, heedless of her nakedness. "There are too many things to do here."

"Then delegate some of them," Lucy suggested gently. "You have an entire staff under you, do you not?"

Pat would have cracked a rude joke, Kat thought. It felt like a stab to the heart. *And I would have elbowed him...*

She pushed the thought aside with an effort. "We'll see," she said, vaguely. In truth, she didn't want to delegate anything. Too much was riding on the occupation's success for her to casually push authority down the chain. And yet, Lucy was right. Ahura Mazda wasn't a starship. A single mind couldn't hope to keep abreast of all the details, let alone make sure the planet ran smoothly. If that was her goal, she'd already failed. "I'll talk to you later."

"I'll have lunch ready for 1300," Lucy said. "You can make it a working lunch if you like."

Kat had to smile, although she knew it wasn't really funny. *All* her lunches were working lunches these days. She rarely got to eat in private with anyone. Even cramming a ration bar into her mouth between meetings wasn't an option. She couldn't help feeling, as she tucked into her scrambled eggs, that she was merely spinning her wheels in mud. She went to countless meetings, she made decisions, again and again and again, and yet... was she actually doing *anything*? She kicked herself, again, for allowing them to promote her off the command deck. The Admiralty probably would have let her take command of a heavy cruiser on deep-space patrol if she'd made enough of a fuss.

It has to be done, she thought as she keyed her console to bring up the latest news reports from home. *And I'm the one the king tapped for the post.*

"Naval spokespeople today confirmed that the search for MV *Supreme* has been finally called off," the talking head said. He was a man so grave that Kat rather suspected he was nothing more than a computer-generated image. "The cruise liner, which went missing in hyperspace six months ago, has been declared lost with all hands. Duke Cavendish issued a statement reassuring investors that the Cavendish Corporation will meet its commitments, but independent analysts are questioning their finances..."

Kat sighed. Trust the media to put a lost cruise liner ahead of anything important. "Next."

"Infighting among refugees on Tarsus has led to a declaration of martial law," the talking head told her. "President Theca has taken personal control of the situation and informed the refugees that any further misbehavior, regardless of the cause, will result in immediate arrest and deportation. The Commonwealth Refugee Commission has blamed the disorder on poor supply lines and has called on Tarsus to make more supplies available to the refugees. However, local protests against refugees have grown..."

"And it could be worse, like it is here," Kat muttered. "Next!"

"Sharon Mackintosh has become the latest starlet to join the Aaron Group Marriage," the talking head said. "She will join fifty-seven other starlets in matrimonial bliss..."

"Off," Kat snapped.

She shook her head in annoyance. The occupied zone was turning into a nightmare, no matter how many meetings she attended, and the news back home was largely trivial. The end of the war had brought confusion in its wake—she knew that better than anyone—but there were times when she thought that the king was the only one trying to hold everything together. The Commonwealth hadn't been designed for a war, and everyone knew it. And now all the tensions that had been put on the back burner while the Commonwealth fought for its very survival were starting to tear it apart.

Standing, she walked over to the window and peered out. Tabernacle City had been a ramshackle mess even before the occupation, but now it was a nightmare. Smoke was rising from a dozen places, marking the latest bombings; below, she could see marines and soldiers heading out on patrol. The civilians seemed to trust the occupiers more than they trusted the warring factions, but they were scared to come into the open and say so. They were afraid, deep inside, that the occupation wouldn't last. Her eyes picked out Government House, standing a short distance from Commonwealth House. Admiral Junayd and his people were trying to put together a provisional government, but it was a slow job. Their authority was weaker than most of the insurgent factions. She didn't envy them.

Her wristcom bleeped from the table. She stalked back to the bed and picked it up. "Go ahead."

"Admiral," Lieutenant Kitty Patterson's voice said. "You have a meeting in thirty minutes."

"Understood," Kat said. She allowed herself a moment of gratitude. Thirty minutes was more than long enough to shower and get dressed. "I'll be there."

She turned and walked into the shower, silently grateful that Commonwealth House had its own water supply. The local water distribution network had been on the verge of failing even before the occupation; now, with pipes smashed by the insurgents and entire pumping stations looted and destroyed, there were overpopulated districts that barely had enough water to keep the population from dying of thirst. Kat didn't understand how anyone could live in such an environment. She thought she would sooner have risked her life in revolt than waste away and die.

But it was never that easy, she thought. *This is how too many people here believe it should be.*

She washed and dressed quickly, inspecting her appearance in the reflector field before she left the suite. Her white uniform was neatly pressed, her medals and her golden hair shone in the light... but there was a *tired* look in her eyes she knew she should lose. She was depressed and she knew it, and she really should talk to the shrinks, but training and experience told her that the psychologists were not to be trusted. None of them had commanded ships in battle, or made life-or-death decisions, or done *anything* that might qualify them to pass judgment on a spacer's life.

She took a long breath, gathering herself as she strapped a pistol to her belt, then walked through the door and down the corridor. The two marine guards at the far end of the corridor saluted her. She returned the gesture as the hatch opened in front of her.

They built the place to resemble a starship, she thought dourly. It had been amusing, once, to contemplate the mind-set of whoever had thought it was a good idea. Were they trying to remind everyone that, one day, the Commonwealth would leave Ahura Mazda? Or did they just want to pretend, for a few hours, that they were designing starships? *But they forgot to include a command deck.*

She drew herself up as she stepped through the next hatch, into the meeting room. It was large and ornate, although she'd managed to clear out the worst of the luxury. She didn't want people to get *too* comfortable in meeting rooms. Thankfully, most of her senior staff had genuine experience, either in combat or repairing and rejuvenating shattered planetary infrastructures. The war had created far too many opportunities to practice.

And I don't have many chairwarmers, she reminded herself as her staff stood to welcome her. *It could be worse.*

"Thank you for coming," she said once she'd taken her chair. "Be seated."

She cast her eye around the table as her staffers sat down. General Timothy Winters, Commonwealth Marines; Colonel Christopher Whitehall, Royal Engineering Corps; Major Shawna Callable, Commonwealth Refugee Commission; Captain Janice Wilson, Office of Naval Intelligence; Lieutenant Kitty Patterson, Kat's personal aide. It was a diverse group, she told herself firmly. And the absence of wallflowers, from junior staffers to senior staffers, allowed everyone to talk freely.

"I was woken this morning by a rocket attack," she said as a server poured tea and coffee. "I assume there was no reason to be alarmed?"

"No, Admiral," Winters said. He was a big, beefy man with a bald head and scarred cheekbones. "It was merely another random attack. The people behind it scarpered before we could catch them."

Because we can't fire shells back into the city, Kat reminded herself sharply. *The insurgents would claim we'd killed civilians, even if we hadn't.*

She felt a flash of hatred deeper than anything she'd ever felt for enemy spacers. She'd never seen her opponents in space, not face-to-face. It had been easy to believe that they weren't that different from her, that they weren't monsters. But here, on the ground, she couldn't avoid the simple fact that the insurgents *were* monsters. They killed anyone who supported the provisional government, raped and mutilated women they caught out of doors, sited heavy weapons emplacements in inhabited homes, used children to carry bombs towards the enemy... Kat wanted them all dead. Ahura Mazda would have no hope of becoming a decent place to live as long as those monsters stalked the streets. But tracking them all down was a long and difficult task.

"At least no one was killed," Major Shawna Callable said. "Admiral, we need more resources for the women's shelters. We're running short of just about everything."

"And they also need more guards," Winters told her. "The last attack nearly broke the perimeter before it was beaten back."

"Draw them from the reserves," Kat ordered. She didn't like deploying her reserves, not when she was all too aware of how badly her forces were overstretched, but she had no choice. The women in the shelters would be assaulted and murdered if one of their compounds was overrun. "And see what we can find in the way of additional supplies."

If we can find anything, her thoughts added. Ahura Mazda produced nothing these days, as far as she could tell. The infrastructure had been literally torn to shreds. Putting the farms back into production was turning into a long, hard slog. Shawna had been right. *We're running short on just about everything.*

She looked at Winters. "Is there anything we can do to make it harder for the insurgents to get to them?"

"Only moving the refugees a long way away," Winters said. "Personally, I'd recommend one of the islands. We could set up a proper security net there and vaporize anything heading in without the right security codes."

"We barely have the resources to keep the cities alive," Colonel Christopher Whitehall said, curtly. He was short, with black skin and penetrating eyes. His record stated that he'd been a marine before he'd been wounded and transferred to the Royal Engineers. "Right now, Admiral, I'm honestly expecting a disaster at any moment."

"So train up some locals and put them to work," Winters snapped. He thumped the table to underline the suggestion. "It's their bloody city. And their people who will die of thirst if we lose the pumping stations completely."

"The training programs are going slowly," Whitehall snapped back. The frustration in his voice was all too clear. "Half the idiots on this wretched ball of mud think that trying to fix a broken piece of machinery is sinful, while the other half can't count to twenty-one without taking off their trousers. We've got a few women who *might* be good at it, if they were given a chance, but we can't send them out on repair jobs."

"It's their schooling," Shawna told them. "They weren't encouraged to actually learn."

Kat nodded in grim understanding. The Theocracy's educational system had been a joke. No, that wasn't entirely true. It had done its job, after all. It had churned out millions of young men who knew nothing, least of all how to *think*. But rote recitals were useless when it came to repairing even a relatively simple machine. It was a mystery to her how the Theocratic Navy had managed to keep its fleet going long enough to actually start the war. Their shortage of trained engineers had to have been an utter nightmare.

They never picked on anyone their own size, she told herself. The Theocracy's first targets had all been stage-one or stage-two worlds. Very few of them had any space-based defenses, let alone the ability to take the fight to the enemy. *And the Theocrats certainly weren't prepared for a long war.*

Whitehall met her eyes. "We need more engineers, Admiral, and more protective troops. If we lose a couple more pumping stations…"

"I know," Kat said. They'd come to the same conclusion time and time again, in pointless meeting after pointless meeting. "Right now, Tyre doesn't seem to be interested in sending either."

"We could try to hire civilian engineers," Kitty suggested. She was the lowest-ranking person at the table, but that didn't stop her from offering her opinions. "They could take up some of the slack."

Whitehall snorted. "I doubt it," he said. "There's work in the Commonwealth for engineers, Lieutenant, and safer too. They won't be in any danger on Tarsus or... well, anywhere. I don't think we could get them out here."

Kitty reddened. "I... sorry, Admiral."

"Don't worry about it," Kat said, briskly. She looked around the table. "Are there any other solutions?"

"Not in the short run," Whitehall said. "We have water and power, Admiral. It's getting both to their destination that is the *real* problem. We've tried setting up purification centers near the sewers and..."

The building shook, gently. Kat tensed, one hand dropping to the pistol at her belt. *That* hadn't been a homemade rocket. A nuke? The Theocracy had supposedly thrown its entire nuclear arsenal at the navy, but she'd never been entirely sure they'd used all their nukes. Hell, the Theocrats themselves hadn't been sure. Their record keeping had been appalling. A nuke wouldn't break the forcefield but would do immense damage to the city.

Winters checked his wristcom, then swore. "Admiral," he said, "there's been an explosion."

"Where?" Kat stood. The blast had been very close. If the insurgents had managed to open a pathway into Commonwealth House, the defenders might be in some trouble. "And what happened?"

"Government House." Winters sounded stunned. "The building is in ruins. Admiral, Admiral Junayd is dead."

"...Shit," Kat said.

CHAPTER TWO

TYRE

Peter Falcone—*Duke* Peter Falcone, he reminded himself savagely—stared at the heavy wooden doors and tried not to let his impatience show on his face. He was no callow youth, although he'd grown up in the shadows of Duke Lucas Falcone; he was one of the single most wealthy and powerful people on Tyre. It hadn't been easy to convince enough of the family to back him, even though he was Lucas's oldest child, but he'd made it. The Falcone family was in his hands now. He had no intention of failing in his duty to his people.

Assuming I ever get through my investiture, he thought as he looked at the doors. They were firmly closed, awaiting the king's pleasure. *Who thought it was a good idea to come up with such... such pageantry?*

He snorted at the thought. The planet's founders, including his great-grandfather, had created a corporate state. There had been fourteen corporations, at the time, and they'd divided the world up between them. It had been simple enough, he'd thought, but, to give the whole enterprise a veneer of legitimacy, they'd turned the planet into a monarchy, with the most powerful CEO declared king. And it had grown from there into a tangled system that worked...mostly. But the founders had never imagined the Breakdown, or the Commonwealth, or, worst of all, the recently concluded war.

And they didn't imagine one of the corporations collapsing either, Peter told himself. The Ducal Fourteen had always seemed too big to fail. But the Cavendish Corporation was on the verge of total collapse, and Peter had a nasty feeling that others might follow. His own corporation was barely treading water. *We never imagined having to splash out so much money on everything from weapons development to force projection.*

It was a sour point, one that had stuck in his craw ever since he'd discovered just how much money had been expended—and just how much remained unaccounted for. The government had raised taxes, as well as asked for voluntary contributions from the big corporations, but its accounting had been poor. The desperate rush to put as many warships into space as possible had done nothing for financial discipline. Peter was uneasily aware that nearly 30 percent of the budget for the last four years had vanished into black projects, projects he wasn't supposed to know about. It was a staggering amount of money, truly unimaginable, and it was one of the bones the House of Lords wanted to pick with the king. And yet, it wasn't the worst of them.

Trumpets blared. The doors were thrown open, revealing a pair of uniformed flunkies and, beyond them, the House of Lords. Peter pasted a neutral expression on his face as he began to walk forward, wondering just how many people were watching him make a fool of himself through the datanet. The entire ceremony was being broadcast live. His father had made the ceremony look solemn and dignified, but Peter suspected he looked like an idiot. The fancy robes and stylized hair came from a bygone era.

And true power lies in money, warships, and troops, he thought as he walked into the chamber. *I could wear rags and Eau de Skunk, and I'd still be one of the most powerful men in the known universe.*

He allowed his eyes to sweep the chamber as the doors were closed behind him. Seven hundred and ninety lords and ladies, crammed into a room that had been designed for only five hundred. For years people had been talking about expanding the House of Lords or rewriting the rules about who could and who couldn't attend via hologram or proxy, but nothing had come of it. The lords who could trace their bloodlines all the way back to the founders had been joined by newer noblemen, some who'd more than earned their right to a title and others who'd been rewarded for services rendered. A cluster of lords, sitting in the upper benches, wore robes to signify that they were colonials. And hadn't there been a thoroughly nasty fight over *their* right to sit in the chamber?

Peter sighed, inwardly, as he picked out a handful of names and faces. Prime Minister Arthur Hampshire, technically a commoner; Israel Harrison, Leader of the Opposition; Duke Jackson Cavendish, trying hard to look confident even though everyone knew he no longer had a pot to piss in… names and faces, some of whom were friends, some allies, and some deadly enemies. Peter wondered, careful not to show even a trace of doubt on his face, if he was *really* up to the task. There were men and women in the chamber who'd been playing politics long before he had been born.

There's no one else, he told himself firmly. *And I dare not fail.*

He sucked in his breath. He wasn't inexperienced. His father had made him work in the family corporation for years, pushing him out of his comfort zone time and time again. And chewing him out, royally, when he'd screwed up. Peter wasn't sure how he felt about that either. His father had been a good man, but he'd also been a *hard* man. The family could not afford weakness in the ranks. Peter, at least, had been given a chance to learn from his mistakes. Not everyone had been so lucky.

And others never had to take up the role, he thought, feeling a flicker of resentment, once again, towards his youngest sister. Kat had never had to study business, never had to take up a position within the family corporation. Instead, she'd gone to war and carved out a life for herself. *Some people have all the luck.*

Peter stopped in the exact center of the chamber and looked up. King Hadrian, first of that name, looked back at him. He was a tall man, with short dark hair and a face that was strikingly calculating. The king, Peter knew from experience, was a man who could move from affability to threat with terrifying speed. He was young too, younger than Peter himself. It was something Peter knew had worried his father. Peter, and the other corporate heirs, could learn their trade without risking everything, but the *king's* heir could not become king until his father had passed away. King Hadrian had been learning his trade on the job. And it was hard to tell, Peter had to admit, just how much was cold calculation versus sheer luck. And inexperience.

A shame the rumors about the king and Kat were groundless, Peter thought as he knelt in front of his monarch. *She would have made a good partner for him...*

He dismissed the thought, ruthlessly. There was no point in crying over the impossible. An affair was one thing, but marriage? The other dukes would have blocked the match without a second thought. And besides, Kat had been in love with a commoner. Peter couldn't help feeling another stab of envy. *His* marriage had been arranged, of course; his parents had organized the match, one of the prices he paid for his position. But Kat was free to fall in love as she pleased. He wasn't sure it was really a good thing. Kat had been devastated by her lover's death.

King Hadrian rose, one hand holding his scepter. He wore a full military dress uniform, although it was black rather than white. Peter thought, rather sourly, that the king had no right to wear so much gold braid, let alone the medals jangling at his breast. But then, the king *was* a hereditary member of a dozen military fraternities. He probably needed to wear the medals his ancestors had won. Some of his supporters would otherwise be alienated.

"It has been a year and a day since Duke Falcone was treacherously killed," King Hadrian said. His words were a grim reminder that nowhere, not even Tyre itself, was safe from attack. The Theocracy's strike teams had done a great deal of damage before they'd been wiped out, but the security measures introduced to combat them had been almost worse. "And now, with the period of mourning officially over, we gather to invest his son with the title and powers that once were his father's."

There was a brief, chilling pause. Peter felt his heart beginning to race, even though he was *sure* there was nothing to worry about. He *was* the

Duke, confirmed by the family council; no one, not even the king, could take it from him. And yet, if the House of Lords refused to seat him, it could cause all manner of trouble back home. The family council might vote to impeach him on the grounds he couldn't work with the rest of the nobility and elect someone else in his place. Peter doubted he'd be permitted to return to the corporation after that! More likely he'd be sent into comfortable exile somewhere.

"But we must decide if he is worthy to join our ranks," the king said calmly. "Honorable members, cast your votes."

Peter tensed, telling himself again that he was perfectly safe. No one would risk alienating him over something so petty, not now. But the vote was anonymous... His family's enemies would vote against him, of course, but what about the others? There were people who might take the opportunity to put him on notice that he couldn't inherit the extensive patronage network his father had built up over the years. And others who would want to renegotiate the terms, now that his father was dead.

He wanted to look around to see the voting totals, but he knew it would be taken as a sign of weakness. He didn't dare look unsure, not now. Weakness invited attack. Instead, all he could do was wait. He silently counted to a hundred under his breath, wishing he didn't feel so exposed. The eyes of the world were upon him.

"The voting has finished," King Hadrian said. "In favor, seven hundred and twelve; against, forty-two."

And a number of abstentions, Peter thought. *Did they refuse to cast a vote because they don't want to take sides, even on something as pointless as this, or because they recognize the whole ceremony for the farce it is?*

"I welcome you to the House of Lords, *Duke* Falcone," King Hadrian said. He reached out and tapped Peter on the shoulder with his scepter. "You may rise."

Peter rose, feeling suddenly stiff. "Thank you, Your Majesty."

"Take your place among us," King Hadrian said. "I'm sure you will find it a very edifying discussion."

A low rustle ran through the chamber as Peter sat down on the bench. It was comfortable, but not too comfortable. Behind him, he heard a handful of lords and ladies leaving now that the *important* business was done. They were too highly ranked not to attend the investment, but neither wealthy nor powerful enough to make themselves heard during a debate. And besides, Peter reflected, they probably knew that half the business conducted in the chamber was meaningless. The real deals would be negotiated in private chambers. By the time they were presented to the Houses of Parliament, various initiatives would already have been revised thoroughly enough to make them broadly acceptable to everyone. The public debates would be largely meaningless.

The speaker came forward, bowed to the king, and took the stand. He was an elderly man, old enough to remember the king's grandfather. Peter felt a little sorry for him, even though he was sure that anyone who'd held such a position for so long had to know where the bodies were buried. The speaker had to wait at the back of the chamber while the king had played his role. But then, that too was part of the ceremony.

"Thank you, Your Majesty," the speaker said. He cleared his throat. "The issue before us..."

Peter glanced down at his datapad as the voice droned on. He'd received more than fifty private messages in the last five minutes, each one requesting a private meeting. Some were just feelers from friends and enemies alike, but others were quite serious. He hadn't expected a PM from Israel Harrison. Technically, Peter was on the Privy Council; practically, he'd been... discouraged... from claiming his father's seat. There'd been too much else to do over the last year for him to let that bother him.

"On a point of order, Mr. Speaker," Israel Harrison said. His voice cut through the hubbub, drawing everyone's eyes to him. "Is the government *seriously* proposing to expand the foreign aid budget?"

He went on before the prime minister could respond. "The emergency taxation and spending program was meant to be terminated with the end of the war. We were *assured*, when we gave our consent, that that would be the case. And yet, here we are, still paying the tax… and hampering our economy in the process. We need to cut back on government spending and resume economic growth."

The prime minister stood. "The fact remains that a vast number of worlds, inside and outside the Commonwealth, have been devastated by the war. Millions upon millions of people have been displaced, cities have been destroyed, food supplies have been sharply reduced or cut off entirely… uncountable numbers of people have had their lives destroyed. Our reconstruction program may be the only thing standing between those people and utter destitution."

"I fully understand why my honorable friend feels that way," Harrison countered. "But I fail to understand why *we* should risk economic collapse, and our own utter destitution, to save those worlds. Many of them were formerly enemy states. Others have been, if I may make so bold, ungrateful."

Peter gritted his teeth as the debate raged backwards and forwards, with government supporters exchanging harsh words with the opposition. It wasn't about the displaced people, he knew, and it wasn't about foreign aid in and of itself. It was the age-old question of just who got to control the budget. The government wanted to keep the emergency taxation program because it gave them more money to spend, while the opposition wanted to get rid of the program because it gave the government a great deal of clout to buy votes. And the hell of it, he knew all too well, was that the opposition, if elected into power, would want to keep the program too.

"The military budget is already too high," Harrison said. "Do we face *any* real threat from an outside power?"

Grand Admiral Tobias Vaughn rose. Peter thought he looked tired. Vaughn had been the navy's senior uniformed officer, which made him *de facto* senior officer for all branches of the military, for the last five years, a term that covered the entirety of the war. Rumor had it that Vaughn wanted to retire, but so far the king had convinced him to stay. Now that the war was over, Peter couldn't help wondering just how long that would last.

"There are two aspects to your question," Vaughn said. He *sounded* tired too. "First, we do not face a peer threat at the moment. However, our neighbors have been building up their own military forces over the last few years. We have reason to believe that they have been pouring resources into duplicating our advanced weapons and technology—unsurprisingly so, as they may regard *us* as a potential threat. It is possible that we may face an alliance of two or more Great Powers in the near future.

"Second, we have a responsibility to provide security for our territory, both within the Commonwealth and the occupied zone. There is, quite simply, no one else who will provide any form of interstellar security. We must deploy starships to protect planets and shipping lanes, and we must deploy troops to protect refugee populations and provide support to various provisional governments. The Jorlem Sector became increasingly lawless as a result of the war, honorable members. Do we really want the Theocratic Sector to go the same way?"

Harrison stood. "Is it going to be a threat to us?"

Vaughn looked back at him, evenly. "We have confiscated the remaining enemy industrial production nodes," he said. "In the short term, chaos in the Theocratic Sector will be very bad for the locals and largely irrelevant to us. However, in the long term, there will be pirates, raiders, and revanchists taking root within the sector. I submit to you, sir, that those forces will eventually become a threat."

"But the Theocracy is dead." Harrison tapped his foot on the ground. "How long do you want to continue to fight the war?"

"Until we win," Vaughn said. "Right now, sir, the sector is unstable, and we're the only thing keeping it under control."

"We have a debt of honor," King Hadrian said.

"A debt of honor we cannot afford to meet," Harrison said curtly. He didn't *quite* glare at the king. "And a debt of honor that was entered into without Parliament's consent."

Peter groaned, inwardly, as the debate grew louder. Harrison was right, of course. The king had promised much and, so far, delivered little. But the king had made promises he'd had no right to make, certainly not without Parliament's approval. No *wonder* his government wanted to keep emergency taxation powers. It was the only way to keep his promises to the Commonwealth.

And yet, we simply cannot afford to rebuild all the Theocracy's infrastructure, he thought. The expenditure would be unimaginably huge. *Even trying would be disastrous.*

He groaned again. It was going to be a very long day.

• • •

PURCHASE FROM 47 NORTH NOW!

Printed in Great Britain
by Amazon